FOREVER

She melted against him, into him, her face turned up to meet his. His lips were warm and sweet against hers, gently coaxing a response from her.

Tess floated away on that dream, knowing on more than one level it was simply that—a dream—but refusing to give it up yet. Her mouth curved into an unconscious smile. If dreaming were the only way she could have Gabriel, then she would dream forever.

And that was how Gabe found her a short while later—a beautiful angel lying in a bed of flowers, her only cover the huge blanket of stars above. His heart ached to look at her. It would be so easy to scoop her up and take her home, to give her anything and everything she wanted, to love her, to make love to her.

To love her.

D1115308

Here Comes the Bride

Laura Drewry

ZEBRA BOOKS
Kensington Publishing Corp.
www.kensingtonbooks.com

ZEBRA BOOKS are published by

Kensington Publishing Corp.
850 Third Avenue
New York, NY 10022

All Kensington titles, imprints and distributed lines are available at special quantity discounts for bulk purchases for sales promotion, premiums, fund-raising, educational or institutional use.

Special book excerpts or customized printings can also be created to fit specific needs. For details, write or phone the office of the Kensington Special Sales Manager: Kensington Publishing Corp., 850 Third Avenue, New York, NY 10022. Attn: Special Sales Department. Phone: 1-800-221-2647.

Zebra and the Z logo Reg. U.S. Pat. & TM Off.

First Printing: May 2005
10 9 8 7 6 5 4 3 2 1

Printed in the United States of America

This book is dedicated to Wendy Evans who inspired, encouraged, and, when necessary, administered perfectly aimed swift kicks. And to Ron. Always.

The author would like to acknowledge with thanks:

My husband, Ron, and our three boys, Thomas, Michael and John, for giving me the space and time to dream.

My editor, Hilary Sares, for giving wings to the dream.

My agent, Jenny Bent, and her assistant, Michelle, for keeping the dreamer focused.

My mom, Arlene, for instilling in me a love of books and Abu Ben Adam; my dad, Doug for keeping the stories *he* could tell to himself; Annie, Don, and Sooze for letting me be the youngest and enjoying all the perks that go with that.

The best group of writers I could hope to be part of. Your honesty is always appreciated (maybe not right when you say it, but certainly after enough time has passed and enough chocolate eaten).

And to the debs who offered an unending supply of guidance, wisdom and apple turnovers.

Chapter 1

Porter Creek, Montana Territory, 1885

Tess Kinley wanted to die. Six days on the stage, driven by the devil himself, was more than a body could be expected to endure. There wasn't a single pothole or creek bed between Butte and Porter Creek she had not been jolted through; not a single filthy station missed; not a single decent meal eaten. She had not bathed in a week, nor had she washed or changed her clothes. Her weakened stomach had long since revolted against the onslaught of such offenses, and although she had not disgraced herself in front of anyone else yet, she would not have cared one little bit if she had.

The stage turned over on two separate occasions, and one of the poor old horses was shot when its left hind leg snapped after becoming entwined in the wreckage. They'd been stuck up to the axles in mud after a three-day downpour, and during this time Tess's vocabulary became significantly extended through the teachings of Mr. Forbes, the stage driver.

She could have gotten off the stage at any point along the way, and probably should have, but with every mile she was able to endure, she had one less mile to go; one mile farther from her nightmare; one mile closer to her dream.

Bumped, bruised, scraped and scratched, she had, by some small miracle, lived through it and arrived at the Porter Creek station in one piece—sicker than she ever would have imagined, but alive nonetheless. Her stomach continued to roll for hours afterward, bile threatening with every intake of breath. At one point Tess was certain she had in fact died and gone to hell, but the elusive peace that comes only with death continued to taunt from within her scattered dreams. A dear old woman bundled Tess in a thin gray blanket and took her to El Cielo where she helped Tess up the stairs and into a huge soft bed.

With filtered sunshine bathing the room in a heavenly glow, Tess's angel appeared. Never in her wildest dreams had she imagined an angel dressed in a beat-up black Stetson or a past-faded chambray shirt, yet there he was, larger than life and more beautiful than any being, human *or* spiritual, had any right to be. For a moment she thought perhaps he was a dream, a figment of her worn-out, defenseless imagination. But then his mouth opened and what came out was certainly not anything one would expect from a guardian of the soul.

"What the hell d'you mean 'it's a girl'? I can see that!" His voice was thunder, beginning as a low rumble and ending in an earth quaking roar that rattled the plate glass windows. "What the hell's she doing here?"

"You no curse to me, Gabe Calloway! Le debo tomar sobre mi rodilla y le da una azotaina buena."

If she hadn't been so tired, Tess would have laughed, or at least offered something to the conversation. But even the thought took too much energy, so she remained as she was, tucked up under the blankets, her amber eyes peering undetected at the huge man-angel and the much shorter, much older woman.

Gabe Calloway, to all outward appearances, seemed the epitome of masculine authority. His solid, six-foot-plus frame fairly filled the doorway when he entered the room—a room he managed to cross in two easy, yet loud, strides. He towered above Tess, his back as straight as could be and his arms, bare to the elbow, crossed over his massive chest. Harsh slate-colored eyes studied her for a moment, his tightened lips paled almost white against sun bronzed skin.

"Why's she here?"

"How I know?" the woman snapped back. "Amos Hubbard say she friend of Bart Calloway and I take home."

A derisive snort sounded from Tess's angel. "Well, you were with her the entire way home. Did she say anything?"

The woman's head shook slowly. "*Nada. La niña* no feel good."

"I can see that, Rosa. Didn't Amos tell you anything else?"

Another head shake. "Amos Hubbard say she friend of Bart Call—"

"You already said that," he interrupted. "Where did she come from?"

"Amos Hubbard say Sherman Forbes say Butte."

"Butte?" Gabe repeated, then muttered, "I don't know anyone in Butte."

"Si," Rosa corrected as she gathered Tess's dirty clothes from the floor. "Bart Calloway in Butte."

"Bart's in Butte?"

"Why you keep say what I say?"

Gabe ignored her. "How do you know where he is?"

"Bart Calloway send letter."

"When?" Honest surprise filled Gabe's voice.

Rosa shrugged indifferently as she turned to leave the room.

"Rosa!" he called after her. "What did it say?"

Tess squeezed her eyes tight to fight back the tears of laughter. So maybe he, the beautiful Angel Gabriel, wasn't the one who reined supreme over all that was Calloway.

"How I know?" Rosa said. "I no read it."

"Then how the hell d'you know he's in Butte?"

"You no curse to me, Gabe Calloway! Le debo tomar . . ." Rosa's reprimand trailed down the stairs behind her.

"Yeah, yeah, okay, okay," he interrupted again, stomping after her.

Tess slept the rest of the day, her dreams filled with fanciful imagery of her Stetson-wearing angel with not a wing or halo in sight. When she awoke, the sun was low in the western sky, leaving her room basking in the brilliance of the last light of day. The distant horizon was almost too perfect to look at, with its contrasting shades of flaming magentas against the cerulean heavens. This was exactly how she had pictured it; exactly how it had been described in all those books she had read, tucked up alone in her room, before her father . . .

"You're awake." Her angel spoke from the open doorway. His voice was so deep, so strong, yet so soft, it sent shivers down her spine.

"Yes," she answered, suddenly overcome by a wave of panic. What on earth was she doing? She didn't even know this man, yet here she was, lying half-naked in the most comfortable bed she could remember, with the full intent of making herself indispensable to the Calloway ranch and everyone who lived there.

If Gabe noticed her discomfort, or the way she slowly tightened the blankets around her, he kept it to himself. He carried in a silver tray loaded down with more food than could feed six people, never mind a lone girl.

"Rosa thought you might be hungry," he stated, avoiding her gaze.

"Thank you." Tess smiled weakly. "I believe I could eat."

She carefully adjusted the blanket, managing, somehow, to hold it with one hand and push herself up with the other. She cringed at the sight of her own skin, still gray with grimy road dust. She could only imagine what the rest of her looked like. Tess Kinley prided herself on always looking her best; her ginger-colored hair had never known a dirty day nor had it ever hung in tatters around her shoulders as it did now. She was under no false illusion that she was a beautiful woman, for she knew she was not, but she was clean and, if nothing else, she was a lady. And to Tess Kinley, that was much more important.

Gabe set the tray on the end of the bed and turned to leave.

"Won't you stay?" The words were out before she realized her mouth was open.

He hesitated but a moment, straightened slightly, then strode to the rocking chair under the window. His long legs stretched out in front of him, boots crossed at the ankles, his hands folded loosely across his belt buckle. His eyes looked everywhere except at her, the muscle in his jaw alternately flexing and relaxing. Tess smiled to herself. He was nervous. Big Gabriel Calloway, master of the house, was uncomfortable sitting in the same room as she. Good.

"Isn't it beautiful?" she asked, biting into a thick slab of warm buttered bread.

"What?" There was a forced gruffness to his voice, but still he avoided her eyes.

"The sunset," she answered. "It's absolutely breathtaking."

"Yeah." Gabe shrugged.

A long moment of silence followed in which Tess could feel his eyes watching her, yet every time she looked over, his face was turned away.

"Rosa's going to want to know your name."

"Oh yes." She smiled, wondering if he felt the faint flush that crept up from beneath his collar. "I suppose that would help, wouldn't it?"

Gabe's only response was to arch his brow impatiently.

"Tess Kinley," she said. "And you are Gabriel Calloway."

At the sound of his name, she watched the fierceness fade from his eyes and the tightness of his jaw relax. What caused him to take in such a huge breath, blink slowly, and exhale in a long, low whistle? The whole episode took but a few heartbeats before his face clouded over again.

"Why don't you tell me why you're here?"

It was certainly not a question, and even though she'd had over a week to perfect her explanation, she knew he would probably laugh her right back to Butte.

"I'm, uh, a . . . friend . . . of Bart's." Not really a lie, but not exactly the truth either.

"I gathered as much," he snipped. "Are you carrying his child?"

Tess choked on her mouthful of bread and took a full two minutes to recover with no help from Gabe.

"Am I *what*?" she cried, wiping her mouth with the blue-checked napkin. "Of all the—"

"Are you?"

"I most certainly am not!" She pushed the tray

back and sat up, barely remembering to grab the blanket. "What gives you the right to come in here and—"

"I'll tell you what gives me the right," Gabe stormed, heaving himself out of the chair so he towered over her once again. "You show up at my ranch, eat my food, sleep in my house and I don't—"

"Okay!" she snapped back. "Quit yelling."

"I'm not yelling!" he roared, then again, only slightly lower, "I'm not yelling."

"I'd hate to hear what you sound like when you *are* yelling," she muttered, forcing several deep breaths into her lungs.

"What?" He grasped the footboard and leaned over, menacingly close.

"Nothing." She should be frightened of this hulking man, but there was something about him that just made her want to hug him.

"Don't mutter then if you don't want me to hear what you're saying."

"Then don't yell at me."

"I'm not yelling!"

The corners of Tess's eyes began to crinkle, her mouth turning up in an increasing smile. It would only make him more angry, but she just couldn't help herself. She started to laugh, a giggle at first, and was soon doubled over holding her aching sides as the tears streamed down her cheeks.

"I'm sorry," she laughed. "It's just . . . I . . . Bart . . ."

Gabe crossed his arms over his chest as he straightened.

"Bart," he snorted. "Tell me how you know him."

Tess's laughter faded. This was the tricky part. How to explain her connection to Bart without being tossed out on her ear. It wasn't hard to see Gabe had little use for his younger brother.

She wiped her eyes and cleared her throat

before she started. "I recently became acquainted with Bart when he came to Butte to . . . attend to some business."

Another snort. "He's a bounty hunter, lady, not a banker."

"Yes, well, in any case, that's how we met."

"You're an outlaw?"

"No!"

"But you just said . . ."

"If you'd let me finish," she muttered. Too late. Most likely he already thought her to be nothing more than a common hoodlum or, worse yet, some kind of tawdry young harlot.

"Speak up."

"Quit interrupting."

She thought she saw the beginnings of a smirk flash across his face before he turned away to take his place in the rocking chair.

"As it turned out," she continued, with more than a little umbrage, "I just so happen to know the man your brother was looking for."

"Who was it?" His steel gaze fixed on her. The look had probably made more than one person squirm, but she was too incensed to let it bother her.

"His name is Barclay Simms."

"How do you know him?"

"Does it really matter?" she shot back.

"You tell me."

"I'm not carrying *his* child either, if that's what you think." Not that he hadn't tried, she shuddered inwardly.

Gabe shrugged. "So?"

"So that's how I met Bart. He was very kind to me."

"Of course he was—you're female!"

"I beg your pardon, Mr. Calloway," she huffed, "but your brother was . . . is . . . every bit the gentleman."

It was Gabe's turn to laugh—a deep, rich sound

that floated up from his throat. "Bart—a gentleman? I've heard him called a lot of things, but a gentleman sure as hell ain't one of them."

Tess lost her train of thought the moment he laughed. He was truly beautiful when he wasn't scowling.

"So if he was so honorable, why are you here instead of with him?"

Tess took a deep breath and released it slowly.

"I've always wanted to come out west, to work the land, to really live instead of just being."

Gabe's eyes narrowed suspiciously. "Where are you from?"

"Boston originally," she said and instantly regretted it. His eyes widened in horror and his head shook slowly back and forth.

"A city girl," he spat out. "Probably come from money, too, don't you?"

Tess straightened. "My father is an attorney, yes."

His blatant disgust almost made her feel guilty. Almost.

"I'll never understand you city folk. What the hell do you think you're doing out here anyway?"

"I want to be here."

"Why? Have you ever done a day's work in your life?" Before Tess could answer, he continued on his rampage. "It's not what you think it is, city girl. This is real life out here. This is hard work, every minute of every day. There's no cotillions or fancy socials out here. You're lucky to see a neighbor once a month, even luckier to get into town to buy supplies every two months. The summers are hotter than hell, and the winters are colder than a witch's . . ."

He stopped. Tess's face flamed in embarrassment and growing fury.

"I will grant you, Mr. Calloway, I have not been raised on a ranch and I may not have the first clue what it's really like to live it every day of my life, but it's what I want. It's what I've always wanted." She paused, swallowing the lump that had inched its way up her throat. "And when I heard Bart speak of El Cielo, and saw the look in his eyes, I knew this was the place for me. This is where I belong. I'm not stupid, you know. I know it's going to be different than what I'm used to, and I fully expect some hard work along the way, but—"

"*Some* hard work?" he sneered. "You don't have the first clue about hard work."

He leaned over, his elbows resting on his knees, and studied her, taking in every inch of her still heated face.

"Oh, for the love of God, say it ain't so." His face fell into his hands, his head shaking back and forth. "Tell me you're not one of those droopy-eyed females who got all these deranged ideas from one of those crazy books they sell at the mercantile."

Tess lifted her chin slightly. She'd never in a million years admit it to him. The fact of the matter was that was exactly where she first discovered her yearning for ranch life.

Gabe lifted his head, rose to his full height, and aimed another piercing stare at her.

"You just get yourself back on the stage and head right back to Boston or Butte or wherever the nearest society page is. You've got no business out here in the middle of nowhere. There is nothing romantic about working out in the dirt all day. It's nothing like how those stupid books describe it."

"But . . ."

"But nothing. Porter Creek's no place for a city girl, especially a little thing like yourself. Bart should've told you that right up front. He knows how I feel about . . ."

"He doesn't know I'm here."

Chapter 2

"What the hell . . ." If he'd been confused before, Gabe was downright stumped now. Who was this little waif of a thing and, more important, what the hell was she doing on his ranch?

"It's hard to explain," she said softly, her eyes lowered to her fidgeting hands.

"Try."

"It's a long story."

Gabe resumed his place in the chair and crossed his legs at the ankles. He did not utter a sound, but the indication was clear. It wasn't that he *wanted* to hear this inevitably long and irrelevant story, but she had traveled all this way by herself. It was the least he could do. And if it meant he'd have to watch those amber eyes of hers snap like firelight again, then so be it. He'd just have to put up with it.

"Would you mind if I got dressed first? I'm not very comfortable."

"Rosa took your clothes to wash them." He watched the color inch its way up her neck and suddenly realized she was nearly naked under that thin blanket. Good God—what was he thinking? He pulled open the wardrobe and yanked out a long red flannel shirt and a pair of well-worn Levi's. He wasn't happy about letting this girl wear his clothes—even if they were his winter stock—but he couldn't very well let her sit there as she was.

Gabe dropped the clothes on the end of the bed and walked wordlessly out the door, straining to hear Tess scramble to get the clothes on before he came back. And he would be back. She was threading her bootlace through the belt loops when he returned. The force of a hundred lightning bolts slammed him right between the eyes the minute he entered the room. How could someone so dirty—no, so *filthy*— look so beautiful in clothes miles too big for her? He could only imagine what she looked like clean.

A wrenching tear pulled unexpectedly at his heart. So help him if Bart had done anything to this girl, there would be hell to pay. Supreme Gabe Calloway hell.

"Better?" he asked, forcing a frown.

"Yes. Thank you."

He waited for her to sit somewhere, but when she began to pace he opted once again for the rocker. It took her a good while before she was able to gather her thoughts enough to speak.

"I don't want to talk about it," she finally blurted. "You'll think I'm horrible."

His flat, unspeaking eyes widened, and his head lolled slightly to the side. Her finely arched brows creased together, her lips pursed into a thin white line. Gabe was beginning to think she really wasn't going to talk about it when she suddenly squared her shoulders and raised her chin a fraction.

"Okay, but please remember it was the circumstances that were horrible, not me. I'm really a very good person."

Gabe tried to hold his frown, but his lips began to twitch upward. Tess rubbed her hands back and forth as she continued to pace.

"Your brother saved me from making a very big mistake."

No response, just a quirked brow. Now he really was intrigued since Bart was usually the one making the mistakes, not preventing them. This might prove interesting after all.

Tess tossed her head, sending a mess of gritty mane back over her shoulder. What on earth could have her in such a tither? For crying out loud, surely a little thing like her couldn't possibly get into *that* much trouble. Could she? Even if it had something to do with Bart . . .

The lilt of her voice rocked him back to his senses.

"My family, well my father really, and I had a disagreement about something, and he made it perfectly clear if I did not see things his way, I would no longer be welcome in his home."

"What was it?"

"What was what?" she asked. "Oh, yes, the disagreement. My father had chosen my husband for me and I disagreed with his choice."

"But marriages are arranged all the time."

"Not mine," she answered stiffly, adjusting the bootlace belt. "I will marry the man I choose, and no one else."

Gabe fought back a smile. So much tenacity in such a little thing. The man was probably lucky she didn't marry him. She continued to fuss with the hugely oversized clothes, rolling cuffs and picking at invisible lint.

"So I was forced to leave my family's home and make my own way."

She appeared to be finished, but Gabe was not about to let it end there.

"What was wrong with him?" he asked.

"Who?"

"General Lee," he quipped.

"Oh." She flushed. "You mean my would-be husband. I'm sure many would think there was nothing wrong with him, that he was perfectly fine. He comes from a respectable family, he has a good job, and I am certain I would have wanted for nothing had I married him."

"But . . ."

"But I didn't love him."

Gabe's laughter boomed through the room and echoed out into the hallway.

"I see nothing funny about this," she said haughtily. "Why are you laughing?"

"You gave up a respectable life of wealth and opportunity because you didn't love the poor sap? Are you crazy?" His laughter ebbed to a chuckle. "You really have been reading too many books, little girl. Nobody loves each other when they get married—they learn to get along, is all."

Tess's mouth fell open and then snapped closed.

"I don't believe that," she finally said. "And I don't believe you do either."

"So let me guess." He smirked. "You believe in love at first sight."

"Yes." The deep gold flecks in her eyes shone brilliantly—too brilliantly, sobering him instantly. He was on his feet in a heartbeat, averting his own gaze as he strode past her.

"I'll have Rosa fix you a bath if you'd like. We'll finish this later."

It was Tess's turn to smirk now. She'd embarrassed him. It was unintentional, but the fact was she did believe in love at first sight. And she had fallen in love the instant she saw her angel.

She was still smiling five minutes later when Rosa bustled in, loaded down with fresh towels and a pink cotton wrapper, followed by a man lugging a huge metal bathtub.

"Senorita," Rosa said, "Miguel bring bath to you."

"Hello, Miguel." Tess smiled. "I'm Tess. It's a pleasure to meet you."

Miguel grinned back. *"Hola,* senorita."

He positioned the tub under the window and hurried from the room to collect buckets full of water. Tess smiled at Rosa.

"Is Miguel your husband?" she asked.

"Sí. We marry many year." She arranged the towels on the bureau and then stood, her arms crossed under her ample bosom, and stared at Tess. There was no hint of accusation in the look, simply curiosity.

"I'm grateful for all your help today," Tess offered. "You are very kind."

Rosa shrugged. "You friend to Bart Calloway, you friend to Rosa."

"I'm afraid Mr. Calloway doesn't see it that way."

Rosa's dark eyes frowned. "Gabe Calloway está muy orgulloso. Very proud."

"Yes," Tess agreed. "I see that."

"He have . . ." Her brow furrowed. "How you say . . . *una corazon triste."*

"I'm afraid I don't understand."

"Gabe Calloway have . . . sad heart."

Rosa shook her head sadly but offered no other explanation. Miguel arrived with two huge buckets of piping hot water and began the arduous task of filling the massive tub. From what Tess could gather, he had engaged the help of the other ranch hands but would only allow them to bring the water to the top of the stairs. He took over from there and carried it into the room. As such, it didn't take the bucket brigade very long to fill the tub.

"Thank you very much." Tess smiled, grasping

Miguel's hand in hers. "And please thank the other men for me."

Miguel smiled as he backed out of the room, his midnight-colored eyes shining first at Rosa and then at Tess. Rosa nodded toward the tray of barely touched food.

"You no feel good. Better?"

"Much better, thank you," Tess sighed. "I will try to eat more."

"Buena niña." Tess had no idea what that meant, but she gathered she was "niña."

After Rosa closed the door behind her, Tess stood in the middle of the room basking in its peace. As much as she longed to jump into the steaming bath, she was reluctant to remove the clothes Gabe had given her to wear. They were so personal, so much a part of him, she hated to lose that link even for a minute.

Eventually she did get in the tub and sank right under the water, head and all, relishing the cleanliness of it all. The new bar of soap Rosa left her was unlike the hard yellow lye soap she'd grown accustomed to in the last few weeks. It was a creamy white color and smelled of fresh honey—something Tess never would have imagined finding in Gabriel Calloway's house.

She began at the top of her head, scrubbing the full length of her hair twice and rinsing it until it squeaked. She continued down over the rest of her body until she was absolutely certain she had scrubbed off every last inch of grime. Then she stood and re-rinsed herself with the extra bucket of water. She could not recall ever feeling as clean as she did at that moment.

"Don't get used to it," she reminded herself. "You no longer have the luxury of daily baths."

Before she was completely dry, she pulled Gabe's

shirt back on and snuggled into its warmth. The rest of the clothes she left in a heap on the rocker while she rummaged through her small carpetbag for her brush. It was a toilsome thing, battling the tangles in her almost waist-length hair, and close to an hour passed before she finished. Satisfied her hair was finally tangle free, Tess donned the pink cotton wrapper and took up the tray of food. She'd been alone long enough; perhaps Rosa would share a snack with her.

The silence in the hallway made Tess tiptoe down the stairs. She had no idea what time it was, but it must have been late for it to be so quiet. To her right she found the kitchen, empty and spotless, as was the living room, the only other room downstairs. Tess frowned.

"Looking for Rosa?" Gabe's deep voice took her by surprise. He had made his way into the kitchen without causing the slightest stir. His jaw clenched and his hands fisted at his sides. Tess's skin tingled under his piercing eyes. No one had ever looked at her with such raw intensity. He took a breath, rested his hands on the back of one of the chairs, and seemed to steady himself.

Tess swallowed. "Yes. I thought perhaps she would like to share a snack with me."

"She's gone home." He cleared his throat twice before managing to finish his sentence.

"Oh, too bad." Tess looked at the tray for another moment then brightened. "Would you like to join me?"

"I don't think . . ." he almost sputtered.

"Come now, Mr. Calloway, we'll take this food outside and enjoy the evening. Just look at that moon." She pointed out the kitchen window to the huge yellow moon. "I've never seen it so bright."

She did not wait for him to answer, just walked

past him through the kitchen door and out onto the huge porch. Her heart swelled when she put the tray down and looked around; the view that greeted her was more spectacular than she had ever imagined. The Calloway land stretched out before her, rolling on for mile after green mile in each direction. Huge pine trees stretched toward the endless clear sky, as though reaching for the stars themselves. A long, deep porch wrapped around the full front of the house, giving the multitude of pink and crimson roses a built-in trellis to climb. Two bamboo rocking chairs, flanking a small square table, faced due east, toward the barn; and adjacent to the main house, about 500 yards off, stood a pretty little apple-green cottage surrounded by a whitewashed picket fence. It was its own little world. Tess smiled. No—Rosa and Miguel's own little world.

Tess inhaled deeply the rich fragrance of the roses mingled with the wild eucalyptus growing near the barn. The night could not have been more perfect. She arranged the tray on the table and settled in one of the rockers, fully expecting Gabe to do the same.

Gabe Calloway had no idea what to make of this woman who'd walked into his life just hours before. She was certainly not like the other women he'd known, and he had known a few. She was not easily intimidated, and God knew most people found Gabe Calloway to be one of the most intimidating people in the county. His size alone was enough to scare the bejeepers out of most folk, but she marched around him like he was nothing more than a piece of furniture. And speaking of which, she had certainly made herself at home in a short amount of time, sitting there in the moonlight as though she'd done it a million times before, as if this were her home.

He lowered himself into the other chair, glancing her way when he was sure she wouldn't notice. Her sweet doll face was pink from her scrubbing; and her long wavy hair, still slightly damp, hung down over her right shoulder. Why couldn't Gabe take his eyes off that head of hair? A far cry from the dull brown it had been an hour before, its natural beauty now began to show. A tawny mix of gold and brown, there was something about it, something that drew his eyes, a beckoning force—daring his fingers to reach out and touch it.

He couldn't help but admire her. It wasn't just any old female who'd take out across the country by herself to follow some foolish idea. After the first day on the stage, most would have hightailed it right back to the city. She still didn't belong here, but he had to give her credit for trying.

Of course, he wouldn't tell *her* that.

"What is it that you do here on your ranch, Mr. Calloway?" she asked, then bit into a crisp red apple.

Gabe watched a trickle of juice slide down her chin before she caught it with a napkin. He swallowed hard.

"We raise cattle."

"Cattle?" She almost beamed. "Wonderful. What kind?"

"Longhorns," he answered, starting to smile as well. "You familiar with them?"

"No. I don't know a thing about cows." She started to laugh then, a light twinkling that floated out through the night and right into Gabe's heart. "But I'm a quick learner."

"You're not staying," he said, still smiling.

"Yes, I am."

"Don't you think Bart's going to have something to say about this when he gets here?"

"Bart?" she asked. "Is he coming home?"

"You tell me."

"I'm sure I have no idea what your brother plans

to do, Mr. Calloway. We didn't exactly part on the best of terms."

"Well, Miss Kinley, I'm sure if Bart is half the . . . man . . . I know him to be, he'll be hot on your trail. He should be here within the week."

"Hmmm." She looked thoughtful, though not particularly distressed. "That could pose a bit of a problem."

"Really?" Gabe couldn't help but smile to himself.

"I must confess something to you, Mr. Calloway." The apple fell into her lap with a thump, leaving her hands free to fidget. "With regard to your brother . . . the thing is . . . I'm afraid . . . well, the long and short of it is this—I belong to him."

Gabe's throat tightened even though he'd half been expecting this.

"You married my brother."

"No, nothing like that."

"Then what?" Why should he care—he had no hold on this woman.

"This is most embarrassing," she said, talking into her lap. "Your brother, Bart . . ."

"Yes, I know who my brother is."

"You needn't be snippy," she mumbled.

"What?"

"Nothing."

"Then don't mutter."

Tess crossed her arms tightly against her chest, her pale pink lips pursed in a deep frown. She had more to say, that was certain, and watching her fight against the urge to say it was more than Gabe could take without laughing. He pushed back his smirk, crossed his own arms, and settled back in the chair.

"What about Bart?" he persisted. "Now that we both know who he is."

Tess exhaled loudly before she spoke.

"Your brother Bart won me in a poker game."

Chapter 3

Gabe nearly tumbled out of his chair. Did she really just say . . .

"Five card draw," Tess continued, sounding very matter-of-fact about it. "He had four aces. That's a good hand, isn't it? It must be, because as soon as everyone saw it, they started groaning and throwing their cards on the table. I've never been one for cards really. My mother, God bless her, tried to teach me the games she played with her ladies' club, but I could never figure them out. I just can't sit still long enough. Do you play cards, Mr. Calloway? I suppose you must; it seems to be the thing men do, doesn't it? Play cards and drink whiskey. Do you drink whiskey? I think it smells absolutely horrid. I just can't imagine having to swallow something that smells so awful, but I guess . . ."

"He won you in a poker game?" Gabe's head spun faster than her words. Bart had done a lot of strange things in his lifetime, but this was way beyond even him.

"Yes." She took in a deep breath, smiled, and sat back against her chair.

"Would you care to explain that?"

"Actually, no," she said. "If you are giving me the option, I'd rather not."

Gabe smiled back with forced politeness. "You misunderstand me—I'm not giving you the option."

"I was afraid of that." Tess sighed. "Well, you see, the thing is I actually belonged to another man who was at the same table as Bart. And when he ran out of money, he was using whatever else he owned for collateral and I just happened to be one of those things. Me and a lovely silver pocket watch, I must admit, I believe he came by through illegal means. He did have a horse as well, a beautiful black gelding named Norman of all things, but he was adamant about holding on to the animal. I guess I should have been insulted he would give me up so easily and not his horse, but frankly I was so happy to be rid of him that I just didn't care one bit."

Gabe squeezed the bridge of his nose between his thumb and forefinger. How much more complicated could this possibly get?

"I'm almost afraid to ask," he groaned, "but how is it you refused to marry a 'perfectly fine' wealthy man in Boston, yet you'd let yourself be owned like a slave by a man who apparently was *not* perfectly fine? President Lincoln did outlaw slavery some years back, didn't he? Or was that whole war thing just a bad dream?"

"A nightmare is more like it, Mr. Calloway," she said. "But you're right, it does sound horrid, doesn't it? It was such a simple idea at first and then everything just sort of fell apart. I'm not afraid to tell you, I thank the good Lord every day for your brother."

"That makes one of us," he grumbled.

"I'm sorry." She smirked. "I didn't hear you—were you mumbling something?"

"Never mind." His grumble turned into a downright growl. "Let's just get this over with."

Tess shifted in her chair, her hands now fumbling with the half-eaten apple in her lap.

"All right then. As I told you, my father disowned me, and I was left on my own without anything, just what I managed to throw in the little carpetbag I have. I had no money, no skills to speak of with which to gain employment. My poor mother would have died much sooner if she'd thought for one moment one of her daughters actually had to work for a living. Her girls were raised to be ladies, and nice ladies did not perform menial tasks. We were raised to sip tea from bone china, play the piano, and have a taste for fashion. My goodness, Mother is probably spinning in her grave as we speak . . ."

"Miss Kinley!"

"Oh, yes, sorry. So what was I to do? I had my dream of moving west and working on a ranch with my husband, having children, that sort of thing, but I was in Boston. Have you been to Boston, Mr. Calloway? It's in Massachusetts, you know."

"Yes, I know."

"It really is lovely. There's theater and carriage rides through the park, people play croquet right out on their lawns. There are horse races and . . . I'm getting off the topic again, aren't I?"

Gabe nodded wearily.

"I do apologize, it's just when I get ner . . . never mind. As you can imagine, my options were very limited. In the time it would take me to find a job and save enough money to come out here on my own, I would be too old for marriage, let alone children, so I did the next best thing."

"Which was?"

"I saw an advertisement in the newspaper that stated there were ranchers looking for wives and I answered it."

"You didn't."

"I most certainly did," she stated, straightening in her chair. "The advertisement said hardworking, honest men would pay quite handsomely for a good wife, and I will make a good wife—a very good wife—the only problem is apparently the money is supposed to go to the woman's family. And that, as you can imagine, is where things began to go terribly wrong."

"No, Miss Kinley," Gabe sighed. "Things started going terribly wrong the minute you chose to defy your father."

"I didn't defy him!" she cried. "I simply did not agree with him! He was being stubborn and unreasonable and I could not allow him to marry me off to the first rich man to come along. Despite what people might think, I believe a woman is entitled to have a say in how her life will be lived. I didn't want to spend my days drinking tea and playing silly games with brainless ninnies who have no opinions on anything going on in the world. I want more than that! I want . . ."

"The life out west. Yes, I know." Gabe tried to wrap his brain around this crazy woman's rationale and it just would not happen; but he'd come this far, he had to hear the rest of it.

"You see," she continued, "I couldn't very well let my family know what I was doing or they would have most certainly had me committed to an insane asylum. Father is on the hospital board, you see, so it would be an easy thing for him to do. Shameful, but easy nonetheless. Come to think of it, Uncle Benjamin might have taken me in. He's more liberal minded than Father and his shortsighted rabble, but I doubt even he would understand my need to do this. At any rate, I had the man—the one I was to marry, I mean—forward all the correspondence to my dear friend Charlotte. She lives on the other side of the city, she does, but we have been friends since we were very little girls. She's such a dear, she is. The oldest of five girls! Can you even imagine having five daughters? I'm very certain my father would have gone completely daft if there had been one more girl in our house. My sister and I were more than enough for him!"

"You don't say." Gabe's hands moved to massage his throbbing temples.

"Sorry." She clearly wasn't. "My plan was a very simple one really. I would use the gentleman's money to make my way out west, and once I met him, I would decide if I loved him or not. If I decided not, then I would simply return the money that was left and get a job until I could repay the rest."

"You're joking, right?"

"No." She shook her head vehemently. "I believe it would have worked, too, except the man came to Boston to collect me personally. He said no man in his right mind would part with that kind of money with no guarantee a bride would show up. Even if he did have a written contract."

"How much money are we talking about here?"

"Two hundred and seventy-five dollars."

Gabe whistled. "Smart man."

"Not smart enough, I'm afraid, but that's simply making a long story longer. By God's good graces, he agreed to hold off on the marriage until we made it west. By and by we made it to Butte where I was used as . . . collateral . . . in the poker game that passed me along to your brother Bart."

She had done her best to tell him as many half-truths as possible, and Gabe knew it full well, but he wasn't sure he could handle the whole truth in one fell swoop anyway, so he decided not to push his luck. There was one thing he couldn't quite get a handle on though.

"So how is it if you're worth almost three hundred

dollars to my brother, he just up and let you walk away?" His face darkened like an August storm. "Or did he exact payment from you in some other way?"

"Oh, no, nothing like that!" Tess's eyes skittered over his and then back down to her lap. "I just left. Well, to be perfectly honest, I didn't just leave, I borrowed some of his winnings before I left—just to get me out here, you see, and then I was going to wire it all back to him."

A huge smile spread across Gabe's face. This story just kept getting better.

"You stole from my brother?"

"Well, I wouldn't exactly call it stealing, Mr. Calloway."

"Did you ask if you could take it?"

"N-no, I didn't."

"Did he offer it to you?"

"No."

"Then that, Miss Kinley, is stealing. You're a thief!"

"I most certainly am not! I fully intend to repay your brother—with interest—once I am able."

Gabe chuckled. "You know what they say about good intentions."

Tess was on her feet in an instant, her fists clenching and unclenching on her hips.

"Mr. Calloway, I assure you—"

"Now don't go getting your knickers all in a bunch, I'm not going to turn you in. Fact is, nothing makes me happier than when someone does a turn to Bart he probably would've done to them if the opportunity presented itself. You were smart to get away when you had the chance."

Tess sunk down into her chair, looking twice as weary than when she first arrived. Gabe watched her fingers twitch in her lap and her teeth chew on her bottom lip.

"How old are you, Miss Kinley?"

"Old enough to know that is not a question a gentleman asks a lady."

He chuckled again, low in his throat. "I never claimed to be a gentleman, Miss Kinley, and you have yet to prove to me you are indeed a lady."

"Why I . . ."

"You what?" he asked, enjoying all too much the way her neck flushed when she became angry. "All I've learned about you is your father should have taken you over his knee and prevented this whole mess from happening. But instead, you've bounced from one man to another to another until you landed here. You know nothing about me and yet here you are, sitting on my porch—only half dressed—and you claim to be a lady? I think the *real* ladies here in town would have a different opinion, don't you?"

"But I've done nothing wrong," she hurriedly explained. "I am a good, virtuous woman who . . ."

"Who happens to be a thief and who doesn't mind sitting here, in make-do night clothes, with a man you've just met and not a chaperone in sight. Hell, the only other woman for miles is Rosa, and since she's not even married to Miguel, she doesn't count either!"

Tess gasped. "She told me he was her husband!"

That piece of news always seemed to cause a stir. "They've lived as man and wife for as long as I've known them, but they are not legally married."

"Oh my!" Shocked at the revelation, Tess thought no less of either Rosa or Miguel. In fact, she actually admired them—it was such a daring thing to do.

They sat in the evening silence, both lost in their own thoughts, both sneaking glances at the other as if sizing each other up. It was very distracting to Tess having him sit so close to her. He did not frighten her in any way, even when he yelled like a maddened bear, but the smell of leather and sunshine that clung to him was more than she could possibly be expected to take and not lose her train of thought. It was no wonder she rambled on like a crazy woman.

Gabe's mind couldn't have been more muddled. She couldn't stay here. He *would* send her back, but there was something about her. She pulled him in every time she batted those bewitching amber eyes at him, every time she went off on one of her tangents, every time she moved and the soft, sweet smell of honey lingered in her place.

"You know Bart will come looking for you." He said it gently, but matter-of-factly.

"But he doesn't know where I went, so why would he come here?" For the first time, she almost sounded worried.

"Because he's a bounty hunter, Miss Kinley. It's his business to find people. And besides, you'd be an easy one to track."

"Why is that?"

"A single woman traveling across most of the territory by herself is a sight most folks take note of."

Tess almost whimpered. "I never thought about that."

"No matter," he said. "You'll be back on next week's stage anyway, so he won't find you here."

"I won't leave."

"Yes, you will."

"No, Mr. Calloway, I will not. I made it all the way out here, didn't I? Don't you think I deserve the chance to make a life out here?"

"I don't honestly know what you deserve, but I do know this is no place for city girls. Sooner or later you're going to realize that, too, so why don't you save everyone a whole lot of trouble and go home? Marry that 'perfectly fine rich man' and live the life you were supposed to live."

"No."

Gabe stared straight at her. "No? Where do you intend to stay while you're in Porter Creek? The hotel costs money."

"I'll stay here."

"That's impossible."

"Why?"

"Because you're a single woman and I'm a single man."

"Yes, but you're an honorable man. I am certain you would not act inappropriately."

"How do you know?"

"Bart told me what a good man you are, how respected you are here in Porter Creek, how conscientious you are, how honorable and upright. . . ."

"Stop!" he cried through his laughter. "You are the worst liar I've ever met. Tell me what he really said."

Tess cleared her throat. "Very well. I believe his exact words were high-minded, staunch, and pompous."

"Now that sounds more like Bart. And out of that, you came up with honorable, upright, and what was the other one?"

"Conscientious."

"Right. Conscientious."

"Regardless," she said, "Rosa would not allow anything untoward to happen."

"Rosa doesn't sleep in the main house."

"Yes, I know, but I do not believe you would try to compromise me in any way."

"Is that right? Have you even thought about what staying here will do to your reputation—even if I was honorable, upright, and what was the other one again?"

"Conscientious."

"Right. Conscientious." He paused. "Well, have you?"

"Of course I have! And as far as I can see, we have two options."

"Really?" Sarcasm dripped from his words. "Would you care to share them with me?"

"Certainly." She smiled. "The first option is for you to sleep in the barn or in the bunkhouse with the other men."

Gabe choked. "This is my house. I'll be damned if I'm going to be kicked out of it by *anyone*— especially a little wisp of a girl like you!"

"That's what I thought you'd say. The other option is much simpler anyway. We can get married."

Chapter 4

It was the scent of honey that snapped Gabe back to his senses. Her scent. It lingered in the air, surrounding him, sapping him of any cognitive thought other than her. He struggled through the fog in his brain, trying to decide if she had, indeed, said what he thought he'd heard. Of course she had not waited for him to offer his own suggestions, but instead collected the tray of food and bolted into the house, leaving him on the porch with his mouth agape.

She had given him two choices, purposely omitting the third and most obvious, which would have Gabe staying in the house with her, reputation be damned. He should do it—just march right in and go on up to bed. This was his house after all, and he certainly had not invited her here. No, he smiled ruefully, he should take her up on her idea and marry her. That would teach her, wouldn't it? Maybe then she'd find out how *un*romantic the ranching life really was and hightail it on out of here. Gabe's smile faded. If it was such a good idea, why did it sit like a rock in the bottom of his belly? Must be the idea of marriage that disagreed with him, because it certainly couldn't be the notion of her leaving. Hell, he didn't even know her. But she sure smelled good.

Cursing under his breath, Gabe cast a final glance toward the kitchen door before trudging out to the barn. Why the hell did his mother—no, Rosa—have to instill such an overactive conscience in him? And how was it she hadn't managed to do the same with his brother? Bart would have been up the stairs and fast asleep by now, his only concern being whether he would have company in his bed or not.

The full moon cast a shimmering yellow light across the yard, but even in the pitch of darkness Gabe would not have taken a misstep. He'd been born and raised right here on the ranch and not a day had gone by when he hadn't made this trek out to the barn at least a half dozen times. He knew, without counting, exactly how many steps it was from the house, the exact angle at which it sat in conjunction with the house, and exactly where every nail had been hammered to keep the structure sound. He spent at least twice as much time out there than he did in the house and, truth be told, it wasn't such a bad place to sleep. It was warm in the winter, cool in the summer, quiet, and at this time of night usually still smelled of clean, fresh hay.

So where was that familiar smell now? And even more disturbing, why the hell did it smell of honey?

Zeus nickered softly and tossed his glossy black mane.

"Hullo, ol' boy," Gabe murmured. "Looks like we're going to be spending a bit more time together."

He scratched the huge stallion's ears and muzzle, whispering nothings to him the whole while. Everyone else in town, including his own ranch hands, referred to his horse as Satan, and that was fine with Gabe. The more wary a body was of an animal, the more they tended to respect it and keep their damn hands to themselves. More than one rancher in Porter Creek had lost horses to thieves in the last few years, but not the Calloways. Zeus was a force to be reckoned with, and the only one up to the challenge was Gabe. No one else would even feed him, let alone clean out his stall or ride him. Not that Gabe would have allowed it anyway, but there was a whole other story.

When Zeus was satisfied he'd not been ignored, Gabe mounted the ladder to the loft and flopped down on the huge pile of straw. The tiny window above his head looked directly back at the house, directly at the bedroom window where Tess lay sleeping. If he peeked out, would he see her there? She seemed to have a thing about looking out at the sky; first it was the sunset, then the full moon. Perhaps she was a stargazer too.

Cussing into the straw, he shifted and twisted in an unsuccessful effort to relax. Why the hell should he care if she was looking out the damned window or not? All that mattered was she was sleeping in the house while he was stuck out in the barn alone with his thoughts. Being alone didn't usually bother Gabe; it gave him the opportunity to focus on the ranch, on what jobs needed to be done first, how much those jobs would cost, and how much profit he would make. Tonight, however, his thoughts were stuck on one thing—Tess Kinley.

She couldn't stay—not in Porter Creek. It was too rough for the likes of her. She needed to live in a place where she could have regular milk baths, go to fancy dances, eat in those fine restaurants he'd heard so much about. She didn't belong here in the middle of nowhere walking through acres of cattle crap and chicken slop. She didn't need to be filthy bloody dirty from sunup to sundown, to sweat like a horse out in the blazing sun or freeze her behind off for months on end in the winter. She needed to be waited on, to be treated like the lady she was born to be. She needed to have servants bring whatever her heart desired, to never have to raise her voice to be heard over the wind or rain or braying of cattle.

Gabe smirked. What she needed was a good whoopin' to put her right. She was far too stubborn for his liking. Far too stubborn. It was a good thing the stage came every week because she'd never last longer than that. Maybe if she was lucky, Bart would arrive before then and take her back to Butte himself. Gabe's easy smirk faded into a deep frown. He didn't even know this girl, but of one thing he was certain—she deserved better than Bart Calloway, a lot better.

He linked his hands behind his head, staring high up into the rafters, seeing nothing but the image of Tess Kinley floating above him. She was a vision all right; her thick, flowing hair tumbling over her shoulder in long graceful waves, her gold-flecked eyes snapping with determination. Yet there was something else that belied her steely resolve. Nobody fidgeted or rambled that much without being fearful of something. Or someone. But who? Bart?

His dark brows drew together. His brother might not be completely virtuous, but he'd never lay a hand to a woman, that much Gabe knew. He might use her and then discard her like a worn-out shoe, but he would never cause her physical harm.

"If she had any sense at all," he mused aloud, "she'd be afraid of me."

Everyone was afraid of Gabe Calloway for one reason or another. His size alone instilled fear in most, his dark scowl and thunderous yell intimidated everyone else. But little Tess hadn't even flinched when he stood over her, towering like one of the huge ponderosa pines so abundant in the Montana Territory. She had, in fact, brushed him aside as though he were nothing more than a spoiled child looking for attention.

Gabe slept fitfully, fighting the haunted memories that plagued him almost nightly and woke him with such a jolt he was certain his heart had leapt from his chest. He wiped his hand slowly across his mouth, knowing the sweat he removed would be replaced just as quickly. The usual torment of his nightmares was even worse tonight. He was still a young boy watching it all happen; the baby, so terribly small, so ghostly blue, and Mama . . . struggling feebly against her own angel of death. She looked to Gabe, the light slowly fading from her gray eyes. Suddenly her eyes were no longer the steel gray of his mother's; they were amber. . . .

Tess tucked herself up into the huge, soft bed and sighed. She was finally home. Whether Gabriel Calloway liked it or not, this was where she belonged—safe at El Cielo with him.

She had, in all honesty, fully expected him to follow her into the house. There was a second bedroom, after all, which he could very easily have slept in. But when she still didn't hear the kitchen door open again, she went to the window and watched, hidden behind the sheer curtains, as Gabe strode purposefully toward the barn. She knew she was right about him; he was a good man. He would make a fine husband.

For all her pomp and display, Tess was more nervous than she ever would have expected or admitted to. She was exactly where she wanted to be, everything was within her grasp, but all it would take was for Gabe to put her sorry behind back on the stage and everything would be ruined. She couldn't let that happen. She belonged here; she was safe here. And best of all, Gabriel was here.

For years Tess had practically devoured the dime novels her friend Charlotte gave her. They filled her with a sense of purpose, a knowledge that life was not meant to be spent drinking tea and playing croquet all day. And it certainly was not meant to be spent with a man you did not love.

Love was something that could neither be helped nor avoided. It happened whether you wanted it to or not, and despite what Mr. Gabriel Calloway thought, it happened immediately. Some people took a little longer to realize it, was all.

She knew she loved him, knew it the moment she opened her eyes and saw him standing in the doorway yelling at Rosa. She also knew nobody would believe her, they'd all think she was a silly little girl living in a dream world.

Well, she huffed, *they can all think whatever they like.* Those dime novels she loved so much might not have been the great literature her mother forced on her, but they were just as—if not more—educational.

She needed a plan, something to make her indispensable both to El Cielo and Gabriel, and something she would be able to put into action right away. After all, the next stage would be back in Porter Creek in one week, and if she didn't prove herself by then, she was certain to be sent packing. And God knew what would happen if Bart happened to show up before then. Or worse . . .

Tess shuddered past the thought, burying herself deeper under the thick, fluffy quilt. Surely it was a good sign Gabe had let her stay in the house. She drifted off into a sound sleep, her dreams a stark contrast to those of Gabe's, save for the fact that he, too, danced through her subconscious.

She was awakened early the next morning by the sound of boot heels—many boot heels—clomping against the hard kitchen floor. She threw back the blankets, taking but a moment to admire the first light of day from her window. With Gabe's old jeans secured tightly around her again, she washed up in the wedgewood chamber set, pulled her hair into one long plait down her back, and hurried, barefoot, down the stairs. Maybe if she learned to be of some use to Rosa . . .

Five pairs of eyes stared back at her, stopping her in her tracks. The two unfamiliar faces seated with Gabe and Miguel openly gaped at her. She must be a sight standing there dwarfed in Gabe's clothes, a strange woman on their turf. Her gaze went immediately to Gabe, who seemed to scowl deeper with every passing second. An eternity passed before Miguel finally spoke.

"*Buenos dias.*" He nodded to her, rising from his seat. "Please." He motioned for her to take his now empty chair.

"Good morning," she answered brightly. "Thank you, Miguel, but you sit and finish your breakfast. I came to see if there was anything I could do to help Rosa."

Gabe returned to his coffee, his scowl staring down into the steaming black brew. When he made no motion to do it himself, Tess took it upon herself to make the introductions.

"Hello," she said to two other men at the table. "My name is Tess Kinley."

The two men—boys really—nearly fell over their chairs in the race to reach her outstretched hand first. They both stopped short, dipped their heads slightly, and spoke at once.

"Joby Dunn."

"Seth Laughton."

"It's very nice to meet you both," she smiled, feeling the heat from Gabe's glare. "Please, finish your breakfast."

The two men flushed profusely and returned to their chairs. Rosa stood with her back to the table, flipping pancakes over the piping hot griddle. The only one who saw her grin was Tess. It was a funny, strange little grin, one that couldn't be easily defined. It had a knowing kind of smirk to it but at the same time seemed to say "be careful what you wish for, *muchacha*, you might just get it."

"Good morning, Rosa," Tess said. "How can I help?"

"You eat," Rosa instructed. "Too skinny."

"I'm fine, really," Tess began, even as Rosa pushed a full plate toward her.

"Eat." She turned from the stove and reached for Joby's and Seth's still full plates.

"We ain't done!" Joby cried, his fork halfway between the plate and his mouth.

"Bup bup bup," Rosa's hands waved them off. "Shoo! *La niña* sit. Eat."

Tess did as she was instructed, enjoying for the moment being fussed over. Once she had a good solid meal in her belly, she'd be ready to take on whatever El Cielo and Gabe threw at her.

"I'm sorry I wasn't up earlier to help you, Rosa," she offered.

"S'okay," Rosa said with a smile. Her black eyes twinkled cheekily. "You eat now. I find you work."

Tess smiled warmly at the older woman as she took Joby's chair.

"You feel better, senorita?" Miguel asked.

"Yes, thank you. It's amazing what a hot bath and a good night's sleep can do for a person." Ignoring the loud snort coming from Gabe's direction, she finished, "Rosa took good care of me."

"Si," he agreed, his smile widening. "Rosa take good care to me, too."

Tess's heart pinched tightly. They loved each other so much, so openly. She longed desperately for that kind of love—the easy, no argument kind of love.

She was more than ready to offer it, but by the look on Gabe's face, he was neither ready to receive nor return it.

She straightened her shoulders. She hadn't come this far to let a little thing like that get in her way. It might take a little work, but she'd have Gabe seeing things her way if it killed her. And judging by his scowl, that was exactly what it might take.

Chapter 5

Gabe pushed back from the table and stood up.

"Rosa," he barked, "Where are her clothes?"

"On the line. They no dry yet."

"Come on." He almost stomped his way to the door before turning to glare at Tess. "Are you coming?"

"Me?" she asked through a mouthful of eggs.

"Who else?"

Miguel smirked over his coffee. Tess looked over to Rosa, who shrugged.

"O-okay," she fumbled, depositing her plate on the counter and hurrying after him, at the same time scrambling to pull on her shoes as she tripped out the door.

The sun shone brilliantly, dancing in the early dew of the new day. Fresh new scents overwhelmed her, filling her with childlike wonder. Who knew dirt could smell so wonderful? So clean, so alive, so . . .

"We don't have time to stand around all day," Gabe snapped.

"Sorry," she answered quickly. "I was . . . oh, never mind. I rather thought I would be helping Rosa today."

It took three of her steps to match Gabe's long stride.

"Rosa doesn't need help; you'd only be in her

way." He pushed open the gate and led her through a throng of squawking chickens to the coop at the back of the pen. "If you're going to stay here, you're going to learn to do the work that needs doing."

"Absolutely," she agreed, following him eagerly inside. "This is amazing."

The coop was alive with the deafening clamor of even more chickens, all perched on nest-covered planks. Gabe snatched a huge wicker basket from a nail by the door and thrust it toward her.

"Reach underneath them and pull out the eggs," he instructed.

Tess stepped up to the first chicken and gently slid her hand underneath.

"There there, girl," she cooed. "I'm going to relieve you of that little old . . . ouch!"

The vexed bird was not pleased at having been disturbed and took her annoyance out on poor Tess's hand—again and again. Tess freed her hand, regarded the injury with more than a little astonishment, and proceeded to push it right back in under the bird. The chicken continued to peck at her but only managed to make contact once or twice before Tess was able to grab the egg and pull it out.

"There!" she said triumphantly. "That wasn't so bad."

Gabe didn't know whether to yell or laugh. He knew the chickens would revolt against a strange hand invading their space and that was precisely why he made her do it. But instead of running from the coop like he expected, Tess plunged her injured hand back in—over and over again—until she had claimed every last egg from the nesting birds. After the first of many unexpected and certainly painful pecks, she hadn't even stopped to examine her hands, but instead became more determined with every wound.

If she knew Gabe was only trying to prove a point, she did not let on. She simply looked up at him with wide-eyed amazement and burst out laughing.

"I did it! I got all the eggs! Isn't that wonderful?" Her whole face lit up like a child's on Christmas morning. "Can I do this again tomorrow?"

Gabe fought to keep his own smile suppressed. No point in letting her think he was happy with her; it would only reinforce her will to stay.

"Not only do you get to collect the eggs," he said dryly, "you get to clean the coop as well. There's fresh hay in the barn and there's feed over in that bucket." He pointed to a large gray pail at the far end of the coop. "When you're done, come find me. There's plenty of work to be done."

"Oh, thank you, Gabriel," she gushed. "I knew I would love this and I do. This is what living is all about!"

Gabe hadn't heard a word she said since speaking his name. When had he been suddenly switched from "Mr. Calloway" to "Gabriel"? Nobody called him Gabriel, it just wasn't done. He had always hated his name, always thought it was the furthest thing from a man's name that could possibly be, yet when spoken by little Tess Kinley, with her silky soft voice, it sent a raging fire through his belly. He wanted to hear it again, exactly as she had just done, with joy that bubbled through her laughter and shone through her eyes. It was as though he had given her a precious gift instead of a hand full of peck marks and a coop full of chicken crap.

Before he opened his mouth and embarrassed himself, which he was sure to do, he turned on his heel and stomped toward the barn where Zeus stood saddled and waiting to go. A good, long ride out to the herd would clear his head of this nonsense.

Tess practically skipped into the house, so happy she was with her collection of dirty eggs.

"Rosa!" she called. "Look what I did! Eggs—and a whole lot of them, too!"

Rosa peered down into the basket and then up at Tess's shining face.

"You do eggs?" she asked, clearly in disbelief. "Gabe Calloway no help?"

Tess shook her head vigorously with more than a little pride.

"No, I did it all by myself."

"Show hands." Rosa demanded, pulling the basket from her tightened grasp. Tess held out her hands, almost apologetically, and waited for the scolding.

"I'm sorry," she said. "I've never done it before and I guess the chickens didn't like having me there."

Rosa clicked her tongue in disgust. "Where Gabe Calloway?"

Tess's heart sank. Rosa was upset with her for disturbing the chickens. Now her only ally would surely convince Gabe to send her away.

"He was walking toward the barn the last I saw of him," she finally answered. "I'm terribly sorry, Rosa, I had no idea . . ."

Rosa wasn't even listening. She pushed past Tess and stormed toward the barn, ranting in her native tongue the entire way. Frantic, Tess ran to catch up.

"Please, Rosa, I'll try to be more gentle tomorrow, don't be angry."

"Where Gabe Calloway?" Rosa yelled as she threw open the barn door.

"He ain't here," Joby answered from the stall he

was cleaning. With his blond curls and freckles, he didn't look any older than sixteen. "Took that horse from hell . . . oh, pardon me, Miz Kinley. . . ." He straightened as soon as he saw her. "He's ridin' out to the herd. Looked like he was in a bit of a mood."

"I give him mood," Rosa snapped as Miguel rounded the corner.

"What is wrong?"

Rosa flew into a Spanish tirade, her arms flailing around her head, speaking faster than Tess had ever heard another human speak. Rosa grabbed Tess's hands and thrust them under Miguel's nose, yelling all the while. Miguel spoke soothingly to her, pried Tess's hands from his wife's and turned her back toward the house. Tess stood where they had left her, wanting very much to cry but refusing to do so in front of Joby.

"Whoo-ey!" Joby whistled. "I'd sure hate to be the boss right now. Rosa's some mad."

"Yes," Tess croaked. "I'm afraid I upset the chickens when I was collecting the eggs. When I told her about it she became quite angry. Do you think she'll ever forgive me?"

"You?" Joby repeated. "Miz Kinley, ma'am, you don't know Spanish real well, do ya?" When Tess shook her head, he grinned broadly. "I reckon Rosa's 'bout mad enough to swallow a horn toad backwards, but she ain't mad at you, ma'am. She's lookin' to peel the hide from the boss."

"But I thought . . ." Tess stopped, glancing from Joby to the house and then back. "But she's so angry at me. She took one look at my hands and flew into a tirade."

"Yeah," the boy chuckled. "'Cuz the boss went 'n' let you collect the eggs knowin' full well they'd try to have you for breakfast."

"What?"

"Them chickens're crazy. They don't let no one but the boss at their eggs. Rosa don't even try, and she ain't sceered of nothin'. 'Cept the boss's horse."

"You mean . . ."

"Yup." Joby nodded, still grinning. "The boss'll be in fer more 'n an earful when he gets back. I best go warn him or sure as hell I'll be gettin' the brunt of his mood when Rosa's done with 'im."

He threw down his pitchfork and closed the stall door.

"'Scuse me, ma'am."

"Joby!" she called after him. "I'm supposed to clean out the coop. Could you please tell me where I'm to put the old straw?"

"The old straw, ma'am?"

"Yes. It's awfully smelly in there, and I mean to re-place all the straw with a fresh batch. But where should I put the smelly bunch?"

Joby chuckled softly. "Why don't you wait 'til I git back, ma'am? I'd be happy to clean the coop."

"No, thank you. I *want* to do it."

The boy's head shook in disbelief. "If you've a mind to clean it yerself, I ain't gonna argue with ya. Just throw what you want in a pile somewhere and I'll tend to it when I git back."

Tess smiled. "Thank you, Joby. I would appreciate it." She waited until he was mounted on his chestnut mare before she added, "Be sure to give Gabriel my regards."

Joby tipped his hat toward her and rode off, a grin still painted across his face.

Tess waited until she was sure he was gone before adjusting her oversized clothes. It just wouldn't do to have it all fall down around her ankles, now would it? She would have to see about purchasing some ready-made clothes at the mercantile, but for now she was quite happy to be wearing Gabriel's.

She searched the barn for anything that might prove useful in her next project and settled on Joby's discarded pitchfork and an old gray horse blanket. Tess had never held a pitchfork in her life and the mere weight of it surprised her. She laid the blanket on the floor of the barn, perfectly square, then attacked the straw pile with the fork, tossing heap after heap on top. When she had piled it as high as she dared, she propped the fork against the wall, took hold of one corner of the blanket, and pulled the entire package out of the barn toward the pen. Walking backward was not the easiest thing when pulling a blanket loaded with straw, but she did manage to stay on her feet, and that in itself was an accomplishment. Surely somewhere there must be a wheelbarrow, but it was certainly well hidden, wherever it was.

She returned for the pitchfork and began the wondrous task of cleaning up after the chickens. They were such funny little things, clucking around her ankles in a maddened frenzy as though she was doing them a grave disservice. Tess clucked right back at them, giggling and twittering as she shooed the lot of them out of their comfortable coop and into the chaos of the pen.

"Just doing a little housecleaning, ladies," she scolded merrily. "I won't be but a shake in here and then you can have it right back."

Unfortunately for the chickens, Tess's "shake" took a little longer than expected. Being a perfectionist didn't help. It was almost an hour later before she had finally cleaned out the smelly coop to her liking and was ready to refill it with fresh straw. She piled the dirty straw neatly near the gate so Joby would have easy access to it, and once she learned what he did with it, she would simply tend to the mess herself.

The fresh straw smelled wonderfully sweet and clean, but again, by the time Tess was satisfied it had been distributed neatly and evenly throughout the coop, another hour had passed and she still hadn't fed the poor birds. Gabe had not advised her on how much feed to put down, so she simply grabbed handful after handful and threw it over the ground until she was sure every chicken would get some.

Her neck and back ached; she was sweating and grimy and her hands were now covered with peck wounds and blisters. She'd never felt better in her life. She stood at the gate, pitchfork in hand, and admired her handiwork. A fine job for someone who had never done it before. Even Gabriel would have to admit that.

The thought was still fresh in her mind when the sound of horses drew her attention away. Gabe and Joby had crested the hill and wasted no time riding directly toward her. Joby tipped his hat slightly as he rode on past to the barn, but Gabe pulled his huge stallion to a stop a few feet away from her. The black Morgan snorted loudly and backed up a step until Gabe's low voice and soothing strokes eased his nerves and settled him.

Tess raised her eyes to find Gabe watching her, his gaze boring into her, taking in every inch of her. She shifted uncomfortably but could not break his hold.

"I'm so sorry, Gabriel," she blurted suddenly. "Joby told me Rosa is furious with you and it's all my fault because I didn't know how to . . ."

Gabe cleared his head with a shake, dragging his eyes away from her. She was covered in straw, head to toe, dirt smudged across her right cheek and nose, and God only knew what was stuck to the bottom of her left shoe. She was an absolute mess and it took every ounce of strength Gabe had not to jump down from his horse and kiss those full, trembling lips of hers. Just swing her up into the circle of his arms and kiss her good and proper.

"Gabriel?" her voice wavered slightly.

"Wh-what?" He hadn't heard a word she'd said.

"I'm . . . I'm sorry," she whispered hoarsely, her voice finding speed and pitch as she spoke. "About Rosa, I mean. She was fit to be tied when she saw my hands and I thought she was angry with me for upsetting the chickens but it turns out she was angry with you and I didn't mean for her to be and I still don't understand exactly why she's angry but she most certainly is and Joby says . . ." she stopped, her head lowered. "I'm sorry. Please don't be angry with me. I wanted to show Rosa how many eggs I got."

Gabe felt his lip begin to twitch. What a funny little creature this Tess Kinley was; so worried about Rosa being angry with him when, in fact, it should have been Tess herself who was furious with him. But instead, she had gone ahead and cleaned out the damn chicken coop—and done a hell of a job, too. Gabe couldn't remember it ever being so clean— even when it was new. Fighting back his smile, he steadied his thundering heart. No point in letting her know she'd done a good job, it would only fuel her resolve to stay.

He bobbed his head toward the coop. "You just finishing this now?"

Tess nodded with a slow, eager smile.

"Took you long enough. Damn near time for dinner." He turned slightly so she wouldn't see his smirk.

"Yes," she retorted. "Well, perhaps if the coop were cleaned out properly more often, it wouldn't take a body quite so long to do it, now would it?"

She turned on her heel and stomped off toward the barn, leaving Gabe to smile after her. He was sure going to miss having her around.

Chapter 6

Rosa lit into Gabe the minute she saw him, her arms flailing.

"¿Que pensaba usted permitir esa pobrecita en el gallinero¿ Para el amor de Dios, que le pasa¿¡ Usted debe estar avergonzado de usted mismo, Gabe Calloway—yo estoy¡"

"Rosa," he said, torn between wanting to laugh at the irate woman and feeling wretched for what he had done.

"You no 'Rosa' to me, Gabe Calloway!"

Tess appeared in the kitchen then. "Please, Rosa," she said softly. "Don't be angry with Gabriel, it wasn't his fault. If I want to live here, I am going to have to learn how everything is done and how to do it myself. I can't expect to be waited on hand and foot, can I? How fair would that be?"

"I no care fair!" Rosa stormed. "Look!"

She grabbed Tess's hands and thrust them under Gabe's nose. Tess fought to free them but Rosa held fast, twisting them over to reveal not only the numerous bruises and blood spots from where the chickens pecked her, but also the filthy weeping blisters covering both palms. Tess squeezed her eyes shut, but the humiliation still burned across her face.

Gabe hadn't looked away from her face, hadn't so

much as glanced toward her hands, which were still being shaken by his crazed housekeeper. With great reluctance, his eyes slowly lowered to the mutilated hands before him. The color drained from his face a mere moment before his stomach rebelled.

"Gabriel," Tess said, her voice gently apologetic. "This is not anyone's fault, for goodness' sake. It's just a few scratches. I want to do this, remember? It was my decision to come here, to work hard, to . . ."

Gabe didn't wait for her to finish. He thrust her hands away, turned on his heel, and disappeared out the door without a word. He didn't stop until he reached the far side of the barn. There he leaned against the wall and slid down to a low squat. Bile scorched his throat, thickening with every breath—breaths that came faster and harder until he was forced to lower his head between his knees to slow them. An eternity passed before he was able to swallow past the acrid disgust. What the hell had he been thinking? Rosa was right—he should be ashamed of himself, and he was. Ashamed, disgusted, and downright sickened.

Yesterday, Tess had the smooth delicate hands of a lady; today, they were scarred, scabbed, and bloody. It was his fault. What made it worse was she didn't blame him; she accepted the wounds almost as though she deserved them. God, how he wished she would yell at him, strike out at him, something. But instead, she had apologized to him.

He'd only wanted her to realize this life was not a silly romantic fairy tale; it was not for ladies or the faint of heart. If she stayed here, those weeping blisters would only be the first of many and probably the least painful injury she would sustain. He couldn't let her stay; God knew what else would happen to her.

Gabe had no idea how long he sat there breathing

through the waves of nausea flooding his stomach. By the time he was finally able to stand without his knees threatening to buckle, the sun had long since passed overhead, which meant he'd missed dinner. Just as well. He wouldn't have been able to hold anything down anyway.

He thrust shaky fingers through his hair and jammed his hat back in place. Inhaling deeply, he rounded the corner of the barn and stopped dead. Tess sat on the porch, rocking gently as she snapped peas into a huge metal bowl.

Air forced its way from his lungs in a loud whoosh. She hadn't seen him yet, he could still . . .

"Oh, hell, Calloway," he growled. "The Lord hates a coward."

As though sensing his presence, Tess's head turned slowly, her gaze locking on his as he made his way toward her. She set the bowl on the small table and pushed up from the chair.

She had washed and changed back into her own clothes, and despite the fact she looked lovely and radiant in her plain blue calico, Gabe couldn't help but feel cheated she'd traded his clothes for her own. Stupid, really, but it ate at him nonetheless.

"Gabriel," she breathed. "I . . ."

"How are your hands?" he asked, his voice thick and unsteady.

"They're fine, really." She tried to conceal them in the folds of her skirt, but the white cloth bandages Rosa had wrapped them in were impossible to miss. "I'm terribly sorry about all of this. It's really not that big of a deal. It's a couple of scratches."

"Stop it!" Gabe's eyes blazed wildly. "Just stop it!"

He grasped her wrists and wrenched them toward him.

"Stop apologizing! I did this to you—and if you

stay here, it's only going to get worse! These . . . blisters . . . are only the beginning."

His gaze bore into her, his grip pinching her wrists, but she did not flinch—not even a little.

"Gabriel," she said again, her voice barely above a whisper. "You didn't do this to me; I did it to myself."

He released her with a thrust, but she did not move away. Instead, her bandaged hand reached to rest lightly on his arm, sending a lightning quick jolt rocketing through him.

"Don't you understand?" she continued. "I want to be here. I want to work hard, to bear the pain and reap the joy of this life. I don't want to sit in a parlor and sip tea. That's not who I am!"

"Then who the hell are you?" Without giving her a chance to answer, he pulled away and stormed into the house, but once inside, he had no idea what to do with himself. Rosa was nowhere to be found, so he stood in the middle of the living room, fighting to retain the slightest hold on his emotions.

What the hell was the matter with him? Why was Tess having such an effect on him? He'd seen other women with injuries—hell, Rosa was blistered all the time—but Tess was different. She'd only been here for a day and already she had gotten to him, gotten inside him to a place he had long ago boarded off to any woman. Damn it, he didn't need this . . . this . . . mess right now.

Lust. That's all it was. Maybe if he tried extra hard, he'd be able to convince himself of that. Maybe. One thing was for damn sure—it was going to be a hellishly long week until the next stage left town. He'd have to keep busier than usual and as far away from her as he possibly could.

With new resolve, he stomped back through the kitchen, poured himself a steaming cup of coffee, and pushed open the door. Without a glance in

Tess's direction, he continued on to the barn, determined to finish shoeing the rest of the horses before supper.

Tess watched him go in silence. She'd caused him enough anguish for one day. He was such a proud man, he'd be mortified if he thought for one second she had seen the haunted look in his eyes, the hidden pain he kept locked up. What—or who—had caused that? And what could she do to unlock that pain and make room in his heart for her?

She continued to snap the peas, staring after Gabriel even when he disappeared through the barn's huge double doors. It was Rosa who finally turned her attention.

"You go church?" the woman asked. She stood at the bottom of the stairs, a huge bolt of plum-colored sateen under one arm.

"I would like to, very much," Tess admitted. "But I don't imagine Gabriel is the churchgoing kind."

Rosa's head shook slowly. "Gabe Calloway no go church, but you go, he go."

"I couldn't ask him to do that," Tess sighed. "I've already been too much trouble."

"No." The woman smiled gently. "Tess Kinley just what Gabe Calloway need."

"But—"

"Come," Rosa interrupted, waving the material a little. "We sew."

Tess sighed wearily and followed her into the house. Sewing—one more thing she wasn't any good at. She had used a needle and thread before, but she was a far cry from being a seamstress. She'd probably stitch poor Rosa right into the cloth.

Rosa walked straight through the house and up to

the bedroom Tess now occupied. She pulled the thin drapes closed and pointed to the far corner of the room.

"I measure," she said.

"But shouldn't I be measuring you?"

Rosa smiled warmly. "No, I measure Tess Kinley. Muchacha need new dress for church."

Tess's eyes widened. "Oh, no, Rosa. I couldn't ask you to . . ."

"Bup bup bup," the woman sputtered, waving away Tess's objections. "I like the sewing. Tess Kinley need dress."

"But there's not enough time to get one made— tomorrow is Sunday."

Rosa stood where she was, smiling at her until Tess resigned herself to the fact she was not going to win this argument. She removed her dress and laid it neatly on the bed. Rosa went to work in a flash, measuring, figuring, re-measuring, and smiling. When she finished, she silently indicated for Tess to get dressed and then took up her measuring tape, scissors, and material and scurried down the stairs to the kitchen.

By the time Tess joined her, the other woman had already spread the material on the table and pinned the newsprint pattern to it.

"You cut; I make tea," she instructed, holding out the shears to Tess.

"I . . . I'm not very good at this sort of thing," Tess confessed.

"You do fine." She turned her back to the table, the decision made, and busied herself with the kettle. Tess studied the scissors for a moment, as though she'd never seen such things before, took a deep breath, and began cutting. She moved slowly, precisely, scared half to death of making a slip and cutting right through the pattern. So deep was her concentration, her eyes didn't blink, her head didn't move, and the tip of her tongue lodged itself between her dry lips.

The tea had already steeped and cooled by the time she made the final cut. She exhaled loudly, unaware she had been holding her breath the whole time. Rosa smiled broadly and handed her a cup of tea.

"Buena," she said, nodding toward the pieces. "Drink, then sew."

Tess sputtered over the rim of her cup. "But I can't! I'm sure to ruin this beautiful fabric, Rosa."

Rosa simply shrugged, removed the excess material and pattern pieces from the table, and threaded a needle. Tess drank slowly, hoping Rosa would change her mind and do the stitching herself, but to no avail. After a few moments, she removed the half full cup from Tess's hand and replaced it with the needle.

"Sew."

"But . . ."

Still smiling, Rosa shook her head and rearranged the material so Tess wouldn't sew the wrong sides together. She showed her how to turn in the edges and press them down with the iron she had heated on the huge kitchen stove. Then she nodded toward the turned-in edges and left the house.

Tess stared after her, more protests dying on her lips. It would be a waste of time to argue. Rosa was obviously used to having people do as she instructed. And besides, Tess thought grimly, she certainly couldn't get hurt sewing, could she?

A dozen needle pricks later, with blood dripping from the last one, Tess set her jaw and struggled to concentrate again. How could something as small as this needle hurt so much? She had lost all track of time, but Rosa had come back and built up the stove's fire to prepare supper. Tess's offer to help was dismissed with Rosa's usual "bup bup bup," so she returned to her sewing, finishing the last stitch as Joby and Seth made their way to the wash bucket at the door.

Tess held up the dress for Rosa's inspection, thrilled with the woman's instant approval.

"We finish after supper," she said.

Finish? Tess rather thought she *was* finished. All the seams had been sewn, the dress was in one piece and it looked just fine. Rather plain, but not bad at all. She hung the dress over the back of the sofa and returned to help Rosa set the table. Miguel arrived shortly after, carrying a straight-backed chair. He set it to the table and indicated for Tess to sit.

"What about Rosa?" she asked.

Joby chuckled. "Rosa don't sit. She hovers."

"But she should sit and eat with the rest of us, shouldn't she?"

It was Seth who answered this time. "I ain't never seen Rosa sit. To the table or nowhere."

"Sit," Rosa ordered, gently pushing Tess into the chair. "Eat."

Tess did as instructed, more than a little aware of Gabe's empty chair.

"Where Gabe Calloway?" asked Rosa, as if reading Tess's thoughts.

"He's jist finishin' up with that horse from hell. Should be here in a bit."

Rosa snorted, mumbled in Spanish, and began dishing up supper. It smelled wonderful—fried chicken, boiled potatoes and peas—and it was then Tess realized how hungry she was. She'd had no appetite at noon, what with the hands episode, but now her stomach was demanding to be sated.

As Joby and Seth kept up an amiable conversation between mouthfuls, Tess couldn't help but laugh. They spoke, unabashed, about their plans, which, being Saturday, included going into town and finding a good card game and a willing woman. She should have been shocked by such talk, or at least pretended to be, but the two were so comical, bantering back and forth about which one would lose out at the card table and which one would lose out with the "ladies."

All too soon they were gone and Rosa had cleared the table, bustling around the kitchen humming softly to herself. After Miguel excused himself, Rosa untied her flowered apron and hung it on its peg.

Tess retrieved the dress and began to lay it out on the table when Rosa stopped her.

"You do enough. I finish."

"But you've done so much already," Tess argued. "Show me what to do next and I'll finish it."

Rosa's ebony eyes glanced out the window. "You talk Gabe Calloway. That be enough for you."

Tess sighed. "I don't think Gabriel wants to talk to me. He's very angry with me."

"No," Rosa said, a little sadly. "Gabe Calloway not angry to you. Gabe Calloway angry to Gabe Calloway."

"Why?" she asked, but Rosa shook her head stubbornly.

"Gabe Calloway tell you when he tell you. Buenas noches, Tess Kinley."

"Good night, Rosa."

She watched Rosa walk toward her own little cottage, to her life with Miguel and the love they shared, wondering if she and Gabriel would ever have that. Gabriel, who carried a deep ache inside his heart, who was terribly angry with her, and who was walking toward the house right at that moment.

Chapter 7

Tess watched him approach, his long stride as certain as ever, but there was a drawn, clenched look to him. She braced for another argument, all the while bustling around the kitchen readying him a plate of supper. It would be harder for him to argue with a mouth full of food.

She poured a cup of Rosa's strong black brew and left it on the table. He didn't offer so much as a nod when he entered the room.

"Hello, Gabriel," she said, trying not to be offended at his mood.

"Tess." He walked past her to the living room, likely to bury himself in the ledgers and other such paperwork.

"I thought you might be hungry."

He stopped in the doorway, opened his mouth, and then clamped it shut when his stomach growled loud enough to shake the window panes.

Tess smirked and set the plate down with a thump. She returned to the stove to pour herself a cup of coffee, which she loaded with sugar, and then slid gracefully into the chair opposite his. She had removed Rosa's bandages but kept her hands in her lap where Gabe wouldn't have to see them.

Almost grudgingly, he returned to the kitchen and took his seat.

"I rather thought you'd have gone to bed already."
He did not look at her or even bother to lift his eyes
from his plate.

"Why on earth would you think that?" she asked.
"It's still early."

Gabe pressed his lips together before answering.
"Because you've had such a . . . trying . . . day."

Tess jerked to her feet, sending the straight-
backed chair clattering to the floor.

"You've got nerve, Gabriel Calloway! You gave me
a job to do and I did it! And I did a damn fine job, I
might add." Her face flushed as the curse flew from
her mouth, but she was too angry to stop. "I'm not
complaining about it nor am I the one making such
a production about a few little scratches. For the love
of God, one would think you'd never seen blisters
before! Let me see your hands!"

She seized his huge left hand in hers and turned
it over to examine the palm. Breath caught in her
throat the second she touched him. A fiery jolt shot
up her arm and lodged itself firmly into her heart.
His fingers and palm were covered in age-old cal-
luses and healed over cuts. There was a strength
to his hand, even as it lay there, huge against her
smaller ones. Something passed between them in
that instant, something Tess could not describe,
but whatever it was, Gabe had obviously felt it too.

He jerked his hand away and wrapped it around
his mug. When Tess spoke again, her voice was much
lower.

"It would seem you've had your own fair share of
blisters and scratches, Gabriel."

"I'm a man, it's different."

"What does being a man have to do with this? Certainly your mother must have sustained a number of
injuries, didn't she?"

Gabe dropped his fork to his plate and pushed

back from the table. He did not stand, but his jaw clenched once, twice, before he spoke.

"My mother had no business living out here in the middle of nowhere and neither do you."

Tess studied the barely controlled storm raging in his eyes, her arms aching to wrap themselves around him.

"What happened to your mother?" It was as though someone else spoke, for Tess certainly had no intention of asking that question.

Gabe was silent for a long moment until Tess wondered if he'd even heard her. When he did speak, his voice teetered on the edge of breaking.

"She was a tiny little thing, my mother." *Like me,* Tess thought. "But my father insisted on dragging her halfway across the country so he could start this damn-fool ranch. Mama never did like it, but she surely did love the old man." Gabe was a million miles and a lifetime away. "She was always sick, always hurt from one thing or another—herding cattle, fending off the Sioux and Cheyenne, birthing babies."

Tess straightened her chair and lowered herself into it, her eyes never leaving Gabriel's face. His pain was so fresh, so real, Tess thought she might be able to reach out and touch it. Her own tears swelled and flowed in tiny rivulets down her cheeks.

"She was never the same after Bart was born, never regained the little strength she had to start with; lost two babies after that. Then she got . . . in a family way . . . again. She never . . . Pa tried . . ." He stopped, took several breaths. "She died trying to birth that little baby girl. Her and the baby."

"Oh, Gabriel," Tess whispered. "I'm so sorry. How old were you?"

"Seven." His voice caught on the word before he could clear his throat past it.

"Dear God. You were so young." Her hands reached to cover his. He stiffened beneath her touch but did not pull away.

Gabe remained silent, his eyes locked on hers as Tess struggled to determine what she was seeing there. It was a horrible mix of anguish, accusation, and anger. He lifted one of his huge hands and gently rubbed his rough thumb across her cheek, wiping away the tears.

Unable to break the contact, Gabe's whole hand cupped the side of Tess's face, marveling at its velvety smoothness. Damn it all to hell but he wanted to kiss her. Right there in the kitchen, right there at the table—and he could see in her eyes she wanted it, too.

He dropped his hand slowly, feeling the disappointment in her eyes.

"Gabriel . . ."

"I best leave." He left his plate, still half-full, and stood, as did Tess, blocking his way.

"I was raised in a house where ladies kept their opinions to themselves and were forced to live by a set of rules I still don't understand." Her amber eyes burned—not with fire but with a deep, all-encompassing warmth—just for him. "We were not permitted to express how we felt, and even my mother and father kept their feelings to themselves. I do not cotton to that way of thinking, Gabriel. I believe people should tell each other how they feel instead of playing silly little games. I . . ."

"Don't." His right index finger pressed against her impossibly soft lips. "You can't stay here, Tess, no matter how much you want to or how you think you feel. You're not built for this kind of life. Women don't belong on a ranch."

"What about Rosa?"

"Rosa's different. Her life here is a damn sight easier than it was in New Mexico. She's used to hard work and hard living. You're not."

"I'm strong." Another tear slipped down her cheek.

A sad smile found Gabe's lips. "Tess."

"I can't go back, Gabriel." She swallowed back more tears, straightened her spine, and lifted her delicate chin defiantly. "I won't."

"Tess . . ."

"No! Don't patronize me, Gabriel. I know in my heart and soul I belong here with you on this ranch."

"You can't possibly know any such thing," he sighed. "You've only been here for one day; you don't even know me."

"Yes, I do. And you know me, too." She closed the distance between them, holding his gaze. "Can you look me in the eye and tell me you don't feel the same way I do? You know there's something between us, Gabriel. Something undeniable, something strong."

"It's called lust, Tess." Gabe's heart hammered against his chest.

"No, it isn't." She smiled softly. "But if it makes you feel better to tell yourself that, then you go right ahead. I know how I feel, Gabriel Calloway. I lo—"

"Stop it! It's lust, pure and simple, and as long as we don't act on it, we'll be fine. So you stay here the week if that's what makes you happy, but come Friday, you'll be back on the stage headed east. That's what *I* know."

He'd almost made it to the door before she caught her breath.

"Gabriel?"

"Yes?" he sighed.

"Will you take me to church in the morning?" She remained with her back to him, speaking as though he were right in front of her still.

"Will I . . .?" Gabe shook his head slowly but

couldn't help the smile that crept over his face. She was such an odd little thing. "Yes, Tess, if you feel you must go to church, I will take you. God knows I couldn't bear another tongue-lashing from Rosa."

She turned and smiled too, even as he left her in the empty house.

He was going to church. Heaven help him not to get struck down by lightning before the opening hymn.

Rosa held up the dress for Tess's inspection. The basic seams Tess completed the day before were now hidden behind dainty white eyelets, and the neckline had been adjusted ever so slightly to reveal a respectable amount of skin without being scandalous. She stepped into the wonderful garment feeling as Cinderella must have, even though Tess had spent her life wearing much finer dresses.

"Oh, Rosa," she breathed, throwing her arms around the grinning woman. "It's beautiful—thank you!"

"Come, I do hair." She steered Tess toward the small stool in the corner of the bedroom. "I leave it down in back."

"But . . ."

"No *but*, Tess Kinley. Gabe Calloway like hair long, no all tied up."

Tess laughed softly. "But shouldn't it be up for church? What will people think?"

"Bup bup bup—who care?" Rosa went to work combing out the long single braid.

"Yes." Tess smiled. "You're right. Who cares what people think? It's going to get their tongues wagging enough seeing a strange woman with Gabriel, isn't it?"

"It get their tongue to wag to see Gabe Calloway to

church," Rosa answered with a decisive nod. "That shock enough to make some dead."

The two women laughed together. Rosa's affection for the younger woman showed in her shimmering eyes and easy smiles. Tess was sure if it had been left to Rosa, Gabe and Tess would be married already. A sudden lump formed in Tess's throat.

"You are very kind, Rosa," she choked. "I am so very grateful—"

"Bup bup bup," Rosa interrupted, waving Tess's words away with the back of her hand. "Estas una buena niña, Tess Kinley. Gabe Calloway need una buena niña. He need strong girl. You take good care to my Gabe Calloway."

"I will, Rosa," she promised solemnly. "If only he'll let me."

Rosa smiled back knowingly. "Gabe Calloway have hard head but soft heart. You no worry of his head, you love to his heart. His head go soft soon enough."

Tess laughed until her sides ached, but try as she may, she could not explain the humor to Rosa. Rosa laughed because Tess did. She finished Tess's hair and held up a mirror for her to see. She had left a fringe of bangs to lay delicately across Tess's forehead while two exquisite mother-of-pearl combs held her hair up on the sides. The rest cascaded down her back in shimmering waves. Tess's cheeks pinked.

"I feel so . . ."

"Muy bonita," Rosa finished for her. She kissed Tess's cheek and took her by the hand. "Come. Gabe Calloway wait."

Tess slid her feet into her tiny, worn slippers, which would be hidden—thank goodness—under the hem of her skirts, and followed Rosa down the stairs. The house was empty since Joby and Seth had the day off and were, in all likelihood, sleeping off hangovers, and Gabe was out hitching up the horses.

Tess watched him from the window, almost afraid to breathe. He was so beautiful in his black suit and string tie with the silver clasp. His dark hair was still damp from his creek bath, and even though a wall and a hundred feet separated them, the scent that was Gabe Calloway filled Tess's senses. Leather, soap, and sunshine.

Rosa smiled wordlessly and left the house, giving Gabe a sly nod as she passed.

He glanced toward the house and caught a glimpse of Tess through the window. If he knew his mouth was hanging open, he made no move to close it but remained rooted, not blinking, not swallowing, not even breathing.

He never would have believed she could be more beautiful, yet there she was, a vision in his window. A vision in his life and in his heart.

An eternity seemed to stretch between them before Tess finally walked outside. Gabe was at her side in less than a heartbeat, offering his hand to assist her down the steps.

"Thank you," she said, her cheeks flushing the softest of pinks.

Gabe cleared his throat and lifted her gently into the wagon. God, how he wished for one of those fancy buggies with the folding top like Widow Dauphin drove instead of this clunky old buckboard with its rough-hewn seats and no protection from the elements. Tess didn't seem to mind one little bit; in fact, from the look on her face, you'd think she was sitting on a cloud.

Gabe climbed up beside her, released the brake, and gave the reins a quick flick, sending the two brown Morgans trotting down the road.

"Might I say, Gabriel," Tess began, smiling gently, "you look very handsome this morning."

Lord Almighty, she was direct, wasn't she? Gabe couldn't help but smile. He hated to admit how refreshing that was in a woman.

"Thank you, Miss Kinley. You don't look half bad yourself. I'm sure you'll give the boys in town something to think about."

"I have no interest in the 'boys in town.'"

"Well, they'll most definitely be interested in you." He glanced over, taking her all in, inch by inch.

"Yes, well, be that as it may," she said, a tiny smile lingering on her lips, "I imagine there'll be more than one single lady shooting daggers my way this morning."

"Don't count on it," Gabe snorted. "I'm not exactly the kind of man the ladies in town look for."

Tess straightened her shoulders, her hands smoothing the ample fabric of her skirts.

"I beg to differ, Gabriel. You are precisely the kind of man a lady looks for. This lady, anyway."

Heat seared up Gabe's neck and right through his scalp. How the hell was he supposed to respond? He knew exactly how he'd like to respond to it—how he'd like to respond to *her,* period—but unless he wanted to find himself married by the day's end, he'd best keep his mouth shut and his responses to himself.

Married. A tiny light flickered deep in his heart.

Chapter 8

The morning could not have been more perfect. Gabe sat beside her in the wagon, his handsome face turning to glance her way when she pretended to look elsewhere. Tess sat as straight as she could considering the fact her bones turned to mush from the heat of his every glance. His thigh brushed hers as the wagon bounced and jerked its way down the road.

Meadowlarks sang brightly from the high pine branches while squirrels scolded them from below. The sky had never been bluer, the air never more fragrant. Tess could not imagine it being any more glorious.

"Oh, Gabriel," she breathed. "Do we have time to stop for a moment? Those wild flowers are too beautiful for words."

She'd never felt life embrace her as it did by the creek. The waters of Porter Creek sparkled brighter than diamonds, and all around them life bloomed. Gabe reined the horses in, set the brake, and moved around the wagon to help Tess down. His huge hands spanned her waist, making her dizzy with their touch. He held her gaze, looking right down into the depths of her very soul, holding her there until he fought his way out and pulled back.

"We only have a minute," he said gruffly. He turned

from her and strode to the creek, his fingers clenched at his sides, his face rigid as stone.

Tess inhaled deeply and tried to focus. If she wasn't careful, she would find herself literally throwing herself at him. She smiled—maybe that wasn't such a bad idea.

She wandered through the wild flowers, picking one, inhaling its sweet fragrance, tucking it through the teeth of her hair comb and moving on to the next. Gabe stood with his back to her, his trancelike stare fixed on the toe of his boots.

"Okay," she said, "I'm ready."

Gabe started, lost his balance, and teetered precariously at the creek's jagged bank. Tess reached out and grasped as much of his jacket as she possibly could. He swayed once, twice, and then regained his balance, bumping right back into Tess. She tripped and went down hard on her backside. Gabe whirled around but wasn't quick enough to prevent her fall.

"Tess!" He stood over her, looking flustered at first and then shocked when she burst into a fit of laughter. There she sat in the middle of a patch of fuchsia fireweed—her hair covered in wayward petals, her dress rumpled—and all she could do was laugh until she cried.

Gabe shook his head slowly, a grin spreading across his face.

"Well, I'll be . . . are you hurt?" he asked, crouching down on his haunches.

"Only my pride." She laughed, her cheeks burning.

Their eyes met and held, her laughter dying on her suddenly parched lips. Her heart jumped, skipped, and then stopped all together. God help her if he didn't . . .

Gabe's mouth eased slowly toward hers until their mouths were but a breath apart. He hesitated, wavered and was about to pull back when Tess moved.

Her hands reached for his face, gently tugging him down until he could no longer fight. His head dipped, barely brushing his lips against hers.

The mere whisper of her touch hit him with the force of a firing cannon. He had to have more, to taste her, to feel her against him. His mouth searched hers, caressing it with gentle yet firm strokes. She leaned into him, her own lips responding with the same deep hunger he felt himself.

Gathering her into the circle of his arms, he pulled her against him, her heart pounding against his own as if they were one, beating the same rhythm. She went willingly, her soft curves molding perfectly to the contours of his hard, lean body.

He had to stop—this was crazy. He shouldn't be kissing her, shouldn't be holding her so close. He shouldn't be reacting this way—what the hell was going on, anyway? He'd kissed plenty of women before Tess Kinley, but none of them had ever wreaked such havoc with his thoughts. Or his heart.

Cussing softly, he released her, his lips reaching for one final caress.

"Oh, Gabriel," she breathed, her lids lowered still as though she were lost in a dream. "I . . ."

"I'm sorry," he rasped. "I shouldn't have done that."

"I . . ." Tess's brain swirled and tumbled as quickly as her heart, until her mouth was unable to form a sentence. Never in her wildest dreams had she imagined she would ever be kissed like that—with such tenderness or such fierceness. Or such love.

"We best be going." Gabe took her hands and eased her to her feet, allowing her a moment to steady her trembling knees. Her beautiful face absolutely glowed, radiant with the evidence of his kisses, her mouth swollen and smiling. He returned her to her spot in the wagon and climbed up beside her.

Lord Almighty, he was in trouble. One kiss would

never be enough. No matter how long he lived, or how many other women he might kiss, he would never be the same. No one would ever touch him the way she had just done. And it tore at his heart he'd let her.

Oh, he wanted her, body and soul, as much as—or perhaps more than—she wanted him; but he could not, would not, give himself to her the way she wanted. He had to send her away, no matter how much it made his insides ache, no matter how much arguing and trouble she might kick up. Letting her stay would only bring more pain.

Despite his misgivings, Gabe was unable to prevent his hardened heart from weakening a little. The light in her eyes was merely a reflection of his soul, and try as he might, he could not wipe the smile off his face. She looked so happy. Did *he* do that to her?

"I'm wondering something, Gabriel," she said, a gentle smile curving her full lips.

Gabe chuckled. "I'm almost afraid to ask."

"However will you explain me to the good citizens of Porter Creek?"

Gabe's smile didn't waver. "Easy. I'll tell them you're my crazy cousin from San Francisco who escaped from the asylum and you're hiding out here until you're found."

"Gabriel!" she gasped. "You wouldn't!"

He laughed. "Yes, I would. Look at you—you're all rumpled and wrinkled. You've got a tangle of flowers in your hair and you look . . ." *Downright good enough to eat!*

Tess smoothed her hair, pulling out mashed flowers as she went. Finished, she turned to face him. He felt his face pale under her gaze, while she glowed more and more every time he looked at her.

"Tess," he said.

"No." She stiffened, clasping her hands in her lap. "Don't say it, Gabriel, because I won't listen."

He sighed softly, his right hand reaching to cover hers.

"You can't stay here."

"Yes, I can!" Tears scorched the back of her eyes, fighting to flow. How could such a perfect moment be ruined so quickly?

"Tess." His voice was gentle, too gentle.

"You can't send me away, Gabriel. We belong together."

"No, we don't. You belong with someone who can take proper care of you, who can offer you whatever your heart desires, someone who can love you the way you deserve to be loved."

Tess choked back a sob but her voice wavered. "You can take proper care of me, you are what my heart desires, and you love me the way I deserve to be loved."

"No." Gabe had to say it twice. The first time wasn't nearly as convincing as it should have been.

"But you kissed me. . . ."

"Yes," he said. "I shouldn't have and I'm sorry. It won't happen again."

"But I want it to happen again!"

"Tess." He chuckled sadly. "Ladies don't say things like that."

"I don't care! It's the truth. And you can't tell me you don't want it to happen again either."

"It's lust, Tess. That's all it is, plain and simple." He had never mastered the art of lying.

"No, it wasn't, Gabriel Calloway, and you know it."

"Tess . . ."

She pulled her hands from his and turned his face to hers.

"Look me in the eye and tell me it was only lust." Her eyes blazed right through him, scorching the lie that lay unspoken on his tongue. After a moment of spark-filled silence, he faced forward and clicked to the horses, sending them off toward town.

The clang of the church bell broke the silence between them. Gabe steered the horses down the dusty main street of Porter Creek past the dozen or so businesses that lined the wooden walkways until he reached the tiny whitewashed schoolhouse, which doubled as the church. Several wagons were already tied to the low-hanging branches of the huge willow tree, while other wagons stood off to the side, their horses hobbled where they stood.

Tongues began wagging before Gabe pulled the wagon to a stop under a willow. In the tree's shade, he threw the reins loosely over the lowest branch. Men and women alike stopped all previous conversation and wondered aloud why Gabe Calloway was gracing them with such a rare visit and who on earth that creature was beside him.

Tess forced back a shiver that skimmed over her flesh as Gabe's hands encircled her waist. Did he hold her a little longer than necessary? Probably not. It must have been her imagination.

"Mornin', Gabe." Apparently the sheriff found it necessary to wear his badge everywhere—church being no exception. An older man with gentle blue eyes and a face full of wrinkles, Tess liked him immediately.

"Sheriff." Gabe shook the man's outstretched hand. "This here's Tess Kinley. She's staying with us for a few days. Tess, this is Fergus Nicholls."

"That so?" His grin was as warm and friendly as his eyes. "Well, it's mighty nice to meet you, Miss Kinley. Hope you enjoy your stay."

"Thank you, Sheriff." Tess smiled. "I'm sure I will."

"Heard from your brother lately?" he asked Gabe, turning toward the church.

Gabe smirked in Tess's direction. "I rather expect to hear from him any day." His brows quickly drew together. "Is there a problem?"

"No." The sheriff laughed. "Not for Bart, but if you hear from him, would you tell him I'd like a word?"

Tess lost track of the conversation as she studied her surroundings. The schoolyard was small, with a set of swings hanging low in the huge weeping willow and a little vegetable garden planted close to the back door. A few women lingered near the swings, staring unabashedly at Tess as she made her way toward the church. Tess smiled politely and carried on, head held high.

She could still feel the warmth of Gabe's lips, the pounding of their hearts pressed close together. She should be ashamed, being this close to the Lord's house and all, but she wasn't. Despite what Gabe might have said afterward, Tess was even more convinced they belonged together. And she was going to do everything in her power to prove that to him.

"Ladies." Gabe tipped his head toward the gossiping threesome near the swing, then to Tess he spoke through gritted teeth. "I can't believe you're making me do this."

"I didn't twist your arm, Gabriel." She smiled sweetly at him.

"No, but Rosa would have if I'd refused."

Tess laughed lightly and took a seat in the back row of benches. More than a few heads turned to stare at them, and to each one, Gabe nodded cordially and sat a little taller. He'd half a mind to take Tess in his arms and kiss her soundly right there in front of God and everyone. That'd give them something to stare at, now wouldn't it?

"What's so funny?" Tess whispered.

Gabe shook his head, motioning toward the good Reverend who was making his entrance.

"Good morning," he said from the pulpit, his eyes fixing immediately on Tess and Gabe. "For those of you I have not had the pleasure of meeting, or for those of you who have been too busy to join us and thus may have forgotten who I am, my name is Reverend Samuel Boswell." He coughed back a laugh. "I welcome one and all to our services here this morning. Perhaps Mrs. Brenner would lead us in an opening hymn."

Mrs. Brenner, seated at the old wooden organ, began to play "Amazing Grace" and soon the entire congregation joined in. Tess's low alto harmonized beautifully with Mrs. Brenner's soprano and the Reverend's deep bass. Gabe could form neither the words nor the tune, but could only listen, awestruck by the unwavering silky voice that sprung from the amazing creature beside him.

So bewildered was he with Tess and his gamut of emotions, Gabe heard not a word of the Reverend's lengthy sermon or any other voice, except Tess's, when Mrs. Brenner ended the service with the Twenty-Third Psalm.

"Gabe Calloway!" Reverend Boswell met them outside the church with a half mocking grin. "I thought perhaps my old eyes were deceiving me when I saw you sitting there."

"Reverend." Gabe nodded.

"And who is this lovely young lady with you this morning? I assume she's the reason you're here today."

"Tess Kinley, this is Reverend Boswell. He's been trying to save my soul for as long as I can remember."

"Not an easy task, I assure you. But I haven't given up the fight yet." The Reverend laughed. "How do you do, Miss Kinley? Are you visiting our good town, or have you come to put down stakes?"

"Well, Reverend," Tess smiled saucily, "that all depends on Gabriel."

The Reverend's eyes moved from Tess to Gabe and then back again.

"I don't understand."

"Miss Kinley has plans to stay right here in Porter Creek," Gabe piped up. "But I've a mind to have her on the next stage out of town."

"Whatever for? This here's a fine town to settle in." The good Reverend winked at Tess. "And I'm sure the single gentlemen of this town would be more than happy to see such a pretty new face."

Gabe's chest tightened, his lips drawn to a thin line.

"If you've a mind for it," the Reverend continued, grinning all the while, "I would be happy to introduce you. . . ."

"Good day to you, Reverend," Gabe muttered, ushering a giggling Tess away.

"Gabriel, that was rude." She laughed. "He was only trying to be nice."

"I know exactly what he was trying to do," Gabe growled. "And you won't be here long enough to have need for introductions."

Tess laid a hand over her breast and batted her lashes coyly.

"Why, Gabriel Calloway, you aren't jealous, are you?"

Gabe lifted her, almost as if she were weightless, and deposited her unceremoniously into the wagon. He seemed to gather the reins, climb up, and release the brake all in one motion. His face was grim and tight. He *was* jealous, damn it, and he had absolutely no right to be. He didn't own her; hell, he didn't even want her here, and yet there it was—the ugly green face of jealousy staring him right in the eye.

Chapter 9

Lonely silence greeted Tess when they arrived home. Gabe marched straight to the barn without so much as a word and, being it was Sunday, everyone else had the day off. She surveyed the house, searching for something—anything—needing to be tended. But to Rosa's credit, there was not a speck of dust, not a dirty dish, not a single thing out of place. In fact, Tess noted, there weren't exactly a lot of things to clutter the house up with or for dust to land on.

The living room furniture consisted of a modest rosewood sofa and matching armchair, both covered in velvety cream-colored upholstery with dainty ivy print. Under the window sat Gabriel's huge oak desk, covered in organized books, ledgers, and an ink well. The wear on the carpeting ended at the desk, leaving Tess to wonder if the living room was ever used.

The only sign a family had actually lived in the house was the lone wedding photograph on the mantel. The young couple, Tess assumed to be Emma and Clayton Calloway, smiled brightly into their future. The man, dressed in a fine-looking dark suit, holding his top hat in hand, bore a striking resemblance to Gabriel, despite his much lighter coloring. Emma Calloway fit the exact image Gabriel had painted of her—a lovely, petite woman dressed in an extravagant and very fashionable white dress adorned with swansdown trim, the perfect contrast to her Gabriel-like dark features.

Tess wandered up the stairs to her room, which, like the rest of the house, had been spared of any homey decorations or designs. The huge oak bed, complete with an amply stuffed tick and two pillows, dwarfed the rest of the room whose only other furnishings were an oak wardrobe that held Gabe's winter wear and a small round table for the chamber set. Above the table hung a plain oval mirror, but other than that the oatmeal-colored walls were completely bare.

She sighed. Surely there was something needing attention. What was the old proverb? Was it idle hands or an idle brain that was the devil's workshop? Either way, she couldn't sit around doing nothing all day. With a twinge of regret, she changed out of her beautiful new dress, pulled her old worn blue dress back on, and tied her hair up on top of her head.

The gentle touch of Gabe's strong hands lingered, in her hair, on her back, around her waist. She shook her head in a vain attempt to release the memory, laced up her boots, and headed out to the garden. Tess retrieved an old hoe lying in the corner by the beans and set to work. Rosa's garden was as neat and orderly as the inside of the house, the rows of vegetables—everything from peas to carrots to onions—set in perfect lines, not a rock out of place. But even Rosa couldn't keep up with the weeds.

Tess knelt in the dirt, basking in the warmth of the sun on her back and the soft breeze on her face. Despite Gabriel's present mood, it was a good day. He had kissed her and that was all that mattered. She would hold that kiss in her heart until the day she died, for Lord only knew if she'd ever experience it again. She bent to her work, relishing in the sheer wonder of it all.

"Thought you might be thirsty." Gabe held out an ice-cold glass of fresh lemonade. He forced his mind to look past the tiny smile that lingered on her lips, past the smudges of dirt across her forehead and cheeks, and past the melody she hummed to the weeds around her. "Sunday's not a work day, you know."

Tess stood, stretched her back and legs, and grinned. "I don't consider this work. Who would have guessed pulling weeds could be so relaxing?"

"Not me."

"Thank you." She smiled and swallowed huge gulps of the refreshing drink. "I didn't know I was so thirsty."

Try though he may, Gabe couldn't help but smile back at her; covered in dirt and muck, she was still the prettiest thing he'd ever seen.

"You should at least have a hat on," he said, trying to sound stern. "You'll get sunstroke out here."

"I don't have one." Tess's brow furrowed slightly. "Perhaps Rosa . . ."

Before she could finish, Gabe removed his Stetson and plunked it on top of her head. It fell down over her ears and covered half her face.

"Yes," she laughed. "I can see how wearing a hat is so very helpful." She pushed it up so it sat back on her head, the large brim still shading her face from the sun. Fire raged through Gabe's stomach and smoldered within his veins. Dazed, angry, and confused, he still could not hold back the smile that tugged the corners of his mouth.

"You don't have to do this you know," he said.

"I want to."

"Wouldn't you rather be in the house where it's cool?" Why did his heart slam against his chest? And why the hell was he standing so close to her?

"N-no," she stammered. "It's too quiet in there. If I have to be by myself, I'd just as soon be outside where at least I'm not alone."

She glanced around, motioning to the black squirrel at the foot of the nearby oak tree, the two red-breasted robins sitting on the fence post, and the quick-moving gopher who poked his head up out of his hole and then dove right back down at the sight of Gabe.

"What are you keeping busy with today?" she asked, her eyes finding their way back to Gabe.

"Nothing now, just tending the animals. D'you want some help?" The words fell from his mouth before he knew he had spoken them.

"Yes." She grinned. "As a matter of fact, I do. The beans and peas need to be picked and the carrots need to be thinned. Think you can manage that?"

Gabe grabbed her glass back playfully. "I've been picking beans longer than you've been alive, Miss Kinley."

"Good," she said. "Then get to work!" She tossed a bowl at him and retrieved her hoe.

They worked in relative silence for a while, Gabe stealing furtive glances at her while she plain out watched him with unabashed pleasure. Every so often she had to stop to adjust the huge hat, and whenever she did, Gabe's gut cinched tighter. Women hated dirt. Hell, even Rosa cursed quietly when she weeded the garden, but not Tess. Her amber eyes twinkled brightly every time she caught him watching her.

"Why don't you get along with Bart?" she asked, catching them both off guard.

Gabe stood up, sighed, and shook his head. "Bart and I have learned it's best if we agree to disagree."

"About what?"

"Everything."

"But he's your brother. Surely you have something in common with him."

Gabe snorted. "We have the same parents, that's about it."

They both returned to their work, a twinge of regret lingering in Gabe's heart.

"He seemed like a nice enough fellow to me."

"Of course he did. You're a woman who expected nothing from him." Gabe sighed. "Bart has never known responsibility his whole life. He's done whatever he wanted whenever he wanted and never bothered to consider the consequences."

"Why didn't your father do something about that?"

"My old man wasn't exactly a pillar of the community, and after Mama died he pretty much left the rearing of Bart and me to Rosa."

"It must have been hard for him to lose your mother and the baby the way he did."

Gabe stopped picking and turned to look at her. "It was his fault they died," he said. "If she'd been in the city where she belonged, where there were doctors readily available, she wouldn't have died. The baby neither."

"You don't know that, Gabriel." Her voice was compassionate yet firm. "Women die during childbirth all the time and there's nothing anyone can do about it; you don't know a doctor could have prevented anything. I'm sure your father did all he could for her."

Gabe's mind raced back to the day, twenty-five years earlier, when his father took Gabe and Bart outside, in the mud and downpour, and the three of them fell to their knees, begging God to spare the lives of Emma Calloway and her newborn baby girl; a baby who had been born too early, who would never take a breath on her own. Their prayers went unanswered. Clayton was left with two young boys he had no idea what to do with and a ranch he no longer had the heart to run.

The last sober decision Clayton Calloway made was to hire Miguel and Rosa to work the ranch with him. Miguel pretty much took over all the decision making of the land and herd, while Rosa took complete charge of the house and the raising of the boys. Clayton came and went as he pleased, a whiskey bottle in one hand and his beloved Emma's picture in the other.

It wasn't long before he no longer commanded or deserved the respect of the other ranchers in town. He spent his days sleeping and his nights drinking and carousing with Dottie Shelton down at the saloon. For her part, Dottie seemed to honestly love Clayton, despite his condition, but he either didn't see it or pretended not to. Miguel did his best to run the ranch single-handedly but to his own detriment—he was too smart of a businessman, and the place grew faster than anyone could have anticipated. He soon began to depend on young Gabe to help out and put in a grown man's days' worth of work, even after other ranch hands were hired.

Bart was still too young to do much, so he spent most of his time in the house being spoiled by Rosa who doted on *el pobrecito*, "the poor thing." As such, he was never expected to take on any more responsibility than was absolutely necessary—and even that was minimal because between Gabe and Miguel, there wasn't much left to look after.

Miguel was an excellent teacher and role model. He taught Gabe everything there was to learn about being a rancher and about being a man. Honor, respect, and integrity were ingrained in him from the start, and nothing was more important than a man's word and his handshake.

"So Bart was never actually given any responsibility around here," Tess said, her head still bent over her work.

"What?" Had he been thinking out loud that whole time?

"Bart," she said, "between you, Miguel, and Rosa, everything was taken care of, so Bart didn't really have to do anything, did he? There was nothing left."

"There was plenty for him to do!" He insisted, though not quite as adamantly as he would have liked.

"Like what?"

"Well, I can't think of anything right now," he snapped, "but there were things."

Tess smiled. "Did you ever think maybe he wanted to be part of things here but you and Miguel were so busy running everything yourselves you didn't give him a chance?"

Gabe shook his head. "You don't know what you're talking about."

"I'm not saying you or Miguel were wrong in what you did or how you did it," she explained. "You were doing what you had to do to keep this place running and pay the bills."

"Damn right."

"But maybe it's time you took a step back and had another look at your little brother. Maybe he felt as though he never really belonged here, that he was simply in the way."

"Really?" Sarcasm dripped like acid from his lips. "And what makes you an expert on my brother all of a sudden?"

"Nothing." She spoke gently, but Gabe's back was

already up. "You obviously know him better than I, but family is family, Gabriel, and he's the only family you have left. The ranch is yours to do with as you please, and Bart has had to go out and make a different life for himself."

"That's not a life—chasing fugitives all over hell's half acre—that's a death wish."

Tess shrugged. "Maybe he's waiting for you to ask him to come home."

"I seriously doubt that."

"Have you asked?"

"No!"

"Maybe you should."

Gabe stared at her in silence for a long while. She continued to pull weeds as she spoke, and not once in the entire exchange had she sounded accusing or judgmental. She had simply pointed out some things perhaps Gabe had been unable—or unwilling—to see. Maybe she was right. Maybe.

A flicker of amusement danced across his face.

"He'd probably be lynched by every girl's father within fifty miles."

"Broke a few hearts, did he?" Tess asked. She smiled, adjusting the hat again.

"More than a few, I'm afraid. Got himself a bit of a reputation before he up and left."

Tess stopped working and looked him straight in the eye.

"What about you, Gabriel? How many hearts have you broken?"

Gabe chuckled. "I'm more of the 'breakee' type than the 'breaker.'"

Tess's smile faded from her lips. "Who was she?"

"Tess . . ."

"Did you love her?" When he didn't answer right away, her face clouded. "Do you still love her?"

The fear in her eyes stabbed straight at his heart.

"I thought I did," he sighed. "But now I'm not so sure."

"Why?"

He couldn't very well tell her the truth—he'd never get her back on the stage if he did. He settled for avoiding the direct question.

"Things change, Tess, people change. It's the way life is."

"Yes," she agreed. "They do. Sometimes for the better."

"And sometimes for the worse."

"Oh, Gabriel," she said quietly. "You don't really feel that way. Look at it this way—if it wasn't for change, we never would have met."

"Yeah," he scoffed, gesturing around the piles of weeds. "And look where that's got us."

Tess laughed lightly and threw a handful of dirt at him.

"What about you, Miss Kinley?" he asked, sobering slightly. "Are you a breakee or a breaker?"

"Neither," she said. "I've never even been courted."

Gabe just about choked. "You're kidding, right?"

"No. Father decided years ago I would marry Harmon. I wasn't permitted to take any gentleman callers."

"So I guess that makes you a breaker."

Tess paused. "No, not really. In all the time Father spent planning my marriage, I never agreed to it, nor did I pretend to. I told Harmon as much the one and only time we were ever alone." A mighty shudder rocked her spine.

"But poor ol' Harm still must have been heart-broken," Gabe said. He forced his arms to his sides to keep them from pulling her into his embrace. He certainly didn't want to have her in his arms, he only wanted to stop her from trembling the way she did. Or so he told himself.

"No. The only thing broken was poor ol' Harm's ego. He refused to believe me when I told him I would not marry him; he assumed I would eventually go along with it. Especially after . . ." She stopped, racked by another shudder.

"After what?"

Tess shook her head. "Nothing. He thought he could convince me in his own little way. That's when I knew I had to leave Boston."

Bile rose in Gabe's throat. "What did he do to you?"

She smiled through the fear that lingered in her voice. "Nothing worse than what I did to him I suppose."

"Did he . . ."

"It's in the past, Gabriel, let's not dwell on it."

God help him if they should ever meet, Gabe fumed. His fist would dwell on ol' Harm's face for a while. He swiped the back of his hand across his brow and ran his fingers through his hair.

"Come on," he said. "That's enough for today. I'm hungry."

"I'm about half starved myself." Tess laughed, the talk of Harmon Stiles left in the dirt.

"Good," Gabe said. He lifted the overflowing bowl of beans with one hand and reached for her hand with the other. "Let's go see what we can rustle up for supper."

Chapter 10

"Bart's here," Gabe announced before taking another bite of his cold ham sandwich.

Tess's gaze flew to the window. "What? I don't see him."

"You always hear Bart first," Gabe explained. "Listen."

Tess strained to pick out the distant whistle. She could barely hear it, and if Gabe hadn't said otherwise, she would have dismissed it as wind.

"What is he whistling?" she asked.

"'Old Dan Tucker.'"

"I don't think I'm familiar with that song."

Gabe shook his head. "Just as well. We'd best make more sandwiches—he'll be hungry."

Tess hurried to gather the bread and ham, her stomach lurching with every passing second. She hardly had time to catch her breath before Bart was at the door, scowling in her direction.

"Howlin' Leonard, woman—did you have to come *all* the way out here? I been on the road damn near a week."

"Hello, Bart," Tess squeaked. "Yes, I'm sorry. I should have told you where I was going, that was very wrong of me, but I had to get away. You understand, don't you? I didn't think you'd mind, although I have to admit I rather expected you to be upset with me for taking your money. I apologize for that too." Her words tumbled out faster than she could breathe. "I see you're still wearing your gun belt. Did you have a hard time finding me? I didn't think you would since I told you I was headed west and you filled me with the notion of how wonderful El Cielo was and, oh dear, you didn't have the ill fortune of staying in that horrid little town called Hidden Valley, did you? It's really no wonder it's called Hidden Valley—it should be hidden from the whole world. I made the mistake of actually taking a meal there in the rat's nest they call a restaurant. I hope you didn't make the same grave error."

Gabe had not so much as raised his head from his plate through the entire exchange, but a huge grin spread wider and wider across his face with every word that flew from her lips.

Bart pulled out the straight-backed chair beside Gabe's, turned it backward and sat astride it, his arms crossed over the back.

"Does she always go on like this?" he asked, reaching for a sandwich.

Gabe shrugged. "Only when she's nervous."

"Why's she nervous? You being your usual prickly self?"

Gabe shook his head and grinned more. "It's you. She's afraid you're going to turn her over to the sheriff or take her back to Butte with you."

"Hello, gentlemen," Tess interrupted, more than a little annoyed. "I'm standing right here you know. I would appreciate it if you spoke to me instead of about me."

"You heard the lady," Gabe chuckled. "Talk to her."

Bart leaned in closer, whispering loudly into his brother's ear. "If she's gonna go on like that again, I'd really rather not."

"I know what you mean—it's enough to test Job,

isn't it?" He shot Tess a teasing wink and went back to his supper. "Took you long enough to get here."

"Hell, Gabe," Bart snorted. "I wouldn't even be here at all if it weren't for her."

"Yes," Tess interrupted again. "You've come for your money, then, is that right? I don't have it all to give back to you yet, Bart, but as soon as I get the rest, I will pay you back—with interest. I used what I needed to get me out here on the stage, and believe you me, if I'd have known what kind of a trip I was in for, I would have seriously considered staying in Butte with you. Of course, I would have had you bring me here eventually, but that is neither here nor there right now, is it? Shall I go get your money now, or will you be staying with us for a while? It's up in the bed . . . it's upstairs. Your money."

"What in tarnation are you goin' on about, woman? I ain't here for my money—although now that you mention it, damn right I want it back—all of it!"

He'd barely finished the sentence when Tess scurried from the room to fetch his money. Bart rubbed his forehead with filthy fingers.

"Do you get this dizzy talkin' to her?" he asked.

"Hell," Gabe muttered. "I get dizzy just lookin' at her."

The minute he heard Bart snort, Gabe realized he'd spoken a little louder than he'd intended. His face flamed, his shoulders tensed, waiting for the ribbing his brother was sure to give him.

"You and her?" Bart laughed. "Hot damn, Gabe, that didn't take you long. Never figured you for a lady's man—especially after Catarina. Figured you'd settle down with a big ol' farm girl and have yerself a whole passel of kids by now."

Gabe's face darkened. "Well, as you can see, you figured wrong."

"Yeah." Bart chuckled again. "But you and her? She's so . . . so . . ."

"She's not staying." Gabe pushed himself away from the table and deposited his dishes on the sideboard. "If you don't take her back with you, she'll be on Friday's stage."

"Where the hell am I supposed to be goin'? And why the hell would I take her with me?" Bart almost shouted.

Gabe stopped and turned to face his brother. "Why wouldn't you? Isn't she why you're here?"

Bart's head bobbed between a half-nod and a half-shrug. "Yes and no," he said.

"Damnation," Gabe snapped. "Why can't anything—*anything*—be easy with her? This isn't going to be a great long-winded story, is it?"

"Hey," Bart said, holding his hand up defensively. "I ain't her. I'll tell you straight out why I'm here. First off, the reason I chased her all the way out here is on account that no good Gribbs broke outta jail and I reckon he'll be hot on her heels, too. So I come out here to warn her. Second reason—"

"Hold on," Gabe interrupted. "Who's Gribbs?"

"Eli Gribbs." When Gabe didn't respond, Bart let out a low curse. "She didn't tell you 'bout him? The poker game . . . ?"

"She said the fella's name was Simms or something."

Bart nodded slowly. "Right, she don't even know the truth herself."

"What truth?"

"Turns out Gribbs killed Simms some months back an' just up an' took over the man's life—everything he owned—includin' his name and Tess."

"Why?"

"Who the hell knows?" Bart shrugged. "Fact is, Gribbs's killed more 'n a few times."

Gabe rubbed his weary eyes with the heel of his hand.

"I should've known it'd be complicated," he grumbled. "What's the other reason you're here?"

Bart swallowed hard. "I'm here 'cause of somethin' she said to me back there in Butte that got me to thinkin'."

"Which was?"

Bart took another deep breath before he continued. "Well, it would seem Miss Tess thinks maybe I bin too hard on you and we should talk it out—man to man."

It was Gabe's turn to laugh now.

"Well I'll be buggered," he said. "I got the same lecture myself not more than a few hours ago. 'Family is family' and all that crap."

"Yup," Bart nodded. "Same lecture."

They sat in silence for a moment, each lost in thought, fighting to find the next words. It was Gabe who spoke first.

"She does have a point, though, I reckon."

"I reckon." Another pregnant pause, then, "She sure don't waste any time gettin' under a body's skin, does she?"

Gabe's neck prickled, his jaw clenched. "Are you saying . . . ?"

"Take it easy, Gabe," Bart chuckled. "I ain't talkin' 'bout that. All I'm sayin' is she sure ain't like the rest of the womenfolk in this sorry little town. There's somethin' different 'bout her; she's got real grit."

"She's headstrong." Gabe's eyes stared blankly.

"She's got spirit."

"Spirits get broken out here."

Bart shook his head again, exhaling loudly. Gabe had never been one to change his mind once it was made up and it was unlikely he would start now—Tess Kinley or no Tess Kinley.

"Are you figuring on staying a while then?" Gabe asked.

"I reckon, if you don't mind."

"Oh hell, Bart, this is your home, too, you know," Gabe said. "Although I was kind of hoping she'd have some company on her trip back to the city."

Tess appeared in the doorway at that moment, looking more defiant than ever.

"Gabriel," she said steadily, "I've told you before—I am not leaving."

"Gabriel?" Bart choked. "You let her call you Gabriel?"

"That is his name, isn't it?" Tess huffed, thrusting the money toward him.

"Well, yeah, a' course it is, but howlin' Leonard, I ain't never heard no one call him that—not even Mama."

"I don't see why not," Tess snipped. "It's a fine name for a man—especially him."

Bart's eyes widened with laughter as he stared from Gabe to Tess and back again. Gabe knew he should be bothered by it, but God help him, he liked hearing her say his name—he couldn't help himself. Still, he had a point to make. . . .

"Yes," he said pointedly at Bart, "she uses my full name, and, yes, Tess"—he turned back to face her—"you will leave."

Tess tossed her head and moved to stand behind Bart. She closed her eyes and mumbled quietly before she spoke.

"Well, Gabriel, I don't really think you have a say in the matter anymore."

"What?" he bellowed. "You're damn right I have a say in the matter—this is my house!"

"It's also Bart's. You just said so yourself."

Gabe's mouth fell open. "That doesn't mean . . ."

"Yes," she said, her voice gaining strength with

each word. "It means everything. If Bart stays, so do I since, if we want to get picky about it, I do belong to him, don't I?"

"What?" It was Bart who hollered this time. "Look here, woman, you don't belong to me or anyone, and I don't give a good God damn if you stay or not. I came out here for two reasons. The first bein' to tell you your old friend Gribbs escaped and is probably gonna come lookin' for you."

"Who's Gribbs?" she asked.

Bart repeated his explanation as quickly as possible and returned his attention to his food.

"Why on earth would he come for me?" Tess asked, eyes widening.

"'Cause I guess he figures you're still his property and you got some sort of value to him."

"But . . ."

"We'll go talk to Sheriff Nicholls tomorrow and see if he's heard anything about Gribbs."

Tess pursed her lips, eyeing each brother in turn. Bart was as stubborn as his older brother, both of them sitting there as if they had the last word in this predicament. She'd show them.

"What was the second reason?" she asked with surprising calm.

"I got some unfinished business with my brother, and I mean to straighten it out once and for all."

"So you will be staying here at El Cielo?"

"Yup."

Tess's brain picked up steam. "If Mr. Gribbs has escaped custody, wouldn't I be safer here with the two of you than on a stage back to Butte by myself?"

Bart looked at Gabe expectantly. When Gabe made no attempt to answer, Bart's brown eyes narrowed first at him, then at Tess.

"Look, Tess, if you got designs on stayin' here,

then you best work something out with my brother 'cause it ain't got nothin' to do with me no more."

Gabe's told-you-so grin made her want to slap both of them.

"Now don't go and get yourself all in a lather, Tess," he chortled in his best I-told-you-so way. "I'll bring in the tub for you and you can have yourself one of those long baths you like so much while Bart and I go have a talk, how's that?"

A warm bath versus slapping the condescending Calloway brothers. Tess weighed the choices and wisely opted for the former. Slapping them would not win her any ground, but at least with a bath she could relax and form a new strategy.

Gabe hauled in the huge metal tub while Bart filled the wood box and Tess busied herself with building up the fire and putting water on to heat. The two men closed the door behind them, and Tess watched from the window as they wandered to the corral and leaned over the fence. You'd never know to look at them that they were brothers unless you saw them walk. They both exhibited a self-assured confidence that to the unfamiliar onlooker seemed almost arrogant. The brothers did not merely walk, they moved with long, purposeful strides, their backs straight, heads high. Even at the corral, they both stood the same—their right feet resting on the lowest rail, their arms crossed over the top one, chins resting on their hands.

With a small sigh, she pulled the drapes closed and set about with her bath. She realized what a luxury this was, having two baths in less than three days. She relished every minute of it, climbing out only when the water had cooled almost to a chill.

Gabe and Bart stared silently out into the empty corral for long moments before Gabe spoke.

"How have you been?"

Bart shrugged. "All right I guess. Busy."

Gabe nodded down toward the other man's gun. "I reckon that there's had a lot of use then, am I right?"

"Not as much as you'd think," he answered. "I only use it when I have to."

Another nod. "You plan on carrying it around with you while you're here?"

Bart smirked. "Well now, that all depends. Am I going to have to defend Miss Kinley's honor from my big bad brother?"

Gabe didn't even pretend to smile. "I wish to hell she hadn't come here, Bart."

Bart's smile faded. "That bad?"

Now Gabe did smile. "That good," he corrected.

"You haven't . . ."

"Hell no!" he bellowed, his smile belying the frown across his brow. "Not that I wouldn't like to, mind you, but then I'd never get her outta here."

Bart scratched his head. "I'm missin' somethin' here, Gabe. If you love her that much, why the hell would you want her to leave?"

Gabe backed away from his perch. "I never said I loved her."

"Yeah, right." Bart looked as though he was going to argue the point further, but thought better of it. "Whatever you say. Either way, why're you so fired up that she leave? A body's just gotta see the way she looks at you to know what's on her mind."

Gabe looked questioningly at his brother.

"You—you stupid ass! God only knows why, but she's got it bad for you, brother. Hell, even I can see that an' I've just got here."

"Doesn't matter. I'm sure she'll get over it."

"I don't think you're givin' her enough credit, Gabe. I say let her stay—if for no other reason than

Rosa could probably use some help 'round here, couldn't she?"

"Women—ladies—don't belong out here, Bart, you know that. Look what happened to Mama."

"Jesus Christ, Gabe, that was twenty-five years ago. It's not like it used to be out here. Hell, there's even talk of the railway goin' through in the next couple years."

Gabe shook his head. "Doesn't matter. Women like her belong with their own kind, not out here slopping pigs and cleaning chicken shit out of coops day after day."

Bart eyed his brother carefully. When he spoke, his voice was low. "She's not Catarina, Gabe."

"I know that!" he bellowed again. "I never said she was—hell, I wouldn't want her to be. But the fact remains, she's Boston high society, not Porter Creek pig slop!"

"Catarina stayed because she thought the Calloway money would be enough for her. She left because it wasn't. She wanted to live in the city; live high, have frilly dresses and silky underthings. Tess obviously don't want that. She wants to be here—with you for some crazy reason. And if you think I'm even gonna think about askin' her why, you're sadly mistaken. Holy-oh-hell, I get a headache just thinkin' 'bout how long it would take her to answer me."

Gabe smiled toward the house. Bart was right, Tess was nothing like Catarina. Nothing at all. She was sexy, smart, funny, and knew exactly what she wanted. Catarina was a looker, there was no doubt about that, but the only thing *she* knew was that she wanted a rich man and it didn't matter if she loved him or not. Money would buy her all the things she needed to be happy. Tess left her money behind to follow a dream she wanted more than anything else in the world. And for some godforsaken reason, that included Gabe Calloway.

Chapter 11

Gabe shook his head sadly. "She can't stay," he repeated more to himself than to Bart. "It's not the place for someone like her."

"Gabe . . ." Bart began.

"Let's talk about something else." Not talking about Tess was one thing, not thinking about her was another.

The sun dipped lower beyond the horizon, emblazing its crimson afterglow across the sky. Gabe couldn't help but wonder if Tess could see it. She would stare in wonder until the very last speck of color disappeared out of sight—you'd think she'd never seen a sunset before. Gabe longed to call her outside, to share the moment, but he forced himself to stay rooted to his spot.

Bart cleared his throat loudly, intruding on Gabe's thoughts.

"I got me somethin' to say then, Gabe, and I'd be obliged if you'd let me get it out."

Gabe nodded.

"I've come to the reasonin' that maybe after Mama died I wasn't the easiest kid in the world to deal with. I did some mighty fool things in my day and never thought 'bout the whys or the wherefores. I just done 'em."

He stopped, inhaling deeply before he continued.

"You and Miguel had this place runnin' like a fresh greased wheel, and I was always just 'the other Calloway kid,' Rosa's little helper." He held up his hand when Gabe started to interrupt. "Now I ain't blamin' you, I know now you were doin' what you needed to do to keep this place runnin' and now that I ain't such a gawkarse, I surely do appreciate it. You had to make a lot of hard decisions and even harder sacrifices for the sake of this damned ranch, and I sure as hell wouldn't change places with you for all the tea in China."

He pushed back his hat and scratched his chin.

"The thing is, Gabe, I ain't the same saphead I used to be. I've had time to look back on how things were and why they were that way. Guess I spent a lot of years bein' pissed 'cuz I never felt like I was part of this place. It was yours. And Miguel's. But now I know, we're just different, you and me. Even if I'd a been you, I still don't think I'd a taken on this place the way you have. It never interested me the way it did you. But even so . . . I want you to know . . . I'm sorry for the trouble I caused. I know it weren't always easy having to chase after me and fix the messes I got myself into, and I'm sorry."

Bart's voice wavered as he trailed off, forcing him to cough over it.

"Oh, hell," Gabe said, exhaling loudly. "It ain't all your fault. I was so hardheaded and set on proving to Miguel and the rest of this damn fool town I wasn't like the old man, I guess I never gave you a chance to prove yourself. It always seemed faster to do it myself than to try and explain how or what needed doing. I guess I figured you'd rather run around and have fun than hang out here and castrate bulls." He paused, a slow smile spreading across his face. "Truth be told, some of the shit you pulled made me wish I could be more like you."

The brothers shared a couple of lopsided grins.

"You'll stay for a while then?" Gabe asked again.

"I reckon." Bart nodded with a wry smile. "Like I said, Rosa could probably use some help around here, and if you're bent on sendin' Tess on her way . . ." He shot Gabe a grin, then added, "I best get my tail over to Rosa's right now or I'll be in for a whoopin' an' a half tomorrow."

Gabe laughed as he watched Bart head off toward the cottage. Rosa would be thrilled—her prodigal son had returned.

"We're bunking with Zeus," he yelled after him. Bart waved his acknowledgment and pushed his way through the gate that led to Rosa and Miguel's house.

Gabe was still chuckling as he made his way to the barn; Zeus and the rest of the horses would be looking for their food and water. He tended to his animals, taking time to speak softly to each one and give them a good rubdown before leaving them to the stillness of the evening.

He needed a good strong cup of coffee if he had any hope of getting through the ledgers tonight. The kitchen curtains remained closed, but surely Tess had finished her bath by now! He knocked softly on the door and when there was no answer, he banged louder.

"Tess?"

No answer. He took a deep, shaky breath and pushed the door open slightly.

"Tess?" he called again. No answer. He stepped inside and cast a quick glance through the room. The metal tub sat vacant in the middle of the kitchen— the only reminder Tess had been there moments before. Regret and relief both flooded through Gabe in waves—regret he'd missed seeing her, and relief he'd avoided the inevitable struggle between his passion and his probity.

While he waited for the coffee to boil, he set about emptying the huge tub and returned it to its corner in the pantry. Tess descended the stairs as though walking on a cloud, her nose sniffing the air eagerly.

"Coffee?" She smiled. "Wonderful idea."

Gabe stared speechless for a moment. Once again she was covered in his old red flannel shirt and Rosa's pink wrapper, her hair in a tousle of tangles around her shoulders. Any other woman, Gabe was certain, would have been well aware of the effect she had on a man, but Tess didn't have the first clue what she did to him.

"Tess," he began, clearing his throat past the sudden hoarseness. "Don't you think you should put something else on?"

She looked blank for a moment, then looked down at the wrapper.

"What's wrong with this?" she asked. "I'm fully covered, Gabriel. I have your shirt on underneath."

"Yes, I know," he seethed through gritted teeth.

Her eyes widened. "Oh, I'm sorry. Do you want me to take it off? It's just that I don't have anything else to wear except my two dresses and—"

"No!" he bellowed straining against his contradictory libido. "I don't want you to take it off. It's not proper, is all."

"Oh, Gabriel." She smiled warmly. "You are so sweet—always thinking of my virtue."

"Yeah," he grunted. "Well, someone has to."

She laughed lightly. Her roughened hands brushed his as she reached for her cup of coffee.

"Thank you," she murmured, her eyes widening with their true innocence. The mere whisper of his touch sent fire raging through her—to places she had never even considered before. His gaze bore right through her, piercing her soul with the torment she saw there. Tess's heart constricted in a painful knot.

She knew, without having any experience to call on, it would be so very easy to seduce him, to have him touch her the way she wanted him to. But she also knew he would grow to resent her for letting that happen. It would be tantamount to trapping him into a marriage and a life he had made clear to her he did not want. Despite her dreams, despite the heartache it would cause her to give it up, she simply could not do that to him, no matter how much she wanted to.

Tess pulled her gaze away and stepped back.

"Perhaps I'll get a blanket to wrap around myself," she said softly. "I was going to take my coffee out on the porch while I try to fight my way through these tangles. Would you like to join me?"

"I have work to do," he muttered.

"Can I help?"

"No, I don't . . . oh, hell," he growled, raking his hand through his own tousled hair. "The biggest help you could be to me is to go sit outside and stay out of my way."

Tess bit her lip, swallowed hard, and nodded. She heard Gabe curse as she retrieved the blue and white crocheted blanket from the sofa and pushed past him out the door. She would not cry. She would not. He would probably expect her to—and God knew she wanted to—but she would not do it. Tears were for the weak and the frail—and she needed to prove she was strong and able-bodied.

She wrapped the thick blanket around her shoulders and sat, shivering, in the warm night air. This was not how she had imagined it would be. One minute Gabe was kissing her senseless and the next he was growling at her like a wild animal. Why couldn't he love her back the way she believed he wanted to? It certainly seemed Gabe was as moved by their shared kiss as she had been, so what could possibly be wrong?

She pulled the comb through her hair slowly, deliberately, as she stared out at the corral, seeing nothing but Gabriel. She jumped when her eyes suddenly focused on Bart standing directly in front of her.

"Oh! You startled me."

Bart smiled. "Looked like you were a thousand miles away, Miss Kinley."

"No," she answered honestly. "I was right here at El Cielo."

Bart mounted the stairs and took up the rocker next to hers.

"He's not an easy man to live with, Tess," he said after a while. "You might want to rethink things."

"I've tried," she said quietly. "I didn't come here with the intention of falling in love with your brother, you have to know that. You made El Cielo seem just as its name implies—heaven on earth. My dream has always been to marry a man I loved—a man who loved me—to have a whole herd of children and to work together to build our life on a beautiful little ranch surrounded by cows, chickens, and sunsets like the one we had tonight."

"Cattle."

Tess frowned. "I beg your pardon?"

"They're called cattle, not cows. Cows are the females in the herd; bulls are the males. Together they're called cattle."

"Cattle," she repeated slowly.

"Right." He leaned over, resting his elbows on his knees. "Can I ask you somethin' kinda personal?"

Tess nodded hesitantly.

"How do you know you really love him?" When she made to argue, he continued, "I mean, how can you be sure it ain't the dream you're in love with and Gabe just happened to be here when you arrived?"

Tess swallowed hard. "I've thought of that myself," she confessed. "But the fact is, when I think about it all—I mean honestly think hard—I realize I would happily give up my dreams and go back to Butte, or Boston for that matter, as long as Gabriel was with me."

Bart watched her as she spoke, seeming to consider what she said.

"I know I've only been here for a couple days," she hurried to explain. "And Gabriel has already tried to convince me there is no such thing as love at first sight, but I don't know how else to explain the way he makes me feel."

"Indigestion?" he asked, smirking.

"No." She smiled back. "Every time I look at him, my heart feels as though it will burst right out of my chest; I can hardly catch a breath and my knees wobble like they were made of soggy bread. I look around this ranch and I feel so many different things for him—admiration, hope, fear. Sorrow." She paused. "He told me about your parents and the baby."

"He did?" Bart's head shook slowly. "Gabe never talks about that."

"I can understand why," she said. "It must have been horrible for both of you."

Bart shrugged. "Was worse for him, I think. I was pretty young."

Tess was silent for a moment.

"Can I ask you something now?"

Bart nodded. "Shoot."

Heat rose up her neck and all through her scalp. "This probably isn't something a lady should ask, especially of a man, but I have no one else to ask, and if anyone would know, you might."

Bart looked solemn. "It'll stay between us then."

Tess's hands fidgeted with the edge of the blanket, her embarrassment blazing across her face.

"Why is it . . . he seems so . . . what I mean is . . ."

"Just say it," he said gently.

"He kissed me."

Bart's expression didn't flinch. He sat where he was, waiting for her to continue.

"Today, before church . . ."

Now his jaw dropped. "He went to church?" he asked incredulously.

"Y-yes," Tess answered.

"But Gabe doesn't go to church," Bart said. "Never."

"He did today."

Bart shook his head again, a slow grin spreading across his face. "Go on."

"Well," Tess said, clearing her throat several times. "It was um . . . well, it was enjoyable. . . ."

"Yes, I'm sure it was." He chuckled.

"This isn't funny, Bart," she snapped. "I'm sorry I even said anything."

She pushed out of her chair and pulled open the kitchen door.

"Wait!" he said. "I'm sorry, you're right. Don't go off mad, Tess. Sit down and tell me what's got you so riled up."

Almost reluctantly, she returned to her chair, the blanket pulled even tighter around her shoulders.

"Tell me," he repeated.

She eyed him warily. At least he wasn't laughing anymore.

"Your brother's reaction to me has been very strange. At first he was angry—very angry—and over the last few days, he seems to flop back and forth between being . . . friendly . . . and being angry with me. Then when he kissed me today, I was certain he felt the same way I did, that he wanted . . . that is to say . . ."

"I know what you mean, Tess."

"Y-yes," she stammered. "Of course. I don't know what to make of him. He's angry with me again, and I can't even begin to imagine what it is I have done to set him off. He was fine when you both left me to my bath, and yet when I spoke to him just now, his eyes are flashing daggers at me. What have I done?"

Bart's grin widened.

"Bart!"

"I'm not laughin' at *you*, Tess. I'm laughin' at *him*. You've got him twisted up so bad he don't know if he's comin' or goin'."

Tess did not smile. "What does that mean? And why do you think it's so funny?"

"Tess," he sighed. "Gabe's a force within himself. He's used to givin' orders, havin' them be followed, and pretty much gettin' his own way on everything. He's the boss in everything—the ranch, the house, his heart." He paused, his brown eyes twinkling mischievously. "Okay, maybe not the house. Rosa's probably got it over him there, but my point is he's used to bein' in control of everything. And then you come along, walk into his life, and wham! He ain't got a clue."

"About what?" she asked, her eyes huge.

"About you!"

"What about me? You're not making any sense."

"You really don't understand any of this, do you?" Bart shook his head in wonder. "Tess, Gabe's in love with you."

Chapter 12

Surely Bart had lost his mind. Gabe might feel something for Tess, but love? She seriously doubted that.

"I'm sorry, Bart," she said. "I don't think you—"

"Don't get me wrong," he interrupted, raising both hands. "He might never admit it, hell, he might not even know it, but it's there. And it scares the crap out of 'im."

"Honestly, Bart, Gabriel is an intelligent man. I think he would know if he loved me or not."

Bart shrugged. "Maybe, maybe not. Truth is, Tess, Gabe's had his fair share of women trouble. There was one in particular who messed him up pretty good. Took him a while to straighten out after that."

"Well, there you go," Tess said. "He's been in love before, so he should know how it feels."

"That's where you're wrong," Bart said. "He ain't never been in love before. Oh, sure, he mighta loved the girl, but he sure as hell weren't in love with her."

Tess considered this for a minute. Gabe had been hurt before. Was that why he was afraid to get close again? But she would never hurt him—she'd rather die first.

"What did this woman do to him?"

"Who—Catarina?" Bart asked.

Tess nodded. Catarina. Just her name made Tess

angry—she sounded like a spoiled brat who needed to be taken over her father's knee. But wasn't that exactly what Gabe had said about Tess herself?

"She worked her way into Gabe's life, had him believin' she loved him, and then she left."

"Why?"

"Didn't wanna be married to a 'dumb rancher' who spent his days and nights thinkin' 'bout cattle. She wanted the high life—the dancin', the fancy restaurants, that sorta thing—an' sure as shootin' she weren't gonna find it here in Porter Creek, that's for danged sure."

"Poor Gabriel," Tess murmured. "Why was she here if she didn't want to be?"

Bart snickered. "Her pa owns the mercantile. Figured she'd marry Gabe—mostly for his money a'-course—an' then convince him to move to Helena or Butte or somewhere a little more lively. Soon as she realized ol' Gabe weren't about to be movin' anywhere, least of all a big city, she hightailed it away from him and cried until her mama and daddy sent her to live with her aunt in Billings."

"That's horrible," she sighed.

Bart nodded. "So, between Catarina and Mama, and the rest of the women who've wandered in and out of his life, he ain't exactly had the best luck."

"But what do any of them have to do with me? Catarina sounds like a perfectly horrible woman and your poor mother couldn't help that she died, for goodness' sake. As for 'the rest of the women,' I can't even imagine how he could compare me to any of them. I would never hurt Gabriel, Bart. You have to believe that."

"Oh, hell, Tess, I know that. But you gotta understand Gabe. When Mama and the baby died, they took a big chunk a' him with them."

"I'm sure you all felt that way." A familiar ache pinched Tess's heart. "When a child loses his parent, especially his mother, it's something that follows him for the rest of his life."

"Rosa tried, God bless 'er, to be a mother to both of us, but Gabe was so sore with Mama and the old man, he took to workin' this damned ranch with Miguel and never stopped long enough to let Rosa love him.

"He hated bein' fussed over, hated anything that showed the least bit of weakness. He was only seven, for cryin' out loud, but he blamed Mama's dyin' on her—for bein' so weak—and on the old man for not seein' it. He's always said weak women got no business out west. Far as he's concerned, they should all be put up in a fancy cushioned room somewhere and forgotten."

"But I'm not weak!" Tess cried. "I'm as strong as anyone, and if he'd give me the chance, I could show him. But, no, I get a couple little blisters and he acts like the sky is falling in, for goodness' sake."

"You got blisters?"

Tess turned her hands palms up and showed him the wounds.

"What the hell happened to you?"

"I was collecting eggs and cleaning out the chicken coop. Your brother and Rosa went on like I'd lost a limb or something equally as foolish."

"Why the hell were you in with the chickens? Nobody goes in there 'cept him."

"Yes," she answered wryly. "I know that now. He was trying to prove a point and all that happened was he became terribly angry with me."

Bart nodded slowly. "That's where you're wrong, Tess. Gabe ain't mad at you 'bout that—he's mad at himself. He prob'ly figured you'd turn tail and run at the first sign of pain instead of workin' with blisters and scratches like that."

"Well, it was me he was yelling at, not himself."

"Yup. That's how he is."

"So you're telling me, when I offered to help him with some work just now and he got angry again, he wasn't angry at me, but with himself?"

"Right."

"Why?"

"Why what?"

"Why is he angry?"

Bart removed his hat and whapped it against his knee, sending a thin cloud of brown dust billowing around both of them.

"That's easy," he replied. "You'd just finished your bath, right?"

Tess nodded.

"Were you standin' there wrapped in a towel or even—"

"I most certainly was not!" she cried indignantly. "I was . . . am . . . completely dressed! I have his shirt and Rosa's wrapper . . ."

"You're wearing his shirt?"

"Yes."

"Well, it's no bloody wonder he's all fired up."

Tess was more confused and frustrated now than before Bart arrived. He seemed to be talking circles around her, and she was getting dizzy from it all.

"Bart," she began impatiently. "I haven't got the slightest clue what you are talking about, but I have to say you are managing to give me a pounding headache."

Bart laughed. "It's prob'ly not near the headache my brother has right now."

"Why?" she seethed. "What have I done?"

"Nothin'," he continued, laughing. "That's just it. Bein' you is drivin' ol' Gabe loco. You're here, he's here, you're both adults, there's obviously something between you if he up an' kissed you on the way to church, for God's sake, and you . . . well . . . how do I put this?"

Tess waited less than a second before her temper got the better of her.

"For goodness' sake, Bart, just say it!"

"Well, okay," he shrugged. "The thing is, Tess, you're a fine lookin' woman and there ain't nothin' more attractive to a man like Gabe than a woman who don't know she's good lookin'."

"Bart Calloway, you are trying to make me crazy! Now be serious, for goodness' sake." She shook her comb threateningly in his face. "Don't try to patronize me—I know full well I am not beautiful. I'm short, I've got this horrible colored hair, my skin is too pale, my—"

"That's exactly what I'm talkin' about, Tess," he argued. "I got no reason to lie to you, so you might as well believe what I say. You're sure as shootin' a good lookin' woman—not my type, but that's a whole different story. Gabe obviously thinks you're somethin' to look at, too, an' seein' you in his shirt is . . . well, let's just say right now, his thoughts alone are enough to send him straight to the hot house."

"Oh, honestly, Bart, I hardly think that's why he got in a huff, because I'm wearing his shirt. Besides, it's not as if I was showing anything—I was completely covered."

Bart shrugged. "Imagination's a wonderful thing."

Tess flushed furiously. "You're making this up!"

"I wouldn't lie to you, Tess," he said through a grin. "Gabe's prob'ly sittin' in there right now fightin' back every urge he has about you and gettin' absolutely no work done at all."

Tess shook her head. "You're wrong, Bart. Everything I do makes him angry, and if I don't get some help from you or someone else, he's going to have me on that darned stage on Friday if it kills him."

"I ain't wrong, Tess, and you're right about one thing—he sure as hell ain't gonna let you stay here.

He's too scared you'll get sick and die on him or you'll plain get sick of bein' here and hotfoot it outta here faster than a long-tailed cat in a room full o' rockin' chairs. He ain't gonna let himself get hurt like that again, even if lettin' you go kills him instead."

"It's not fair," she sighed. "It's just not fair."

"No, ma'am, it ain't. But that's what you get for fallin' in love with stupid Gabe Calloway."

"Bart," she began, but his twinkling eyes stopped her.

"I'm kiddin', Tess. Just kiddin'. He ain't that stupid, I reckon. After all, he's got good taste in women, don't he?"

Tess flushed at the compliment but did not respond. She picked up the comb from her lap and resumed the fight with the tangles. They rocked in companionable silence for a while, the only sound being the steady creaking of the porch floorboards.

"So what d'you think of the place anyway?" Bart asked.

Tess shrugged. "I've not actually seen anything yet, except the chicken coop. I haven't even been invited past the barn door yet. But I guess if what you say is true and Gabriel really will make me leave, then it's probably best if I don't—"

"The hell with that!" Bart boomed. "You came halfway 'round the country to see the ranchin' way of life, and I'll be damned if I'm gonna let you go home still wonderin' what it's all about."

"But what about . . ."

"The hell with everythin' else! Startin' tomorrow, Tess Kinley, you are gonna learn what ranchin' life is really like—hell, I might even teach you how to castrate bulls!"

"Bart!" she gasped, but she was laughing too hard to be ashamed.

"It's settled then," he chortled. "You be ready first

thing, little missy, and we'll ride out to check the herd after breakfast. How's that sound?"

"Really?" she almost squealed with delight. "I'd love it! Can I milk one of the cows? Can I learn how to shoe a horse?" She bounced up and down in her chair, her hands clapping together. "Ooh, ooh, can I learn how to play poker?"

Bart's laughter echoed through the still air.

"I don't think . . ."

"Oh, please, Bart, not for money or anything, but will you teach me? Please?"

"Well now, little missy, if you're gonna play cards with Bart Calloway, you play for money or you don't play. I'll spot you enough to get you through a couple a' hands; but if you can't manage to win some back, then you're out, got it?"

"That's wonderful!" she giggled. "I can't wait. Do you think Gabriel will want to play, too?" Her excitement waned. "On second thought, maybe we shouldn't even ask him. The less I see of him, the easier it will be to leave on Friday, right?"

Bart sobered. "I ain't makin' no bets on that, Tess."

"No," she sighed. "Me neither."

He reached out and patted her hand lightly. "You still got a few days, Tess. Try and enjoy 'em while you're here."

Though her eyes burned with tears, she refused to let them fall. Instead, she lifted her head high and smiled as brightly as she could.

"I'll be ready and waiting tomorrow morning," she said. "Is there anything I should bring with me?"

"Nope. I'll make sure the horses are saddled and ready to go; you just make sure you're ready for a full day of work."

"Oh, I will be," she promised. "Thank you, Bart."

"My pleasure, ma'am. Now you best go get some

shut-eye if you expect to keep up tomorrow. I'll walk you in so Gabe don't bite your head off again."

She smiled her thanks this time and followed him in through the kitchen. Gabe was seated at his desk, his long legs stretched out, his right ankle crossed over his left. A deep frown creased his brow and was made even more pronounced by his blind stare and his arms crossed tightly over his chest.

"Good night," Tess said quietly as she tiptoed up the stairs. Bart nodded back, but Gabe remained stoic.

"Any coffee left?" Bart asked, eyeing Gabe's mug. "Hell, you ain't even touched yours. That bad?"

Gabe finally blinked. "Forgot about it, I guess."

"*You* forgot about coffee?" Bart echoed. "Must got a lot on your mind. Wanna tell me about it?"

"There's nothing to tell." He pulled himself upright and leaned over the open ledger in front of him. "Did you two have a nice talk out there?"

Bart pulled in a chair from the kitchen and straddled it.

"She told me you kissed her."

"Damn it!" Gabe hissed, slamming his pen down on the desk. "It was a mistake, Bart, that's all."

"No shit," he agreed. "But for some reason she seems to think it wasn't."

"Yeah, well, she also thinks she's in love with me, so there you go."

"She is," Bart stated matter-of-factly.

"No, she's not. She might think she is, but the truth is she's been reading too many of those dime store novels and now her head's all full of crazy ideas."

"Nope," Bart said, shaking his head. "You're wrong. I can't for the life of me figure out why, but she's really and truly in love with you. Poor girl. Maybe we ought to have Doc Bender come and have a look at her—all that jostlin' on the stage must have rattled her brain or somethin'."

Gabe rolled his eyes. "This isn't funny, Bart."

"You're right, it ain't funny at all. That little girl's got her whole heart wrapped up in thoughts of you, and what do you do? You kiss her, for God's sake, and then tell her she can't stay. You got her so confused she don't know what to think."

"She should be thinkin' about her trip home," Gabe snapped.

"She is."

Every last bit of color drained from Gabe's face.

"She knows you're gonna send her away, even if you do love her. She knows with every single passin' minute her dream dies a little bit more, and come Friday she's gonna have to say good-bye to everythin' she ever wanted."

"That's not my fault!" Gabe growled. "I didn't ask her to come here—she just arrived. I didn't ask her to get all droopy eyed and declare her love for me. She did that all on her own."

"You're right," Bart agreed. "It ain't your fault. She brung all this misery on herself, didn't she? You're an innocent bystander."

"Damn right," Gabe nodded.

"She prob'ly asked you to kiss her, too."

"That was a mistake," he repeated. "One I won't let happen again."

Bart pushed himself up from his chair and shrugged.

"Don't rightly matter if it happens again or not, Gabe. Fact is, it happened once and that's all it took."

Gabe stared after his brother as he strode from the house. When the hell had Bart started giving a hot tinker's damn about anyone except himself? And why the hell did Gabe's heart suddenly ache with the same fierce intensity as the pain in his pounding head?

Chapter 13

"Good morning, Rosa," Tess called brightly as she hurried into the kitchen. The inviting aromas of sizzling bacon and hot coffee filled the house, making her stomach gurgle obnoxiously.

Rosa smiled. "La niña hungry, no?"

"Yes," she grinned back. "I'm starved. What can I do to help?"

"Nada. Bart Calloway say you go ride today."

"Yes," Tess almost gushed. "I'm going to get to ride a horse and see the cows and the land and—"

"Bup bup bup," Rosa interrupted, her hands waving away Tess's words. "No ride in dress. I bring for you."

She pointed to the living room where a pile of clothes lay stacked on the back of the sofa. Tess lifted each piece one by one and examined them. A lovely soft blue blouse with a fitted bodice, a matching riding skirt, and a blue and white checked bandana.

"Are these yours, Rosa?"

"Si," the woman nodded. "Many year back. I no more little—I big."

She patted her broad stomach and chuckled.

"Thank you, Rosa." Tess choked back a tiny sob. "I promise I will look after them today."

"Go," Rosa said, again waving away Tess's thanks. "You hurry, eat soon."

Tess scampered back upstairs and changed her

clothes as quickly as she could. The riding skirt was still a little too big, but with the aid of the belt from the pink wrapper, it would work just fine. After a quick glance in the mirror, Tess had to admit if she had a hat and some real boots, she'd almost look like she fit in here. Almost.

She tossed the thought from her head and returned to the kitchen where everyone except Gabe had already gathered.

"Good morning." She smiled around the room. Rosa nodded her approval and indicated the chair next to Bart's.

"Goin' ridin' today, miss?" Joby asked.

"Yes." Tess smiled. "Bart has kindly offered to show me around the ranch today."

Joby nodded and stuffed another forkful of eggs into his already full mouth. Seth didn't comment, but his eyes shifted uneasily between Bart and Tess. With the exception of an odd smile, Bart held his remarks to himself, but the grin broadened significantly when Gabe entered the room.

"Good morning, Gabriel." Tess smiled.

Gabe nodded his greeting to the room as a whole, but his eyes lingered a moment longer on Tess.

"Sit," Rosa ordered as she pulled Joby's and Seth's plates out from under them.

"Damn it, Rosa," Seth whined. "We ain't done yet. Ain't we never gonna be able to finish a danged meal?"

Rosa's spatula whirled through the air, striking Seth on the back of the head.

"Ow!" he hollered. "What d'ya do that for?"

"You no curse to me, Seth Laughton!" Her two fists—the right one still wrapped around the spatula—settled on her ample hips, bracing for a fight.

Bart and Joby laughed right out loud, but Miguel only smirked.

"Well jeez, ya didn't hafta hit me!"

Rosa waved the spatula at him again, sending him racing from the house, with Joby tripping behind him. She dished up a huge plate of bacon, eggs and hotcakes for Gabe and served it up with a mug of strong black coffee. She nudged Miguel gently and nodded toward the door. He immediately rose and took his plate to the sideboard.

He waited for her to dry her hands before leading the way to the door. Rosa turned and shot Bart a look.

"You take care," she warned, wagging her finger at him. "Buena niña."

Bart grinned broadly, a sly twinkle glowing in his deep brown eyes. "I'll bring 'er back without a scratch—or a blister."

Rosa tsk-tsked at him before she left, but her smile pretty much contradicted the sound.

Gabe swallowed a mouthful of coffee and fixed his glare on Tess.

"You two got plans for today?" he grunted.

Tess lifted her chin and smiled bravely. "Yes," she said. "Bart is going to show me around the ranch. I might even get to milk a cow."

Gabe's face clouded, his eyes narrowed, and his lips drew into a thin, pale line.

"That is," she continued dryly, "unless you need me here for some reason."

She knew Bart was fighting back his laugh, could feel the tension tighten among the three of them. She'd been up all night rethinking her plan and she couldn't back down now. She was going to take in everything she possibly could, learn every last detail about cows—cattle—and ranching she was able in the short time she had left at El Cielo.

"You'd be in the way here," he grunted, pushing his still-full plate away. "Do what you like."

Bart no longer tried to hide his smile as he chewed

his food and guzzled his coffee. He was obviously enjoying this exchange.

"Thank you," Tess replied evenly. "I will."

Gabe shoved away from the table and stormed from the room, leaving her trembling in his wake. Guilt immediately flooded her, making her both angry and confused. Why on earth should she feel any guilt whatsoever toward him? He'd made himself fairly clear he had no intention of letting her do any type of work—no matter how menial—so why shouldn't she go riding with Bart? At least *he* was friendly.

"You know," Bart chuckled. "I don't think I know anyone who'd talk to him in that kinda tone. Most folk are scared right dumb when he gets to lookin' that way."

"Oh pish," Tess scoffed. "The last person in the world I would be afraid of is Gabriel. He would never hurt me. Not physically anyway." Her eyes filled with unshed tears but she pushed them back. No sense crying over what couldn't be helped.

Bart's grin faded. "Come on, let's get outta here. Horses are waitin'."

Tess forced a smile and stacked the remaining dishes on the sideboard. "Right," she said. "Let's go."

Outside, she caught sight of Gabe leaning in the shadows of the barn door, his arms crossed over his chest, his hat pulled low over his eyes. Bart ignored him and strode straight to the waiting horses.

"I saddled Hera for you. She's a pretty easy ride—gentle and not terribly jumpy."

Tess smiled and climbed up into the saddle. Bart adjusted the stirrups and waited until she was comfortably settled atop her mount before he hopped up on his own mare.

"Tess!" Gabe's voice boomed from across the yard.

"Knew we wouldn't get away clean," Bart whispered, turning Tess's forced smile into a genuine one.

"Yes, Gabriel?" she answered calmly. "What is it?"

He was beside her in a flash, his stony expression not giving anything away. In one swift motion he removed his hat and jammed it down on her head, covering her eyes. Tess pushed the brim up enough to peek out. Then he turned on his heel and stomped back to the barn without looking back.

"Is he gone?" She giggled.

Bart's eyes couldn't have gotten any bigger. "Yeah."

"Let's go then."

Bart shook his head slowly and clicked to his horse, sending her off across the yard, past the chickens and toward the northeast rise. They rode at a gentle trot, letting Tess take in every minute detail.

Acres of grassland stretched out in front of her, dotted here and there with vast groves of ponderosa pines and sagebrush. Squirrels scurried through the branches, while jackrabbits and gophers darted in and out of barely visible holes in the underbrush.

"Do you grow any crops here?" she asked, scanning the horizon.

"Nope. Just raise cattle—that's enough."

"But they're cows," she said. "How much work can they be?"

Bart chuckled. "Well, it ain't them that's the work. Besides brandin', milkin', castratin', and the general muckin' that goes with cattle, a lot of work goes into runnin' off rustlers and fixin' the fence over an' over again."

"What happens to the fence?"

"Rustlers," he said. "Neighbors. They cut it to get onto the land whenever they please."

"Neighbors!" she gasped. "Why on earth would your own neighbors destroy your fence?"

"You ain't been here long enough to meet the Langmans, have ya? That's prob'ly for the best, I reckon." Bart shook his head in disgust. "Sorriest bunch of men I ever did meet."

"What's wrong with them?" Tess pushed Gabe's hat back again.

"Besides bein' plain stupid ya mean?" He spat his tobacco onto the ground. "Wyatt Langman and the old man got into it one night at the saloon—this was a few years after Mama died—and somehow in the kerfuffle, Wyatt's oldest son Adam took a bullet. Died on the spot."

"That's horrible." Tess shuddered.

Bart nodded. "Ol' Wyatt swore he'd get even with the old man one day, an' even though he never meant it, his boys took him at his word."

"What do you mean?"

"Stupid things." He shrugged. "The boys sneak over to do us damage, but it always backfires on 'em. One time they cut through the fence tryin' to rustle some of our herd and Beau somehow managed to get himself gored. A' course that was our fault, too."

"Who is Beau?"

"Langman's next oldest son."

"How many are there? Langmans, I mean."

Bart scratched his head. "Let's see, Adam and Mrs. Langman are long dead, so that leaves Wyatt, Beau, Clint . . . Damon an' Evan . . . Stupid Frankie . . . Garth and . . . Collette. She's the baby of the family. How many's that? Eight, I guess."

Tess rolled her eyes heavenward. "Have mercy—eight children! Do they all still live on the ranch?"

"Hell yeah." Bart laughed. "Most of 'em are married with kids of their own now, 'cept for Stupid Frankie and Collette a'course."

"Why do you say that?"

"No woman with half a grain of sense would marry

a gawkarse like Stupid Frankie Langman, and as for Collette . . ." Bart's eyes twinkled merrily as he swiped his sleeve across his brow. "Let's just say she's always been a bit of a challenge."

Tess's jaw dropped. "Bart Calloway! Are you saying . . ."

"Whoa up there, missy," he laughed, at least showing the good sense to blush. "I ain't never touched her. Did my fair share of lookin', though, but she was still a baby the last time I seen her—barely seventeen."

"Seventeen is hardly a baby," Tess replied. "Many women are married with children at that age."

"Not Collette Langman. A man wouldn't just be marryin' her, he'd be marryin' the whole herd of 'em, and there ain't a man alive up to that job."

"Not even you?"

Bart's grin widened.

"My my my," she said knowingly. "A smile like that can only mean one thing. Have you set your sights on courting Miss Langman?"

Bart shrugged. "Like I said, I ain't seen her in a spell."

"How long exactly?"

"I been gone over two years."

"Two years isn't long, Bart. Perhaps she's sweet on you as well."

Bart reined in his mare and leaned over the saddle horn. "Who said I'm sweet on 'er?"

"You didn't have to say it, Bart, it's written plain as day across your face. You should see yourself."

"Tell me somethin'," he said, nudging his horse ahead. "How is it you can see it so clear on me but you don't see it in Gabe?"

Tess looked stunned, then hurt. "Don't tease me, Bart. Gabriel doesn't look at me like that. Well, he did once—before he kissed me—but other than that . . ."

"I'm sorry," Bart said. "I didn't mean . . . oh, hell, Tess . . . have you decided what you're gonna do?"

Tess brightened. "Yes, as a matter of fact, I have. I'm staying right here."

"Here?"

"Not here at El Cielo, but here in Porter Creek. I'm going to go into town tomorrow and find myself a job and a place to live and I'm going to build a life for myself right here just like I planned." She paused, smiled sadly, and added, "Well, almost like I planned."

"So I guess that means you'll up an' marry some other knot head here in town—just make sure it ain't Stupid Frankie Langman!"

"You won't have to worry about that, Bart. I have no intention of getting married."

"But . . ."

Tess shook her head resolutely. "I will only marry a man I love, and I love Gabriel. I can't even imagine being married to anyone else." She took a deep breath, forcing another smile. "So I'm going to save my money and start my own farm here in Porter Creek. Of course it won't be nearly as grand as El Cielo, but it'll be big enough to support me into my old age."

"You can't be thinkin' straight, Tess. Farmin' an' ranchin' are hard ways to live, especially if you're a woman."

"I can do it. I know about gardens and such, and now, thanks to your brother, I've learned about chickens as well. I'll get some cows, some pigs, and whatever else I need and I'll make it work somehow."

"It's not easy, Tess."

"I know."

Bart was silent a long time before asking his next question.

"Why here? I mean it's gonna be hard enough for

you bein' a single lady an' all in a town full of gawkarses but to have to see Gabe all the time, ain't that gonna make it even harder? I mean what if . . ."

His voice trailed off, but the unasked question hung between them, like a noose around her heart. Her eyes burned in their sockets, but she lifted her chin a little higher, straightened her shoulders, and pushed Gabe's hat back on her head a little more.

"Living in the same town as Gabriel may prove difficult, yes. More so if he should find and marry another, but I came here with a goal, Bart, and I intend to achieve that goal—with or without him. I will admit, though, there is a small part of me that hopes one day your boneheaded brother will come to his senses and see the light, so to speak. I know it is unlikely, but you never know. Miracles happen every day."

She was shocked to hear how confident she sounded, for she certainly did not feel it in her heart. Seeing Gabriel married to another would likely kill her on the spot.

Bart shook his head slowly. "But you could start a farm in any of a hundred towns. Why make it harder on yourself by stayin' here?"

"This is where I belong. You and Rosa are the only friends I have left in the world, except for Charlotte, but she's back in Boston, and I *am not* going back there."

"Why not go back to Boston? You'd be taken care of there, you wouldn't have to scrape and scrounge for every penny. . . ."

"No," she said resolutely. "I'd rather die than go back there. Now let's not talk about it anymore and please, Bart, don't mention this to Gabriel; he's sure to try and stop me."

"Tess . . ."

"Please, Bart."

He nodded hesitantly and dismounted.

"Come on then," he sighed. "Let's get these animals watered. I think Rosa tucked some food in your saddlebag there."

Tess dismounted beside him and led her horse down the gentle slope to the pond's cool water. As the animals drank, she reached into her saddlebag and withdrew a cloth-wrapped bundle. Inside was a piece of dried apple pie, some bread, and a handful of jerky.

"This is delicious," she marveled through a mouthful of jerky. "Want some?"

Bart laughed right out loud. "Try living on it for a week or so and then tell me that again."

She sank down in the soft grass under the shade of a huge pine and removed Gabe's hat—one of a cowboy's most prized possessions. He might never admit to that, but she'd read enough about the west to know there were three things a rancher was most proud of—his horse, his boots, and his hat. And here she sat with his hat in her hands, leaving his head bare—unheard of for a rancher.

Her heart squeezed in anguish knowing Gabe must feel something for her—he couldn't kiss her the way he did and not feel something—but it wouldn't make any difference. He would never let himself give in to those feelings.

Chapter 14

The magnificence of the herd took Tess's breath away. In all her imaginings, she never considered a herd of cattle to be a beautiful sight, yet there they were, twenty-five hundred longhorns, give or take, milling over acres and acres of prime Montana grazing land. It did not seem possible the thin needle grass and balsamroot scattered throughout the sagebrush could possibly contain enough sustenance to support any living creature, but the cattle devoured it as if it were manna from heaven.

From their viewpoint atop a dry, grassy butte, Tess and Bart remained a safe distance from the herd.

"Just ask Beau how smart it is to get too near the herd," Bart scoffed.

She marveled at the animals, struck by the mere size and number of them.

"What happens to them?" she asked, almost afraid of the answer.

"Gabe holds an annual contract with the army where they buy a certain percentage of the herd every year and of that, 'bout half goes to the Indians and the other half goes to feed themselves."

"Does Gabriel drive the cattle to the forts himself?"

Bart chuckled. "Gabe ain't that stupid. There ain't nothin' more ugly than a cattle drive. Oh sure, you read all that crap 'bout how a cowboy comes to know life once he's been on a drive, but that's a load of malarkey. Cattle drives ain't nothin' but back-breakin' hard work and headaches."

"So how do you move them?"

"The army sends a trail boss to town and he hires on however many hands he wants. Then they come and drive the herd themselves."

"It sounds like a smart plan," she murmured.

"Like I said, Gabe ain't stupid." Bart grinned. "A little thickheaded maybe and not too bright in some areas, but when it comes to cattle . . ."

They stared out over the herd for a while, Tess's thoughts whisking her back to the grassy bank of Porter Creek, Gabe's arms wrapped around her, his heart pounding in rhythm with hers. If she never felt that again in her entire life, at least she had the memory—one glorious moment when everything was perfect; her dream had taken life, in the form of Gabriel Calloway, and she was loved, protected, and cherished.

"Tess?" Bart's look was of genuine concern. "You okay?"

"Yes," she answered, a little too quickly. "I'm fine. Why don't you tell me more about this Collette Langman?"

"Ah, yes." He smiled lazily. "The fair Collette. She's as close to perfect as I ever seen, Tess."

"Close to perfect?"

"Well, she *is* a Langman. But I reckon that ain't her fault. Just dumb luck."

Tess studied Bart's face. A peaceful calm fell over him, his nut-brown eyes crinkled at the corners. He was obviously quite taken with the girl, despite her one shortcoming.

"So why is it, according to you, her entire family is pretty much worthless, yet she is not?"

"You've never met the fair Collette," he sighed

happily. "She's the only one out o' the whole knot-head bunch who got any schoolin'. She's quick as a whip, that girl, and that there's one girl who's got pluck; she ain't afraid of nothin'."

"And?" she prompted.

"And," he chuckled, "she's 'bout the prettiest thing I ever seen in my life."

Tess couldn't help but smile. Her heart yearned for Gabe to look at her that way, to feel that way about her, to think her being brave was a good thing, but she was happy for Bart. He was such a likable man, so easy to talk to, so easy to be with.

"Have you told her any of this?"

"Hell, Tess, I only got to town yesterday. For all I know, she's up and married one of the other gawk-arses here in town already."

"So what are we doing here when you have a lady's heart to win? You just get yourself over to the Lang-man place right this instant, Bart Calloway, and make your intentions plain."

Bart's eyes laughed as he shook his head.

"You've been reading too many of them silly books," he said. "That ain't exactly how it works, you know."

"Why on earth not? It's obvious you love her, so why not tell her? For goodness' sake, Bart, life is far too precious to waste time playing coy with each other for months on end. Women prefer a man who states plainly how he feels."

"An' I'd be happy to do just that," he answered, "if I could get past her brothers. They don't let nobody near her, and what with the old man's history with Wyatt, I ain't expectin' them to be terribly welcomin' when it comes to me."

"That's ridiculous," she said. "You had nothing to do with what happened—you were still a child."

"Don't much matter," he shrugged. "Far as they're concerned, it might as well a' been me or Gabe."

Tess pondered the predicament for a moment, her brain grappling for an idea until suddenly it hit her—it would be the easiest thing in the world.

"I'll go." She stood up and unwound the horses' reins from the tree branch. "I'll tell them I'm new in town and I heard Collette was about the same age as me so I thought I would introduce myself." She smiled at her own ingenuity. "It's not even a lie! I'd truly love to meet this girl."

"Tess." He laughed, starting after her.

The two horses nickered nervously. Hera stamped her hooves and pulled back, rearing slightly. It was in that instant Tess heard it—a sound so frightening it stopped her heart dead in mid-beat. She dropped the reins and the horses both bolted, leaving Tess standing frozen to the spot. She had never heard the deadly rattle before, but it was unmistakable.

"Stop, Bart!" she cried in a hoarse whisper. "Where's your gun?"

"My gun?" he repeated. "What the hell d'you . . . ho-lee shit, Tess, don't move!"

"I'm not even breathing!" she snapped. "Shoot it!"

"I can't," he whispered back. "My gun's in my saddlebag."

Cold beads of sweat dripped down Tess's brow. The huge snake lay less than two feet away, coiled and ready to strike, its rattle waving menacingly in the air.

"What do I do?" she asked, trying to steady her voice.

"Don't move!"

"I couldn't even if I wanted to," she muttered.

"I'll try to get it from behind." The sound of Bart's voice moved to her left side and then stopped. Tess fought back the scream that welled in her throat—after all she'd been through, she'd be damned if she was going to let herself die this way.

He crept toward the snake, lowering himself

enough to reach out and grab its back end. The moment that followed was without question the slowest one in Tess's life. The snake whirled away from her and struck at Bart, its fangs piercing through the skin of his right forearm. In the same instant, Tess had it by the rattle and hurled it into the valley below, not giving a thought to what effect a rattlesnake could have on a herd of cattle.

"Oh, Lord," she prayed out loud. "Please don't do this." She was already ripping Bart's shirt from his arm. She pushed him backward to the ground and removed the belt from her waist.

"Tess," he said, his voice already fading.

"Shut up!" she ordered. "Lay still and keep quiet."

She wound her belt around his arm, just under his elbow, and cinched it as tightly as she could. A knife—she needed a knife. Her hands moved down the pockets in Bart's shirt and jeans, propriety be damned, and came up empty. A soft nickering answered her prayers—Bart's horse, Meg, had returned and stood pawing the ground just feet away. Tess inched toward her, careful not to spook the animal further.

"Good girl," she murmured. "I need into that bag you've got there. Good girl . . . steady . . . steady . . . that's it." She took the reins gingerly in one hand and moved to the saddlebag, clawing desperately through the tobacco pouch, past the Colt .45, under a handful of jerky and a thin metal container until her hand closed around a small knife at the bottom of the bag.

"Thank you, God," she prayed. The reins still clutched in her hand, she tugged the horse back to Bart, threw the reins over a branch, and dropped back down to her patient. Bart's eyes rolled back in their sockets, but he did not make a sound. Tess tried to believe that was a good thing. She knew better.

"This is going to hurt," she said, warning herself more than him. She held her breath as she pulled the knife down his already swelling arm. Then she leaned over, put her mouth over the angry red wound and sucked for all she was worth, spitting and sputtering every last drop of poison to the ground beside her. She had no idea how many times she repeated the procedure, but she was drenched with perspiration and fear by the time she stopped.

Bart had long since faded in unconsciousness, his head rolled to the left. Tess wanted to scream in frustration. Should she leave the tourniquet in place or should she remove it? Damn it—she couldn't remember.

"Better to leave it there," she reasoned aloud. "If I missed any poison, it'll have a harder time getting through. I hope."

She sat for a moment, staring at Bart, willing him to give her some idea of what to do next, not knowing whether she should ride back to the ranch and get Gabe, or stay here. *Stay,* she decided quickly. She couldn't leave him here—what if there were more snakes lurking nearby, or God only knew what else. Someone would have to come and check the herd eventually, wouldn't they?

Whiskey! Tess hurried back to Meg and pulled the saddlebag right off the mare's back. Her right hand went immediately to the thin metal container at the bottom—a flask!

"Thank you, Bart," she said. "You might have saved your own life."

She twisted open the flask and poured the amber liquid directly over the wound, offering a silent prayer of thanks he was not conscious, for certainly the pain of the alcohol would have driven him over the edge. She saved the last bit of whiskey and tipped a tiny bit gently into his mouth. If ever there was a time a man needed a drink, she reasoned, this would be it. At that moment she almost wished she were a drinker herself.

Before her hand even touched his brow, she knew he had a raging fever. Her eyes flew back to the horse, her prayers answered once more. The full canteen hung loosely from the saddle horn. She pulled the bandana from around her neck, soaked it with the cool liquid, and mopped Bart's burning brow.

It had little effect, and for the first time Tess realized how close Bart was to dying. She needed to get him home, to a doctor.

She hurried back to the butte where they had sat moments ago and scanned the valley below. It was so huge, so vast, there was no way she would be able to pick out a horse from a steer. Nevertheless, if she didn't try . . .

"Hello!" she bellowed as loud as she could. "Hello! Is anyone down there?"

No answer.

"Hello! I need some help up here! Hello!"

Nothing. She returned to Bart, mopped his brow again with more water, and then hurried back to the edge.

"Hello! Hello!" Her throat ached, her head pounded, but she could not—would not—give up. "Hello!"

Below, the herd began to move, all at once, brawling and snorting. She opened her mouth to yell again, doubting she would be heard above the rising din, but willing to try anyway, when she saw something move. A rider!

"Thank God!" she whispered, then let loose again with another whoop. "Hello! Up here!" Her arms waved frantically above her head, the bandana flapping in the air.

The closer Joby came, the more defined his expression became, and it was not a friendly one.

"Lord A'mighty, Miss Tess," he scolded, "yer spookin' the cattle. What in tarnation is all the . . ."

His eyes zeroed in on Bart lying motionless in the shade.

"What the hell?"

"He's been bitten by a rattler," she quickly explained. "I need you to ride back and get Gabriel and a wagon or something to put him in so we can get him home."

"Jumpin' jehoshaphat! Did you tie—"

"Yes," she answered impatiently.

"Did you suck out—"

"Yes! For the love of God, Joby, would you please just go?"

The man made like he was to dismount. "Why don't you ride home? I'll stay here with Bart."

"No! You can ride faster and you know your way better. Go!"

"You sure?"

"Yes!"

He threw his leg back over his saddle and turned the horse toward home, kicking it into a dead run. There was nothing to do now but wait. She tried to calculate how long it would take them to return. She and Bart had taken their time riding out to the herd, in fact, their horses had walked most of the way, and they'd only arrived about midday. If her luck held, Gabe and Joby would be back in a couple hours.

She lowered herself into the grass beside Bart and mopped his brow over and over again.

"Hold on, Bart," she ordered. "You have unfinished business with Miss Langman. You've just returned home—Gabriel can't lose you now. He needs his brother. You're the only family he has left in the whole world."

Bart remained motionless and Tess knew that was not a good sign. The longer he remained unconscious, the worse it was.

"Come on, Bart," she pleaded. "Wake up. Please please please. Do it for me—you know your brother is going to blame me for this, and I could really use you on my side when he gets here. Please?"

She took his hand in hers and rocked back and forth, at first humming softly, and then outright singing. She'd read somewhere even unconscious people could hear voices. She began with the Twenty-Third Psalm but quickly decided that might get him to thinking he was already dead, so she immediately switched to "Amazing Grace" and every other song she could think of, from "Battle Hymn of the Republic" to "Oh! Susannah" and "Camptown Races." When she ran out of songs, she started back with "Amazing Grace" until her throat became too parched and sore to squeak out another sound. She didn't dare take a sip from the canteen in case Bart needed it.

She mopped his brow for what seemed like the hundredth time, dribbled the last of the whiskey down his throat, and stood to stretch her aching muscles.

Across the acres, riding as though carried on wings, Gabriel raced toward them. He leapt from his horse before the animal even stopped.

Without a word, he dropped to Bart's side, his eyes taking in everything—the wet bandana draped across his brother's forehead; the thin cotton belt wrapped around his arm; the wound itself, still red and angry; and finally, Tess. Her hair had loosened from its plait and now blew around her face in the breeze. Her eyes, wide with fear, stared straight back at him.

Gabe felt Bart's brow, frowned, and took a closer

look at the wound. Then he raised himself to his full height and in the span of a heartbeat pulled Tess roughly into his arms, one hand cupping the back of her head, the other tightening around her waist. She buried her face against his shirt, her own hands clenching the material as though her very life depended on it. She had no idea she was crying until Gabe lifted her chin gently and kissed away the tears.

Chapter 15

"Are you okay?" he asked, his voice a raspy whisper.

"Y-yes, but Bart . . . oh, Gabriel . . . what if . . ."

"Don't," he said, stroking her back gently. "It looks like you did all you could."

Why did she have to fit so perfectly into his embrace? It was as though she was made for this single purpose, for him alone. Gabe tucked the thought away to the very deep recesses of his mind—not gone completely, but to a place where he could pretend it had disappeared.

"How on earth did a city girl like you learn how to treat a snakebite anyway?" Gabe asked. "Don't imagine you come across many snakes in the city."

"Only the two-legged kind," she said softly. When he looked quizzically at her, she flushed crimson and reluctantly confessed. "I read it in one of my books."

Gabe's laughter rippled through her heart.

"Not one of those dime store novels," he teased. "I thought they were full of Cinderella types who sat around all day waiting for their Prince Charming to ride up and sweep them off their feet."

"I suppose some of them are," she admitted with a smile. "But the ones I read are full of intrigue and adventure. And romance."

He stiffened, the warmth in his heart chilling to the icy wall he needed it to be. After another moment, he slowly released her and returned to his brother.

"Any whiskey left?" he asked, glancing at the flask on the ground.

"No, I used the last of it just before you arrived."

Gabe strode over to Zeus and pulled his own flask from his saddlebag. He emptied half of it into the open wound and then recapped it. The flesh on Bart's arm was still red and swollen—an angrier looking wound he couldn't recall seeing—but at least Tess had known what to do. Thank God for that.

Tess.

Gabe's heart nearly jumped through his chest. What if it had been her who was bitten? Bart was a big man, he could surely fight off any remaining venom, but Tess . . . she was so small, so fragile. There was no way she would survive such an injury. God help them both, she could have been killed today.

A cold knot formed in the pit of his stomach, the muscle along his jawline flexing in barely controlled rage.

"From now on," he said flatly, "you'd best stay near the house where I can keep an eye on you."

"What?" Her confusion played across her face. "I knew it," she muttered. "I told Bart you would blame this on me. I . . ."

"Stop mumbling and speak up." He ached to ease the frown from her brow, to thank her for saving Bart's life and to thank God for saving hers. But he didn't.

"I said I knew you would blame me for this. It's my fault Bart got bit by a rattlesnake. It's my fault the snake was here in the first place, isn't it? It's my fault . . ."

"Well, how is it that he was bitten then? I'm not stupid enough to believe you were not somehow involved."

Tess stiffened, her cheeks flaming.

"I . . . we were about to head back and the horses . . . they got spooked." She stopped long enough to swallow and furrow her brow deeper. "The snake was between Hera and me. Bart crept around the tree there to get at the snake from behind."

"Why the hell didn't he shoot it? God knows he never makes a move without that damn .45."

"It was in his saddlebag."

"And the saddlebag was . . ."

"The horses ran as soon as the reins were untied from the tree."

"Of course." Gabe shook his head in disgust. "So what you're telling me is Bart was trying to get the snake away from you, is that right?"

"Y-yes. But . . ."

Gabe turned his back to her, mostly so she wouldn't see his face. It could have easily been Tess lying in the grass. He leaned over his brother, felt his brow again, and frowned himself. The fever had all but vanished, leaving Bart cool and clammy.

"He's getting chilled," Gabe muttered. "Where the hell is Joby with the wagon?"

Tess marched over to Meg and fought to uncinch the saddle. She threw it to the ground and pulled the blanket off the horse's back, unfolding it as she moved. It wasn't nearly large enough to cover him, but it would do for now. Gabe snatched it from her hands and wrapped it around Bart, tucking it underneath to keep him up off the ground. Before he'd finished, the sound of pounding hooves could be heard in the distance.

Tess exhaled loudly. "Hurry, Joby."

Joby reined in the team a few feet away and jumped down.

"How's he doin'?" he asked.

Gabe shrugged. "We'll see how he takes the ride home. Let's get him loaded."

Tess scrambled into the back that had been filled with straw and blankets. She arranged it as best she could, lying one of the old, worn horse blankets down on top of the straw.

Gabe and Joby lifted him gingerly into the back of the wagon and then straightened him out. Tess immediately wrapped him in the remaining blankets, praying they would be enough to keep him warm on the long ride home. It would be slow going because they had to take care not to jostle him too much lest any remaining poison get moved around.

"Pass me that canteen and cloth," she ordered, expecting Joby to respond. Gabe tossed it up and tied Zeus to the back of the wagon before climbing up himself. He re-claimed his Stetson, and it now sat beside him. Tess wondered briefly why he didn't put it on, but that was the least of her concerns right now.

"Joby," Gabe barked, "saddle up Meg there and get home. Tell Rosa what's going on, that we'll need a bed ready when we get there. Then go fetch Doc Bender and have him waiting for us. Feed him if you have to—but don't let him at the whiskey."

Joby nodded and hurried to do as he was told. Gabe clicked to the horses and sent the wagon off across the vast expanse of land that still separated them from the house. It wasn't five minutes later when Joby flew past, racing to beat hell—or, as it were, Gabe.

Tess took Bart's hand again. It lay cold and limp in her lap, giving her chills of her own.

"It's going to be okay now, Bart," she said gently. "We're going home. You're going to be fine, you hear me? Of course Rosa's going to tan your hide for scaring us this way, but I won't let her beat you up too badly. I'll tell her it was my fault, how you were only trying to protect me from my sorry little self."

She stopped, unable to speak past the lump in her throat. Gabe was right; if Bart died, it would be her fault. If he hadn't been showing her the herd, he never would have been near that damned snake.

"You saved my life," she whispered hoarsely. "Oh, Bart . . . I . . ."

Bart's lids fluttered briefly, then stilled. His tongue ventured out slowly, trying in vain to moisten his parched lips. Tess nearly dropped the canteen in her hurry to help. She wet the cloth and held it against his mouth.

"Drink," she said softly. "Oh, thank God, Bart. Drink."

Gabe spun in his seat, managing to keep the team moving forward.

"Is he awake?"

"Yes." She was crying again. "Yes, he is. Bart, can you hear me?"

This time he managed to lick his lips. "'Course," he mumbled. "Now will ya shut up? I'm tryin' to sleep."

"Oh, yes." Tess laughed. "Whatever you want. Do you want more water? Here." She didn't wait for him to answer, but pressed the wet cloth against his mouth again.

"Why . . ." he struggled, "why you cryin'?"

"Because I'm so happy." She laughed, swiping at the river of tears that flowed down her face.

"Why, did he kiss ya again?" Bart's mouth fought to smile but only managed a twitch before he fell back under the blanket of sleep.

Gabe turned front again. Neither he nor Tess spoke for a long time afterward. She sat in the straw, her back to Gabe, and continued to cry, though unlike her happy tears, these stung her eyes and throat and scorched her cheeks where they flowed.

"Tess." Gabe's brittle voice broke through the deafening quiet. "Now do you see why it's not safe for you to stay here? You don't belong here."

Tess did not answer, did not even blink. Maybe

Gabe was right; this was dangerous country for a girl to be living in, but at least she could make her own decisions. She didn't belong here. How many times had she heard that in the last few days?

By the time they neared the house, the sun had long since set behind the mountain. Tess was shivering almost as badly as Bart. He had not opened his eyes again, and her concern deepened with every passing minute. Rosa, Miguel, and Dr. Bender met them at the bottom of the porch steps.

"How is he?" Bender asked. "Did he wake up yet?"

"Once," Gabe answered before Tess could open her mouth. "But it wasn't for very long and there's been nothing since."

He threw the reins over the post and stepped into the back of the wagon. Miguel joined him and the two men lifted Bart out as gently as they could. Tess remained in the wagon, watching as Rosa took over, clucking her way into the house ahead of them, holding the door, and ushering them up to the far bedroom.

An overpowering emptiness filled Tess, a void that left her drained physically and emotionally. She climbed out of the wagon and made her way quietly up to her room. She changed her clothes and folded the dirty riding outfit on the foot of the bed. Certain it was safe, she tiptoed back downstairs and sat at Gabe's desk. She removed five dollars from the pay envelope and left a hastily written note on the kitchen table where it wouldn't be missed.

She closed the door quietly behind her and started down the road, glancing back over her shoulder only once. Or twice.

"Damn it!" Gabe crumpled the note into a tight ball and threw it across the room.

"She's gone, ain't she?" Bart's voice was still weak but he'd gained considerable strength in the short time he'd been home.

Pacing, Gabe nodded, his fingers trying in vain to ease the throbbing in his temples.

"She's gone, all right, but only to stay at the hotel. What the hell is she thinking going off in the middle of the night like that?"

"She's prob'ly thinkin' it's what you want her to do."

"I don't want her out there in the pitch dark . . ."

"So go get her."

"No bloody way!" he bellowed. "She doesn't belong here! Hell, Bart, she nearly got you killed."

"That ain't fair," Bart said. "It weren't her fault."

"Of course it is! You were trying to save her life."

"Gabe, you know that ain't true. She saved *my* life."

Gabe didn't answer; he paced faster, rubbed harder. Maybe it wasn't true, but hell's bells, she didn't belong here. It was better this way—well, safer anyway. So why was the ache in his belly ten times worse than the ache in his head? And why did he feel like a huge part of him just died? She was gone, out of the house, off the ranch, out of his sight. Out of his sight.

"You should go talk to 'er, Gabe. She's prob'ly right upset."

"I'm not her mother, Bart," he snapped, not quite as sharply as he would have liked. Bart must have sensed it, because the look he gave his brother was all it took to make Gabe bend—a little. "I have to go to town tomorrow anyway to see Brolin. I'll check on her then."

Tomorrow seemed like an eternity away when, in fact, according to his internal clock, the rooster'd be crowing in a matter of a few hours.

"What are you talkin' to him for?" Bart asked.

"I sold him the timber rights to the five acres in

the south corner," he answered distractedly. "Just have to sign the papers."

"You mean he actually got his mill runnin'?" Bart smirked. "Never thought I'd live to see the day."

"You almost didn't," Gabe reminded him.

"What does Wyatt have to say 'bout him buyin' timber from you?"

Gabe shrugged. "I don't see how Langman's got any say in the matter at all. He had his chance to make a deal with Brolin, but he was too greedy and wouldn't budge on his price. Brolin's in business to make money, not lose it."

"I know that, but I don't reckon Wyatt's gonna take this lyin' down."

"What's he gonna do?" Gabe smirked. "Send one of his other idiot sons over here to get gored? Let him send the whole damn lot of them and we'll take care of them all at once."

Bart's lips tightened. "Gabe . . ."

He tried to sit up but Gabe put a hand out to stop him.

"You're supposed to be resting, so shut up and go back to sleep or Rosa'll skin us both alive."

For a moment, he thought Bart was going to put up a fight, but then his brother slumped back against the pillows and fell asleep, a small frown creasing his forehead. Gabe flopped in the chair beside the bed, rubbing his left palm over his mouth.

What the hell was he going to do? His conscience would not allow him to let her go like this, let her walk away without any real understanding of why she couldn't stay. She deserved at least that much. Hell, she deserved even more—a lot more than what he had to offer.

Chapter 16

Tess covered her face with trembling hands and gave vent to the agony of her loss. Gabriel did not love her. He probably hated her. She almost killed his only brother, and it was all because of a silly dream she insisted on following—a dream she had dragged the Calloway brothers into without even asking for their opinions on the subject. She was no better than her father.

Gabriel did not love her. Her mind repeated the statement over and over, forcing her to swallow it and acknowledge it for the truth it was. He was angry with her and was going to be a great deal angrier when he discovered he was missing five dollars.

She managed to walk as far as the bridge that crossed over the creek to the bed of wildflowers where Gabriel had kissed her not so very long ago. She knew now it had not been love he felt for her then, it had been lust. Plain and simple lust. He'd told her as much himself that he believed in lust at first sight, but certainly not love. Tess sighed. Gabriel was so terribly busy on the ranch he probably didn't have time to find a nice woman, to court her properly, or to fall in love with her. He probably didn't even have enough time to take company with one of the working girls at the saloon for that matter.

So when Tess arrived at the ranch, he was probably so happy to see a female of any sorts, he would have kissed her if she'd had green teeth and a third eye. Lust did strange things to a man, or so she'd been told.

Tess had never experienced true heartache before—at least not this kind. She'd been devastated by the sudden loss of her mother some years ago, but that was a completely different kind of pain. This was an all-encompassing misery—so acute, in fact, it was an actual physical pain. She was a woman alone, facing the harsh realities of being alone—of being lonely.

"You can have everything," her mother had told her more than once. "Everything is there for the taking, you just have to want it badly enough to take it."

"Well, Mother," she sighed aloud, "apparently you were wrong on this one. I can't have everything."

Tess fell to her knees in the middle of the field, surrounding herself with the intoxicating aroma of eucalyptus and sweet green grass. A million stars and a moon close enough to touch illuminated the immense blackness of the sky. This was most definitely not the same starless sky that loomed dauntingly over Boston.

Boston, an entire world away, a completely different life ago, and yet Tess knew one day she would have to make peace with that old life. One day she would write to her father and let him know where she was and that she was well. Not today, not tomorrow, and probably not anytime in the near future, but one day.

In all her twenty-one years, Tess had been absolutely certain of two things. The first was had she stayed in Boston and agreed to marry Harmon Stiles, the devil incarnate, she would have been dead before her next birthday; the second was this town, this western haven,

was exactly where she belonged—here with her angel
Gabriel.

If only she'd been able to convince him.

Tess closed her weary eyes and lay back among the
dew-laden flowers. She would rest for a while and
when the sun came up she would go to town and
start building her new life without her angel. Her
mind swirled into dream, filled with the sweet fragrance of the earth, mingling with the sunshine and
leather scent of Gabriel, his strong arms cradling her
against him, protecting her, loving her.

Tender and light as a summer breeze, his lips
brushed across her brow, the tip of her nose, then
both eyes. Her breath held in her throat, her legs no
longer able to hold her. She melted against him, into
him, her face turned up to meet his. His lips were
warm and sweet against hers, gently coaxing a response from her.

Tess floated away on that dream, knowing on more
than one level it was simply that—a dream—but refusing to give it up yet. Her mouth curved into an unconscious smile. If dreaming were the only way she
could have Gabriel, then she would dream forever.

And that was how Gabe found her a short while
later—a beautiful angel lying in a bed of flowers, her
only cover the huge blanket of stars above. His heart
ached to look at her. It would be so easy to scoop her
up and take her home, to give her anything and
everything she wanted, to love her, to make love to
her.

To love her. He could not let himself do that knowing eventually, whether she knew it or not right then,
she would leave him. Whether it be on the stagecoach
out of town or on the wings of an angel, she would

leave him. Either way, whatever the circumstances, it would mean the certain death of Gabe Calloway.

He climbed down from his saddle, leaving Zeus to graze freely, and slowly lowered himself to the grass beside her. Even asleep she radiated such a glowing vitality, an intense magnetism, Gabe had to fight the urge to wake her up and abandon himself to the pleasures of her flesh. God help him, he wanted to, but . . .

But he couldn't very well leave her there either, so he pulled off his thin canvas jacket and draped it over her, then lay down in the grass and pulled her gently into his arms. He was only trying to keep her warm, was all. It didn't matter it was the warmest night of the year so far, or his jacket alone would have sufficed in keeping her warm, he couldn't risk her catching a chill, because then she wouldn't be able to leave on Friday.

She snuggled closer against him, the top of her head resting under his chin, her small left hand pressing flat against his chest. Gabe's pulse leapt, his heart hammered, and every last drop of blood raced south of his belt. He should let her go, lay her back in the grass and get as far away from her as he could. But damn it all if she didn't smell like heaven itself. And she fit against him like nothing he could ever imagine.

She mumbled in her sleep, but Gabe was unable to make out what she said. Whatever it was, it made her press closer to him, pulled a soft quivering moan from her throat, and left her sighing contentedly. Gabe's whole body stiffened—including parts he couldn't relax if he wanted to.

He inhaled deeply, breathing in her honey-scented sweetness. He squeezed his eyes shut, trying in vain to do the same with his heart, and tried to convince himself that holding her that way did not really feel as good—or as right—as it actually did. He would just hold her for another minute, a few more heartbeats, until the stars disappeared, until . . .

"Gabriel?"

She couldn't possibly realize how sensual her voice sounded speaking those three syllables.

"Hmm?" It was the best he could do without opening his mouth and making a complete fool of himself.

"Am I still dreaming?"

"Not unless we're having the same dream," he muttered, silently berating himself for being caught in this predicament.

Tess sighed softly. "I wish."

For the life of him, Gabe could not bring himself to release her or even to sit up. Neither one of them moved or spoke for long, heart-hammering minutes.

"I'm sorry about Bart," she murmured, barely loud enough to be heard.

"I know," he shushed her. "I'm sorry I yelled."

Against his mind's screaming objections, Gabe's fingers trailed down her temple to trace the outline of her cheekbone and jaw.

"Tess," he breathed. "Now do you see why you can't stay here? That snake could have easily bitten you instead of Bart, and you're not strong enough to survive something like that."

"How do you know?" she asked quietly. "You might be surprised how strong I am."

"Okay." He sighed. "*I'm* not strong enough to survive you getting bitten."

Tess laughed. "That's okay, I'm strong enough for the both of us."

Gabe's breath caught in his throat.

"Tess . . ."

"Don't," she said, her voice as tight as his heart. Her fingers played idly with the button of his shirt, unknowingly driving him closer to the brink of insanity. "I know what you're going to say and you're right."

"What?" Gabe pushed himself up to sit, thereby dropping her onto the grass. He was quick to recover and pull her up beside him.

"You're right," she repeated. "If all I'm going to do is cause problems for everyone, then maybe I don't belong out on the ranch. Well, not your ranch anyway."

"What the hell is that supposed to mean?" His voice, though not yet a full-out yell, boomed through the stillness.

"Gabriel," she said gently, "you've done your best to convince me I have no place on El Cielo and that come hel . . ." She took a moment to swallow. "Come Friday you mean to have me on the stage."

"Y-yeah," he said hesitantly, eyeing her uneasily.

"Well, I can't fight you on that. It's your ranch and I can't very well stay where I'm not welcome. So I'll stay in town."

"Until Friday," he finished for her.

"No," she said, shaking her head. "Until I can save enough money to buy my own farm."

"What?" He bolted to his feet and now he *was* yelling. "Are you crazy? Have you not heard a single word I've said to you?"

"It's a little hard not to hear you, Gabriel, since most of the time you're yelling."

"I'm not yelling!" he thundered.

"Yes," she corrected, keeping her own voice even, "you are."

"You *cannot* stay here! Haven't I made that clear?"

"Oh, yes, you have made yourself perfectly clear. And now I'm going to do the same."

She pushed up to her full height, bringing her nose in direct line with the center of his chest, and lifted her chin, meeting his steely gaze straight on.

"You know how I feel about you, Gabriel Calloway, and I'm not ashamed to admit it to you or anyone else who cares to know. But no matter how I feel, I cannot make you feel the same way about me, no matter what I do or how hard I try. So I give up. If you don't love me, there's nothing I can do about that, but I'll be . . . damned . . . if I'm going to give up the rest of my dream of living out here."

"But . . ."

"I'm not finished!" she snapped. "I intend to take myself into town, find myself a job—or two if I must—and save enough money to buy my own home, my own land, my own livestock. I intend to live how I want and where I want—and you, Gabriel Calloway, have absolutely no say in the matter whatsoever."

She stood toe to toe with him, her fists balled tightly on her hips, her amber eyes glowing fiercely with an inner fire.

"But . . ." he repeated.

"But what?" Her delicate brows arched, daring him to argue with her.

"B-but . . ." he stammered, his words tripping over his heart that had somehow lodged itself in his throat. Damn, she was a feisty little thing, and hot double-damn how he wanted to kiss her then. Her entire being emitted a steadfast strength he not only admired, but envied. It took him a minute before he was able to spit out, "How do you know you'll be able to find work?"

Tess straightened her shoulders even more. "I believe there is always work if you're willing to do it. It might not be clean or easy, but work is work."

Gabe's glare faltered slightly. She had a point, he believed in that very same idea, but still . . .

"You can't live in town." Why couldn't he force even the slightest bit of strength into his voice?

"I most certainly can," she said, nodding defiantly. "I will get a room at the hotel or at Miss Hattie's boardinghouse."

Gabe found his vocal strength again. "You are not living at the hotel!"

Tess took a deep breath to control her own anger before she spoke again.

"Gabriel," she finally said. "Unless I am mistaken, a woman still has certain rights in this country. Granted, we have not been given the right to vote—yet—but since I am no longer living under my father's roof and I am not married, I do not have to take orders from anyone, including you. I can—and will—do as I please. Now if you'll excuse me."

She pushed his jacket against his chest, letting it fall to the ground when he did not immediately reach for it. She lifted her skirts a touch and resumed her walk toward the town of Porter Creek. The stars had begun to fade, the sun would soon begin its rise, and as such, the restaurant must certainly be open by now, gearing up for the breakfast rush. At least that's what she prayed for. She'd offer up the entire five dollars for a strong cup of coffee right then.

"Tess . . ." he called after her, though he remained rooted to the spot.

She waved a dismissing hand at him and kept walking. Who did he think he was telling her what she could and could not do? He had a lot of nerve! A lot of nerves . . . and muscles, her traitorous mind recalled. He certainly was a daunting presence with his broad chest and massive shoulders. He literally towered over her, trying his darnedest to appear intimidating, yet it was his glare that faltered first, not hers.

And how was it, she wondered, that God had given the man such huge strong hands, *and* the ability to be so tender, so gentle, and so able to drive her to distraction with just the slightest touch? It was a wonder, all right, something she would wonder about for too many long, lonely nights.

Chapter 17

Gabe stared after her until she rounded the curve out of sight. How could someone so little be so damned irritating, so stubborn, so . . . so irresistible? If she'd have lifted her chin any higher, she'd have toppled backward, he mused, a slow grin finding his lips.

He couldn't let her live in town. And he sure as hell couldn't let her go out and get a job! Gabe's brow creased across his forehead. Though she was right. He had no say in the matter unless they were married. And he sure as hell wasn't about to marry her—although he did have to admit the idea had some merit. It had nothing to do with him loving her, because that was out of the question; but at least if he were her husband, he could forbid her to do asinine things like taking a job in town or worse, rooming at the hotel.

And, of course, if she were his wife, he would be permitted certain conjugal rights afforded to a husband. That would be reason enough right there.

Gabe shook his head clear and rubbed his weary eyes. How had she managed to get him thinking such crazy thoughts? He'd always been so levelheaded until she walked into his life, but now he couldn't form a coherent thought if his life depended on it. Everywhere he looked, everything he did, she was there, hovering in the forefront of his mind, muddling his brain and throwing his insides into a horrendous ravel; his heart spent most of its time racing from the depths of his belly to the middle of his throat instead of staying where it belonged—lodged between two traitorous lungs that had recently forgotten how to function on their own.

Maybe time spent away from her would straighten him out. "Out of sight, out of mind" and all that. Besides, he thought with a deepening frown, maybe a few days in town would make her rethink her plan and see things his way.

He took up Zeus's reins and swung up into the saddle. A stiff cup of coffee, a big breakfast, and a shave, that's what he needed. Then he'd be able to think straight when he met up with Brolin in a few hours. Of course, while he was in town anyway, he'd probably check on Tess to make sure she was all right.

He forced his thoughts to the deal he made with Brolin. With the expected boom the railroad would bring to Porter Creek, there would soon be a greater demand for lumber here and in the surrounding towns. Businesses were sure to start up quicker than a june bug on a hot griddle, and the Calloway ranch boasted prime timber over more acres than not. Of course, so did the Langman place, Gabe reflected, but if Wyatt was too dim-witted to see an opportunity when it presented itself, that wasn't Gabe's fault.

He let Zeus into the barn, removed the saddle, and threw him some fresh oats before heading to the house for his own breakfast. Rosa met him at the door with the darkest glare he'd ever seen.

"Where Tess Kinley?" she demanded.

"She's taken herself to town," he answered, dreading the inevitable lecture. "Figures she's better off there than out here getting herself—and everyone else—into trouble."

"Gabe Calloway . . ." Rosa started, her voice rising at the same speed as the spatula in her hand.

"Don't start," he groaned. "She's got no business living out here anyway and she's finally seen that."

"*La niña. . .*"

"That's enough!" he snarled. "Tess is a grown woman, Rosa. If she chooses to move into town that's her business—it's got nothing to do with me!"

Rosa snorted in a most unladylike way and turned her back to him.

Gabe sighed wearily. He hated arguing with Rosa, hated having her angry with him, and *really* hated the overdeveloped conscience she had raised him to have. "How's Bart?"

"Okay," she answered stiffly.

"Do I have time to go see him before breakfast?"

"Si."

Gabe cringed. As much as Rosa liked to yell and lecture, her one-word answers were worse than any of her hour-long tirades.

"Rosa," he began gently. "I—"

"Bup bup bup," she stopped him with a wave of her thick, stubby hand. "You go tend Bart Calloway."

Why did Rosa have to be right all the time? He fumed as he headed up the stairs. And worse, why did she have to know he knew she was right?

Bart lay wide awake in his bed, with his hands cupped behind his head.

"Well, look at you," Gabe grinned. "You don't look near as dead as you did a couple hours ago."

"Don't feel near as dead neither," Bart grinned back at him. "But don't tell Rosa. Been a long time since I had any woman fuss over me like this, and I intend to enjoy every minute I can of it."

Gabe couldn't hold back his laughter. "Hell, Bart,

Rosa'd fuss over you if you got a hangnail, for Pete's sake. Now if it was me that got bit by some ol' snake, she'd have me up ridin' herd already."

"That's 'cuz I'm nice to her," Bart answered, his brown eyes dancing cheekily. "But you . . . hell, you couldn't charm yer way outta a wet sack."

Gabe's face darkened through his forced smile. He didn't want to be charming. Did he?

"D'you find Tess?" Bart asked.

"Yeah." His jaw tightened, but a tiny light flickered in his soul. "Damned if she's not the orneriest female I've ever met."

"She is that," Bart agreed. "Ain't nothin' worse than a female with an opinion."

Gabe nodded distractedly.

"'Nuff to drive ya crazy, ain't it?"

Another nod.

"So why don't ya just marry 'er and be done with it already?"

It took an extra second for the words Bart spoke to register in Gabe's brain.

"What?" he yelped. "I think that venom went straight to your brain, Bart."

Bart shrugged. "That may be, but you're the only one who can't seem to see how much you love the girl, so just do it. Go get Reverend Boswell and get it over with."

"What the hell are you talking about?" Gabe gaped. "I'm not going to marry Tess. Though I'll admit she does need a strong hand to put her back where she belongs, but it's not going to be me!"

Bart grinned devilishly. "We'll see, brother. We'll see."

Gabe eyed him warily. "You must be overtired or something. I'll have Rosa bring you up some warm milk—that'll put you to sleep right quick."

"Fine," Bart nodded. "I can always use more fussin'

over, but it don't change what I said, Gabe. An' you know I'm right. Yer 'bout as crazed as a coon dog right now an' we both know why."

"It's because I have to deal with halfwits like you who think you know more about me than I do!"

Bart shrugged. "Never said I knew more, just that I can see more, was all."

"My eyesight's as good as yours," he snapped.

"Don't seem that way to me."

"Well who the hell asked you anyway?" Gabe turned on his heel and stormed from the room, leaving Bart to smirk after him. Why didn't everyone mind their own damned business?

Tess pressed her hands down the front of her dress and then reached to tidy her hair. Several pins had worked themselves loose and she struggled, without the aid of a mirror, to straighten herself as best she could. She'd never find a job looking like the homeless little waif she was.

The town of Porter Creek stretched before her, its one narrow street a nightmare of potholes left over from the abundance of spring rain months earlier. She picked her way through the dirt and muck, lifting her skirts enough to keep them from dragging. When she reached the boardwalk, she let them fall and lifted her chin a notch, keeping her eyes forward. She could do this. Of course she could.

The hotel, with its adjoining restaurant, was the first building on the street. Tess's face broke out in a wide grin when she spotted the neatly written sign in the window: Help Wanted. It was a sign—literally and figuratively—she told herself; she was meant to stay in this town and make her life here.

With a deep breath, she pushed open the door to the restaurant and walked in, her head high. A middle-aged woman sat at the table nearest the kitchen, her graying hair pulled back into the tightest knot Tess had ever seen. When she looked up from her ledger, lifeless blue eyes stared down a long, pointed nose.

"Yes?" she said, hardly politely, but not completely rude either.

"Good morning." Tess smiled. "I would like to speak to the proprietor if I may."

The woman stood and eyed Tess with one raised brow.

"I am the proprietress," she answered. "What do you want?"

Tess forced the smile to remain on her lips, despite her immediate reaction to snap back.

"I'm here to apply for the job," she said simply.

The woman sniffed. "Really? Have you ever worked in a restaurant before?"

"No, I haven't," she answered. "But I'm a hard worker and I learn quickly."

"What other types of jobs have you done?"

"Actually," she admitted, "this is my first."

The thin woman clicked her tongue and picked imaginary lint from her high-necked black dress.

"How do I know you are worth hiring?"

Tess's jaw dropped, unable to form a single word for a long moment.

"I guess you'll have to trust me," she finally said.

"I don't trust anyone," the woman stated, continuing to eye Tess. "Who are you anyway?"

"My name is Tess Kinley. I've only been in town a few days."

"Yes," the woman said dryly. "I've heard about you. You're living out at El Cielo with those Calloway boys."

Those Calloway boys. Tess's skin prickled from her toes all the way up to her scalp.

"I'm sorry," she said, fighting to control her anger. "I do not know your name."

"Pauline Lutz. You may call me Miss Lutz."

"Yes, well, Miss Lutz, I don't know what you've heard about me—or the Calloways for that matter—but I will not stand here and defend myself—or them—to a complete stranger. However, I will say what I do or do not do in my personal life is no one else's business but my own. It will not matter here nor there what I say to convince you I am trustworthy; in the end, the decision is yours. So you can hire me or not, it's entirely up to you."

"Yes," Miss Lutz sniffed again. "It is up to me, so here is my offer. You work the breakfast and lunch shifts today and I will decide if you are up to my standards. If I decide you are acceptable, then we will discuss future wages. If not, neither one of us has lost anything."

"I'm sorry, Miss Lutz," Tess said, shaking her head. "That is not acceptable to me. I will not work for free and I don't expect anyone else in this town will either. I am more than happy to start work immediately for you, but I will expect to be paid for my work today and any other days I work for you. And I expect an honest wage for an honest day's work."

"Is that right?" Miss Lutz folded her arms across her bosom.

"Yes."

The woman's eyes narrowed. "You're certainly willful, aren't you?"

Tess's smile was genuine this time. "Yes, I've been told I am many things—willful being one of them."

Miss Lutz did not smile. "Fine," she said. "You can start right now. Here are the rules. You will not be late, you will dress appropriately, you will not tend to personal matters on my time, and you will not consort with the customers."

"Fine." Tess nodded. "Where do I start?"

"Right here." Miss Lutz pushed through the swinging doors to the kitchen and pointed to an empty cupboard. "You may store your . . . bag . . . in there for today. Here's an apron and there's the cutlery tray. I do the cooking, so stay out of the way of the stove unless I instruct you otherwise. Your duties are to tend to the customers and clean up after them, resetting the tables once they are cleared. Understand?"

Tess nodded again. "Yes, ma'am."

"Have you had breakfast?"

"No, I haven't."

Miss Lutz sighed. "Get yourself something to eat—quickly, mind you—and then get to work."

Tess almost smiled at the woman until Miss Lutz added to her last offer.

"After today, any meals you take at my restaurant will be paid for by you. I do not offer handouts to anyone. Understood?"

"Yes, ma'am." She nodded again, helping herself to a cup of coffee and a thick slab of bread. "Thank you."

Pauline Lutz set to work in her spotless kitchen, stoking the fires in the stove, cracking dozens of eggs into a huge metal bowl, and sifting flour for biscuits. Tess donned her apron, swallowed her bread almost whole, and took a huge drink of coffee. Then off she set for her first day of work.

At the first scent of bacon, men started filling the restaurant in throngs. Tess filled their mugs, took orders, delivered food, collected money, and wiped empty tables with a speed and precision that surprised even herself. She actually found herself enjoying the work, despite the snide comments and whistles delivered by most of her customers.

Then, as suddenly as they appeared, they disappeared back out the door, leaving the restaurant eerily empty. Tess continued about her work with quick and steady fingers until the last table was cleaned, reset and ready for the next customer. Then she returned to the kitchen where the piles of dirty dishes were waiting. Miss Lutz's sleeves were rolled to her elbows and her arms dripped with water from the dishpan, but her apron and her hair were as neat as though she'd just dressed herself. Tess never would have guessed the woman had spent the last two hours bent over a hot griddle tossing out pancakes and sausages as fast as the orders came in.

Tess pulled the dishtowel from the hook and began drying the growing stack of dishes.

"This is not part of your job," Miss Lutz said.

"That's all right," Tess smiled. "It will go faster if the two of us do it together. How soon until the lunch crowd starts?"

Miss Lutz shrugged. "An hour, I suppose. Is the front ready?"

Tess nodded. "Ready and waiting."

"Good. Now suppose you tell me why you're in town looking for work when I'm certain those Calloway boys would be more than happy to put you up in their fine house. Of course, they wouldn't do it for free. I'm sure they would expect payment in one form or another."

Tess's faced flamed at the woman's insult. She should tell Miss Lutz exactly what she thought of her opinion and exactly what she could do with it. Why on earth couldn't people mind their own business?

Chapter 18

Gabe's frown deepened as the day progressed. Marry Tess Kinley—what the hell was Bart talking about? If Tess needed marrying so badly, why didn't Bart do the job himself? He certainly had an easy time talking with the woman; she never yelled at him the way she did Gabe. And she didn't drive Bart half as crazy as she did him either. Why was that?

He tied Zeus's reins to the post outside the sheriff's office and took himself inside.

"Mornin', Fergus," he said. "How's it going here in town these days?"

The sheriff rose from behind his undersized desk, as always buried in mounds of paperwork, and shook Gabe's outstretched hand.

"Hullo, Gabe." He smiled. "Nothin' too exciting goin' on here. Heard from your brother yet?"

"That's why I stopped." He nodded. "Bart arrived home the other day, but he's been laid up with a snakebite, so he won't be able to get to town for a few days."

"That's too bad. He's gonna be okay, though?"

Gabe nodded again. "He knows about that Gribbs fellow escaping if that's what's on your mind."

"That and more," Fergus answered. "Maybe I'll swing by this afternoon or tomorrow and see how he's doin'."

"Better yet," Gabe suggested, "why don't you take supper with us tonight and you can talk to him then? I'm sure Rosa'll be glad to see you."

Fergus's eyes glimmered saucily. "Yes," he answered slowly. "And I just might get to see your young Miss Kinley again, won't I?"

Gabe's jaw tightened. "'Fraid not, Fergus. Miss Kinley left the ranch last night and is staying somewhere in town now."

"What? Why the hell would she do a fool thing like that?" He obviously had more to say, but one look at Gabe's face and his mouth snapped closed.

"She's figuring on getting herself a job and buying a farm outside of town," Gabe said flatly, his eyes darting around the room.

"I see. Well, that's too bad, but I'd be much obliged for the meal tonight anyway. My cookin' ain't what it used to be."

Gabe's head bobbed in response. "Good, then we'll see you tonight."

The sheriff nodded again as Gabe made his retreat. He still had a few minutes before his meeting with Brolin and thanks to Bart's foolish talk about marrying Tess, Gabe had no appetite for his morning meal, but now his stomach was hollering for some attention.

Directly across the street was the saloon, where warm-hearted Dottie would surely fix him something halfway edible, or he could venture into the restaurant for a plate of damn fine cooking prepared and served by the most hostile woman he'd ever met. Pauline Lutz had never once in all the years she'd lived in Porter Creek smiled in Gabe's direction. In fact, most times she made no secret of her tsking at either him or Bart and usually sniffed at them as she stared down that long, skinny nose of hers. But she could cook a damn fine meal.

He started toward the saloon but quickly changed his mind. He was in no mood to be social, and Dottie could talk the ear off of Job if given the chance. He veered to the left and headed down to the end of the street where no doubt his mood would only worsen, but at least his stomach would be happy.

He pushed through the door and took the table nearest the window without even looking up. His Stetson came off the second his hand touched the door and it now sat on the table across from him. Doc Bender and Sheriff Nicholls met up across the street, outside the mercantile, smiling and nodding at the passing townsfolk.

From the corner of his eye, Gabe saw a menu pass under his chin and a coffee cup lowered in front of him.

"Thank you, Miss Lutz," he mumbled, catching a brief glance at the hand that pulled back. Tess.

His head whipped around and sure as hell, there she stood, a told-you-so grin on her face, loose tendrils of hair falling from her pins, and today's lunch special wiped all over her apron—beef stew and dumplings with blueberry cobbler.

"Tess!" he blurted. "What in blazes are you doing here?"

The midday sun paled in comparison to her smile.

"I told you I would get myself a job and I did. Why are you so surprised?'

"But here?" he whispered loudly. "Are you crazy? Lutz is about the meanest woman this side of the Mississippi. Couldn't you find something else?"

Tess shrugged. "I like it here."

Gabe's head shook slowly. "You must be a bugger for punishment or something."

"Yes," she answered. "I must be."

"Tess!" Pauline Lutz's voice snipped from the kitchen

doorway. "No consorting with the customers—you know the rules."

"Yes, Miss Lutz, I know. Mr. Calloway is having a difficult time deciding what he'd like."

Gabe's eyes widened in surprise. She was talking about lunch, wasn't she? Before he could speak, Miss Lutz clicked her tongue in disgust.

"I'll give him what he always orders—steak, fried eggs, and mashed potatoes. Now get back to work."

Tess's smile widened, making his own mouth dip into a deeper frown. Without a word, she swiveled away from him and continued on with her work as if he wasn't sitting less than ten feet from her. Most of the lunch customers had come and gone by then, leaving only Gabe and the Hubbards in the corner, who were soaking up every word Gabe and Tess spoke to each other.

Gabe scowled into his coffee mug. Damn well should have gone to the saloon and put up with Dottie's nattering is what he should have done. But instead, he was being eyed like a side of beef by the station master and his nosy wife, who probably noticed every time Gabe's eyes wandered away from the window and over in Tess's direction.

Tess's smile hadn't faded one tiny bit when she arrived with his lunch.

"Here you are, Gabriel. Let me know if there's anything else you need."

She placed it on the table, refilled his coffee cup, and made to leave again.

"Tess," he whispered hoarsely.

"Yes? Is there something wrong with your lunch?"

"No," he answered automatically without even having looked at the plate.

"Then what is it?"

I want you to come home, his mind hollered, take off that ridiculous apron and come home. Home?

The ranch wasn't her home, it was his. She didn't have a home.

"Where are you staying?" he fumbled. "I mean, have you found a room to rent?"

"No," she said, "not yet. I haven't had time, but once I've finished work today I'll find something. The hotel is right here, so there's always that."

Gabe's neck flamed, his eyes nearly bulging from their sockets. "You are not taking a room at the hotel," he seethed.

"I'm sorry, Mr. Calloway," she smiled sweetly, completely ignoring the steam he was certain pumped ferociously from his ears. "I'm not to consort with the customers. If there's anything I can get you, please let me know; otherwise, I'll get back to my work."

Gabe's chin nearly hit his plate, and it probably would have remained there, too, if Marylynn Hubbard's snickering hadn't rocked him back to his senses. He snapped his jaw shut and forced his glare away from both Tess and Mrs. Hubbard.

He wrapped his fist around his fork and shoveled the food into his mouth with fierce determination. He'd be damned if he'd let on how much she drove him nuts. He cleaned his plate without tasting a bite, swallowed the steaming coffee in one gulp, and pushed himself away from the table. He tossed enough money down to cover the cost of the meal and a tip for Tess, jammed his hat back on his head, and strode from the restaurant without so much as a glance back.

She could go stay at the damned hotel if that's what she wanted to do. What the hell did he care?

One look at the clientele coming and going from the hotel was enough to change Tess's mind about staying there. Filthy, cursing men stumbled in and out the front door, spitting tobacco as they made rude remarks to passersby and then guffawing at their own jokes. Their foul stench alone was enough to make her stomach churn.

She witnessed one woman exiting the hotel and even she looked slightly less than questionable. The smudged rouge on her lips and cheeks gave evidence to what her occupation most likely was, but Tess refused to judge her on that alone. Perhaps she was a wife of one of the men staying there, or perhaps she was traveling through town herself. Perhaps.

Miss Hattie's boardinghouse was a mile outside of town, so that was where Tess headed as soon as she finished at the restaurant. The road, though dusty and full of ruts, was flat and easy to follow. It led her along the other side of the creek and along its bank where she awed at the peaceful majesty of the swaying willows and the boundless number of daisies dancing in the breeze.

The picturesque view immediately relaxed her, melting away what remained of the lingering tension from that morning. Miss Lutz had completely taken her by surprise, with her sideways insinuations that Tess had somehow scandalized herself by simply knowing Gabriel. She would have to work hard to prove her worth to Miss Lutz before the woman passed along whatever ill-gotten gossip she had heard.

Miss Hattie's house was an olive green, two-story Victorian surrounded by a huge wraparound porch and more flowers than Tess could even name. A white picket fence bordered an extensive yard that played host to a huge vegetable garden and a heavy-laden cherry tree.

Inhaling deeply, she unlatched the gate and stepped through. Though she had never personally met anyone who operated a boardinghouse, she had heard plenty of stories and none of them were particularly encouraging. Her heart ached to be back at the ranch, safely ensconced in the kitchen with Rosa or out fighting with the chickens again. How she longed to ride gentle Hera across the open plain, to feel the sun on her face, the wind in her hair, and Gabriel's strong arms wrapped gently around her.

But that was not what Gabriel wanted. If he had things his way, she would never have even set foot in Porter Creek, let alone spent any time at El Cielo. A sudden sob caught in her throat, stopping her at the bottom of the steps. She couldn't very well appear weepy and pathetic when she met her prospective landlady, now could she?

She dashed the back of her hand across her eyes, swallowed hard, and marched up the steps. The white wood door opened before she even knocked, making her gasp in surprise.

"Yes?" Water-blue eyes, sunken amid a mass of pale wrinkles, peered up at Tess. "What do you want?"

"Are you Miss Hattie?" Tess asked.

"Who wants to know?" The door opened wider, revealing an older woman who was much more round than she was tall.

Tess cleared her throat. "My name is Tess Kinley, ma'am, and I'm looking for a room to rent. I was told . . ."

"*You!*" the woman almost hissed. "I've heard all about you and those Calloway boys. What are you doing at my door?"

Tess stood speechless for what seemed half an eternity. Surely, this kindly looking woman wasn't insinuating what Tess thought she was.

"I-I beg your pardon, ma'am," she said, fighting to keep her voice steady. "I don't know what you might have heard, but as I said, I am here looking for a room to rent."

"I don't rent rooms to the likes of you." The woman made to close the door but Tess pressed her hand against it, holding it open.

"And what kind of person am I?" she asked, heat flooding up her neck into her scalp.

The woman sniffed. "The kind that would take up with those Calloway boys and live out there at El Cielo—unchaperoned—doing God only knows what. That's what kind."

Tess's face flamed crimson. "Yes," she bit out through gritted teeth, knowing full well she should keep her mouth clamped shut. "I did stay, unchaperoned, at El Cielo for several days, and if it was any of your business, which it isn't, you would know both Gabriel and Bart were perfect gentlemen the entire time. They both stayed out in the barn with the horses until yesterday when Bart was bitten by a rattlesnake and moved into the house, which is part of the reason why I am here."

A very small part, she reasoned, but nevertheless, a part.

"Now," she continued, her confidence increasing with every breath. "Do you have a room? My money is as good as anyone else's."

The woman's eyes grew wide.

"Why, I never . . ." she sputtered. "How dare you speak to me like this?"

"And how dare you speak to me the way you have!" Tess snapped back. "You know nothing about me and yet you have already jumped to judge me. I assure you I am as trustworthy as anyone you might know and—"

"I rent my rooms to respectable ladies and gentlemen," Miss Hattie interrupted. "I do not allow any type of carrying on by my tenants, whether it be in my home or elsewhere. I will not have my reputation tarnished."

"Miss Hattie," Tess's ire was reaching epic proportions now. "I will have you know—"

"Good day." The door closed and Tess was left standing on the porch, her mouth agape, her hands fisted at her sides.

Never before had she been spoken to in such a manner—or accused of such things. The woman may as well have come right out and called her a harlot. Of all the nerve!

She stomped back down the stairs and slammed the gate behind her. She would show this town exactly what kind of lady she was—they'd all be surprised if they knew where she came from and who her father was. But, she thought with a slow sigh, it didn't matter who she used to be, it only mattered who she was now, and how she carried herself in public. She never would have guessed such a small town would hold the same views and opinions as the high society of Boston and other large cities.

She'd been in town a few days and already the town had labeled her anything but a lady. Tears burned the back of Tess's eyes. She was respectable, she was virtuous, and she'd be darned if she'd feel any other way—even though she would gladly give herself to Gabriel in a heartbeat if only he'd ask. If only he'd ask.

She shook her head, trying in vain to push Gabriel from her thoughts so she could focus on the problem at hand. It was closing in on supper time, it would be getting dark soon, and she had nowhere to sleep for the night. She could go back to El Cielo, but that would be tantamount to admitting defeat, and she absolutely would not do that—not today or any other day.

Her only other choice was taking a room at the hotel for now until she could make other arrangements. There must be one decent person in town who would rent her a room, she'd just have to ask around is all. Of course, if her new reputation hadn't already preceded her, it might be easier; nevertheless, she would somehow make do.

With a lift of her chin and a wipe of her eyes, she began the walk back into town. She would make this work if it was the last thing she did.

Chapter 19

The Porter Creek Hotel was far worse than Tess ever could have imagined. The man at the desk, who said his name was Jasper and refused to offer anything further by way of introduction, openly leered at her as she wrote her name in the register.

"Yer in luck there, lass," he grinned at her through blackened teeth. "I gots one empty room left, but if'n someone else comes a'lookin' for a room, yer gonna hafta double up."

Jasper made his way out from behind the desk, his huge belly straining against the confines of his grease-stained shirt and belt buckle. Sweat—yesterday's and today's—dripped from his thick brow and chin, as his beefy hand reached for the key hanging behind him.

"Come on then," he grunted, leading Tess through what might be considered a lobby.

Red and gold carpeting, threadbare in most spots, covered the wooden floor, and a huge potted fern stood dying in the far corner of the room. The one window in the room faced the street, but the grime and filth was too thick to see through it anyway. As such, the room remained dingy and depressing even in the full light of day.

Tess followed Jasper up a flight of stairs and down the hall to the last room on the left. The door opened grudgingly into the most disgusting sight Tess had ever seen.

The room couldn't have been bigger than most pantries. She didn't dare do it, but she was certain if she stood in the middle, she would have been able to touch the walls on either side of her. The pillowless bed, or rather, cot, was pushed up against the north wall, right underneath the tiny, curtainless window. A thin stained sheet covered the sagging mattress and a small round table stood against the adjacent wall, barely large enough to support the chipped blue enamel chamber set that sat on it. A motley framed mirror hung above it, complete with a long, thick crack running the entire length of it diagonally. The bare floor had obviously not seen a broom in more days than Tess cared to consider, and the thought of what was probably living in the room with her sent a rolling shudder down her spine.

She could put up with a lot of things, but a rat was not one of them.

"Dollar a week," Jasper nodded. "In advance."

Tess pulled one of Gabe's silver dollars from her pocket and dropped it in his outstretched hand.

"I don't allow no carryin' on in these rooms," he said matter-of-factly, amazing Tess by saying it with a straight face. "You keep your men out of my hotel."

Tess's hand pressed against her mouth, fighting back the bile that began to build in her throat. If he didn't stop breathing on her, she was most certainly going to lose her dinner on his already dilapidated shoes. He stared at her for a moment longer, then handed her the key and walked out, leaving her to stare about herself in horrifying despair. This was not what she had planned—not even close.

It was then Tess realized how exhausted she was. The work at the restaurant had proved tiring, but it was exhilarating too, knowing she was working toward her goal, each hour worked putting her that much closer to making her dream a reality. The confrontations with both Miss Lutz and Miss Hattie, however, had left her drained and weary. What she needed was a little bit of food and a good night's sleep, but she still had plenty of work to do first.

With key in hand, she closed the door behind her and boldly walked out of the hotel and into the mercantile. A pale young girl smiled weakly and offered her assistance in cutting the length of white flannel Tess requested and then wrapped it up along with a bar of honey-scented soap and a small oil lamp, complete with whale oil.

"I don't suppose you sell brooms?" Tess asked as she paid for her purchase.

The girl shook her head. "Pa forgot to get some last time. Be another couple weeks 'fore he gets any more goods."

Tess sighed. "You wouldn't have one I could borrow, would you? Just for a few minutes?"

The girl didn't answer, just stared blankly.

"I'm only taking it to the hotel for a moment," Tess explained. "I need to sweep out my room so I can see what's there. Not that I really want to know, I'll admit, but it's better than not knowing, don't you think?"

The girl still did not answer, but reached for the broom and handed it to Tess.

"Thank you." She smiled. "I'll have it back to you in a shake."

She hurried back to her room and set to work. She ripped off a small square of the flannel, dipped it in the murky water of the chamber bowl, and scrubbed the grit from the window. It was truly amazing how much light such a small window could let in.

With that completed, she rinsed the cloth and took to washing down the walls, the table and the mirror, and finally, the chamber set itself. When she finished, she took the broom and swept the floor until new blisters formed on her hands. She pushed the filth out into the hallway and closed the door again. The remaining flannel was soon transformed into a plain curtain and matching sheet for the bed with enough left to lay over her as a blanket. It wasn't much to look at, but it was a darn sight better than it was an hour before.

She returned the broom to the girl at the store and made her way back to Miss Lutz's restaurant. She needed to eat and since there was nowhere else . . .

An unfamiliar woman greeted her with a weary smile and a cup of coffee.

"Hi," Tess smiled back. "I'm Tess. Miss Lutz hired me for the breakfast and lunch shifts."

"Lucky you," she chuckled. "I'm Lily, it's nice to meet you."

Her white-blond hair, held back in a single plait by a raveling pink ribbon, needed a good brushing, and her moss green eyes appeared almost lifeless behind the dark circles that shadowed them. Her smile was friendly enough, though, and her hands and face had been scrubbed pink.

"How long have you worked here?" Tess asked, eager to make a new friend.

"Seems like forever," Lily whispered back, "but it's only been a couple months, since my Charlie passed."

"Oh," Tess sighed. "I'm sorry."

"Not your fault," she smiled sadly. "He's the one who got himself drunker 'n a skunk and fell into the creek. Weren't for the little ones, I'd hardly notice he was gone."

"You have children? How many?"

"Three." Lily's face lit up like the north star. "Betsy, Fredrick, and little Aggie. She was a year last week."

"My goodness," Tess breathed. "How do you manage with three children, a home and having to work? You must be run ragged."

Lily chuckled sadly. "My kids are the only thing that keep me going everyday. I'd be workin' the breakfast and lunch shifts if I could, but I have to wait for Betsy to get home from school before I can leave. She's such a good girl, watchin' over her little brother and sister."

"How old is she?"

"Just turned nine."

Tess inhaled sharply. The poor thing was still a child herself and already she was forced to take on the responsibilities of a grown woman.

"Lily!" Miss Lutz's voice sliced through the restaurant. "It doesn't matter that she is the only customer, there is still work to be done. Now take her order and move on."

Tess fought back the urge to stick her tongue out at the nasty woman, but Lily, who stood with her back to Miss Lutz, grinned openly.

"Not exactly the warmest woman in the world, is she?" Lily whispered.

"I've met warmer December mornings."

Lily didn't even try to suppress her laughter. "It's going to be so nice having someone on my side."

Tess caught sight of Miss Lutz glaring at them from the kitchen doorway.

"If I don't get us both fired first," Tess whispered back. "I'll have a ham sandwich, please, with a glass of milk."

Lily nodded and hesitated a moment before she left.

"Don't let her get to you," she said quietly. "I know who you are and what she thinks about you, but it's none of her business. It ain't anybody's business, Tess, except yours. Remember that, because this town is awful small and it seems everybody thinks they're better 'n everybody else. You just keep your chin up and pay no mind to what she thinks."

Tess couldn't speak past the lump in her throat. She forced a smile, but it only served to push out the tears that shimmered against her lower lids. She wiped them away quickly and looked down at the table. Lily patted her shoulder gently and walked away to the kitchen.

A friend, Tess thought. That's exactly what she needed after the day she'd had. Now if she could find a different place to stay. A wave of guilt immediately washed over her. Here she was feeling sorry for herself when poor Lily had three children and a house to look after and no husband to help her. Well, if Lily could make it work and keep a smile on her face, then so could she.

She took a deep breath, wiped away the last tear, and lifted her chin. Her circumstances could be a lot worse, that was for certain, so she would make the best of what she had to work with and carry on.

Lily returned with her meal and refilled Tess's coffee cup.

"I'm done here in a few minutes," she said. "Would you mind if I joined you for a cup of coffee?"

"I'd like that." Tess smiled.

Lily returned to her duties, wiping up the last of the tables and setting out the cutlery for the next day. When she finished, she untied her apron and disappeared into the kitchen, returning a moment later with a steaming cup of coffee in one hand and a small bowl of pea soup in the other.

They huddled over the table, keeping their voices low.

"How long've you been in town?" Lily asked.

"Less than a week. I was staying out at El Cielo with the Calloways, but . . ." Tess stopped.

"Tess, you don't have to explain anything to me.

Like I said, it's none of my business or anyone else's."
She reached out to cover Tess's arm with a dry, cal-
lused hand. "If you want to tell me about it, I'm happy
to listen, but . . ."

"No," Tess hurried to explain. "It's nothing like
that. It's . . ." Again she stopped.

Lily looked up from her bowl, a knowing look
coming over her face. "Which one is it?" she asked.

"Which one is what?"

The other woman's eyes flooded with emotion—
sympathy, empathy, and experience.

"Which one of them Calloway boys are you in love
with?"

Tess's chin dropped. "How did you know?"

"There ain't a woman in the world who'd stay in
a place like Porter Creek, working for a woman like
Pauline Lutz, unless there was something—or
someone—holding her here. So which one—Bart
or Gabe?"

Tess's face flamed. "I . . . I . . . oh, heavens, it's
Gabriel."

Lily sat back in her chair and crossed her arms
over her chest. "Thought so. Does he know?"

"Oh, yes," she sighed. "He knows all right. I've
made it abundantly clear to him how I feel, but all he
can think about is getting me on the first stage out
of town."

"Mm-hmm." Lily nodded.

"I guess I should have played coy with him or something," Tess admitted. "But I don't believe in playing
foolish games. Life is too precious and far too short to
waste time pretending you don't feel something when
you really do. I guess it doesn't matter, though, does
it? All I managed to do was make him angry and more
determined to get me out of his life."

"And yet here you are, still in town, with a job."

"Yes." She nodded frankly. "I'm determined to

save myself enough money to buy my own place and live off the land."

Lily eyed her carefully for a moment before she spoke. "You're serious, aren't you?"

"Absolutely. Do you think I'd be working here and living at the hotel next door if I wasn't?"

"You're living at the hotel?" Lily gasped. "Good Lord, Tess, that place is worse than hell itself!"

"I know," she sighed. "But Miss Hattie . . ."

Lily's tongue clicked loudly. "The old boot wouldn't rent you a room, would she?"

Tess shook her head.

"That nosy old woman should have her secrets aired to the whole world and then we'd see who was considered 'respectable.'"

"Oh, Lily, I can't really blame her. After all, I stay at El Cielo without a chaperone. . . ."

"What about Rosa? She lives there too."

"Yes." Tess smiled. "Rosa is wonderful, but I guess she's not considered proper either since she and Miguel have never actually married."

"Oh pish! They don't make women any better than Rosa, I don't care what anyone says. She raised those two boys like they were her own, and despite their faults, she did a darn fine job."

Tess pursed her lips. "Can I ask you something, Lily?"

"Of course."

"Every time the Calloway name came up today, both with Miss Lutz and Miss Hattie, it was greeted with a sniff and a look of disdain. Why is that?"

Lily grinned wickedly. "It's a toss-up between old man Calloway and Bart. The old man drank himself stupid after Emma died. And Bart, well, he was a bit of a wild one growing up. Seen more than his fair share of women come and go. The old biddies in town blame him for ruining more than a few of their precious young girls. But if you ask me, it takes two to make an argument, and I didn't see any of them precious young girls telling him no."

Tess couldn't help but grin; Bart did have a certain charm about him.

"But what about Gabriel?" she asked tentatively. "Was he the same?"

"Gabe? Lord no! Straight as an arrow, that boy. In fact, I've only ever known two or three women who have ever gotten close to him, and none since high-falutin Catarina left him."

"Then why do the ladies in town consider him to be such a rogue?"

"Guilty by virtue of his name, Tess. After his mama died, his pa sort of fell by the wayside, keeping company with Dottie and her girls over at the saloon. And then came Bart with his charm and his way with the ladies. The Calloway name eventually lost the respect it once commanded. Nothin' Gabe did or didn't do."

"It's not right."

"Nope, it ain't," Lily agreed, "but there ain't much either one of us can do about it."

She finished the last of her coffee and stood to leave.

"Listen, Tess, I wish I could invite you to stay with me and the kids, but the house already ain't big enough for the four of us. I'm real sorry."

"Don't you be sorry one bit, Lily." Tess smiled. "I'll be just fine."

"I'm sure you will." Lily nodded. "I'm sure you will."

Chapter 20

The next several days all seemed to blend together in a murky blur for Tess. After working her shifts at the restaurant, she would haul two huge buckets full of water up to her room and sponge herself down from head to toe, trying to wash off as much grit and grime as she could. What she wouldn't give for a nice hot bath and completely clean hair.

The other hotel guests stumbled into their rooms at all hours of the night, falling up and down the stairs, crashing into the walls and generally making enough noise to raise the dead. Tess did not sleep but rather dozed off and on, terrified one of the drunken rascals would come barreling through her door at any time during the night and pass out in her room. Or worse.

She had not seen Gabriel since he showed up in the restaurant her first day there, and her heart ached more and more every day. How she longed to see him again, to look at his face, to look in his eyes—those stormy, smoke-colored eyes that looked right down into her very soul.

Ironically, it was the very day Gabe would have had her on the stage that Tess's luck finally changed for the better. She was fairly certain Gabe would disagree, but in her opinion, the events of that fateful

Friday were the best thing to happen to her since
first laying eyes on her angel himself.

It was the day she met the Langman family.

The restaurant was buzzing with lunch customers
in various stages of their meals when the door
opened and in walked a pretty young girl accompa-
nied by a man who easily could have passed for her
twin brother. Tess showed them to the nearest clean
table and hurried to fill their coffee cups.

"You're new." The man's voice bounced around
the room until every other customer looked up from
their meal.

"Yes." Tess smiled hurriedly. "I am. Have you decided what you would like?"

"I'm Collette Langman," the girl said, offering her
hand. "And this is my tactless brother Frankie."

Tess's eyes flew to the kitchen door. She'd already
been snapped at twice this morning for talking to
customers.

"Collette . . ." Tess faltered. The infamous Collette
Langman. The girl's eyes were bluer than anything
Tess had ever seen, and her golden hair fell in shim-
mering waves down her back. Bart was right, this girl
was absolutely stunning. Tess's smile brightened.
"It's nice to meet you. I'm Tess Kinley."

It was the other girl's turn to smile now. "Really?
You're Tess Kinley? I've heard so much . . . what I
mean is, I was told . . ." Collette flushed. "I must
sound as bad as Frankie. I'm sorry."

"Nonsense," Tess said, glancing back at the kitchen.
"I'm afraid I can't talk right now, but I would very
much like to speak with you later. Would you mind?"

"Would I mind?" she repeated. "Why on earth
would I mind? I have so many questions for you myself that I could go on for days."

"I'll have a steak with potatoes and peas," Frankie

interrupted. "And bread. Lots of bread. And a piece of cherry pie. Got that?"

"Yes," Tess nodded absently, her focus still on Collette. "Would you be able to meet me later?"

"Oooh, I'd like that." Collette giggled. "I'll come back in a few hours, how would that be?"

"Fine," she answered. "Just fine."

Miss Lutz cleared her throat behind Tess.

"And what would you like, miss?" Tess's eyes danced with excitement. She was going to get to know Collette Langman, and perhaps in the process, play matchmaker.

Collette's mouth twitched against a laugh. "I'll have a bowl of soup and some bread, please."

"Of course. I'll bring your lunches right out."

Tess's heart seemed to float in her chest. She already liked Collette Langman and she'd only just met her. Frankie, on the other hand, appeared a little rough, but what did that matter?

She flew through the rest of her shift, counting the minutes until she would learn more about Collette and her family. She hoped she would be able to bring her new friend and Bart together somehow.

With the final plate washed and returned to its place, and all the tables washed and reset for Lily's supper shift, Tess washed quickly in the kitchen basin and hurried outside to wait for Collette. Within moments the other girl was walking toward her from the livery.

"Tess!" she called. "Come on, let's walk."

The two women instinctively linked arms and headed out toward the creek, both giddy with excitement.

"I have to admit," Tess said, "I've heard a little about you, too, Collette."

Collette's pretty face pinked. "I hope what you've heard is favorable."

"Oh yes." Tess laughed. "Very favorable."

"Tell me!" the girl cried. "Tell me everything. How is he? Is he staying this time? He's not up and married some little . . ."

"Slow down." Tess laughed. "I'll tell you everything I know, which might not be much, but it could prove helpful."

"Oh, yes, tell me everything."

They neared the creek now and Tess could smell the sweet bouquet of the wild flowers.

"Let's sit here," she said, "and I'll tell you what I know, okay?"

Collette would have dropped to the ground right there if Tess hadn't pulled her along to a grassy spot under a huge willow.

"Now," she began, "I hope I'm not overstepping myself here, but it seems to me you and Bart need a little help, so here it is."

Collette clasped her hands under her chin and gazed up at Tess with open eagerness.

"Yes," she continued, "Bart is home, and as far as I know, he plans on staying. At least for some time. No, he did not go off and get himself married and, in fact, he hasn't even courted a woman for quite some time."

Collette's grin widened.

"It would seem," Tess grinned back, "he is quite taken with a certain someone right here in Porter Creek. Someone whom he considers close to perfect and, now let me think, what were his exact words? Oh, yes, 'the prettiest thing he ever did see.'"

Collette's smile faded, her bottom lip trembled. "I knew it!" she cried. "I knew he'd find someone before I ever had a chance to . . ."

"Collette!" Tess laughed gently, placing her hand over the girl's. "It's you! Bart wants you!"

"M-me?" she stammered. "Bart is interested in *me*?

But I'm not pretty and I'm certainly not even close to perfect!"

"Yes." Tess nodded. "Your one imperfection, according to Bart, is your family name, but he supposes that can't be helped. As for the other, Collette, you most certainly are pretty and, in fact, I'd say you are the loveliest girl I've seen in a very long time."

"Oh." Collette blushed. "You're just saying that."

"No, I'm not. You truly are beautiful, Collette, and if you don't know that, then I suppose that's what makes you even more attractive to him."

"Really?"

"Well, I can't honestly say I am familiar with the way a man's mind works," she confessed, "but from what Bart himself has told me, you are his main distraction."

Collette threw her arms in the air and flopped backward into the grass.

"Oh, thank goodness," she gushed. "I had myself convinced he didn't even know I was alive."

"He knows." Tess laughed. "He knows all too well."

Collette sat back up, her eyes suddenly troubled.

"But if what you say is true, then why hasn't he come calling? Is he sick?"

Tess's chin dropped to her chest. "Yes," she finally said. "He has been sick and I'm afraid it's all my fault."

"Whatever do you mean?"

Tess explained about the snakebite and how if Bart hadn't been trying to save her, he never would have been bitten in the first place.

"But you saved his life," Collette breathed in amazement.

"Hardly," Tess said, shaking her head. "If it hadn't been for me—"

"If it hadn't been for you," she interrupted, "Bart would be dead right now. Oh, my Lord, Tess, I don't know what to say."

Tess shrugged. "You're very kind, Collette. I wish Gabriel shared the same view as you."

"What do you mean? Isn't he grateful you saved his only brother's life?"

"Oh, I'm sure he is," Tess hastened to explain. "But the whole incident only furthered his resolve to send me back to Boston where, according to him, I belong."

"You're from Boston?" Collette's eyes rounded. "Really? What on earth are you doing here then?"

Tess could not hide her smile. "I belong here. One day when I've saved enough money, I'm going to buy my own farm and live the life I've always dreamed of."

"But what about Gabe . . . ?"

"Yes, Gabriel, he is a bit of a problem, but since I'm not living at El Cielo anymore, I'm hopeful by not seeing him I'll be able to put him out of my mind."

"You're not at El Cielo anymore?" Collette asked, obviously surprised. "Where are you staying—at Miss Hattie's boardinghouse?"

Tess grimaced. "No, actually, Miss Hattie wouldn't have me."

"You're not serious!" When Tess nodded, Collette's brow furrowed. "Then where . . . oh, no, Tess, you're not staying at that dreadful hotel, are you?"

"Yes," she answered, lifting her chin a notch. "I am. It's not the nicest place I've ever stayed, but it will do for now."

"It most certainly will not!" Collette declared, bolting to her feet and dragging Tess along with her. "You are coming home with me."

"But . . ."

"No buts about it. It's the least I can do, Tess. After all, you saved Bart's life, and I don't care a lick what anybody—including nosy old Hattie—thinks about you. Nobody deserves to live in a place like that . . . that . . . hell!"

"Collette . . ."

"Hush now," the girl ordered, pulling Tess back down the road to town. "There's plenty of room at our house, and I'd be so happy to have female company. I won't take no for an answer."

"Don't you think you should check with your family first? I'm told you have quite a large family and I can't imagine there would be enough room for any more . . ."

"Nonsense! Most of my brothers are married and living in their own houses on the ranch anyway. There's only Pa, Frankie, and me living in that big old house. Now come on."

"Wait!" Tess pulled her arm free and stopped in her tracks.

"What is it—do you like living at the hotel?"

"No, of course not, it's just . . ." She hesitated.

"Tell me." Collette took a step toward her, her hand reaching for Tess's.

"Two things, really. The first is I must be allowed to pay my own way. I will pay your father for room and board and do my fair share of chores. Agreed?"

Collette nodded. "If Pa agrees."

"And the second thing is . . . well . . . I don't know how to say this delicately."

"Just say it, Tess. I won't be offended."

Tess sighed. "If you and Bart should manage to . . . well, you know what I mean . . . I don't want to be caught between the two of you. I consider both of you my friends now and I can't be asked to take sides in any kind of disagreement or anything else."

Collette laughed. "Is that all? Land sakes, Tess, if Bart ever does make his intentions known to me, I am certainly not going to let him go for anything in the world. I've waited too long for this, and I intend to dig in my heels and keep him no matter what.

That is, of course, if what you've told me is true and he does intend to court me."

"Oh, it's true, Collette. The problem is, well, may I be frank?"

"I wish you would."

"He's concerned about your family. He told me about the problems that have lingered between yours and his, and he's not so sure he can get past your brothers and your father."

Collette's eyes narrowed defiantly. "I'll take care of my family. If they so much as even think about getting in my way over this, they will rue the day they were born!"

Tess laughed and took the girl's arm.

"I think this is going to work out splendidly," she said. "It would seem you and I think along the same lines. What a refreshing change!"

The two women walked back into town, broad smiles across both of their faces. They marched straight up to Tess's room at the hotel, collected her few belongings, and left.

"I need to stop at the mercantile and purchase a ready-made dress," Tess said, her first week's pay clutched in her palm.

"Pish," Collette said. "I have plenty of dresses, there's sure to be some you can wear. You save your money for that farm of yours, you hear me?"

"Oh, Collette," Tess sighed. "I don't know what I ever did to deserve a friend like you, and I'm certain I can never repay your kindness to me."

"Being my friend is more than enough payment," she said, squeezing Tess's arm. "You and I are going to be the best of friends."

"Yes." Tess nodded. "I think you're right."

Frankie Langman was waiting for them outside the livery with the horses and buggy. Collette climbed in first and then nodded toward Tess.

"You remember Tess, don't you, Frankie?"

Frankie grunted some kind of greeting as he took Tess's hand and helped her into the buggy. She was so happy, so thrilled to be getting out of the hotel and into a real home again that she took no notice of the people around them.

"Boss!" Miguel hollered. "Boss!"

Gabe strode out of the barn, a horseshoe in one hand and a metal file in the other. Miguel's horse frothed at the mouth, and Miguel fought for breath himself.

"What in blazes has you all fired up?" he asked, taking the exhausted horse by the bit.

"Trouble, boss. You ain't gonna like it."

"What?"

Miguel dismounted, still shaking his head in disbelief.

"It's Miss Tess," he said. "I seen her in town just now and . . ."

"And what, Miguel?" Gabe demanded, his whole face darkening like a July storm.

"She was gettin' in the Langman buggy with Stupid Frankie."

"Hell and damnation!" Gabe bellowed. "What the hell is she thinking taking up with the likes of Stupid Frankie Langman?"

"I don't know, boss, but it can only mean trouble. What if . . ."

Gabe was already heading back to the barn. "Bart! Bart! Come on, I'm going to need your help on this one."

"What's up?" Bart rounded the corner as he spoke. His color still wasn't what it should be, but it was a lot better.

"Seems Tess has taken up with Stupid Frankie.

Miguel saw her getting in his buggy. I'm going over to the Langman place to get her. You coming?"

Color and life flooded back into Bart's face.

"You bet yer ass I am." He grinned. "Let's go."

Chapter 21

Gabe had Zeus saddled and moving inside of two minutes with Bart right behind him.

"Stupid Frankie?" Bart said, shaking his head. "*Stupid Frankie?*"

"Will you shut up already!" Gabe snapped. "I need to think."

"Okay, okay," he muttered, more to the wind. "But Stupid Frankie?"

The Langman place was almost upon them and Gabe still had no idea what he was going to do when he got there. Most likely he'd be shot out of his saddle before he knew what hit him anyway.

Around the corner, the house loomed larger and larger with various horses and wagons tied randomly to whatever was closest. Gabe rode Zeus right up to the front steps and dismounted, almost tripping over Bart as he did.

"Watch it!"

"Sorry," Bart said, ducking his head slightly. "Now what do we do?"

"I don't have one damned idea," Gabe muttered as he banged on the door.

"Good," Bart snickered. "I like a well thought-out plan."

Before Gabe could fire back, the door opened and there stood Collette Langman. Gabe hardly noticed her—or his brother—as he craned his neck to look past her into the huge foyer.

"Is Tess here?" he demanded.

"Yes," Collette answered politely, her eyes never leaving Bart's. "Would you like to come in?"

Gabe didn't answer, just pushed through the doorway, barely remembering to remove his hat as he did.

"Hello, Bart," Collette said, a soft blush finding her cheeks. "How are you?"

"Collette." He grinned back. "I'm 'bout as healthy as a hound dog now."

"It's nice to see you again." Her left hand wrapped itself around her tiny waist while her right hand fiddled idly at her neck.

"I been meanin' to come by an' see you," he said, a heated flush climbing up his neck.

"Yes, Tess told me what happened. You were very lucky—"

"Where is she?" Gabe broke in unapologetically.

Collette pulled her eyes from Bart's. "I'm sorry?"

"Where is Tess?"

Collette's face softened. "She's getting settled in her room upstairs. She . . ."

"She's what?" This time he did bellow.

"She's getting settled . . ."

"Gabriel? What on earth are you doing here?" Tess appeared at the top of the staircase, her eyes scanning the room. Suddenly a smile lit across her face. "Bart. I'm so glad you're here. How are you?"

"Couldn't be better." He grinned foolishly. "You?"

"I'm just fine, thank you for asking." She turned her attention back to Gabriel who stood frozen in his place. "Did you need something, Gabriel?"

Gabe's mouth clamped shut, his fists bunching his hat between them. She'd moved into the Langman house. That could only mean one thing. His heart was ready to explode right there in the foyer. How could this have happened? How could she be so goldarned stupid? How could he?

"Perhaps we should step outside," Tess said. She didn't wait for him to agree or disagree. He simply exhaled loudly and followed her out the door, slamming it behind him.

"What the hell do you think you're doing?"

"Please, Gabriel, keep your voice down."

"Don't tell me to keep my voice down!" he yelled. "I'll damn well yell if I want to yell, and damn it, I *want* to yell!"

"Very well," she said, crossing her arms over her chest. "Go right ahead, but if we're suddenly surrounded by a whole herd of Langmans, all armed to the teeth, that will be one thing you won't be able to blame me for."

Gabe resisted the urge to take her by the shoulders and shake some sense into her.

"What are you doing here?" he asked again, his voice considerably lower this time.

"Isn't it wonderful?" Tess asked, her eyes dancing with excitement. "Collette has offered to let me stay here with them until I'm able to buy my own place. She's such a dear girl."

"Collette?" Gabe's brow furrowed. "But I thought . . . Miguel said . . . what about Stupid Frankie?"

"Stupid Frankie?" she repeated. "Honestly, Gabriel, I hardly think that's a neighborly thing to call the man. He was kind enough to drive Collette and me home this afternoon and . . . oh, I see."

"What?"

"Miguel saw me get into the buggy, didn't he?"

"I . . . he . . ."

"And he naturally assumed I was taking a ride with Frankie, is that it?"

Gabe slapped his hat against his thigh. "Thunderation, woman, what was he supposed to think?"

"That is completely irrelevant, isn't it? The question I have is this: What business is it of yours if I did take a ride with Frankie or any other man, for that matter?"

"What?" His fury weakened slightly, his pride kicking him in the stomach.

"Well, honestly, Gabriel, I think you've made yourself fairly clear on the point that you are not interested in a future with me, so what do you expect me to do?"

"That doesn't mean you should take up with the first idiot to come along!" The second the words were out of his mouth, Gabe regretted them. "I'm sorry. I didn't mean that like it sounded."

To his surprise, Tess was smiling at him.

"Why, Gabriel Calloway," she said softly. "You truly are jealous."

"I am not!"

"Then what on earth would possess you to come riding all the way over here, to a place you can't even bear to talk about, never mind the people who live here?"

"I . . . I . . ." he fumbled, inhaled deeply, and set his jaw. "I was worried."

"Worried?" she repeated.

"Yes," he nodded. "You have no idea what these Langman people are like. I didn't want you to get yourself into trouble is all."

"I see."

"But so long as I'm here, tell me. Are you and Stupid Frankie . . . ?"

"No, Gabriel, Frankie only drove us home. I'm here as Collette's guest and nothing more. Are you happy now?"

Gabe scuffed his boots against the porch boards. "If you're so hell-bent on living in Porter Creek, there must be somewhere else you can stay."

Tess's smile tightened. "Actually, no, there isn't. Miss Hattie won't have me, and I've stayed at the hotel for several nights now and I'd rather not do that again. So this is the only option left, and frankly, I quite like Collette."

"What do you mean Hattie wouldn't have you?" Gabe seemed to double in size right before her.

"It's not her fault, Gabriel. She has a reputation to uphold, and if she let just anyone rent . . ."

"What did she say to you?" he demanded, towering over her.

"Nothing that hasn't been said before, or won't be said again, I'm sure."

"Tess . . ."

She shook her head. "No, Gabriel. I have no one to blame but myself for the opinions people might hold of me. I was the one who arrived at El Cielo without a chaperone, knowing full well what the consequences might be."

"I don't give a damn . . ."

"I'm fine." She turned her gaze away from him. She was still the worst liar he'd ever met. "I have a decent job, a nice place to sleep now, and pretty soon I'll have enough money to buy my own place. You needn't worry about me."

"Easier said than done," he muttered, then louder, "Why can't you go back to Boston?"

Tess's fingers fumbled at her collar, but she straightened upright and swallowed hard.

"I don't want to. I want to be here."

"Damn it, Tess . . ."

Before he could finish, tears rolled over her lashes.

"I don't expect anything from you, Gabriel," she said. "You've made yourself clear and I respect your feelings. I don't mean to impose myself on you or your hospitality anymore, and I'm so very sorry for the grief I've already caused you. And Bart." She swiped the back of her hand across her eyes. "But I will not go back to Boston. I have chosen to stay here and that's exactly what I mean to do. How I feel about you has not changed, nor do I ever expect it to, but that certainly doesn't mean you are beholden to me or are in any way responsible for me." Her trembling hand rested against his chest as she choked out the words. "Please, Gabriel, please don't ever feel you are responsible for me. I'm a grown woman and I'm fully capable of looking after myself. You certainly don't owe me anything."

Gabe's huge hand covered hers, the reflection of his own breaking heart mirrored in her eyes.

"Tess," he murmured, pulling her into his embrace. "God, Tess, don't you see? As long as you're here, I can't help myself but look after you. It doesn't matter whether I want to or not, I can't seem to get you out of my system."

He stepped back, locking her shoulders between his hands. Tears flowed freely down her face, her eyes already swollen.

"I can't let myself love you, Tess," he rasped. "God knows I want to, but I can't."

"I know," she said, a forced smile trembling on her lips. "I know."

"Tess . . ."

"I'm fine," she lied again. "Really, I am. I don't know why I'm crying, just tired I guess. I think I should go lie down for a while."

Neither one of them moved for a long moment, Gabe's eyes searching her face for something, but what?

"Good-bye, Gabriel." She moved to step around him, but he caught her by the wrist and pulled her back.

"I'm sorry, Tess," he murmured, gazing down into her still-damp eyes. "I . . ."

His hands cupped her cheeks, his thumbs rubbed along her cheekbones. Damn, she was irresistible.

His head dipped, her eyes lowered, and suddenly he was kissing her, tenderly, slowly, hungrily, with an urgency that rocked him to his very core. Her lips responded instantly, molding against his. Her arms slipped around his back and held him as though he were her life support.

She was so soft, so fragile, so . . .

"No," he muttered against her hair, pulling away. "We can't."

Tess stumbled back, unable to regain her balance for a moment. When her eyes opened, the blatant pain he saw there just about dropped him to his knees.

"You're right," she said. "We can't. I can't do this, Gabriel. I can't let you kiss me like this knowing you will never want me the way I need you to." Her head lowered, the tears falling straight to the porch now. "Please don't ever kiss me again."

Gabe swallowed hard, fighting not to take her back into his arms right there and then.

"Tess . . ." he choked out. "I . . ."

"Good-bye, Gabriel." She moved around him and fled through the door before he could even catch his next breath. When he finally gained his senses, she had disappeared up the huge oak staircase, leaving him alone on the porch.

"What the hell happened?" Bart asked, barreling through the door. "What did you say to her?'

"None of your damn business." Gabe jammed his hat back on his head and stumbled down the steps. "You coming?"

Bart glanced back at the open doorway, but Collette was already gone, having followed Tess up the stairs to her room.

"Yeah," he grumbled. "I'm comin'. Waited this long, guess a little while longer won't kill me." Gabe had already disappeared around the bend before Bart even hoisted himself up into the saddle.

A bitter cold settled in the depths of Gabe's soul. In his mind's eye, all he saw was Tess, the trembling tears on her eyelids magnifying the raw misery she tried so valiantly to hide.

Damn it, he cursed silently, his shoulders slumping forward. Why did it have to be this way? Why did she have to be so honest, so unlike most women? If she'd try to force herself on him, make him feel guilty about pushing her away, he'd feel so much better. But instead, she accepted his rejection and forged on. He kept going back to her, kept kissing her, kept needing her.

Why the hell couldn't he leave her alone? They'd both be better off.

"Gabe!" Bart barked, riding up beside him. "You listenin' to me?"

"What?" he muttered, blinking his glazed over eyes again and again. "What'd you say?"

"Holy-oh-hell, Gabe, just go back there an' fix it."

"Fix what? There's nothing . . ."

"That's a load of crap an' you know it. That girl's 'bout as heartbroke as I ever seen and you ain't lookin' much better."

"Doesn't matter," he said, his voice void of all conviction. "I can't . . ."

"Don't be such an ass! A' course you can. Just turn that damn animal 'round and go back."

"No, I can't."

"Why? 'Cuz yer damn fool pride won't let you? Because you like bein' miserable?"

"You don't understand. . . ."

"Yer right." Bart nodded. "I ain't got a friggin' notion what the hell's goin' on in that thick skull o' yours, but if I was you, I'd be ridin' fast as I could back to that ranch 'fore one of them other stupid gawkarses takes a likin' to her. She ain't gonna wait fer you forever you know."

"I didn't ask her to." Gabe's voice remained low, his stomach lurching with every word his brother spoke.

"No, you didn't," Bart agreed. "'Cuz somewhere in that little pea brain o' yours, you think she's better off somewhere else. Well, I'm tellin' ya right now, brother, that little girl ain't goin' anywhere whether you like it or not. So these are your choices: get the hell back there right now and make her yours once and for all, or sit back and watch her marry up with one of the other jackasses in town an' then you'll have to watch her be with someone else for the rest of your life. You willin' to do that?"

Gabe's eyes never looked up once. His blind gaze remained on the saddle horn, and if it weren't for Zeus's own instincts and direction, Gabe probably would have ended up in Mexico. Not that he would have cared either way.

"Damn it, Gabe!" Bart snarled. "She loves you! Don't that mean anything to you?"

"Doesn't matter."

"What the hell d'you mean it don't matter? A' course it matters."

"No, it doesn't." Gabe's head shook slowly. "She deserves better than this, she . . ."

He stopped, shrugging his shoulders in resignation.

"You mean she deserves better 'n you." Bart's frustration boiled over. "An' yer right. She deserves a man who's willin' to fight for her, who ain't sittin' here feelin' sorry for himself when he ain't got no right to be. She deserves a man who ain't scared of 'er."

"I'm not scared of her!" Gabe snapped, sitting a little straighter. "It's . . ."

"It's just you're scared she's gonna up an' die on ya." Gabe stopped his horse with a jerk.

"What the hell are you talking about?" he demanded, Zeus rebelling against the hold Gabe had on the reins.

Bart pulled up beside him and stopped.

"Come on, Gabe, I know I ain't the brightest star in the sky, but hell, this is as plain as the day is long. You think 'cause she's a city girl like Mama and Catarina, she's got no business living out here."

"It's not just that. . . ."

"No, I know it ain't. Yer so damn scared that even if she could stand livin' out here, she'd prob'ly up and die on you anyway. Well, I got news for you, big brother—we're all gonna die one day."

"I know that!"

"So wouldn't you rather spend what time you got here with someone worthwhile rather than a bunch a stinkin' ol' cow punchers?"

Gabe set his jaw before he spoke.

"But what if . . ."

"What if she decides tomorrow or next week or next year she can't stand livin' out here? What if she decides you ain't the man for her? Or what if she's the next one to get bit by a rattler?"

"Yeah, Bart, now that you mention it, what if any one of those things?"

"The hell with all of those things, Gabe! I coulda easily said what if she decides this here's heaven right on earth? Or what if she decides for some crazy reason yer the only man she's ever gonna want? Or what if she lives to be a hundred? Sure it's a gamble, but hell, Gabe, if you don't take that gamble, how you ever gonna know?"

"I'm not the gambler in the family," Gabe said cynically.

"Yeah, well, I ain't usually the one talkin' sense neither and look at me go."

Bart spat into the dirt below him and spurred his

horse forward, leaving Gabe to stare in wonderment after him. Who was that man and what the hell did he do with the old Bart?

Chapter 22

"Frankie tells me yer acquainted with them Calloways." Wyatt Langman made no attempt to disguise his accusatory tone.

The Langman kitchen fell deathly quiet.

"Yes," Tess answered tentatively, peering over her coffee cup.

"Don't much like them boys," he said, picking his teeth with his long, yellowed fingernail. "Their pa weren't good fer nothin'."

Tess arched her brow. "I'm afraid I never met the man."

Wyatt grunted. "Man murdered my boy Adam, right there in Dottie's saloon."

"Now, Pa," Collette intervened. "The judge ruled that an accident. Besides, you and Adam—and probably Clayton, too, as far as that goes—were too drunk to know what was going on or why."

Tess thought she caught something strange in Collette's expression but it passed too quickly to be sure.

"Don't you talk to Pa that way!" One of the brothers, Tess guessed it was Evan, was on his feet, his pasty face splotched in anger. "You ain't got no idea . . ."

"Sit down, son," Wyatt ordered. "I won't have no one raisin' their voice to a lady in my house. It ain't right."

The man sat down, but his glare only darkened.

"She shouldn't be talkin' to you like that, Pa. She don't know what happened. She weren't there."

"Neither were you, Evan," Collette pointed out. "The only witnesses were either already passed out or too drunk to see clearly, so we'll never know what really happened, will we? Besides it was almost twenty years ago, why can't we let it go?"

"Let it go?" Wyatt repeated. Tess noticed the blue vein on the side of his neck begin to throb. "Now you listen here, Lettie. Adam was your brother, whether you remember him or not, and I don't care what no one says no how, murder is murder, and so help me God, Clayton Calloway should rot in hell fer what he done."

"Pa . . ."

"That's the end of it." He turned his attention back to Tess who had to force her eyes to blink back the fear she felt lurking within them.

"Now, Miss Tess," he said. "I won't have those Calloways on my land, you hear? As long as yer a guest in this house, you keep that in mind. I can't stop you from seein' them in town but if I ever see them on my land again, I'll shoot 'em both deader 'n a can of corned beef. Understand?"

Tess could only nod for fear if she opened her mouth she would scream.

"Good." Wyatt pushed back from the table. "Come on, boys, we got us some work to do."

The Langman boys, all six of them, filed out of the house behind Wyatt, leaving Tess and Collette alone in the kitchen. Tess had been living at the Langman ranch for over a week but still was not accustomed to the Langman brothers.

"Don't mind Pa," Collette said softly, her voice shaking. "As Damon says, he's more gurgle than guts. He'd never do anything to Bart or Gabe."

"He sounded very convincing to me." Tess lowered

her cup and reached for Collette's hand. "You can't have Bart coming to call on you here if that is how your father feels about him."

The girl nodded. "I know, but if Pa finds out I've seen Bart on the side, he'll be even angrier. Oh, Tess, what am I going to do?"

Tess inhaled deeply, patted Collette's arm, and smiled her determined smile.

"Don't you fret, we'll figure something out. Now why don't you explain your family to me?"

"What do you mean?" Collette asked. She lifted the coffeepot from the stove and filled their cups.

"I don't mean to pry," Tess was quick to say, "but if Adam was already grown by the time you were born and he's been dead almost twenty years, your mother must have been an incredibly strong and durable woman."

Collette laughed. "My mother was, yes. Adam's mother on the other hand . . ."

"I don't understand."

"My pa's been married four times, Tess." She laughed harder at Tess's shock. "Yes, it was quite the scandal, I suppose, but it's so long ago it doesn't really matter anymore, does it?"

"Four times?" Tess asked. "He doesn't seem old enough. . . ."

"He's close to sixty." Collette nodded. "You'd never guess it to look at him, but he is. He married his first wife, Adeline, when he was eighteen. Adam was born within a year, and then a year later she died birthing Beau."

"That's awful," Tess sighed, her thoughts straying to Emma Calloway and her own tragic demise.

"Yes," Collette agreed, "but that's only the beginning. Pa had no idea how to look after babies, nor did he have any interest, I suspect, so he remarried right away."

"That's not so unusual," Tess said. "Don't men usually remarry quickly when they have young children?"

"Maybe, but they don't usually marry their dead wife's sister!" She giggled. "It's okay, Tess, I think it's all rather amusing myself. Pa married Adeline's sister, Virginia, less than a month after Adeline died. Virginia soon found herself in the motherly way as well, and over the next seven or eight years, they had Clint, Damon, and Evan. Apparently, she was unable to carry any more children after that, though God knows they tried. To hear Beau tell it, poor Virginia lost at least one child every year after that until her death."

"How did she die?" Tess asked, shaking her head in disbelief.

"I believe she bled to death after losing one of the babies."

"Oh my Lord."

Collette nodded. "Anyway, Pa took his time in remarrying after her. Evan was the youngest at that point, I think he was about three or four. Then Pa married Harriet, who gave him Frankie and Garth, and finally he married my mother, Margaret. She passed when I was fourteen."

"My goodness, Collette, that's quite a story."

"I know there's more to the stories than what I've been told, but I'm almost afraid to ask."

"What do you mean?"

Collette's face flushed. "There's been talk in town for as long as I can remember that my parents were . . . that they . . . knew each other long before they were married. Long before Harriet ever died."

"Oh dear," Tess breathed. "That must have given the old biddies in town something to flap about, I'm sure. Has your father ever said anything to you about it?"

Collette shook her head. "I've never asked. He did marry my mother, after all, whether it was out of love or duty, I don't know, and quite frankly, I don't think I want to know."

"You're probably right," she nodded. They sat in silence for a few moments, sipping their coffee. "May I ask you something?"

"Of course."

"It's really none of my business."

"Tess," Collette smiled. "I have no secrets from you. Go ahead."

"Okay." She chewed her lip for a moment, unable to find a tactful way to phrase her question. "What is it about Adam's death that has you so guilt ridden?"

Collette blanched.

"I'm sorry, Collette," Tess hurried on. "You don't have to answer; it's none of my business. I just . . ."

"No, Tess. I'll tell you." Tess waited patiently while Collette gathered herself. "There was talk, just talk mind you, that my mother wasn't as faithful to Pa as she should have been."

"You mean . . ."

Collette nodded. "People started talking about how much time she was spending away from the ranch, away from Pa, and how much time she was spending with . . . with . . ."

"Collette?"

She cleared her throat. "With Clayton Calloway."

"What?" Tess's jaw dropped nearly to the table. "Surely . . ."

"No," Collette hurried to say, "it turned out she was going over to El Cielo quite often, but it was because of Rosa. She and Rosa had become close friends, but to the snoops in town all they saw was a married woman spending time at a widower's ranch. They even went so far as to accuse her of trying to pass me off as Pa's child when I was really Clayton's."

"But you look just like your pa!" Tess cried. "How could they even think such things?"

Collette shrugged. "People are nasty. Anyway, Clint and Damon say I looked more like Mama when I was a baby so there was really no way to tell. Pa met up with Clayton at the saloon one night and they got into it pretty badly. Pa can get terribly mean when he's been drinking, and I believe Adam was trying to keep the two of them apart when he got caught in the middle." She paused, took a sip of her now tepid coffee, and continued. "So you see, Tess, if it hadn't been for me, Adam would still be alive today."

"Oh, Collette, that's not true! It wasn't your fault, for goodness' sake. You had nothing to do with it."

"I'd like to believe that, but my stomach tumbles and rolls every time I think about it."

Tess studied the girl's face. She was sure just by the look in Collette's eyes that Wyatt Langman had done next to nothing to assuage the girl's worries.

"Mama told me the truth," Collette almost whispered, "but I still can't help but feel responsible."

"You see?" Tess smiled back. "There you go—your mother would never lie to you about something like that, would she?"

"No," she said. "Especially since she knew how I felt about Bart. If he and I shared the same father, I would need to know."

"But you said your mother passed away when you were fourteen. Surely . . ."

Collette flushed clear up to her scalp. "I've always loved Bart," she confessed. "For as long as I can remember, he's always been the one. I have always hoped and dreamed one day . . . well, that one day I would be more to him than just another stupid Langman."

"Collette!"

"It's true." The girl laughed. "I know what people say about my family, and when it comes to my brothers, they're usually right. Please don't misunderstand me, Tess. I love my brothers to death—all of them—but they do tend to be a little thick sometimes. And Bart knows it, too."

Tess's heart tightened in her chest. "You've known your whole life Bart was the one for you?"

Collette nodded.

"And you've waited all this time, even when he left town and stayed away all this while?"

Another nod. "I love him. I've always believed in the power of love, even if it seemed impossible."

Tess sighed. "That's exactly how Gabriel makes it seem—impossible."

"You haven't given up on him, have you?"

"I don't know, Collette. I know I love him, I know I will always love him, but he's determined not to love me back, so what can I do? I can't force him to love me any more than I can force myself not to love him."

"Maybe he'll come around."

"I don't think so." Tess lifted her chin a notch and tried to smile. "He's a very determined man."

"And you, Tess Kinley, are a very determined woman. If it's Gabe Calloway you want, then you have to believe it is Gabe Calloway you will have."

"It takes two, Collette, and he will not let himself get close to me."

"So what will you do? Find another man to love?"

"It's not quite that simple I'm afraid. I wish it was, though." Tess frowned down to her soul. "I won't ever love another man the way I love Gabriel. And I will not marry unless I'm in love."

Collette nodded. "We are so alike, you and I. Pa has tried, God bless him, to marry me off more times than I can count, but I always refused. I knew what I wanted; I just had to wait for him. Maybe that's all you have to do, too."

"I'd wait forever if I thought for one minute

Gabriel would eventually love me, but I don't think he ever will. I sound so pathetic, I know, but the only man I will ever marry is Gabriel. Unless he can let himself feel the same way about me, I will die an old spinster."

"Oh, Tess, there must be something we can do."

"I'm afraid not," she answered, her heart breaking as hard as her voice. "But enough moping about me. Tell me about you and Bart. What happened the other night? I was so caught up in my own selfishness, I never thought to ask."

Collette's face lit up like the morning sun.

"Oh, Tess, it was so wonderful." She closed her eyes, her hands clutched under her chin. "He told me he means to court me, to woo me, to make himself the only man in my life."

"That's wonderful!" Tess cried. "You must be so happy."

"I am," she gushed. "It's . . . well, you heard Pa. Bart Calloway is not exactly the man Pa ever envisioned me married to."

"Yes, well, I'm sure he never envisioned he'd be married to his own sister-in-law either. We can't always control our fate, Collette."

"I know, but it's going to take some time before Pa is ready to accept the fact I am going to marry Bart. Maybe not today or tomorrow, but some day."

"What about your brothers?"

Collette waved her hand through the air. "Pish. Who cares what they think? They do what Pa tells them to do and that's it. I don't think they could come up with a single idea between them."

Tess laughed. "That's an awful thing to say."

"I know, but it's true. The last great idea they had was to sneak onto El Cielo and rustle some of Gabe's herd. Just ask Beau how well that went—and he's supposed to be the smart one of the bunch."

"Bart told me about Beau and his . . . mishap," Tess admitted guiltily. "It must have hurt something awful."

"He deserved it." Collette shrugged. "Now, what do you say you and I walk into town? I hear Mrs. Clark got in a whole passel of fancy dresses and I'm dying to see them."

Tess smiled warmly. It had been a long time since she had enjoyed a relaxing afternoon with a good friend, and since Lily had agreed to share the Saturday shifts, Tess had the whole day off.

"I think that sounds wonderful. I'll go freshen up a little."

"Good idea." Collette smirked. "You never know who you might see in town, do you?"

"I . . ." Tess fumbled, a guilty grin finding its way to her mouth.

"Never you mind." She laughed. "Get yourself upstairs and make yourself as pretty as you can. If nothing else, getting all gussied up will make you feel better, and that's half the battle right there, isn't it?"

Tess flew up the stairs on featherlight feet, marveling at her good fortune. So maybe she would never have Gabriel to herself. She did have a good friend, a clean place to sleep, and a half decent job. Things could be a lot worse.

And they soon would be.

Chapter 23

"I should warn you," Collette laughed lightly, "Pa will no doubt have a great deal to say about you and I walking to town like this."

They had walked about a mile or so, the morning air still fresh with dew, when she made this announcement. Tess sighed; she couldn't seem to stay out of trouble for some reason.

"He doesn't like you going to town?" she asked.

"Oh, it's not that, although he would much prefer it if I stayed locked up in my room, I'm sure. He thinks it's too dangerous for ladies to be out walking on their own."

"But we're in the middle of nowhere, for goodness' sake," Tess said. "What on earth could happen to us out here? I mean, if we were back in Boston or somewhere like that, I could understand his concern, but what is the worst thing that can happen to us here?"

Collette shrugged jovially. "Bee sting?"

Tess laughed with her as they looped arms. "I can't imagine there being any crime at all in a town like this."

"Oh, there's trouble all right," Collette said soberly. "That's what worries me."

"What do you mean?"

Collette stopped suddenly, pulling Tess back with her.

"You mean you don't know?"

"Know what?"

"Bart," Collette said, as if that answered any question. When the confusion remained on Tess's face, Collette continued. "Sheriff Nicholls has offered Bart a job."

"What?" Tess yelped. "What are you talking about?"

Collette began to walk again. "It seems the sheriff is set on retiring and moving to Amarillo to be near his sister. He asked Bart if he'd consider taking over his duties."

"What did Bart say?" Tess was thunderstruck.

"He said yes, of course."

"He what? Is he crazy or something?"

Collette shrugged. "He's always wanted to be a lawman, Tess, you know that. That's why he became a bounty hunter."

"Being a bounty hunter is a far cry from being a sheriff," Tess said, a little too stiffly.

"Maybe," Collette agreed, "but it's either take the sheriff's job here in Porter Creek or move to Texas and join the Rangers."

"He wouldn't!"

"Yes," Collette answered, chewing her bottom lip. "He would. That's what he told me, anyway. If he can be sheriff right here, then he can settle down and get married and . . . ."

"I thought he was going to work at El Cielo with Gabriel."

The girl shook her head. "Bart has never had the ranching itch like Gabe. He's always wanted to be a lawman of some kind."

"But it's so dangerous! Even out here where it seems so peaceful . . . I'm sorry, Collette, I'm worrying you more, aren't I?"

"It's okay," Collette sighed. "You're not saying anything I haven't already thought myself. But this is what he wants to do, it's what he has always wanted. Knowing that, how can I ask him to give it up?"

"Oh, Collette," Tess sighed. "I had no idea. You must be a wreck. Finally, Bart comes home, makes his intentions clear to you, and now this. What will you do?"

"There's nothing I can do, Tess. Loving Bart means loving all of him. If he didn't have that need to make things right, he wouldn't be the Bart I know and love." She paused, smiling ruefully. "Isn't it strange how the traits that make me love him so are also the things that make me want to run screaming away from him?"

"Yes." Tess nodded. "I know exactly what you mean. It's a strange thing, love."

"What's even stranger is Bart being a lawman. No one would have guessed that's what he wanted when he was a child." Collette's smile deepened. "He was a touch wild."

"So I heard. But he doesn't seem wild now."

"No," Collette said. "He's finally settling down."

They walked a moment in silence, each lost in her own thoughts of the infamous Calloway brothers and how, frustrating as it was, they wouldn't change a thing about either one of them.

"Tell me about Boston," Collette said suddenly. "What's it like?"

Tess inhaled deeply. "Boston is a whole other world away," she said. "It's nothing like it is here, and yet both places are so wonderful, so enchanting. So scary."

"What do you mean?"

"I don't know if I can talk about it, Collette. Not yet, anyway. I . . ."

In the recesses of her mind, Tess heard the horse

approaching before her ears actually took in the sound. Whatever trouble was coming, it was coming for her. She knew that, knew there was nothing she could do to stop it, and knew in the same instant a small part of her had been expecting it.

The world around her grayed, her knees began to buckle, but before she could fall to the ground, she was scooped up from behind and hauled into the front of a saddle, the smell of stale whiskey warm against her face.

"Hello, Tess," the thick voice whispered against her hair. "I been lookin' fer you."

"Eli Gribbs." Tess didn't know if she actually said the name out loud or if her brain had simply yelled it loud enough for her ears to hear.

In the distance, Collette's cries followed the galloping horse.

"Tess! Tess!" With every passing second, the girl's voice faded further and further back in the distance.

She tried to straighten herself in the saddle, but Eli held her fast, pulling her tighter against his filth.

"What do you want, Eli?" she asked, struggling against him.

"Well, now," he sneered. "I want what's mine, and that means you, don't it?"

"I don't belong to you, Eli, so let me go."

"Can't do that," he said, his smelly breath assaulting her senses. "I got the law lookin' fer me now, and as long as I got me a hostage, they ain't gonna git their hands on me, are they?"

"Please, Eli," she pleaded, hating herself for sounding so weak. "If you just turn yourself back into the authorities, I'm sure they will . . ."

"They'll what? Hang me quicker?" He snorted. "I ain't gonna hang today, Tess. An' as long as I got you, I figure I'm safe."

The jolting of the horse and the horrid stench of

Gribbs worked together to make Tess's head pound inside her skull. She couldn't let him take her away; she'd never see Gabriel again, she'd never have her own little farm, her own cows, her own . . .

"I been a long time without a woman, Tess, and I mean to fix that right quick like."

Tess's spine went rigid; for a moment she thought she would be sick, but she quickly regained her senses and forced herself to think. She couldn't let him touch her! Heaven help her, what would Gabriel think if another man . . . why would Gabriel care? He didn't want her.

She quelled the shudder that raced from the base of her spine to her scalp.

"Why don't you go back to Dottie's saloon? I'm sure there's a . . . someone . . . there who would be quite happy to . . . to . . ."

She swallowed hard, unable to push the words out.

Gribbs laughed—a loud, thick, filthy laugh.

"To what Tess? Touch me? Let me . . ." His thick tongue lapped at her earlobe, slurping along her neck as though he were a child with a new candy.

Bile rose in Tess's throat. She struggled furiously against him, but his grip was surprisingly strong.

"I don't want a whore to do that to me, Tess," he gritted, his lips pressing against her neck. "I want a lady—a real lady. I ain't never had me a real lady before. I know you want it. . . ."

"Let go of me!" she screeched, reaching to claw at his face. "You are a pig, Eli Gribbs! I wouldn't let you touch me if you were the last man on earth!"

The harder she fought him, the tighter his grip became. He grasped her wrists with one hand, somehow managing to control the reins at the same time. His other arm wrapped around her middle, pulling her tight against him. To her shock and horror, she realized Eli was already disgustingly aroused and eager to have his way with her. She struggled and squirmed against him, her screams echoing back to her. She was wasting her breath. There wasn't another soul around for miles; no one to hear her cries.

"Go ahead and scream, Tess," he hissed. "By the time I'm done with you, you won't have any voice left. I'm gonna . . ."

Tess's terror blocked out the rest of his words. She couldn't let this happen—she wouldn't let him touch her.

Think! If she didn't get away from him, there was no telling what he'd do to her. And how on earth would she ever face Gabriel again if she didn't do everything in her power to get away from this animal?

Gabriel. She willed him to hear her pleas, willed him to come after her, to take her in his arms and chase this nightmare away. She kept his face in the forefront of her mind—her reason to fight. The minute Gribbs loosened his grip just a bit she'd make her escape. Somehow.

Gribbs reined the horse to a stop in front of an old rundown shack about fifteen miles out of town. He yanked Tess down from the saddle, keeping her wrists bound within his grasp.

"Please, Eli," she said, forcing her voice steady. "Don't do this. Just let me go. I swear I won't say anything to anyone. You can ride out of here and no one will ever know. Please . . ."

"I love to hear women beg," he sneered, ignoring her pleas. "Come on."

He yanked her through the fallen-in doorway and shoved her across the room, his hands finally releasing their grip on her. She tripped over a three-legged bench and an old decaying straw tick before she regained her balance. Her eyes searched the room frantically for anything—an escape, a weapon, anything. There was nothing. Not a pot, not a gun, nothing.

The one-room shack was barely large enough to be considered a house, but apparently some poor soul had lived there at one time. A shredded piece of blue cotton dangled from above the only window in the room—a window that was closer to the door than it was to Tess. A wooden crate stood upended under the window, and other than the bench and tick, the room was empty.

Glancing swiftly around again, her eye caught sight of something—a tiny framed picture lying amid the rubble. Not a single shard of glass remained to protect the picture, but the image was unmarked. She reached to pick it up, keeping one eye on Gribbs who had somehow managed to get his horse in through the doorway and was now tethering it to the door handle.

Tess's fingers wrapped around the frame, then opened to reveal the image. An angel. Tess's heart sang with relief—it had to be a sign of some kind. The tiny body of the cherub had been drawn with the finest of inks, its wings from silver, and the halo shone brilliantly golden even in the dim light of the shack.

An angel—her Angel Gabriel. Surely he would come for her, wouldn't he? This had to mean something, it just had to.

Eli turned and faced Tess, his boots scuffing against the dirt floor as he inched his way toward her, like a vulture closing in on its prey. Tess backed into the wall, still searching for anything that might help her. She clutched the drawing in her hand, willing it to give her strength. Gribbs took another step closer. Then another.

Tess couldn't breathe. Her heart tried to pound its way out of her chest, and her knees threatened to buckle out from under her at any moment. And still Gribbs moved closer.

"I don't wanna hafta get rough." He grinned, his black teeth seeming to drip with tobacco juice. His greasy black hair hung to his shoulders, his unshaven cheeks covered in scars and bruises. He took another step closer and Tess ducked, trying to run past him. Quick as lightning, his arm closed around her, hauling her up against him again.

"Where d'ya think yer goin'?" he chuckled. "I ain't near done with you yet."

He shoved her down on the old tick, never lessening his hold. His right leg moved over so he straddled her middle, and then he released her wrists. She immediately flailed against him, dropping the angel and tossing and twisting in a vain attempt to free herself.

"I like a gal with spirit," he sneered as he unbuttoned his pants and pulled his shirt out of the way. Tess's eyes slammed shut, but her mouth opened wider, forcing out still louder screams.

"Ain't no one gonna hear ya, Tess, 'cept me, and I like a little fight." His grimy hands pawed her face and neck, then stilled against the collar of her dress. It was Collette's dress, a dainty yellow calico with lace edging and hem.

Collette! Tess's mind raced. Of course—Collette would have sent help! Assuming, of course, she'd made it either back home or to town by then.

Gribbs's fingers tightened on the top button of Tess's collar. In one lightning fast tear, he ripped the front of the dress wide open, exposing the flimsy camisole beneath. Tess's throat, now screamed raw, was unable to make another sound. She pounded against Gribbs with her fists, clawed at him with her nails, and twisted beneath him but was still unable to budge him an inch.

He raised himself to his knees long enough to rip open the rest of the dress. Then he captured her wrists again and bound them to the broken bench with his belt.

"That oughta hold ya for a minute," he growled. He raised himself to his feet, still towering over her, and removed his pants altogether. Tess turned her head and retched onto the tick—this couldn't be happening. It just couldn't be.

Gribbs sank back to his knees, this time forcing Tess's legs wide.

"Please," she begged again. "Please . . ."

"That's it," he grinned. "Beg. I love that."

Tess's face burned with fire-hot tears of fury.

"I bet yer real soft," he tormented her. "Real soft. An' I ain't gonna hand you over 'til I find out fer myself. Let's have a feel, shall we?"

His hands reached for the camisole, his fingers finding the lace edging and tugging at it—surprisingly gently.

Tess's bound hands tugged frantically at their bonds, her whole body thrashing beneath him, but he was completely unmoved by it. In fact, he didn't even seem to notice, so intent was he on what lay beneath her camisole. *So* intent, in fact, he either didn't notice or chose to ignore the way the horse nickered and stamped its feet.

"Tess!"

The door flew open and in burst Gabriel and Bart—both with guns drawn.

"What the—" Before Gribbs could finish, Gabe smashed him across the side of the head with the butt of his gun and hauled Tess into his arms, tearing her free of her bonds as he did so. He dropped the gun to the floor and carried her out of the shack, lowering her gently to the grass, his gray eyes searching her face silently.

"Are you hurt?" he asked, his hands making short work of what was left of the belt.

Tess shook her head, the terror in her eyes haunting him like nothing before had. With the belt tossed away, Gabe's hands twitched, not knowing what to do or where to touch. He wanted to take her in his arms, to kiss away her fear and her trembling. He wanted to . . .

Tess threw her arms around his neck and sobbed like a child. Never had his heart pounded so fast, never had he been so scared, never had he been so relieved.

Chapter 24

"Oh, Gabriel," she cried. "I was so scared. I . . ."

"Shh," he murmured against her hair, his trembling arms circling around her. "It's all right now. You're going to be fine."

"But he . . . how did you . . . Collette!"

"Collette's fine," he said. "She's resting at the ranch, waiting for us to bring you back."

"But how did you know where he'd bring me?"

"It doesn't matter, Tess," he soothed, smoothing her hair back from her cheek. "All that matters is you're safe now. Are you sure you're not hurt?"

"I'm okay." She nodded, unable to force even a small smile. "I . . . oh, Gabriel . . ." She eased back, her eyes lowered, and saw the state of her dress—of Collette's dress. "Oh, no—look at this!"

Suddenly she realized she was half-naked, covered only by her thin camisole and drawers. She hastened to pull the ripped sides of the dress together, but Gabe's huge hands covered hers. His tenderness only made Tess cry harder.

"Here," he said softly. He quickly unbuttoned his own shirt and wrapped her in it, gently pushing away her hands when she tried to button it. "Let me do it."

His fingers fumbled over every button, but at last they were all secured. Her cold hand turned Gabe's cheek until his eyes met hers, and it was then Tess saw it—the terror she herself had felt just moments before mirrored in Gabe's face.

"I'm okay," she said softly, finally able to force her lips into a weak smile. "Thanks to you."

A strange chill ran up her spine at the sight of the man in front of her. His broad, bare chest, bronzed by the sun, beckoned her toward it, toward the man who had literally given her the shirt from his own back in order to protect her dignity. He wore a strange look—the same look she'd seen some weeks ago when she'd donned the clothes from his wardrobe. It was a look of confusion, of longing, and of an almost tangible sorrow.

Tess's hands, quivering and small, reached tentatively toward him, needing to touch him.

"Tess," he said, his voice choking on the single word. "I . . ."

Bart shoved the hastily dressed Gribbs out of the shack ahead of him and waved his Colt in the man's sweaty face. Blood trickled down his left temple where Gabe had hit him with the gun, and his right eye had already begun to swell—from what injury, Tess had no idea.

Her hands fell back to her sides, her entire being consumed with guilt and shame for the lust-filled thoughts she'd had just a moment before.

Bart slammed Gribbs against the side of the building, face first, sending shingles flying from the roof.

"You even think about breathin' the wrong way, Gribbs, and I swear I'll kill you right where you stand." He ducked back in the shack long enough to retrieve Gribbs's horse. He bound the man's wrists with a rope from his saddlebag and shoved him toward his animal. "Get on."

Without a word, Gribbs grasped the horn with both hands and hauled himself into the saddle. Bart fastened the end of the rope to the horn, securing Gribbs in place before taking the reins in his hands and climbing up on his own mount, pulling Gribbs's animal alongside him. He turned to look at his brother and Tess.

"You okay?"

Tess couldn't decide if his question was aimed at her or at Gabe, but either way, she couldn't find a voice to answer him. The sight of Eli Gribbs and the thought of what he had intended to do to her, in fact would have done to her, rendered her speechless once again.

"Fine." Gabe's voice sounded as weak as a baby's. Bart bobbed his head in a nod before he turned both horses back the way they'd come and spurred them toward Porter Creek, his shiny black Colt pointed menacingly at the man to his left.

The silence that followed nearly consumed Tess. Her angel had come for her; her angel had saved her from a fate worse than death; and now her angel stood behind her, his breath as ragged as her own, his chest heaving with each intake of breath. She wished she knew what he was thinking, wished he was thinking the same thing she was—how the only thing she wanted was to throw herself back into his embrace and stay there, warm and secure, for the rest of her days.

But she couldn't let herself do it. He had made himself clear on the fact he could not let himself love her, and she was certainly not going to force herself on him or make him feel responsible for her. If he ever came to her, he would have to come willingly and because he loved her as much as she loved him.

Tess's stomach tossed and threatened, so great was her fear. Fear not only because of her encounter with Eli Gribbs, but because of what she would see when she turned to face Gabriel. Now that she was safe once again, he would no doubt be angry with her for walking into town with Collette the way she had, and he would very probably insist she be on the next stage. In fact, she wouldn't be surprised if he . . .

"Come on, I'll take you home." Gabe's voice was so soft it felt like velvet against Tess's ears.

His reaction surprised her such that she was unable to move and remained frozen where she stood.

"Are you all right?" he asked, walking around in front of her. "If he . . ."

"I . . . I'm fine," she stammered. "J-just a little shaky, I guess."

Without a moment's hesitation, Gabe lifted her effortlessly from where she stood and swung her up into Zeus's saddle before climbing up himself. He shifted back as far as he could and without a word pulled Tess gently against him, her legs dangling over the left side of the horse.

"Relax," he murmured above her head. "I've got you."

I know you do, Tess's heart cried. *I know you do.*

He urged Zeus into a slow walk, so unlike the thundering ride she'd been forced to endure with Gribbs a short while ago. Tess forced herself not to lean against him, not to notice the warmth of his skin or his acute, masculine fragrance. She had to be strong; she had to resist her urges and refuse her heart. She could not let him pity her.

"Gabriel," she said, though it was so soft she feared perhaps she hadn't spoken at all. She cleared her throat and tried to sit up a little straighter, but Gabe's arms held her fast.

"Gabriel," she repeated, slightly louder.

"Hmmm?"

"I want to thank you for coming for me." She felt the lump beginning to build at the base of her throat, but she forced it back—twice. "You didn't have to, I know, and I can't even imagine what would have happened if you hadn't. . . ."

Her voice broke at the memory of Gribbs, straddled over her wearing only his unbuttoned filthy shirt. She squeezed her eyes shut against it and took another deep breath.

"I don't know how I can ever repay you for coming," she said. "I owe you my life."

Gabe's response was to place his hand gently along the side of her head and ease it toward his chest. He spoke not a word, but his hand repeatedly stroked the side of her face with a tenderness she had never experienced before.

Gabe's throat ached with the tears he forced back. He knew if he so much as opened his mouth, he'd fall apart right there in the saddle for all the world to see. Big Gabe Calloway crying like a baby. But damn it, he'd never been so scared in all his life. He couldn't remember a thing Collette had said past "Tess was taken." It was as though his whole world stopped right there and then. He might well have stopped breathing himself, so great was his fear.

For the millionth time since hearing Collette's frantic cries, Gabe thanked God for the good fortune he had not removed Zeus's saddle after checking the herd that morning. The few precious minutes it would have taken him to get the saddle on would have been all Gribbs needed to finish what he had started with Tess. An icy shiver raced through Gabe's veins. If he'd been a minute longer, if Collette hadn't made it back to the ranch, if Zeus had thrown a shoe, if Gribbs had ridden a little faster—that's all it would have taken.

Gabe had never killed another man—had never even considered it—but he would have done it today without a second thought. His mind flashed to the sight of Gribbs leaning over Tess, exposing himself and bent on taking her whether she wanted to or not. He could have shot him right there—and would have, too, if it weren't for the fact Gribbs would have fallen right on top of Tess.

He'd never felt rage like that before; never not cared what a man's life was worth. But Gribbs was not a man, he was an animal. An animal who had put his hands on Tess; who had touched her, put his mouth on her. On Tess, on *his* Tess.

Gabe's jaw tightened. Here she was, this strong, frightened little angel, sitting in his lap after what was probably the worst ordeal of her life. And it was his fault. He knew Gribbs was on the loose—hell, both Bart and Sheriff Nicholls had told him that much—and yet he had done nothing to protect her. He'd let her leave the ranch and live in town of all places! He should have known Gribbs would come looking for her. He should have kept her at El Cielo until the law hunted Gribbs down and put him where he belonged—in hell.

But he hadn't done that. He had let Tess wander unknowingly into danger when he could have very well prevented it. And what was she doing now? Thanking him for saving her! If it wasn't for him, she wouldn't have been in that situation to start with, and all she could do was thank him. Damn it all anyway, she should be mad as hell but she wasn't.

She sat in front of him, her petite body trembling, and tried to pretend she was as brave as she could be, lifting her chin, straightening her spine, and swallowing back her tears.

God, but he loved this woman.

The realization nearly knocked him out of the saddle. He really and honestly loved Tess Kinley. He was *in love* with her and would have gladly died today if it meant she would have been safe and unharmed.

Every knot in his heart loosened and an unfamiliar warmth spread over him like a flannel blanket on a winter's day.

He loved Tess Kinley. He would never be able to let her go, even if she wanted him to. How could he have been so stupid to try and send her away? What the hell had he been thinking? He needed her, he *wanted* her—hell, he didn't honestly think he could take another breath without her.

He was no longer concerned about her leaving him—it was a distant worry, one so tiny it was barely a flicker in his heart. He would do everything in his power to keep her right there with him, beside him, as they journeyed through life together. She would bear his children, God willing, and he would love and cherish every single minute they had together. If that was one day, one week, or one hundred years, he would spend every waking moment making her happy.

He could barely contain his excitement now. They would get married and start on a family right away—tonight if at all possible. But wait. A lady like Tess needed to be pampered, she needed a home, not just a house like he had at El Cielo. Of course, she would deny the notion and insist she'd be happy as the house was, but it wasn't a home. It needed something . . . something that would help make it hers . . . something like that new-fangled, built-in tub Harvey Clark had on display in the mercantile!

Gabe's smile lit up his heart. Tess loved to be clean, to soak in a tub full of hot water. He'd buy her that fancy tub for a wedding gift and have it installed right away. Maybe Rosa could help him make the place look a little more . . . lived in . . . instead of just stayed in.

Of course, Tess would have to agree to all of this.

And right now she was being decidedly more quiet than he would have liked. It wasn't like her to not have something to say.

"Tess," he said, barely above a whisper. No answer. "Tess?"

Then he heard it—the soft, even breathing of a sleeping angel. He shifted her gently, moving her closer to him until she snuggled right up against his chest, tucking her face into the curve of his neck. Nothing in all his thirty-two years had ever felt as good as that. Nothing had ever felt as right, as perfect, as if that was how God had meant it to be.

He chuckled softly. How could she sleep at a time like this? He'd finally realized and accepted what his heart had been yelling at him all this time, and she was sound asleep. If she hadn't been through such an ugly ordeal, he'd have woken her up right there and yelled it out for the whole world to hear.

Maybe it was for the best. He'd keep his little secret for a few more days while he talked to Rosa and got the tub installed. Then he'd tell Tess. If he told her any sooner, she'd insist he save his money, and then he wouldn't be able to get her the tub or any other of the fancy things she deserved, like honey-scented soap and fancy satin bonnets. Hot damn, he might even shock the hell out of Mrs. Clark and buy Tess some of those red silk petticoats he'd seen in Rosa's catalog. He'd be more than happy to go flat broke buying the woman anything and everything to make her happy.

He couldn't wait to tell her all about his plan, about the undeniable extent of his love for her, and about the love he was going to show her—on their wedding night and every night for the rest of his life. It was going to be perfect, he'd make damn sure of that, and if he had to wait a couple days before he told her, then so be it. Better he have it all figured out than go off half-cocked and have her refuse the surprises he had in store for her.

For now, he would settle for having her in his arms, her honey scent all around them, as he took her safely home.

Chapter 25

Tess's senses returned one by one. The first thing she felt was the warmth of his skin where her face was pressed against him. She savored it for a long moment before letting anything else intrude. Next she inhaled his scent, the all-Gabriel scent of leather and sunshine. What was that sound? Was Gabriel humming? Tess's eyes flew open—he was humming! She glanced around quickly, trying to get her bearings, but it only took a moment to realize where she was.

El Cielo. He was supposed to have taken her home but he brought her here instead.

"How are you feeling?" His voice startled her, making her jump. Huge, warm hands soothed her back down, easing her head back to his shoulder. "Sorry, didn't mean to scare you."

"I . . . I . . ."

"You were sleeping."

"Yes," she answered, more than a little embarrassed.

"That's good," he said softly. "It's what you needed."

"How did you know I was awake?" she asked, still tucked up against his bare chest.

Gabe chuckled, low and throaty. "Your eyelashes."

"My what?" She made to pull away again, but he held her close.

"Your eyelashes brush against my neck when you blink," he said.

Tess gulped. "Oh, sorry."

"Why? I'm not."

Gabriel actually sounded happy; something must be wrong. Surely it wasn't her he was happy with.

"Why are we here?" she asked, then suddenly realized exactly where they were, "And why are we sitting on your horse?"

"I told you I was going to take you home," he said. "And you were asleep, so we were just resting here until you woke up."

Tess's eyes darted around the bit of yard she could see. "How long have we been sitting here?" she asked.

She felt Gabe shrug. "Dunno, about half an hour, I guess."

"What?" This time she did pull away from him and sat up. "We've been sitting here in the yard for half an hour?"

Gabe's eyes twinkled merrily. "Yup."

"Why didn't you wake me?"

"You were sleeping."

"Yes, I know, but you could have woken me, for goodness' sake. People must think we're as crazy as a couple of loons sitting here like this."

"Who cares what people think? You've had a . . . trying . . . morning, you were tired and so I let you sleep."

Tess couldn't for the life of her decipher what that grin meant. She'd never seen him behave so oddly before and, quite frankly, she was more than just a little concerned.

"Well, I'm awake now. Perhaps we should get down."

Gabe shrugged again. "If you want. No hurry."

Tess eyed him carefully. Something wasn't quite right, something he obviously wasn't about to share with her just yet.

"Is Collette still here?" she asked, none too eager to leave the confines of Gabe's arms.

"She's in the house with Bart." Gabe's brows drew together in a frown. "Is there something going on there I don't know about? Something between her and my brother?"

Tess couldn't hide her own smile this time. "I hope so," she breathed.

"What the hell's that supposed to mean?" he blurted. "She's a Langman, you know?"

"Oh, who cares? She loves Bart, and as for him, well, I've never seen a man quite so taken with a woman before."

Tess cringed. She hadn't meant to insinuate anything by the remark, but Gabe was sure to think she had. When she finally worked up the courage to look up at him, he was looking right back at her with the silliest grin spread across his face.

"So Bart's in love with a Langman, is he?" he said, shaking his head. "I wager he's in for a world of trouble."

"And I'll wager he already knows that. But love does strange things to people, Gabriel. It gives them a strength they never knew they had, and yet scares the bejeepers out of them all at the same time."

Gabe's grin widened even more. "Is that so?" he said. "Interesting."

The shine in Gabe's eyes never wavered for a moment and, in fact, seemed to grow stronger the longer he looked at her. With every last ounce of willpower, Tess finally dragged her gaze away from his, only to look straight into his still bare chest.

"Oh, dear Lord," she gasped. "Perhaps you should . . . oh, I have it, don't I?"

Her trembling fingers found the buttonhole at her neck and began to free the buttons of Gabe's shirt.

"Hold on there." He chuckled. "As tempting as it

is to have you take it off, I think my shirt should stay right where it is for now. Your dress isn't exactly in the best of condition."

"Oh! I wasn't even thinking." Her eyes remained transfixed on his skin. It was as though she were in a trance, unable to blink or even think. Her hand moved of its own accord, reaching for him, pressing against the expanse of his muscled body. The minute her fingers touched him, lightning surged up her arm, scorching her through to her soul. Her arm jerked, but her hand remained where it was as if permanently fixed there. She tried to lift it off, but it would not move.

Gabe raised his own hand slowly and covered hers with it. A tiny gasp escaped Tess's throat.

"Oh," she sighed. "I'm sorry. I didn't mean . . ."

"Don't be sorry," he said again, the same shine glowing in his gray eyes. "I'm not."

Tess's mortification glowed fire red against her cheeks. What was the matter with her anyway?

"I-I don't know what I was thinking," she stammered, her chin dropping to her chest.

"Don't worry about it." His voice was so close Tess thought she should be able to physically touch it. "Come on, Collette's probably about ready to send out the cavalry looking for you."

He slid down from the saddle, easing Tess down after him, and lifted her chin with the crook of his finger.

"You have nothing to be ashamed of," he said. "Nothing that happened today was your fault. Not with Gribbs and not now."

"But I . . ." Tess flushed even more.

"Shh." Gabe touched his finger to her mouth. "*Nothing* was your fault."

Tess shivered against the warmth of his finger. If she'd had even an ounce of strength left, she would have been able to suppress the soft groan that escaped her lips.

"Come on," he urged gently, giving her hand a soft squeeze. "Let's go in. Are you okay to walk?"

"Yes," she squeaked, her humiliation growing with every second he looked at her that way. It wasn't quite a mocking grin, but it definitely had something behind it.

She hurried up the stairs ahead of him and let herself in through the kitchen.

"Tess!" Collette nearly flew across the kitchen at her. "Are you hurt?"

"No." Tess smiled softly, glancing at Bart. "Thanks to those Calloway boys."

"Bart's been telling me about that awful man Eli Gribbs. How horrible! Why didn't you tell me any of this before, Tess?"

Tess sighed. "I think I was about to when all of this happened. It's over now, though, so can we please just put it behind us?"

Collette nodded and reached for the coffeepot.

"Rosa made us a fresh pot, although it has been sitting for a while." She hesitated a moment, then fought to stifle a giggle. "I didn't think you two were ever going to come in the house."

Tess flushed again. "I was sleeping," she said guiltily, "and Gabriel . . ."

Collette nudged her gently and whispered, "It wasn't sleep I witnessed, Tess, so don't be trying to fool me."

"Oh dear." Tess slumped into the nearest chair, her forehead falling onto the table in front of her. "I'm so embarrassed. I . . ."

Collette patted her shoulder softly. "You don't have to explain yourself to me, Tess. I know exactly how you feel."

Tess sat back up and accepted the strong brew.

Gabe had not come into the house but stood in the kitchen doorway, his eyes never leaving Tess.

"I better go tell Rosa we're back," he said quietly. "Bart, you coming?"

"What for? I'm havin' some coffee."

"Bart." All three of them turned at Gabe's voice. There was a quiet insistence in it that had Bart on his feet and headed toward the door in a flash.

Letting Bart out ahead of him, Gabe nodded and smiled at the women. "Be right back."

They watched him go in silence, then Collette took the chair across from Tess.

"What was that all about?" she asked. "With Gabe, I mean?"

Tess shrugged wearily. "I have no idea, Collette. He's been acting very strange and I haven't a clue what to make of it."

"What do you mean?"

Tess took a long drink of coffee. "He was humming."

"Gabe?" Collette choked. "Humming?"

"Yes." She nodded. "And that's not all. He's been smiling, too—a strange sort of smile I can't even begin to decipher."

"Strange," Collette agreed over her mug. "Very strange, indeed. But tell me truthfully: Did that horrible animal hurt you?"

"No, not really," Tess said. "He certainly scared me, I'll say that much for him, and if it weren't for Gabriel and Bart, there's no telling what he would have done, but it's over now. I just want to forget about it."

"Oh, Tess, it's so awful. I was so frightened, I didn't think I'd make it back here in time. I kept tripping on my silly skirt and screaming like a crazy woman until Gabe came running up the road to see what was going on."

"Thank you, Collette." Tess took her friend's hands in hers. "If you hadn't made it back here when you did, I'm afraid . . ." Her throat closed and her eyes burned. "Thank you."

"You're like the sister I never had," Collette answered, her huge blue eyes glistening with tears. "I want us to stay that way forever."

"And we will," Tess assured her, "if I have anything to say about it."

Despite having a head start, Bart had to hurry to keep up with Gabe.

"What's so goldarned important I had to leave a perfectly good cup a' joe?" he asked.

Gabe didn't turn to look at him or even miss a stride. "I'm going to marry Tess."

He pulled a clean shirt from the line as he walked and shrugged into it.

"You're what?" Bart grabbed his brother by the arm and whirled him back around, nearly colliding with him in the process.

Gabe stopped, laughed out loud, and shrugged. "I'm gonna marry her, Bart."

"But . . . what? When?"

"I haven't figured that out yet," he said. "But when I do, you'll be the second to know."

"What the hell d'ya mean second? Who's first?"

"Tess, of course." He started toward Rosa's cabin again.

"Gabe!" Bart shouted. "Would you stop for just a flippin' second? You mean she doesn't know? You haven't asked her?"

"You ask enough questions for the both of us." Gabe laughed, never slowing his pace. "And, no, she doesn't know yet, so I'd be thankful for you not saying anything yet. To anyone."

"I don't know what the hell you're goin' on about, brother. You can't marry a girl 'less you ask her first you know. That's the way it's done. 'Sides, what are ya waitin' for? Why not just ask 'er?"

"I've got a plan, Bart, that's why." He pushed through the gate to the cabin and marched on ahead.

"This I've gotta hear," Bart mumbled, hustling behind him.

"Rosa!" Gabe called, banging on the front door. "Rosa, you here?"

"Si," the woman's voice called back through the door. "Come."

Rosa was in the kitchen, as usual, baking Miguel's favorite cherry pie.

"Ah, Gabe Calloway," she half smiled. "La niña?"

"She's fine," he answered quickly. "Listen, I need your help with something, and we have to be able to get it all figured out in a few days. Can you help me?"

"Si."

"He's gettin' married!" Bart burst out. "Can you believe that shit, Rosa? *Gabe* is gettin' married. Or he hopes he is anyway."

"Jeez, Bart! Just can't keep that damned mouth shut, can you?"

"What you talk 'bout?" Rosa asked, her fingers resting on the pastry. "Who Gabe Calloway marry?"

Gabe's face-wide grin returned. "I'm hoping to marry Tess, but I'm going to need your help."

"What you mean—hope? What that?" She rubbed her hands across her apron and crossed the room, eyeing him suspiciously the entire time.

"Okay," he sighed. "Here's the thing. I want to marry her but I haven't asked yet because, well, I just realized it today, and after what happened this morning it doesn't seem like quite the right time, if you know what I mean. But before I ask her, I want to do some changes around here—make it more lady friendly."

Rosa's face positively glowed. "Gabe Calloway marry Tess Kinley? La niña?"

Gabe nodded, proud as a peacock.

"He thinks he's gonna anyway," Bart snickered. "I think he's puttin' the cart before the horse myself. How d'you know she even wants you anymore? You ain't exactly been eager for her attention lately."

"I know, I know, but it's going to happen, Bart. Mark my words."

"What you need?" Rosa asked. "I do."

The three of them sat down in the tiny living room area as Gabe spilled forth his plan.

"What I want to do is get that fancy tub ol' Harvey has in his store and put it inside the house."

"Where?" Bart chuckled. "In the kitchen?"

Gabe shook his head. "That's where you come in, Bart. I need a room added on to the house. Big enough for the tub and whatever else I can think to put in there."

"A new room? In a few days?"

"Yeah." Gabe nodded. "It's not like you have a job or anything to get to. You've got lots of time and we've got plenty of lumber, so that's not a problem."

"Well, actually," Bart began, "I, um . . ."

"What?"

"Ferget it." He grinned with a shrug. "Ain't important."

"And, Rosa," Gabe continued, "I need some girly stuff—like lacy things, you know. Got any ideas?"

Rosa laughed and reached beside her chair for her stack of outdated magazines. "You look," she said, pointing to the inside pages. "You pick."

Gabe at least had the decency to blush a little. "Later. I need some stuff for the house, too."

"Like what?" Bart snickered. "A new room with a built-in tub ain't gonna be enough? I don't think Tess'll really care what the hell's inside the house as long as you're there."

"Maybe." Gabe nodded. "But I'm going to make damn good and sure there's everything in that house she could ever want. And then some."

Bart sobered. "She won't leave you, Gabe. You don't gotta try and win her by flashin' around all yer money."

"I know, and it's *our* money. The ranch is part yours."

"Now hold on there just a second, Gabe," Bart said, rising to his feet. "I ain't earned one red cent of that money and you know it. If anyone deserves part of this stupid ranch, it's Miguel. He's the one worked it all these years."

"Sit down for crying out loud," Gabe sighed. "I know damn well who this ranch belongs to, and if anything should happen to me, Tess gets my third."

"Your *third*?"

"Of course," he answered a little impatiently. "Had a lawyer draw up papers years ago putting the ranch in all three of our names—you, me, and Miguel."

"Does he know?"

"Of course he knows! Mad as a peeled rattler when I told him, but he knows."

The three of them laughed together for a moment, then Gabe spoke again.

"So are you two going to help me?"

Chapter 26

"Perhaps it would be better if Miguel took us home," Collette said when Bart and Gabe returned a while later.

"I'll take you," the brothers chorused in unison.

Collette laughed softly, but it was Tess who answered.

"No, Collette's right. Mr. Langman wouldn't be very receptive to having either one of you on his land again this soon."

"I don't give a . . ."

"Bart." Tess's voice was low but firm. "Please."

"All right," he grumbled. "I'll go find him."

Collette followed him out into the yard, leaving Tess alone in the house with Gabe. Consumed with guilt for her shameless act earlier, she could not bring herself to look at him.

"You sure you're okay?" he asked softly, keeping his distance from her.

Tess nodded. "Yes, thank you. I'm sorry for all the trouble. It seems to follow me around, doesn't it?"

Gabe chuckled. "So it would seem."

From the corner of her eye, she spotted Miguel leading the team of horses from the barn.

"Well," she said, swallowing hard. "I guess I'll be going now. Thank you again for . . . for today. If there's anything I can ever do for you or Bart, you will ask, won't you?"

"Oh, yeah," he answered, that silly grin spread across his face again. "I'll be sure and ask. Probably sooner than you think."

Tess's eyes shot upward, locking on his.

"I don't understand," she said.

"You will." He stepped out the door, holding it open for her to pass. "I'll see you tomorrow."

"Tomorrow?"

"You are going to church tomorrow, aren't you?"

"Y-yes," she answered, "but . . ."

"So I'll see you there. If you need a lift into town, send word and I'll come pick you up."

Tess stared agape for what felt like hours. Gabe smiled and went to talk to Miguel. Bart had already handed Collette up into the wagon and then turned to help a still stunned Tess.

"Don't bother tryin' to figure him out," Bart said, shaking his head slowly. "I ain't figured him out yet and I've known him a helluva lot longer than you have."

Tess sat down beside Collette. "Bart," she said softly, reaching for his hand, "thank you for your help today. If there's anything I can ever do for you . . ."

A dazzling glint flashed in his brown eyes. "I think you already have, Miss Tess. We'll call it square, okay?"

Tess released his hand and asked with feigned innocence, "We'll see you soon then?"

Bart laughed as he and Gabe waved them off. But then they did the most curious thing; they picked up the axe and saw at the barn door and headed off to the area of dense tree growth directly behind the house. What on earth were they doing? Even Tess had noticed how much firewood was stacked beside the house—they certainly wouldn't be needing any more for weeks to come.

They rode back to Langman's ranch in relative silence, although several times Tess caught Miguel looking at her in the most peculiar way—almost as if he knew something about her, but what? She pushed the thought from her mind and tried equally hard not to think too much about church services the next morning. She should be looking forward to going to church so she could hear the Lord's word, not because Gabe was going to be there. But still, it did add a little more to the day knowing he would be.

Miguel helped them both down from the wagon and bid them farewell with a short bow and a broad smile.

"Something very strange is going on," Tess mused. "Very strange indeed."

She did not have a moment to ponder the situation. The moment they opened the door to the house, they were met head-on by Wyatt Langman and three of his sons. One was Stupid Frankie and the other one she remembered was Evan, but the third one she couldn't remember—Garth or Clint?

"You been spendin' time with them Calloways again?" he demanded.

"Yes, Pa," Collette said with a sigh, "but it's not how it looks."

"If it ain't what it looks like, girl, then what the hell is it?"

"I hear'd y'all spent the afternoon over there," said the unknown brother.

"An' you." Evan nodded toward Tess. "You was ridin' 'round with the oldest one there an' he weren't wearin' no shirt!"

"Please," Collette said calmly. "Let us explain what happened. It was all very innocent."

"Bullshit."

Wyatt's hand flew up and cracked Stupid Frankie on the back of the head.

"Won't have no cursin' in front of the ladies."

"But Pa—"

"Shut up, Frankie." He turned a pointed finger back at Collette. "You best get to explainin'."

Tess put her hand out to stop Collette. "Please, let me."

Collette began to protest, but Tess shook her head. Finally, Collette agreed.

"Mr. Langman," Tess began, "the fault is mine. You see, before I moved to Porter Creek, I had the bad fortune of making enemies with a loathsome man who apparently thought it worth his while to track me down here. It's a rather long story, but the gist of it is while Collette and I were walking into town this morning, this . . . er, man . . . rode up behind us and grabbed me. God knows what would have happened to me if your daughter had not made her way to El Cielo and told the Calloways what had happened. They immediately set off to find me, which they did, thank goodness, and now we are all home safe and sound."

She took a deep breath, only just realizing she had not inhaled since she started her story. She braced herself for Wyatt Langman's interrogation—surely he would question her virtue now, if he hadn't already. After all, how many women made enemies with men who tracked them down like animals and kidnapped them?

"You walked into town?" Wyatt's question wasn't even directed at Tess, but at his daughter.

"Y-yes," she answered. "It was such a nice morning, and Tess has never had the opportunity to . . ."

"You walked into town?" he repeated, his tone distinctly sharper. "Alone?"

"Yes, Pa."

"Damn it all to hell, Lettie," he shouted, apparently forgetting his own no-cursing and no-yelling rules. "How many times I gotta tell ya it ain't safe?"

"Yeah, Lettie," the unknown brother piped in, pushing more tobacco into his already swollen lip.

"Shut up, Clint," Collette snapped. "Pa, I'm nine-teen years old. For goodness' sake, when am I going to be old enough to look after myself?"

"Never! 'Long as yer livin' under my roof, I make the rules, ya hear?" He pointed his crooked finger at Tess. "That goes fer you, too, hear? I won't have no daughter of mine keepin' time with the likes of them there Calloways, so you jus' stay as far away from them no good varmints as you can. Hear?"

"But, Pa," Collette moaned, taking a step toward him.

"You hear?" he bellowed.

Collette and Tess nodded in unison and watched, blanched, as the four men stomped out of the house. Only then did poor Collette burst into tears.

"You see, Tess? What am I going to do? He hates Bart and Bart hates him . . . oh, it's the worst!"

"No, it isn't, Collette. Things can always be worse." Tess smiled down at the poor girl who had crumpled to the floor. "Believe me, it can always be worse."

Collette laughed through her tears, and they each retired to their rooms for the evening. Tess spent most of the night flat on her back, wide awake. Gabriel was going to be at church. He even offered her a ride if she needed one. What on earth was going on in the man's head? As far as that went, what on earth had gone on in her own mind all day? Just thinking about how shamelessly she'd reached out and touched his bare chest mortified her all over again, yet even the memory of the touch made her whole arm quake as it had earlier.

Everything about the day brought on waves of emotions she couldn't control. The terror when she realized exactly what Gribbs planned to do to her, the relief when Gabriel burst through the doorway, the need she had to touch him, to have him hold her. The touch of his hand against her cheek had been almost unbearable in its tenderness, so much so that even now it brought tears to her eyes and made her soul ache with wanting to be touched like that again. Just once.

She covered her wet face with her hands and sobbed quietly. Why couldn't she let him go? He didn't love her, he was simply being kind today. It was in his nature to feel responsible for everyone else, which was the reason he had chased after her and Gribbs. But why hadn't he yelled at her? She'd been expecting it ever since Bart left them standing alone outside the shack, but it had never come to pass. Instead, he had been gentle, kind, and compassionate.

It made Tess nervous. Very, very nervous.

Stupid Frankie took them to church in the Langmans' fancy carriage, with the parting instructions he would pick them up right where he left them. Collette stuck out her tongue at him and turned around, looping her arm through Tess's as she did so. They ascended the first step when a familiar voice tickled Tess's ear.

"Morning, ladies. Beautiful day, isn't it?"

"Good morning, Gabe." Collette smiled, tossing Tess a quick wink. "Yes, it is a glorious morning. Is your brother with you?"

Her eyes scoured the surrounding area in vain.

"No, Miss Langman," he said. "I'm afraid it's just me this morning. I've got Bart working on a project at the ranch."

"Working on Sunday?" Collette mocked. "Honestly, Gabe Calloway, you're asking for fire and brimstone, you are, making him work on the Sabbath. It's sacrilege."

Gabe smiled brightly. "I'm sure the good Lord will give His blessing to this, Miss Langman, don't you worry. Bart'd be happy to have company for lunch, though, if you knew of anyone who might be interested."

Collette scowled. "Yes, well, I'm afraid your brother will have to eat his meal alone today. And every day, unless I can figure out a plan."

"We'll come up with something," Tess said, speaking for the first time. "It'll work itself out. Somehow."

"I wish I had your faith," Collette muttered. "I really do."

"Speaking of faith," Tess said, turning to Gabe. "What brings you to church this morning, Gabriel? I got the distinct impression Sunday services were not exactly something you cottoned to."

Gabe hooked his thumbs through his belt loops and puffed out his chest, grinning his strange grin. "I'm a changed man, Miss Kinley. I've come to do right this morning, and I mean to work a change in a number of other things as well."

"Really?" Tess's brow quirked cynically. "Like what?"

Gabe pulled open the door to the church and motioned them both inside.

"I'm afraid you'll have to wait and see," he answered.

He escorted them to the same pew they had occupied the week before and sat himself down right beside Tess, close enough to brush shoulders with her. If she didn't already know what half the town thought of her, she might have asked him to move over a touch, but since they all thought she was of loose virtue anyway, she didn't bother. Well, that, and she plain enjoyed having him so close.

Collette didn't even try to hide her smirk and offered, in a hushed whisper, to change pews so they could be alone, but Tess swatted her arm and shot her a scolding look.

Almost two hours later, Tess hadn't heard one word of Reverend Boswell's sermon. In fact, she didn't even remember which hymns had been sung, and that was always her favorite part of church services.

"Ladies," Gabe said when they'd made their way back outside. "Would you like me to see you home?"

"That's very kind of you," Collette answered when Tess's mouth fell open wordlessly. "But my brother will be here shortly, and I don't think he or Pa would take very kindly to seeing us with you again."

"That's unfortunate." He smiled. "I'll tell Bart you said hello."

"Yes." She nodded eagerly. "Please do."

"Tess? May I speak to you for a moment?" Gabe motioned toward the tree where Zeus was tethered and waited until she moved before he followed.

"How are you feeling?" he asked when they were finally out of range of most of the busybodies. "Did you get some rest last night?"

"A little," she answered hesitantly. Her eyes narrowed, studying his grin for some kind of clue. Finally, she gave up. "What is going on with you, Gabriel?"

"What do you mean?"

"You know very well what I mean!" she whispered sharply, jabbing him with the end of her finger. "You're being nice to me, you came to church this morning—something's not right, now what is it?"

"Tess," he laughed. "You worry too much. There's nothing going on you need worry about. I told you, I'm a changed man and I'm looking to . . ."

Tess's stomach lurched and her knees began to buckle. "Oh, dear Lord," she gasped. "I've been making such a fool out of myself, haven't I?"

"What are you talking about?" he asked, reaching to steady her.

She pulled out of his grasp and leaned back against the huge willow. Tears burned her eyes and throat, but she couldn't let them loose, she *wouldn't* let them loose. An icy knot tightened her stomach as the dull ache of foreboding filled her soul.

"You're in love, aren't you?" she asked in a voice so fragile it sounded as if it would shatter at any moment.

Gabe's mouth dropped, then broke into that stupid grin again.

"Yes," he said. "As a matter of fact, I am."

"I see." She cleared her throat and fought to remain on her feet. "Does she live here in town? Have I met her?"

"Yes," he repeated. "To both questions."

Stunned and sickened, she forced her eyes up to meet his and there it was, that strange, indescribable glow that had lingered over his magnetic gaze since yesterday. He was in love—madly, wildly, passionately in love with another woman. Twice she opened her mouth to speak and twice all she could manage was a barely audible squeak. Finally she was able to fight back the suffocating sensation in her throat and form a lie.

"I'm happy for you, Gabriel," she said, her lips now as dry as the dust at her feet. "I hope she makes you very happy. You deserve at least that much."

Something flickered across Gabe's face, but Tess tore her eyes away. She couldn't bear for him to see her pain.

"I've never loved this way before," he said softly. "I'm hoping to make her my wife before the week's end."

Tess's hand flew to her mouth in a vain attempt to

stifle the sob that tore free from the back of her throat.

"That's wonderful for you, Gabriel," she said, knowing the tears were only a heartbeat away from falling. "Collette and Frankie are waiting for me. Please offer my congratulations to your bride. I wish you the best."

She hurtled away from the tree—and Gabriel—and raced toward the Langman carriage, with Gabriel's voice echoing through the black void between them.

"Tess! Come back!"

"Just go," she cried when Frankie turned to look at her. "Go!"

Tess continued to sob uncontrollably long after they arrived back at the ranch. Collette fretted and fussed over her, unable to make any sense out of Tess's incoherent sobs until finally Beau appeared and hauled both women out of the carriage and into the house. Unable to walk, let alone stand, Tess's legs would have collapsed under her if Collette hadn't insisted Beau carry the distraught woman up the stairs to her room.

Hours passed, tea went cold, food went uneaten, and the only word Collette could decipher through her friend's anguish was "angel."

Chapter 27

Gabe reined Zeus to a walk as he neared the Langman ranch. He'd taken enough cues from both Collette and Tess to understand Wyatt would probably greet him with his shotgun shoulder high and the safety off.

Instead, it was Stupid Frankie who met him halfway down the road to the house.

"What d'you want?" he demanded, resting his right hand on the butt of his Colt.

"I need to see Tess."

"I don't reckon she wants to see you right now, Calloway."

"This isn't any of your business, Frankie. It's between me and Tess, now let me by."

"You're trespassin' on Langman land and you know how we deal with trespassers."

Gabe sighed, but his glare never wavered. "I don't want to fight you, but I will if I have to."

"There ain't gonna be no fightin', Calloway, only one shot. And since you ain't armed, it's pretty easy to see who'll be doin' the shootin'."

"Take your best shot then, Frankie." He nudged Zeus on ahead, his eyes still fixed on Frankie's Colt.

Gabe saw him swallow hard, once, twice, his hand twitching against the revolver.

"If he don't shoot you, I will, and you know I ain't

bluffin'." Wyatt Langman rode out of the trees ahead of Gabe. "Now get off my land, Calloway."

"I need to speak to Tess," Gabe said, keeping his voice even. "I won't be here any longer than needs be. . . ."

"You've already outstayed yer welcome. Now git." Wyatt waved his gun in the air, pointing back down the road.

"Wyatt . . ."

"Git." He released the safety on the gun, leveling the barrel at Gabe's chest.

Still Gabe hesitated. He needed to talk to Tess, to explain. He couldn't bear seeing her that upset, even if he knew it would only last a short while. He had to tell her everything, but Wyatt Langman was making that a little difficult at the moment. Gabe knew Frankie never would have shot him, but Wyatt, well, he wouldn't put anything past the old man. Ornery as the day is long, that was Wyatt Langman.

Gabe nodded. "Fine. Would you at least give her a message for me?"

"No. I done told both her and Lettie they ain't to have anythin' to do with you or your no good brother, so you just ride on outta here and I won't hafta shoot ya fer trespassin'."

Gabe gritted his teeth and turned Zeus around.

"I'll be back," he promised, eyeing Wyatt steadily.

"An' I'll be waitin'." The old man nodded back.

Gabe spurred Zeus down the road, a string of curses trailing out behind him. Now what the hell was he going to do? How the hell was he ever going to get to talk to Tess with her holed-up at the crazy Langmans' place? Maybe Bart . . . no, Wyatt'd shoot Bart long before he thought to ask any questions.

Gabe was stuck. He'd made one hell of a mess out of this. If Tess hadn't run off so quickly, he'd have been able to explain it to her, make her see the humor in it. But now he'd be lucky if she ever wanted to speak to him again—no matter what the reason.

He needed a plan; he needed to think. Hell, what he needed was a miracle.

He found Bart on the side of the house, unloading the rest of the planed boards from the wagon.

"Your lady friend sends her regards," he said with a slight sneer.

"Wha . . . ?" Bart started, then shrugged. "How'd you know?"

"Wasn't hard to figure out, Bart. You get the stupidest look on your face when she's around, and she ain't exactly ugly."

"No." Bart grinned, wiping the sweat from his brow. "She sure ain't. How'd it go with Tess?"

Gabe shook his head. "You're not going to believe it."

Bart eyed his brother for a moment and adjusted his hat.

"If it's somethin' stupid you did, I sure as hell will believe it."

"Stupid doesn't even begin to describe it," he muttered. "It started out all right, was actually kind of funny, but then . . ."

"Then you blew it. Right when you had it all figured out, you blew it." Bart pulled another board from the wagon and laid it on the ground behind him. "What the hell d'you say to her?"

Gabe heaved a heavy sigh and filled his brother in on what had happened.

"So you figured it'd be best if you didn't let Wyatt shoot you, is that it?"

"Something like that. But now how the hell am I going to get near her? There's no one here that can get onto Langman land without meeting the angry end of a shotgun."

"You really are stupid, ain't ya?" Bart never stopped moving; it was beginning to drive Gabe crazy. "Go to the restaurant tomorrow, talk to her there."

"The restaurant," Gabe repeated. "Bart, my boy, you're not as dumb as you look! That might just work."

"'Course cranky ol' lady Lutz's likely to fire her if she sees you anywhere near the place, but that ain't a worry, is it? I mean, Tess will marry you, won't she?"

Uncertainty suddenly crept into Gabe's brain.

"Y-yes," he stammered. "Of course she will. Why wouldn't she?"

Bart quirked his brow. "D'you really want me to answer that?"

"Bart," he snapped. "I'm serious."

"So am I," Bart said, laughing all the while. "If today went half as bad as you made out, you'd best tread lightly with 'er or she's likely to bolt again."

Gabe set his jaw and walked away, leaving Bart to his work. Tomorrow was an eternity away.

Shadows deepened under Tess's eyes; her face was ghostly pale and pinched. Still, she had to go to work. She washed and dressed with stiff movements, refused any breakfast, and wordlessly climbed into the wagon so Mr. Langman could take her into town. No more walking for her or Collette.

"You shouldn't be goin' anywhere, young lady," Wyatt said, climbing up beside her. "I'll go to town and tell Lutz you won't be in today."

Tess forced her lips to smile. "Thank you, Mr. Langman, but I need to stay busy, to keep my mind thinking of something else."

"I tol' ya them Calloways weren't good fer nothin'."

"It isn't Gabriel's fault," she said quietly. "He can't help how he feels. Or doesn't feel. I've known that from the very beginning."

"Cur dogs, the whole lot o' them."

"Mr. Langman," she said gently but firmly. "You've been so kind to me, letting me stay at your home, and I do appreciate your generosity, but I cannot allow you to speak that way of either Gabriel or Bart. They've been more generous with me than they ever needed to be, and although I'm sure no one in town would ever believe it, they were perfect gentlemen when I stayed at their ranch."

"I ain't buyin' that fer a minute, Tess. There ain't a man's bone in either of them coward's bodies."

"You're wrong." Tess held up her hand when he meant to argue further. "Clayton Calloway made a few bad decisions after his wife died. So deep was his sorrow he forgot everything else, including his own children. Have you never loved someone so deeply that losing them was the same as losing your entire being?"

Wyatt's face paled. He cleared his throat and clicked to the horses.

"Lettie's mother, my Maggie. When she died, I wished I'd a died, too. Only thing that kept me goin' was my girl, Collette." His face crinkled into a sad smile. "She's so much of her ma in 'er."

"I'm sorry," Tess murmured. "It must have been terrible for you. Collette told me about her mother, about how much Margaret loved you. She told me the story about her and Clayton, too."

Wyatt's lips tightened.

Tess touched his arm. "You know that was a lie, don't you? Silly, idle gossip started by someone with far too much time on her hands."

Wyatt barely nodded. "I know that now."

"You're a good man, Wyatt Langman." Tess

reached for his hand and squeezed it gently. "And so are the Calloways. You should take another look at them one day."

Wyatt didn't answer, just bobbed his head and pulled the wagon to a stop in front of the restaurant.

"Thank you, Mr. Langman," Tess said, forcing strength into her voice. "For the ride, for your home, and for listening."

"One of us'll pick you up at three o'clock."

Tess smiled weakly and stepped toward the restaurant, no longer interested in the job, the money, or the farm she dreamed of. It meant nothing now. Gabriel was marrying someone else; it was real now, he didn't love her, and he never would.

"You look like you've died and just haven't fallen over yet," Miss Lutz said. "What's the matter with you—are you sick?"

"No," Tess answered flatly. "I'm fine."

"You're not fine," the woman snipped. "And if you intend on keeping your job, you'd best find a way to look like you're still alive or take your bag right now and leave here. I won't have my employees looking like death itself."

Tess nodded silently. She stood before the small mirror in the kitchen and pinched her cheeks as hard as she could, but they would not pink up. Instead, her face became blotchy and swollen. Heaving a resigned sigh, she tied on her apron and set to work. With her arms loaded down with clean plates, she pushed through the kitchen door out into the restaurant.

"Tess." Gabriel's voice cut through her faster than any bullet, stopping her heart in mid-beat. The stack of dishes tumbled from her trembling arms, crashing to the floor in a million pieces. Neither Tess nor Gabe even flinched.

"What the . . ." Miss Lutz ran out of the kitchen, wiping her hands on her impeccable apron. "You!"

Her accusatory tone went completely unnoticed.

"You will pay for those, Tess." She pushed a broom toward Tess who let it fall to the floor in front of her. "I don't pay you to stand around talking."

In the back of her mind, Tess could hear someone talking, like a faraway buzz, but she had no interest in whatever was being said. Gabriel was there, standing in front of her, dressed in his Sunday best, a bouquet of daisies clutched in one fist. The buzz faded farther and farther away.

"Gabriel," Tess breathed, reaching for the nearest chair. He was getting married today. Why else would he be dressed like that and carrying flowers? "What are you doing here?"

Gabe's face paled slightly. He licked his lips over and over before speaking.

"I, um . . . I think maybe I made a bit of a mess of things yesterday and I wanted to talk to you for a minute."

"I can't," she croaked. "Miss Lutz . . ."

"It's you," he said, taking hesitant steps toward her. "You're the one."

"What . . . what one?" Her voice shook harder than her hands. She felt certain she would throw up.

Gabe was in front of her now, a nervous smile on his face. With painstaking languor, he lowered himself to one knee.

"You," he said softly, taking her cold hand in his. "You're the one I love. You're the one I need. You're the one I want to marry, the one who makes me happier than I've ever been in my life."

The room blackened around her, swirling and dipping until she thought she'd fall off the chair.

"But . . ."

"No buts," he said, pressing his finger against her

mouth. "I love you, Tess Kinley, more than I can even begin to tell you."

"But yesterday . . ."

"Yesterday didn't go well," he admitted with a slight blush. "I wanted to tell you, but you took off so fast, and then Wyatt wouldn't let me . . . well, never mind about that."

"I thought you said . . ."

"Don't think," he whispered. "And forget anything I've ever said before now. I love you."

"Oh, Gabriel." Her heart leaped in her chest and began to beat again, harder, faster, and larger than ever before. "I don't know what to say . . . I never thought . . . after the other day . . . and you came for me . . . but you said . . . what about . . . ?"

"Tess." He laughed softly. "Forget everything else. Do you love me?"

His smile faded when she hesitated.

"Tess?" He searched her face looking for a hint of an answer, but all she did was cry. Huge, hot tears rolled down her cheeks, landing on their folded hands.

When minutes passed in painful silence, Gabe stiffened.

"I guess I made a mistake coming here," he said, rising to his feet. "I'm sorry, Tess."

He turned to leave but Tess grasped his hand and pulled him back, knocking the flowers to the floor.

"Gabriel," she said, "how do I know this isn't just another dream? How do I know I won't wake up crying again like I have every night since I came to Porter Creek? How do I . . ."

Tess's words were smothered by Gabe's lips. His kiss was urgent and hungry, demanding and yet exquisitely tender. Knees quaking, she leaned into him for support. His huge hands locked against her spine, pulling her closer until she could no longer determine where she ended and he began.

Her fingers wound themselves through his thick, still-damp hair as she returned his kiss with reckless abandon, oblivious to everything else around her. This was a kiss for her hardened, weary soul to meld with, a kiss that joined their hearts forever, a kiss that was in no way a dream.

"Miss Kinley!" Pauline Lutz gasped in horror. "Just what do you think you're doing?"

The kiss ended, but barely. Their lips still pressed gently against each other, both of them afraid to break the connection. Tess's eyes remained closed, but she smiled.

"I'm certainly not dreaming," she breathed.

"No," Gabe murmured back. "You're not dreaming."

"Miss Kinley! Get hold of yourself, for goodness' sake."

"I've got a good enough hold on her for the both of us, thank you very much," Gabe smirked. "And I'm not about to let her go."

Tess laughed lightly, feeling awash with new life.

"She has work to do!" Miss Lutz snipped in a tight voice.

"Sorry," Gabe said, shaking his head. "Tess doesn't work here anymore, ma'am. I'm taking her home right now."

"Gabriel," Tess said softly, finally opening her eyes. "I can't leave her without any help. She was kind enough to give me a job when I needed one, the least I can do is finish my shifts for today."

"But . . ." His voice bordered on a whine.

"Gabriel." Tess's amber eyes crackled with fire. "I have to do this. You be here at three o'clock sharp and I'll be waiting."

Gabe groaned. "I don't know if I can wait that long."

"I'm sure you'll survive." She laughed. "Now let me get back to work."

It was as though her heart had somehow left her body and was floating around her; it felt so light, so happy, so loved. Her hands cupped his cheeks and pulled him down to meet her lips once more.

"Three o'clock?" he whispered against her mouth. "That seems like an eternity away."

With marked reluctance, she released him, but not before he planted a hundred kisses across her brow, down her nose, and over each eye.

"I love you, Tess Kinley."

"So you said." She smiled saucily. "Does that mean those flowers are for me?"

"Oh, yeah, they are." He picked them up, blew invisible dust from the petals, and held them out to her. As he pressed the bouquet into her right hand, he pressed her left hand to his lips and kissed it ever so gently.

"Three o'clock," he said, backing away slowly.

Tess's tears blurred her vision of him, but her mind's eye saw him perfectly—halo, wings, and all.

"Tess," he called from the doorway, grinning that stupid grin of his. "Does this mean you'll marry me?"

She half ran, half flew, across the restaurant, threw herself back into his arms, and buried her face in the warmth of his neck.

"Yes," she sobbed. "Absolutely, yes. Forever and a day, yes."

"Good," he choked, wrapping his arms around her again. "Just had to double check."

They stood in the doorway, locked in each other's arms, until Miss Lutz cleared her throat loudly. Tess loosened her hold around his neck and he lowered her to the floor.

"Three o'clock," he repeated.

"Three o'clock."

"Tess." Miss Lutz's voice got shriller with every breath.

Gabe backed out the door slowly, holding Tess's gaze until the glass closed between them. Her hand lingered against its smoothness for several more moments before she turned back to her work. She found a vase, filled it with water, and arranged the dew-covered daisies in it. Then she set about cleaning up the pile of broken dishes on the floor.

It was the longest eight hours of Tess's life. More than once, she was certain Miss Lutz had turned the clock back—it was not possible that time could move that slowly.

Stupid Frankie arrived shortly before the appointed time and short of yelling, Tess finally convinced him she did not need a ride back to the ranch.

And then, suddenly, it was three o'clock and Gabe was standing in the doorway, looking more handsome than he ever had before. Tess's cheeks flushed against his gaze. She made her good-byes to her employer, retrieved her daisies from the vase, and followed Gabe out the door.

Not a word was spoken between them. Gabe lifted her up on Zeus's back and climbed behind her, his arms circling her waist, his lips exploring the soft delicate skin behind her earlobe. She leaned back against him and sighed happily, wrapped in the arms of love.

Chapter 28

"Why are we stopping?" Tess asked, lifting her head from Gabe's shoulder.

Zeus's head lowered to gnaw the lush green grass at the creek side. The sparkling clear water tripped and danced along merrily; the long, flowing branches of the willows swayed gently in the breeze.

"We've got a lot to talk about, a lot of decisions to make, and I'd just as soon do it without Wyatt's rifle pointed at me."

"Wyatt?" she asked as Gabe lowered her to the ground. "But I thought . . ."

Gabe laughed. "You really have to stop that. Thinking I mean."

"But . . ."

"Okay, listen," he sighed, still smiling. "I can't take you home with me today because I'm not ready for you yet. And I can't take you to Langman's because Wyatt made it pretty clear if I stepped on his land again I'd be leaving in a pine box."

Tess smiled. "Yes, he's become very protective of me lately. More than my own father ever was." Her brow wrinkled. "What do you mean you're not ready for me yet?"

Gabe took her by the hand and led her to the bank of the creek. They sat in the grass, side by side, her small body tucked beside him and held tightly by the strength of his arm.

"I've got some surprises in store for you, Miss Kinley," he said, his gray eyes sparkling like the creek. "And they're not ready yet, so you can't come with me."

"You didn't have to—"

"I know I didn't," he interrupted again. "I wanted to. I want to make you happy, Tess—as happy as you make me."

Tess lifted her face to his and kissed his chin with feather-soft lips. "You already have made me happy, Gabriel. There's nothing else I could possibly want."

"You weren't so happy yesterday," he said quietly. "I didn't honestly think you'd ever speak to me again."

Tess's throat tightened. "Why did you do that? Why didn't you tell me yesterday?"

"I'm sorry, darlin'," he sighed. "I didn't want to say anything to you until I had everything ready for you at El Cielo, but then you started off on how I was in love, and you're right, I am."

"But I thought you meant . . ."

"That's what you get for thinking again." He chuckled softly and kissed the tip of her nose. "I'm sorry, Tess. The last thing I wanted was to hurt you, but you ran off so fast I couldn't explain anything to you, and then Wyatt . . ."

"Wouldn't let you see me," she finished for him. "I heard Stupid Frankie telling Beau."

"Exactly." Gabe lifted Tess off the ground and lowered her down on his lap. "I love you, Tess. I want to marry you and give you everything."

Tess's face flushed. "I love you, Gabriel, and I want to marry you, but I don't know what I have that I can give to you. Everything I own I left in Boston."

"Not everything," he answered, his voice low and husky.

"What do you mean?"

Gabe swallowed hard. "Kids, Tess. I want kids and I want a whole passel of 'em. I want to be trippin' over them every time I turn around. And I want them all to look exactly like you."

Tears welled in her eyes—blissful, exhilarated, overwhelmed tears.

"Oh, Gabriel," she cried. "I want that, too—although I don't think I want them to look like me, poor things. They should all look exactly like their father, but maybe get their common sense from their mother."

"What?" His laughter shook his whole body. "You're the one who traveled halfway around the country all alone to come to some godforsaken town in the middle of nowhere, remember? D'you call that common sense?"

"Yes," she said with a sharp nod and a smile. "Because look what I found when I got here."

Gabe wrapped her in his arms and sighed again. "Yeah, look what you found—a man with a cussed sense of pride who's more stubborn than a ten-year-old mule, who . . ."

"Who takes a while to figure out what's best for himself, even if it's right under his nose."

Gabe's stomach tightened. "When I think about how I almost lost you, how I would have put you on that stupid stage and seen you out of town. How Gribbs . . ."

"Shush," she said, curling against him. "That's all behind us now. You've finally come to your senses and admitted I was right."

Gabe could hear the smirk in her voice, even if he couldn't see it.

"Okay." He laughed. "You were right. And you need to straighten me out on something else, too."

"What's that?"

"When are we going to get married?" He tilted her chin back so she looked up into his face. A smoldering fire burned in his eyes. "I'd like to get to work on those kids we were talking about."

Tess's eyes lowered, her cheeks flaming beneath his gaze.

"What?" he teased lightly. "That embarrasses you? Not one day after meeting me, you told me you loved me and that didn't embarrass you."

Tess couldn't look at him.

"I know," she whispered, "but it's just, well, you see, I've never . . ."

"Tess," he said, his voice as tender as the fingers that brushed against her cheek. "Look at me."

Slowly, she lifted her gaze to his. All teasing had vanished from his eyes until all she saw was a gentle passion that warmed her through to her soul.

"I won't deny how happy it makes me to know I'll be your first," he said. "But even if I wasn't, it wouldn't matter to me. I love you. And I promise you this, Tess. I will never do anything you don't want me to do, okay?"

More tears cascaded down her cheeks and Gabe simply wiped them away with the pad of his thumb.

"Enough of these." He smiled. "Now answer the question."

"Which one?"

"Which one?" he groaned, falling on his back in the grass. "When are we going to get married? Pick a day—any day."

"How about . . ."

Suddenly, Gabe jerked back up. "Or do you want to wait for your family to come out for it?"

Tess noted the panic in his eyes and smiled. "No, Gabriel, I'm not about to wait for them to get on a train and make their way out here."

"Oh, thank God," he breathed, glancing heavenward. "I don't think I could've waited that long anyway."

"Tomorrow?"

"Tomorrow?" he yelped. "Don't toy with me, Tess. You don't have a dress yet, we haven't even talked to Reverend Boswell, the house . . . my surprises aren't done yet."

"I don't need a fancy dress, Gabriel, I need you. I can't imagine Reverend Boswell is run off his feet with things to do and I don't want any surprises. Marry me. Tomorrow."

"But . . ."

"Tomorrow," she repeated, a mischievous sparkle glinting in her smile. "Or we wait for my family to come out."

"Tomorrow it is!" In one fluid motion, he lifted her from his lap and stood up. "Come on then, we've got work to do."

"What work?" She laughed. "Let's sit back down and . . ."

"Nope," he said, shaking his head. "Too many things to do."

He hoisted her back up into the saddle and climbed up behind her, turning Zeus back toward town.

"Where are we going?" She laughed. "I thought you said we had work to do."

"You'll see." He held her fast with one arm while urging Zeus into an even run. He spoke not one more word until he'd tethered the horse to the post outside the mercantile.

"Go on in and see what Mrs. Clark has for dresses. I'll go talk to the Reverend."

"But Gabriel . . ." She began to protest, but he cut her off.

"Don't argue with me, woman!" he teased. "Now come on."

He took her by the hand and half pulled her inside the store.

"Mrs. Clark?" he called, marching toward the counter. "Mrs. Clark?"

"Yes?" The middle-aged, portly woman scuttled out from the back room. "What's the matter?"

"Nothing," he answered, "unless you don't have any ready-made dresses."

Mrs. Clark's eyes narrowed slightly as she studied Gabe first and then Tess.

"What kind of a dress?" she asked, forcing a sugary smile.

"I don't need . . ."

"A pretty one," Gabe said with a definitive nod. "A real pretty one. And put it on my account."

With that, he turned on his heel, shot Tess an amused wink, and strode out of the store. Both women stared after him, their mouths hanging open. Mrs. Clark was the first to regain her thoughts.

"All right then, Miss . . . ?"

"Kinley," Tess replied. "Tess Kinley."

"Oh!" The woman's eyes flew open wide, her right hand resting on her bosom. "Of course, I should have known."

In that instant, Tess's anger flared. "What is that supposed to mean, exactly?" she demanded.

"Well," Mrs. Clark started with a sniff, "it's no secret you have been living out at El Cielo with those Calloway boys. So I guess it shouldn't come as a surprise to anyone he wants you to look your best."

"I beg your pardon," Tess seethed. "But if it's any of your business, which I assure you it is not, Gabriel and I are to be married. Now that might not mean much to you right at this moment, Mrs. Clark, but I'm sure it will when I tell him how you have treated me. The Calloways must do a fair amount of business in your store, am I right?"

"Y-yes," the woman answered falteringly.

"Believe me, then, when I say unless you change your attitude toward me and anyone else whom you judge, all transactions between the entire Calloway family and your business will stop." Tess's voice grew louder and louder. "I have no problem ordering everything I need from a catalog or—better yet—taking trips into Helena to purchase the goods I need. Do I make myself clear?"

"Is there a problem out here?" Mr. Clark came out from the back room, his eyes fixed on his wife.

Tess raised her eyebrow in the other woman's direction as well, waiting for her to answer.

"Is there a problem, Mrs. Clark?" she asked.

"N-no," the woman answered slowly. "I was about to show Miss Kinley our selection of dresses. Right this way, dear."

Tess smiled sweetly at Mr. Clark and followed his wife to the far counter where the ready-made clothes were kept.

"I have a selection of different styles," Mrs. Clark said, then faltered. "And colors."

"White will do fine, thank you very much."

"Yes, of course." She held up three different dresses for Tess to examine, each varying greatly from the others.

She chose a plain white satin gown, fitted at the waist, with long puffy sleeves and a full skirt. Tiny pearls edged the curved neckline and delicate ivory lace finished the hem and cuffs. She did not bother to look at veils, but opted to wear roses from the ranch in her hair. It was certainly not the dress—or the look—she would have worn if she'd ended up married to Harmon Stiles, and that was perhaps one of the reasons she loved it so much.

Mrs. Clark nodded approvingly and quickly wrapped the garment in brown paper.

"Will you be needing any . . ." She hesitated, glancing around the room for her husband. "Any pretty underthings? I have a lovely selection of lace camisoles and the like if you'd care to look."

A genuine smile found Tess's lips. "Thank you, Mrs. Clark, but I don't think so. Not today, anyway. But perhaps another day."

Mrs. Clark's round face beamed back at her. "Yes." She nodded. "Perhaps."

She handed the package to Tess and followed her out of the store.

"I apologize if I offended you before," she said, her cheeks pinking slightly. "I tend to forget what the Good Book preaches—judge not lest ye be judged. I think you'll be a welcome addition to the town of Porter Creek."

Tess patted the woman's hand softly. "Thank you, Mrs. Clark, that was very kind. I look forward to seeing you again soon."

Gabe strode up the boardwalk then, his even white teeth flashing in the sunlight.

"Congratulations, Mr. Calloway," Mrs. Clark offered. "You're a very lucky man."

"Yup," he agreed. "I am. Are you ready?"

Tess nodded, thanked Mrs. Clark again for her help, and let Gabe lift her up on Zeus's back.

"Are we set for tomorrow?" she asked.

"One o'clock," he grinned, "at the creek."

"At the creek?" she repeated. "Why . . . oh, that's lovely."

A hint of a blush colored her cheeks as the memory of their first kiss warmed her veins.

They rode in silence for a while, secretive smiles playing against both their mouths.

"I'll walk from here," Tess said with a smirk as they neared the turnoff to the Langman ranch. "I'd hate to lose you this close to our wedding day."

"No bloody way," he snorted. "I'll take you in. You shouldn't . . ."

"Gabriel," she said softly. "I don't think it's a good idea to antagonize Mr. Langman any more than necessary. I'd rather you be in one piece tomorrow, if it's all the same to you."

"But . . ."

"Hush now. Let me down, and I'll see you tomorrow."

Reluctantly, Gabe slid from the saddle and lifted her down. But he didn't release her right away.

"Tess," he said, his voice low and shaky. "I . . ." His slate-gray eyes glowed with an inner fire that filled her with a whole rash of emotions—love and passion, anxiety and fear.

"Tomorrow, Gabriel. I'll see you tomorrow."

Gabe's head lowered slowly, his hands pulling her closer. She tipped her head back and met his kiss with a gentle intensity that told him everything he needed to know.

When he finally released her, there was an aching look in his face that melted her heart into a pool of molten love.

"Tomorrow," he rasped.

She nodded slowly, backing away from him one tiny step at a time.

"I love you, Gabriel," she said, her eyes illuminating that very fact. "And I'll see you tomorrow, one o'clock, at the creek."

She watched him swallow, open his mouth to speak, and then shut it again. For a moment she thought he was going to cry, but then he turned away and climbed back on his horse. With a lightning quick wink, he shot her a dazzling smile and sent Zeus racing toward El Cielo, whooping all the while.

Chapter 29

Asking Collette to stand up for her was the easiest thing in the world. Convincing one of the Langman men to take them into town, however, proved more of a challenge—especially when they discovered the reason.

Surprisingly, it was Wyatt Langman himself who finally agreed to it. After all, he reasoned, if they all refused to saddle up and take the girls to town themselves, the cussed females would probably head out on their own again anyway, and God knew what trouble they'd find themselves in then.

"I ain't sayin' I approve of you marryin' that cur dog," he warned Tess. "But I reckon you ain't my daughter and it don't matter a lick what I got to say on it. Hear this, though. If'n you come to yer senses and need a place to go, you git yerself back here to us, you hear?"

"Thank you, Mr. Langman." Tess smiled softly. "I don't believe I'll need to impose on you again, but I thank you for your concern."

Wyatt nodded and went to hitch up the carriage. No bride deserved to ride in an open wagon on her wedding day, he explained.

Gabe was already pacing by the bridge when they rounded the corner near the creek. At the first sound of horse hooves, he and Bart both stopped and turned, the tension in their faces visibly disappearing.

Rosa and Miguel stood off to the side, under the shade of a willow. He with his hat twisting in his hands, and she looking as proud as a mother hen.

Gabe stepped up on the bridge and took the near horse by the bit.

"Wyatt," he nodded, "I appreciate you bringing her for me."

"I done told her what I think 'bout her marryin' a fool like you, Calloway, but she's got it in her head she loves you and there ain't no convincin' her otherwise."

"I'm sure you tried your best." Gabe smiled, and to his surprise, Wyatt Langman smiled back.

"Damn right I did."

Both men walked to the side of the carriage and held out a hand for the women. Collette was the first to step out, her cornflower blue eyes sparkling—more for Bart's benefit than anyone else's.

Bart immediately stepped up and took her hand, ignoring the fierce glare of her father.

"You do look lovely," he murmured to her, causing her face to pink becomingly.

Tess stepped out next, her shimmering white dress flowing around her like a cloud. Collette had secretly dashed off to El Cielo earlier and pinched a handful of coral-colored rosebuds from their bushes, and they were now arranged throughout Tess's hair like a crown.

Gabe's smile sent shivers up and down her spine. He was pleased, which, in turn, pleased her. She tucked her hand under his arm and walked with him to the bank of the creek, never taking her eyes off him. He was so beautiful, just looking at him hurt her eyes.

The others joined them, each one offering hugs

and words of thanks that the two of them had finally found their way to each other. Reverend Boswell arrived, made his way down to the creek, and smiled warmly at Tess.

"I can't recall a lovelier bride," he said.

Tess flushed and Gabe grinned even more.

"Are we ready then?" asked the Reverend.

"Just a moment," Tess said. She took Miguel by the arm and led him a short distance away, their heads tucked low.

Gabe watched them, Tess speaking softly, Miguel nodding in agreement and then looking past the small group of people to the carriage on the bridge. He spoke a few words, kissed Tess on the cheek, and strode back to stand beside his wife.

Tess, too, walked back toward the group, but then passed them by and hurried back up the slope to the bridge and Wyatt Langman. After a moment, Wyatt removed his hat, swiped his arm across his brow, and nodded briefly. Then the two of them returned to the creek.

"I'll be givin' Miss Tess away today," he announced, proud as could be. "So remember that, Calloway—if anythin' should happen to upset this little girl, you got me to answer to. Got it?"

"Yes, sir," Gabe answered solemnly. "Thank you, sir."

"Let us begin then," the Reverend said, opening his Bible. "Dearly beloved . . ."

Tess looked up into Gabe's eyes and in that instant the entire world stopped. There was no one else, there was only the two of them, standing by the creek bed pledging their love and commitment to each other for all time. Collette cried and Bart cleared his throat every time he breathed, it seemed, but Tess and Gabe stared into each other's eyes, each knowing this was how it was meant to be. Be it fate or the good Lord himself that brought them together, it no longer mattered—they were together, bonded forever and forever, certain they were exactly where they were supposed to be.

"Congratulations, Mrs. Calloway," Reverend Boswell said, extending his hand. "May you have a long, happy life together."

For the first time, Tess pulled her gaze from Gabriel's and looked down at the shiny gold band on her finger. It was real, she was married; she was Gabriel Calloway's wife.

"Thank you, Reverend." She ignored his hand and kissed him on his weathered cheek, making him smile. He nodded to Gabe, shook his hand, and made his good-byes. The Widow Brenner was waiting on him, he explained shyly.

Collette sniffled behind Tess. "I'm so happy for you both," she cried. "It was a beautiful ceremony."

"Yes, it was," Tess agreed, her own eyes beginning to fill. "And from the looks of things, we might be having another wedding sometime soon."

She nodded her head toward the bridge where Collette's father was in deep conversation with Bart.

"Oh dear," Collette sighed.

"Now now," Tess soothed. "Nobody's yelling, so let's take that as a good sign."

Even as she spoke, Bart smiled at whatever Wyatt said to him and the two men shook hands.

"You see?" Tess laughed. "Everything is going to be fine. Why don't you go find out what's going on?"

Collette had already lifted her skirts and was hurrying back up to the bridge.

Gabe wrapped his arm around Tess and pulled her close. She wondered if there would ever come a time when she didn't marvel at the love she felt for this man, when her heart no longer flipped and twittered every time he touched her. She prayed not.

"Well, Mrs. Calloway," he murmured into her hair. "Shall we go home?"

"Home," Tess sighed. "Yes, let's go home."

Miguel had already brought the buggy around and now stood near Wyatt's carriage, holding the reins.

"He insisted on bringing the wagon," Gabe explained, "even though I told him it wasn't necessary."

Heat flooded Tess's face. With lowered lashes, she smiled shyly.

"I would prefer riding home with you." She spoke so softly Gabe had to strain to hear her.

"That's my girl." He laughed, hoisted her into the air, and marched off to the stand of willows to fetch Zeus. "I knew you'd see things my way."

Rosa clicked her tongue at them but still couldn't hide the smile that spread across her face. Gabe Calloway had found his *corazon*.

Tess waved to Collette, blowing kisses as they rode by.

"Save those for me," Gabe groaned softly in her ear. "Any kisses you're looking to give away belong to me now and no one else."

"Yes, my love." She snuggled back against him, basking in his strength and his tenderness.

A soft quiet fell between them as Zeus carried them toward El Cielo.

"Have I mentioned lately how much I love you?"

"No," he answered. "As a matter of fact you haven't."

"I do, Gabriel. I love you more with every breath I take. Sometimes I'm almost certain my heart is going to burst right out of my body."

"Go on," he said, smiling against her hair.

"You make me feel safe and warm and loved and cherished and . . . I don't think I could love you any more if I tried."

"Try." He reined in Zeus at the barn door and lifted Tess down. "Wait here, I'll be right back."

With the speed of a man in love, he tended to Zeus and had Tess back in his arms before she could think. As they walked back toward the house, hand in hand, she noticed the addition on the side of the house, just off the kitchen.

"What on earth?"

"My gift to you," Gabe beamed. "Come have a look."

He led her in through the kitchen, past the pantry, and through an oak door that hadn't been there the last time Tess was. He pushed opened the door and stood back, giving her room to walk through.

"Oh my!" Tess breathed. "A real bathtub? Oh, Gabriel, you shouldn't have done this! It's too much!"

"No, it's not," he said, taking her by the hand. "And look, Bart piped it through to the kitchen so the water in the pump'll be hot when it gets here."

"How on earth did he manage that?"

"Who knows?" Gabe laughed. "But leave it to Bart to come up with it."

Tess walked around the tub slowly, running her fingers along the edge. It was huge, absolutely huge. In fact, it was big enough for two! Her cheeks burned crimson at her wicked thoughts, horrifying her more when she realized Gabe was watching her.

"Had the same thought myself," he murmured, taking her in his arms. "But the tub can wait. Right now, I've got a much . . . softer . . . surprise I want to show you."

Taking her hand again, he led her back through the kitchen and up the stairs, past the room she had occupied not so very long ago, and into his bedroom at the end of the hall. Tess's heart careened out of control, pounding so loud she was certain it would shake the house down around them.

The room had been completely transformed. Gabe's huge four-poster bed, once the only piece of furniture in the room, was now joined by a beautiful ornate vanity and a huge wardrobe carved from the same oak as the new door downstairs. White lace curtains hung in the window, and a beautiful blue and yellow patchwork quilt covered the bed.

A new white porcelain chamber set sat on the vanity beside a vase of heavenly smelling wild flowers. She took it all in, marveling at the changes, yet humbled by the knowledge Gabe loved her enough to do it in the first place.

"It's beautiful," she said, exhaling softly. A tiny shiver raced up her spine as Gabe came up behind her and wrapped his arms around her middle.

"You're beautiful," he murmured, inhaling the sweet scent that lingered all around her.

Tess turned in his arms and gazed up lovingly. There was an eagerness in his eyes, a patient, loving eagerness she, herself, felt in her own blood.

"Are you nervous?" he asked, brushing her hair back from her cheek.

Tess shook her head. She'd heard plenty of horror stories about . . . this part of marriage . . . mostly from her mother's lady friends who thought Tess wasn't listening. To hear them tell, laying with a man was quite possibly the most horrible thing in the world, yet for some reason, Tess knew it would be just the opposite with Gabriel; theirs would be true love making, not anything like what the ladies spoke of.

Her hands trembled as they reached for his, but it was not nerves that caused them to do so, it was the sheer anticipation of what was to come, of knowing once and for all she and Gabriel would be joined in the most intimate and primal way possible.

Gabriel's lips whispered against hers, pulling a soft moan from deep within her. Her knees weakened, her heart expanded, and suddenly she was lifted as though carried on the wings of an angel. Her angel.

He lowered her to the bed and pulled back, brushing his trembling knuckles against her cheek.

"Gabriel?" Tess's whisper echoed back. "What is it?"

Gabe's clouded gray eyes searched her face. He swallowed hard—twice.

"Is there something wrong?" Tess sat bolt up.

"Yeah," he said, then cleared his throat. "There is."

"What?" She fought back the tightness that crept around her heart.

Gabe rubbed his palm across his mouth. "I, uh . . ." He paused, ducking his head, but not before color crept up his neck and across his face. "I don't know what to do."

Tess gaped. "But I thought you had . . . I mean, you've never . . . ?"

He chuckled quietly and lifted his gaze back to Tess who had inched her way closer. "I mean I don't know what to do *with you*. You're different, Tess. You've got this hold on me somehow, and I don't have the first clue what to do about it."

"Then don't do anything," she murmured. "Let me do it."

With deft fingers, she loosened his string tie and slid it from around his neck. Gabriel's Adam's apple bobbed, bringing a smile to Tess's lips. She released each of his shirt buttons leisurely, gaining more confidence with every hitch of his breath. With deliberate movements, she eased the shirt from his shoulders, then ran her hands delicately over the broad expanse of muscle before her.

Gabe sucked in a breath, fighting to release his wrists from the constraints of his shirt.

"Tess . . ."

"Shhh," she breathed, pressing her lips against the hollow at the base of his throat. Her hands reached to her own neck, to the top of a long row of tiny pearl buttons, and began the arduous task of releasing them one by one.

Gabe's eyes followed her fingers, button by button, until she sat in front of him, her dress open from neck to waist.

"Oh God, Tess."

She smiled cheekily. "Are you getting any ideas about what you should do with . . ."

Gabe's mouth swallowed her words, devouring her senses right along with them. Someone shuddered, but she couldn't begin to guess which one of them it was. His lips trailed over her cheeks, her nose, and her eyes. Tingling warmth washed over her. And through her. In one lightning fast motion, Tess's dress fell to the floor in a puddle of silk. Gabe knelt beside the bed, easing the satin slippers from Tess's feet. His eyes never left hers, even as his hands reached for her stockings.

The touch of his huge hand against her thigh pulled a sharp gasp from her throat. Inch by slow inch, he lowered each stocking and tossed it over his shoulder. Tess reached for him, urging him toward her, until she felt his lips on hers again. She filled her hands with him, pulling him closer yet, but Gabe resisted, moving his mouth down her neck to the swell of her breast above the chemise. She arched toward him, aching, desperate for his touch. And he didn't disappoint her. Tess gulped for air, but found none. She spiraled toward something she'd never known, never even imagined, and Gabriel was not about to stop until she burst through.

He made short work of what was left of her underthings, leaving her in silky nakedness. She was even more beautiful than he'd ever imagined. Her soft, creamy skin, now pinked with arousal, tingled under his touch. He'd never wanted another woman so much, never needed another so much. She stirred his soul and made him crazy. And now that he had her, he would never let her go.

Gabriel's fingers moved over every inch of her, caressing, loving, and awakening her every cell. She moved beneath him, urging him on, needing more of everything he offered. His mouth followed the trail of fire left by his hands, his lips leaving their own moist trail down her throat, across her shoulders, and between her breasts. Surely a body couldn't bear such sweet torture without exploding.

Gabe released her briefly, just long enough to remove the rest of his clothes, then pulled her into his arms again, pressing tender kisses against her hair. When he thought how close he came to letting her go—to *making* her go—he could barely breathe. He ached to be in her, to have her. His tongue circled each breast, his own arousal increased by her soft moans. He moved his hand lower, across her silky belly and over her thigh, seeking out her desire.

"Oh, Gabriel," she moaned.

"Say it again," he choked. "Say my name."

She was so soft, so sweet, so warm. His teeth gritted, he held his own need in check, easing Tess through the first painful moment of their joining and on through to their final glorious moment.

"Gabriel!"

Light splintered into a rainbow of stars. Her insides convulsed at the same moment Gabriel shuddered and moaned. She'd never felt more alive or more exhausted in her entire life. She wrapped her arms around his shoulders and held tight—she could spend the rest of her life just as she was—wrapped around him and filled with enormous love and fulfillment. Gabriel's sweat-dampened body slumped over her, his heart pounding through his chest against hers.

"Gabriel," she murmured. "I can't breathe."

"Mmmm." He chuckled low in his throat. "I guess I knew what I was doing after all then, didn't I?"

"Well, yes, but I mean you're crushing me."

Gabe wrapped his arms around his wife and rolled over onto his back, pulling her with him. He had no intention of releasing her any time soon. In fact, he smirked, it might be interesting to start all over again just the way they were.

Brilliant sunshine poured through the window when Tess finally woke the next morning. Gabe's heart beat beneath her ear, his hand gently stroking her bare shoulder.

"Good morning," he said.

"Mmm," she sighed. "How did you know . . . ?"

"Eyelashes."

Tess's fingers traced a path up his chest to his beard-stubbled face. Life was good.

"Did you sleep well?" she asked, enjoying the roughness of his beard against her hand.

"Like a baby." He smiled. "I had an exhausting afternoon—and night."

Tess knew she should be ashamed of the way she'd carried on the night before, but she couldn't help herself. The things he did to her . . . well, mercy, her mother's lady friends obviously had never done that!

"Do you think . . ." She stopped, suddenly feeling shy.

"Do I think we made a baby last night?" he said tenderly, lifting her chin back up with his finger. "I don't rightly know, but if it takes a lot more practice before we finally make one, that's fine with me."

Tess couldn't help but giggle.

"You're awful," she scolded happily. "Just awful."

"And you're beautiful," he growled, pulling her in for a long, mind-drugging kiss. "I'm not going to get any work done if you keep this up."

"Me?" She laughed. "I was just lying here innocently, minding my own business, when you . . ."

"There's nothing innocent about you, Tess Calloway. Not anymore."

"And whose fault is that?"

Gabe threw his hands above his head in surrender. "Guilty as charged."

"All right then," she said, her eyes dancing. "What should your punishment be?"

"Life. Nothing less than a life sentence."

"Life then." Tess nodded, her eyes smoldering in passion. "And not a minute less."

Chapter 30

Nothing Tess had read or hoped to be true could have prepared her for the life she and Gabriel embarked on together.

She'd read about love, laughed and cried right along with the characters in the novels she read, but those emotions were nothing compared with what she lived every second. Her heart swelled at the sight of her new husband, ached at his absence, and the slightest touch of his hand sent volcanic eruptions through her entire being.

For every ounce of love she felt, she saw it reciprocated in Gabriel's eyes; for every quiver that rocked her soul, she felt it reverberate in his kiss. It still didn't seem possible to her the very man who had done all he could to send her away was the same man who loved her so freely now.

Every night she prayed she would conceive Gabriel's child, and with every passing day she felt more and more certain she was, indeed, carrying his son.

While Gabe went about his work on the ranch, Rosa set her mind to teaching Tess the finer points of running a house—western style. Although she never went back into the chicken coop, Tess did learn how to feed the animals, when to feed them, and how to catch one without losing a finger. When it came to actually killing the bird, however, Tess could not bring herself to do it. Rosa laughed at her silliness, took the chicken firmly by the head and body, and gave it a quick twist. The resulting noise was enough to send Tess running around to the back of the house.

From that day on, it fell to Gabe or Miguel to kill and pluck the bird before Tess would touch it. She learned how to cook all Gabe's favorite meals, including roast chicken with dumplings and boiled potatoes; she learned how to make bread and bake pies and, eventually, with a lot of practice, she mastered the fine art of coffee making—plenty strong and lots of it.

She weeded the garden with a vengeance, refusing even the smallest of pests or weeds any space. The vegetables were put up, with the help of Rosa, and every room of the house was adorned with the most fragrant of flowers picked from the yard or out by the creek.

It was a tremendous amount of work to keep the men fed and the house in order, but Tess relished every minute of it. This was, after all, what she had dreamt about for so many years, and now here she was living that very dream. As much as she tried to refuse it, Tess did enjoy the pampering she received from her husband. He insisted on her taking her nightly bath, as she used to in her previous life, and more often than not, he was the one who lathered her hair and rinsed it clean.

He made a point of being home for every meal, no matter where he was or what he was doing; he never entered or left the room without kissing his wife; and he strutted around the ranch as though he had the world by the tail. Even Rosa commented on the change.

"La chica give Gabe Calloway mucha felicidad."

"I hope so." Tess smiled. "I love him so, Rosa."

"Si." Rosa nodded, eyed Tess carefully from head to toe, pausing at her midsection, and then broke out into a wide grin.

"What is it?" Tess asked.

"Nada," the woman said, shaking her head. "La niña give Gabe Calloway *mucha felicidad*."

Before Tess could press her further, Rosa folded her apron and left the house, pausing long enough to kiss an unexpecting Gabe on the cheek as he opened the door for her.

He stared after her, shook his head slowly, and turned a quizzical look at his wife.

"Has she been drinking?" he asked, half joking.

"No." Tess laughed. "But she has been acting a little queer this afternoon."

Gabe scooped Tess up in his arms and twirled her around in a circle.

"Come on," he said. "Let's go for a ride."

"What about supper?"

"Forget supper—it's Saturday, they can eat in town. Lord knows they'll be heading there anyway."

No further argument was needed. Tess hurried out behind him, feeling only the slightest bit guilty at leaving without feeding the men. Bart met them at the barn door.

"Goin' somewhere?" he asked.

"Just for a ride. You're on your own for supper." Gabe lifted Tess into Zeus's saddle.

"That's where yer wrong, big brother." Bart grinned. "I'm takin' supper with Miss Collette Langman tonight."

"Oh, Bart," Tess cried, clapping her hands together. "That's wonderful! How did you ever manage to convince Mr. Langman?"

"Seems I got you to thank fer that, Tess. Wyatt figured if a nice girl like you would hook up with the likes of us Calloways, and stick it out the way you have all these weeks, then he supposes we can't be all that bad. Told me I could call on Collette on Saturday nights as long as he was there to keep an eye on things."

Tess's eyes brimmed with tears. "Collette must be so happy, I'll have to stop for a visit tomorrow. Give her my love, will you?"

"Rather give 'er mine." He grinned. "But I'll pass along your thoughts."

Gabe clicked to Zeus and sent him off at a gentle run toward the rise in the east.

"This poor animal," Tess cooed lightly. "I should probably start riding my own horse and give him a break from the extra weight."

"Not a chance," Gabe growled. "You'll stay right where you are until this beast is ridden into the ground."

She inched her way back until she was pressed right up against him. "You're the boss," she said.

"Damn right I am." He laughed, planting light kisses on the top of her head. "And don't you forget it."

They rode for over an hour, surrounded by the still of the early evening. Following his own direction, Zeus took them to the same crystal clear pool where Bart had been bitten by the snake, and waited patiently while they dismounted. Gabe tossed the reins to the ground and dropped to his knees in the thick buffalo grass.

"It's everything I ever dreamed of," Tess sighed wistfully. "And more."

Gabe took her hand and tugged her down beside him.

"Takes some getting used to for some folks," he said. "It can get pretty lonely out here."

"How could anyone be lonely with all this beauty around them?" she asked. "The trees, the mountains, the sky—I never would have guessed the sky was so big."

"It's the same sky they see in Boston, Tess."

She shook her head vehemently. "No, it's not. This sky is alive with stars and clean air and . . . and space. Boston's sky is dark and haunting. And the land—you'd never see this much untouched land anywhere near Boston. There's so many people there, so much turmoil. It's like a whole other world out here."

Gabe's heart surged. That was exactly how he felt himself, but to hear her say it meant more to him than anything else. She loved the land as much as he did; and just when he thought he couldn't love her any more than he already did, his heart expanded even more.

The howling of a lone wolf, far off in the distance, made her shiver.

"You're not afraid of a little thing like a wolf, now are you?" Gabe teased, resting his arm around her shoulders.

"Who me?" she said teasingly. "I'm not afraid of anything, remember?"

"I almost believe that to be the truth," he murmured. "Is there anything you *are* afraid of?"

"Losing you."

Gabe couldn't breathe for a whole minute. Her answer had been so quick, so sure, it was obviously something she'd been thinking about.

"You're not going to lose me," he said softly. "I'm real easy to find. Just look beside you."

She swallowed hard, catching her bottom lip between her teeth. She'd always known the fear was there, that one day she could in fact lose Gabriel, but until that moment she hadn't realized how much she depended on him for her every breath. Now that she had him, she couldn't imagine not having him, and just the thought scared her more than death.

"We should get away for a few days," Gabe announced suddenly. "Take a trip to Helena or somewhere. Where would you like to go?"

"Nowhere," she answered honestly. "I want to stay right here. Besides, we couldn't leave if we wanted to."

"Of course we can! Bart is more than capable . . ."

"Bart?" she said. "But he's going . . ."

She stopped. It was Bart's news to tell, not hers, but why wouldn't he have told Gabe yet? Gabe sat up, searching her face.

"What? What's Bart up to now? He's not going to lead on Collette Langman and then skip town like he always does, is he? Damn it anyway, I should have known . . ."

"No!" she cried. "It's nothing like that. I don't know why he hasn't told you yet."

"Told me what?" he persisted.

Tess pursed her lips. Gabriel was her husband, and she couldn't keep secrets from him.

"Bart has been offered a job," she said hesitantly.

"Where?" Gabe's face began to color angrily. "Back in Butte with all those crazy miners? Worse?"

"If you'll stop yelling for a minute, I'll tell you."

"I'm not yelling!"

"Gabriel."

"Okay," he relented. "I'm not yelling. Where is he going now?"

"Nowhere," she said. "Apparently Sheriff Nicholls has offered him his job right here in Porter Creek."

"What? Where's Fergus going?"

"His sister in Amarillo is ailing and he wants to be closer to her, so he asked Bart if he was interested in the job."

"And of course Bart said yes." Gabe was obviously not happy.

"Of course." Tess nodded. "Why wouldn't he? It's what he wants."

"Sounds to me like he's wanting to get himself killed is all."

"Gabriel, I'm sure your brother wouldn't do anything to put his life in danger—especially if he's set on marrying Collette."

"You don't know my brother the way I do," he snapped.

"And I don't think you know your brother quite as well as you think you do. He loves Collette, he wants to make a life with her. But he doesn't have the ranching blood you have, he never has. You can see it in his eyes, Gabriel. He doesn't look at the land the way you do; he doesn't stop and enjoy the smell of horse manure or fresh hay—to him those things don't even exist. He wants to be a lawman."

Gabe listened in wonder to what she said. How had she pegged both him and Bart so well in such a short time? Hell, he knew Bart wanted to be the law, but he'd never noticed his brother not wanting to work the ranch. In fact, he'd never even given it a second thought. Bart was a Calloway, this was his legacy—the land, the stock, everything. How could it not mean something to him?

"Guess I better have a talk with him," he grumbled. "If he's serious about this sheriff job, I'll have to buy him out I guess. Unless he wants to keep his share."

Tess knew he was thinking out loud, so she kept her thoughts to herself, but she also knew Bart would never accept money for his "share" of the ranch. He never felt a part of it anyway and he hadn't put in the sweat and headaches either Gabe or Miguel had. As far as Bart was concerned, the ranch was his brother's to do with as he pleased.

"When's he supposed to start?"

"First of the month, I believe."

Gabe's jaw tightened, his gray eyes staring blindly across the open land.

"He's a grown man," Tess said softly, running her fingers through Gabe's tousled hair. "You can't make decisions for him anymore. If this is what he wants . . ."

"I know, I know. But why couldn't he choose something a little less deadly? Like wrestling grizzly bears?"

Tess laughed and kissed his cheek. "You're a good man, Gabriel Calloway."

Gabe snorted and lay back in the grass. Tess lay down next to him with her head on his chest, breathing in time to his heartbeat. He closed his eyes and inhaled deeply, basking in the contentment of the moment. It was so quiet, so peaceful, so damn near perfect.

He sat up with a jerk.

"What is it?" Tess asked with clear alarm.

He held up his hand to silence her for a minute, his ears straining for the sound of anything—a bird, a squirrel—but there was nothing. Dead silence.

"Gabriel?"

"It's too quiet," he finally answered, surveying the surrounding area.

"What does that mean?" she asked, growing more and more frightened.

"Maybe nothing."

"Maybe something, Gabriel. What?"

There was no obvious reason for the eerie calm, no bear or other predatory animal lurking nearby, no storm clouds billowing in from the south. Zeus nickered nervously and pawed the ground, his head tossing back and forth.

Gabe immediately stood up and seized the horse's reins, his eyes still focused on the surrounding area. Slowly, so very slowly, he turned in a circle, watching, waiting. The sun had begun to set low in the western sky, blazing its dusky scarlet across the horizon. He continued in his circle, froze, and turned back to the west.

"Dear God," he breathed, leaping into the saddle. "Come on!"

He hauled Tess up unceremoniously behind him.

"Hang on!" he ordered, spurring Zeus back toward the ranch house.

"Gabriel," she cried, terrified now. "What is it?"

"Fire."

One word had never frightened her so much. She craned to see past Gabriel's hulking form but was unable to discern anything that even slightly resembled a fire. There were no flames, no visible smoke. She blinked against the blinding light of the sunset—the odd-colored, just slightly too bright sunset.

Gabe's heart pounded beneath her hands. His breath came in fast gasps that matched the overburdened animal beneath them. Zeus snorted and huffed, but never slowed for an instant. Gabe pushed him all the way home, riding him as close to the flames as he dared, then leapt from his back, pulling Tess down with him.

"Gee-up!" he bellowed, slapping Zeus on the backside. The animal immediately bolted back the way they'd come.

Tess couldn't move. Wild with fright, her eyes wouldn't even blink. The main house and the cottage were both engulfed in flames with the fire edging nearer and nearer to the barn.

"Stay here!" Gabe ordered, running toward the barn.

"What are you doing?" she screamed. "Don't go in there!"

But it was too late, he was already inside throwing

open all the doors, unlatching gates, and chasing the rest of the horses out. The horses, spooked by the smoke and flames, needed little encouragement and took off in the same direction Zeus had gone.

"Where is everyone?" Tess cried. "Joby! Seth!"

Even as she heard her own pleas, she knew where they were—in town. Saturday was drinking and gambling night. But where were Rosa and Miguel? They usually stayed home . . .

Tess raced toward the cottage, screaming their names. The flames licked at the front window and the door, but it had already made its way in through the roof. She pushed through the gate, racing straight for the door when Gabe grabbed her from behind.

"Get away from here!" he yelled. "I'll go . . ."

Tess turned to follow his wide-eyed stare. Miguel. She fell to her knees beside the man, lying face down on the singed grass. A dark liquid oozed over his back and pooled beneath him. Tess took his shoulders and tried to turn him but Gabe was suddenly there, stopping her.

"Don't," he said, his voice nothing more than a hoarse whisper now. "He's dead."

"No!" she sobbed. "No! Miguel . . . Rosa!"

Gabe bolted for the cabin, barreling through the door as if it weren't even there. The heat was overwhelming; the smoke was choking him ferociously. He searched the front room on his hands and knees, reaching blindly through the fire. Nothing. With Tess's screams echoing in his ears, he moved on instinct now, into the kitchen and then down the narrow hall to the bedroom. His eyes felt as though they were seared to his lids, his throat barely able to swallow. He'd all but given up when his fingers slid into something thick and almost gooey. Blood.

A deep sob ripped from his throat as he grasped the woman by the ankles and hauled her out from beside the bed. Boards above his head began to fall inward, the flames now eating their way through the inside walls and furniture. Gabe tried to inhale but there was simply no oxygen left. With a final tug, he lifted Rosa's bound, lifeless body from the floor and raced blindly back to the front door.

Tess was dragging Miguel across the grass toward the gate when Gabe finally lit through the flames.

"Gabriel!" she cried. "No—she's not—oh no!"

Gabe ran past her, lowered Rosa's body on the dirt out of danger, and went back for Miguel.

"Come on," he rasped, pulling her by the arm as well. "There's nothing we can do."

"But can't we get some water . . ."

"We're too far from the creek and there's no way we could pump fast enough to keep up."

He gently lowered Miguel beside his wife and reached for Tess, trying in vain to ease the wrenching sobs that echoed in his head. It was only later he realized they had come from within himself, not Tess.

Chapter 31

By the time Bart made it to El Cielo, both the house and cottage had been reduced to little more than piles of ash, while the barn, smoking and smoldering in some places, had been saved by the pump Gabe had at first considered useless.

Tess was bent over a small blaze in the yard, beating it down with an old horse blanket, while Gabe continued to fill buckets at the pump and empty them against the walls. The pair of them looked as though they'd surfaced from deep within a coal mine, so covered were they in soot, dirt, and smoke.

"Ho-lee shit." Bart clamped his jaw shut, wiped his eyes with the back of his sleeve, and dropped his horse's reins.

Gabe straightened and watched as Bart made his way toward him.

"What the hell happened?"

Gabe shrugged. "Wasn't an accident, that much I know."

"Where's Miguel and Rosa?" Bart raised his brow, a knowing dread slowly covering his face even as the words crossed his lips. With painstaking reluctance, he followed Gabe's sober gaze to the grassless patch of earth.

"Rosa?" he whispered. "No . . ."

Gabe watched his brother hurtle toward the two

lifeless figures on the ground—the only parents either one of them had ever really known. Throwing down his bucket, he trudged over to Bart, motioning for Tess to stay where she was.

Bart's brown eyes were wild with fury, the vein in his neck pulsing rapidly.

"Someone tied her up and shot her."

Gabe nodded grimly.

"And Miguel?" Bart asked. "The fire get him?"

"Shot in the back."

"Holy jumpin' . . ." Bart glanced back at Tess, still bent over the intermittent fires. "How's she taking it?"

"Not good," Gabe answered. "I don't know if she realizes what happened here or not. I haven't said anything."

"Just as well." He nodded. "No point in spookin' her any more than she already is. 'Sides, it coulda been drifters or . . ."

"Drifters don't usually bar doors and leave untended horses in the barn."

Bart started. "What're you talkin' about?"

Gabe sighed wearily. "The cottage door was tied shut from the outside—I tripped over the rope when I broke it down—and all the horses were still in the barn. Wasn't drifters."

"Any ideas?"

"You're the sheriff, you tell me." Gabe's voice was brittle to the point of breaking.

"Gabe, listen," Bart began, straightening to face his brother.

"Forget it," he said, waving Bart off. "We'll yell at each other later, right now you've got a job to do. I want whoever did this tracked down like a wild dog, and so help me if I find him before you do . . ."

"I can't let you go off half-cocked, Gabe, or you'll get yerself into a heap load o' trouble."

"I'm not just going to sit on my ass and wait for

him to come back!" Gabe fought to keep his voice down. "He's already killed two of us."

"I know," Bart choked, then cleared his throat and closed his eyes. "We should get them buried."

"Not until Boswell does his thing, and they both need proper caskets." He inhaled deeply and pointed toward his lost friends. "We're not burying them like that."

"I'll ride into town and get Nate Brolin. He can put caskets together faster 'n anyone."

"Wait," Gabe said. "We need to move them out of the open, it's getting dark and . . ."

"Yeah, okay." Bart shuddered visibly and Gabe was only too happy he didn't need to finish his sentence.

Without another word, Gabe bent to Miguel and Bart lifted Rosa. They carried them straight to the barn and fought to make it up the ladder to the loft. With the ladder removed it would be next to impossible for wildlife to get at them. They covered them with what remained of the horse blankets and tucked extra straw around them.

"I'll be back as soon as I can."

Without a word to Tess, Bart leapt back on his horse and rode out, his shoulders considerably more slumped than usual.

When Gabe came out of the barn, Tess was standing in the middle of the yard, surveying the damage. There was nothing left of the house, save the brick chimney. Not a single board remained intact, not a single piece of furniture discernable among the ashes.

He walked up behind her and wrapped his arms around her, resting his chin on her head. Her sooty hands caressed his arms while huge muddied tears slipped down her cheeks. Remarkably, Gabe could still smell the scent of her honey soap beneath her smoke-filled hair.

"We'll be okay," he murmured. "We've got plenty of money to rebuild and . . ."

"I don't care about that!" she cried, turning in his arms. "Rosa and Miguel are dead—somebody killed them! Who would do such a thing? Who could be that evil?"

So she did know the truth. Gabe sighed; maybe it was for the best.

"I don't know," he answered, shaking his head. "But I'm damn well going to find out, I can tell you that much."

"Oh, Gabriel," she sobbed, leaning into him again. "What are we going to do?"

"We're going to rebuild," he answered, forcing conviction into his feeble voice. "We're going to start over with a brand new house, a brand new . . ."

"What are we going to do without Rosa and Miguel?"

Gabe exhaled slowly. "I wish I knew, sweetheart, I wish I knew."

Locked in each other's embrace, they were vaguely aware of approaching horses. To their stunned surprise, the entire Langman family rode up, each one armed with a shotgun, including Collette.

"You all right, Calloway?" Wyatt asked, glancing around the yard.

Gabe nodded shortly.

"Met up with yer brother on his way to town, told us what happened. Any sign of the culprit?"

"Haven't even looked," Gabe admitted. "We had to save the barn and . . . then . . ."

"Bart told us." Wyatt climbed down from his horse, removed his hat, and swiped at his brow. "Real sorry to hear 'bout that, Calloway. They was good people."

"The best."

The rest of the family, taking their cue from their father, dismounted and wandered around the yard, kicking dirt, shaking their heads, and mumbling incoherently. Collette walked straight to Tess and took her in her arms.

"We'd barely finished supper," she said, "and Bart kept looking out the window. He knew something was wrong but he didn't know what. It wasn't until we went outside that he saw the smoke—I guess our kitchen faces the other way because we had no idea . . ."

Tess nodded against her friend's shoulder, her eyes burning with smoke and tears.

"Anyway, Bart was long gone before Pa had a chance to round up the boys."

"Guess it were lucky the wind weren't blowin' the other way," Stupid Frankie said flatly, nodding toward the stand of trees behind the house. "If it'd got in there, the whole town woulda been in trouble."

"Yeah," Gabe snorted. "We're real lucky."

Stupid Frankie nodded and spat tobacco juice on the ground, Gabe's sarcasm lost on him completely.

Wyatt clicked his tongue at his boy and spoke again.

"You got a posse together yet? 'Cuz we're ready, willin', an' able to hunt this bastard down fer ya."

"I appreciate that, Wyatt," Gabe said. "But Bart and Fergus'll take care of that. Right now I have other things to think about."

His gaze fell to Tess, still clinging to Collette.

"A' course," Wyatt nodded. "We'll take 'er home with us and get 'er settled for the night. Lettie can make 'er some tea or somethin' to calm 'er down."

"I'd be much obliged. I'll come for her in the morning once we get this mess figured out."

Tess's head rose from Collette's shoulder with a sudden jerk.

"I'm not going anywhere, Gabriel. I'm staying right here with you."

"Now, Tess," he began, reigning in his patience. "You need . . ."

"Don't you tell me what I need!" she snapped. "I'm a grown woman and perfectly capable of making my own decisions."

"Tess . . ."

"No! You are my husband, Gabriel, and it was my vow to stand beside you in good times *and in bad*. Well, guess what? It's time for the bad."

"But you could get a hot meal and a good night's sleep."

Tess's temper erupted like a volcano.

"Do you honestly think I could eat a bite of food right now—or get a wink of sleep? Are you going to do either? No—probably not. So don't you tell me where I should be. I know my place, Gabriel Calloway, and it's right here with you!"

A flash of guilt swept across her face as she turned to face Wyatt.

"Please, Mr. Langman," she said, much softer. She took the man's hand in hers and looked him straight in the eye. "I mean no disrespect, and I do appreciate your offer, but you must understand . . ."

"I understand perfectly, little lady, and I couldn't agree more. 'Course if you were *my* wife, I'd hog-tie you to the nearest saddle and get you the hell outta here. But y'ain't my wife, now are ya?"

"No," she smiled weakly. "I'm not. And I defy anyone here to even try hog-tying me to anything. I may be little, but I promise you you'll live to regret it."

Gabe sighed. "There's nowhere for you to sleep here, Tess. And it's going to be a long night banging caskets together and digging their graves. You don't want to be here for that."

"Yes, I do. They were your family, Gabriel, and as such, they were mine." She crossed her arms over her chest and straightened her spine. "I'm not leaving."

"Okay, okay," he surrendered, throwing up his hands. "You've made your point. Thank you, Wyatt, but it would appear my wife is going to be difficult about this, and I'm too beat to fight her on it. If she wants to stay, so be it."

"Right then. C'mon boys, we're only in the way here right now." He helped Collette back into her saddle and turned back to Gabe. "You let me know when yer ready to git buildin' again, Calloway. A body can always use an extra pair o' hands."

Gabe nodded silently, his throat too tight to speak. Tess lifted her chin and forced a smile.

"Thank you, Mr. Langman. We'll be sure to let you know."

Wyatt tipped his hat back on his head, clicked to his old mare, and led the herd of Langmans back down the road into the looming darkness.

"Come on," Gabe said softly. "If you're so hell-bent on staying, we've got work to do."

He reached inside the barn door and pulled out two shovels and a hoe, took Tess by the hand, and led her through the thick stand of trees behind the house. About fifty feet in, she recognized the outline of three headstones—Emma and Clayton Calloway's and their stillborn daughter.

A small patch of trees had been cleared away from the area some time ago, leaving a large open space for the family burial. Icy shivers raced through Tess's veins. Lord, how she prayed she wouldn't have to make this trek very often.

"Do you think you can do this?" Gabe asked, watching her expression.

"Yes," she answered, a little too quickly. "Of course I can. Just show me where."

He outlined two plots with the edge of the hoe, and they set to work piling the dirt alongside the holes. It was hard, backbreaking work, but Tess didn't utter one complaint. She put her back into it more and heaved shovel after shovel out of the hole. It wasn't long before Bart rode back into the yard flanked by Reverend Boswell and Sheriff Nicholls. While the sheriff walked around the ruins, studying the mess, Bart led the Reverend into the barn and up the ladder to the loft.

Nate Brolin was next to arrive, looking like he'd been rousted out of a deep sleep. Gabe helped Tess out of the hole and went to speak to the man who would act as undertaker.

"Nate," he said by way of greeting.

"Jeez Louise, Gabe, I'm sorry as hell 'bout Rosa and Miguel. Must be quite a shock."

Gabe nodded solemnly and led the way to the barn. Bart and the Reverend met them on their way out.

"They're in a better place," Reverend Boswell said, his right hand resting on his well-worn black Bible. "They walk with the Lord now."

"Thank you, Reverend," Tess answered quickly when she felt Gabe stiffen. "I'm sure you're right. If you'll excuse us for a moment, Mr. Brolin needs to . . . uh . . ."

"Yes, yes, of course." The Reverend nodded. "Please." He stepped to the side, giving them all room to pass. "May God bless you all."

Gabe opened his mouth but clamped it shut when he felt Tess's nails dig into the flesh of his arm.

Nate went about his work with speedy precision, mumbling softly to himself and scribbling furiously on a small tablet he clutched in his left hand.

"What about headstones?" he asked.

Gabe nodded. "They need to match Mama's and the old man's. I'll show you on the way out."

"Fine," Nate said. "I'm done here."

Gabe led him out to the trees where Bart had

taken up his shovel and was busy throwing dirt with the speed of a man possessed. Tess regained her own shovel and jumped back down into the other hole while Gabe and Nate discussed dates for the headstones. By the time Nate left, Bart had finished the hole he was in and was now helping Tess. With two of them working together, the work was done in half the time.

Sheriff Nicholls wandered around the yard, taking mental notes and clucking sadly to himself. Several times he stopped to talk to Gabe or Bart and then returned to his work. It was a long couple of hours before he finally took his leave.

With their work done, there was nothing to do now but wait until morning, when they could begin the process of rebuilding—the house and their lives without the two most steadfast people they'd ever known.

Bart set about building a small rock pit, filled it with dry grass and twigs, and then set a match to it. The irony was not lost on any of them. They had just fought to put out the fire that had taken their home from them, and yet now they built their own fire to keep warm until morning.

Gabe sat on the ground, his knees tucked up to his chest, staring blindly into the flames. Tess's heart ached to look at him. As much as she would miss Rosa and Miguel, it was nothing compared with what Gabriel and Bart must be feeling. She knelt behind him, wrapped her arms around his huge shoulders, and tried to blanket him with her tiny body. How she wished she could take even a tiny bit of his pain and carry it for him; but she knew she couldn't. The best she could do was to love him even more.

They sat that way for a long, long time, not a word spoken, not a sound uttered. Finally, when she thought he'd never give in to it, Gabe's forehead lowered to his knees and his whole body convulsed with anguished sobs. Tess tightened her hold around his body, using every last bit of her strength not to break down with him. He needed to let it out, to grieve his loss, to be comforted; what he didn't need was to have to comfort anyone else right then. Not even his wife.

Chapter 32

News of their loss spread faster than the fire itself, bringing the entire town out for the burial of Rosa and Miguel. Even Miss Hattie from the boardinghouse came, bringing with her enough food to feed the Fifth Regiment. Tess made a point of greeting everyone and thanking them for coming, leaving Gabriel and Bart to themselves. Neither one had said more than half a dozen words since the previous night, and Tess feared things would get worse for them before they got better.

Reverend Boswell blessed both caskets and the souls of the dearly departed, then turned and added an extra blessing to all who had cared for Rosa and Miguel. Tess sat rod straight between Gabriel and Bart, grasping their hands in hers. Neither one of them so much as blinked through the entire service. When Reverend Boswell finished, Bart immediately rose from his seat, searching the crowd until his eyes lit upon the only person he cared to see. Collette.

As if he'd spoken his thoughts aloud, she, too, rose and made her way directly toward him, ignoring the stares and soft gasps around her. Wyatt Langman was on his feet in a flash, his mouth open to object, when he must have thought better of it and sat back down. Collette walked right up to Bart, put her arms around his middle, and held him, in front of all to see, comforting him with an inner strength Tess prayed for.

Bart tucked his face in the crook of her neck and shoulder and held on to her for a long time.

"Come on, everyone," Tess said, rising to her feet with Gabriel. "There's coffee and cakes in the barn."

As though one, the entire crowd turned their stares from Bart and Collette and wandered toward the barn, picking their way through the ashes of the house.

"Why don't you go for a ride?" Tess whispered to Gabe softly. "I'll deal with these people."

"The horses . . ." he began, but Tess stopped him with the point of her finger.

Far enough away to make a dash for safety if need be, Zeus stamped his feet and tossed his head. Gabe sighed with regret.

"I can't," he said. "All these folks came out . . ."

"Never you mind about these folks," she said. "They'll understand, and if they don't then they should be ashamed of themselves."

"But . . ."

"Go, Gabriel." She kissed his cheek tenderly. "I think you need to be by yourself for a while."

Gabe looked down at his wife with dead eyes. She was the reason he'd made it through the night with his sanity intact.

"You sure?"

"Yes." She smiled through glassy eyes, then added with a note of teasing, "Just remember to come back."

Gabe ran his finger gently down her cheek. "I love you, Tess Calloway."

"I know," she said definitely. "And I love you. Now get out of here."

He kissed the top of her head and both hands before making his way out of the crowd toward Zeus.

Bart watched in silence for a moment, kissed Collette on the cheek, and took out after Gabe, taking his own horse by the bit and hauling himself into the saddle.

Tess and Collette watched the two brothers ride out across the land they'd only ever worked with Miguel; the land Rosa had worked and tilled to provide food for the lot of them.

Joby and Seth approached Tess, their hats twisting nervously in their hands.

"Miss Tess," Joby said, his head ducked low. "We best get out to the herd now, unless you be needin' us for somethin'."

"Thank you, Joby. But I think Gabriel would want you to look after the herd for him. Be sure to take some food with you, though. There's plenty."

The two men nodded meekly and backed away.

"Oh, Tess," Collette sighed ruefully. "This is so awful for you. How is it you're holding up so well?"

Tess's chest heaved. "I'd like nothing more than to fall in a heap right here and cry for a week," she admitted. "But Gabriel needs me to be strong, as you were strong for Bart just now."

"I wasn't." Collette shook her head. "I needed him to hold me as much as he needed to be held."

"Still," Tess insisted, "most ladies I know wouldn't have done it, walked up in front of everyone like that. You must really love him."

"I do," she choked. "It breaks my heart to see him like this. I wish there was something I could do, some way I could unburden him."

Tess nodded sadly, patting the other girl's arm. "I know exactly what you're feeling. Now come, I'm going to need your help to get through this afternoon."

Collette wiped her eyes with her white lace handkerchief, lifted her chin, and plastered a smile across her pale lips.

"Right," she said. "Let's go receive your guests together, shall we?"

"Thank you, Collette," Tess said softly, swallowing hard. "You are a dear friend."

"As are you. Now come, let's get this over with."

Every minute of the afternoon dragged by with painstaking slowness until finally the only ones left were Reverend Boswell and the Widow Brenner, but with a little smile and a great deal of insistence from Tess and Collette, they too finally made their way back toward town.

And still Gabe and Bart did not return.

Joby and Seth finished with the herd and then busied themselves doing nothing until it was painfully obvious to all of them they were just killing time.

And still Gabe and Bart did not return.

"You boys should head back into town," Tess said. "There's nothing to do here but wait for Gabriel and Bart, and I'm certain they'll be along shortly."

Her forced conviction was much stronger than it sounded in her head.

"Don't reckon the boss'd be too pleased with us if'n we up and left you to yerself, Miss Tess," Seth said.

"I'm not alone," she said. "Collette is here with me and what's the worst that can happen?"

"Lots," Seth said, his eyes wide.

"Seth," she smiled. "We'll be fine. Now away you go. I'll be sure to tell Gabriel how you wanted to stay."

"Miss Tess . . ." Joby started, looked into her face, and closed his mouth. "Yes, ma'am."

"Thank you for your help today, boys. We're all very grateful."

"Ma'am." They both half-nodded, half-bowed, and took their leave.

Tess linked arms with Collette and they strolled

around the yard, saying nothing but fearing the same thing. Finally, Collette, near tears, begged for conversation.

"Tell me more about Boston. What was so horrible you felt you had to leave?"

"It's a little complicated," she sighed. "But regardless of what happened, I would have left eventually anyway. I was meant to be here, I know that."

Collette did not speak, but urged her on with her inquisitive look.

"You see, Collette, I come from a very affluent family. My father is a lawyer in one of the largest firms in Boston and he knows everyone and everything about them. My mother, God bless her, did her best, but she was no match for him when it came to decision making. He chose my sister's husband and thought he should be able to do the same for me, without my having a say in the matter."

"I take it you did not agree with his choice."

"I most certainly did not. The man he chose, Harmon Stiles, is also an attorney and *his* father, as it happens, is one of *my* father's partners. I guess he thought it would be a good business decision on his part and did not take kindly to the fact I had no interest in his business—or the Stiles' family business for that matter. Harmon Stiles is a horrible, horrible man. He makes Eli Gribbs look like an addle-headed child.

"Anyway," she continued, "needless to say, both Father and Harmon considered me a 'silly little girl' and believed they could arrange the entire wedding without so much as my consent. So I was forced to take matters into my own hands."

"What did you do?" Collette breathed, her eyes wide.

"I told my father I would not then, now, or at any time marry Harmon Stiles, and he, in turn, told me if I did not go through with the wedding, he would immediately disown me and cut me off of any inheritance. Like that meant anything to me at all." She shook her head in disgust.

"Father apparently did not believe I meant what I said because he continued on as if I'd not said a word."

"So you left?"

"Yes. But it wasn't quite that easy. You see, I have always wanted to live out west, on a ranch like this, and raise a family here. But since I had no money myself, it was all Father's, I couldn't very well jump on a train and head out, so I did something that, in hindsight, might not have been the smartest thing to do, but it got me here. Eventually."

"What?" Collette's eyes were as wide as dishplates.

"I answered an ad for a mail order bride."

"You didn't!" she gasped.

"I did. And that's when things started going horribly wrong. You see, the man who placed the ad, Mr. Barclay Simms, ended up murdered by Eli Gribbs . . ."

"That man . . ."

Tess nodded. "Yes, but Bart explained all of this to you, didn't he?"

"Goodness, no. All he said was that horrible man was someone from your past who was bent on causing trouble. He certainly didn't tell me any of this!"

Knowing Bart had tried to save her the embarrassment of her past, Tess felt the tiniest bit better.

"Anyway," she said, "Eli Gribbs showed up pretending to be Mr. Simms, and how was I to know the difference? Well, I have to admit, I was horrified when I saw him and thought perhaps once we got out west I could somehow get away from him. Thank goodness I was able to convince him to wait until we made it west before getting married."

"And . . ."

"And we ended up in Butte where he lost me in a poker game to Bart."

Another gasp. "Dear Lord, you must have been terrified."

Tess nodded. "I was at first, but once I met Bart and heard him speak of El Cielo, I had to come. And then I saw Gabriel and knew I'd done the right thing. Took a little while to convince him, of course, but he came around."

She smiled happily, although her eyes cast a worried glance across the empty acres around her.

"And then Eli Gribbs came looking for you. Aren't you afraid your father and Mr. Stiles will do the same?"

"I've thought about it, but I've been here long enough now. If they were looking for me, they certainly would have found me by now, don't you think?"

Collette nodded. "I'm sure you're right."

"I must confess, though, the idea of him finding me . . ." she trailed off.

"Tess?" Collette's worried gaze searched Tess's frightened face. "What is it?"

Tess shuddered.

"Tess," Collette persisted. "Did he do something . . . ?"

"No," she breathed shakily. "He threatened, though, and the look in his eyes when he said it, Collette . . . I swear he is possessed by the devil himself. I had heard talk about other women Harmon had 'dealt' with and that was enough to convince me I wanted no part of him. I've never met anyone as evil as Harmon Stiles."

"What happened?" Collette's frightened voice chilled Tess even more.

Tess shook her head. "It's in the past now, let's not dwell on it."

The sun was setting low in the sky, the calm of the evening settling around them.

"Oh, Tess," Collette suddenly wailed. "You don't

suppose Bart and Gabe . . . that they . . . they wouldn't . . ."

Tess set her jaw and straightened her spine.

"The thought did cross my mind," she confessed. "But surely they wouldn't go after whoever did this without telling us, would they?"

"No," Collette said. "I hope not, anyway."

"Let's talk about something else," Tess said. "Tell me about the change in your father. I have to say I am more than a little surprised in the turn around."

"It's you, Tess." Collette's smile was a welcome change from the grim faces they'd seen all day. "Pa has taken a shine to you like I've never seen before. I'm sure he'd take you in and adopt you in a flash, maybe even trade his own children if he could call you his."

The women laughed lightly together.

"I doubt that's true," Tess said, "but if I had anything to do with the change, I'm happy about that."

"You did," Collette insisted with a nod. "Once Pa saw how much you were in love with Gabe, it was as though he'd suddenly seen the light, so to speak. He really believes if someone like you, a good, virtuous lady, could see the good in one of *those Calloways*, then they must not be so bad. Of course, he's not completely ready to yield to Bart yet, but he's getting there."

"I'm so glad," Tess said, squeezing her friend's hand. "You make Bart so happy, and he needs you more than anything right now. I hope you know that."

"I do," she replied. "I hope I can be of some comfort to him."

"I think you already have been."

Collette's sharp intake of breath made Tess turn, warily, dreading the worst. But there, shadows stretching out before them, rode Bart and Gabe, both tall in their saddles.

Tess lifted her skirts, higher than she should have, and raced across the field with Collette right beside her. Gabe was off Zeus and running toward her before his animal had even stopped. He scooped her up into his arms and held her tight against his chest.

"Oh, Gabriel," she cried. "I was so worried. Are you all right?"

"I'm fine," he murmured. "I'm sorry I frightened you."

Collette was sobbing against Bart's shoulder as he whispered soft soothing words into her ear. Gabe released Tess but kept his arm around her waist, keeping her close. He whistled for Zeus who joined them shortly, and they walked back to the barn, leaving Bart and Collette to follow when they were ready.

"Where did you go?" Tess asked, her heart feeling a hundred pounds lighter now that he was home.

"We rode all over the ranch, back and forth, looking at nothing in particular and seeing everything. I really can't explain it."

Tess sighed. "I'm so happy you're home. We thought you'd decided to go after whoever did this. You wouldn't do that, would you?"

Gabe's head lowered. "I won't lie to you, Tess, we did talk about it. In fact, we were this close to doing just that." He held his finger and thumb in a pinch, demonstrating his point. "But Bart thought it best if I didn't get myself involved. God knows I tried to convince him otherwise, though."

"Thank God for Bart," Tess breathed. "Promise me you won't ever do that, Gabriel. Promise me you'll leave it to the lawmen to find them. I couldn't bear it if I lost you."

Gabe took her by the shoulders and forced her to look into his eyes.

"I will never leave you, Tess. You and Bart are the

only family I have left, and I'm not about to do anything stupid that'll get me killed."

"Promise?"

Gabe pulled her close and kissed her, hardly
brushing his lips against hers at first. His head lifted
slightly, then lowered again to recapture the softness
of her mouth, the velvety warmth of her lips.

"Come on," he rasped. "I'm too tired to stand anymore, let's go find somewhere to sit down."

She took him by the hand and led him up to the
loft, to the very place his slain friends had lain the
night before, and eased him down into the straw.
Then she curled herself into the crook of his arm
and rested the side of her face on his chest.

Gabe was asleep before she had even closed her
eyes. But unlike the night before, his body did not
twitch, toss or turn once.

Chapter 33

In the days that followed, Gabe and Bart felled buggy load after buggy load of trees and hauled them off to town where Nate Brolin cut them into boards and planed the whole lot of it smooth. Then it was hauled back to El Cielo and stacked inside the barn to keep dry. The horses had since been rounded up and corralled behind the barn.

Collette arrived every morning with enough food for everyone, and it seemed to Tess, more often than not, Wyatt allowed her to make the trip alone. *He must be softening*, she thought happily.

Tess worked to help clear an untried piece of land where the new house would stand, and every morning she took a handful of fresh wild flowers to the graves. More than once Wyatt Langman had offered his hospitality to them, insisting he had plenty of room on his spread for them all to stay, but Gabe continued to politely refuse. He simply would not be run off his ranch, and Tess, ever the dutiful wife, remained by his side, even after Bart finally gave in and accepted a bed in the Langman bunkhouse. Of course, Bart did have other incentives for his decision, but he couldn't be blamed for that.

Gabe and Tess continued to sleep in the loft, with straw for a bed and a coarse horse blanket for covers. Joby and Seth rode into town every night to stay at the hotel, an expense Gabe insisted on paying himself. The two ranch hands seemed to anticipate Gabe's wishes before he spoke, and every day they rode out to tend the herd and ride fences.

It was during one of these early mornings when Gabe had taken a fresh load of lumber into town that Tess's world came crashing down around her. As she stood over Rosa's grave, she was surprised by the sound of horses coming down the road. It was too soon for Gabriel to be back and Collette had already come and gone with the morning meal. So who . . .

Tess's feet froze beneath her; it couldn't be. Her first instinct was to turn and run back through the woods, but where would she go? And what would they do when they found her? Lifting her chin, she stepped out of the trees and marched toward them.

"Hello, Father," she said, not a trace of emotion in her voice. "How nice to see you."

She turned her face to the other rider, his thin, lanky features sitting tall in his saddle.

"Hello, Harmon," she said dryly.

"We've been looking for you, Tess," her father said. "You've certainly come a long way from home."

"This is home," she said. "And I'm sorry you wasted your time looking for me."

Harmon Stiles dismounted slowly, his menacing gaze raking over his former fiancée.

"It's hardly been a waste of time, Tess, since we did find you, didn't we?" He removed his leather riding gloves and stepped toward her. Tess refused to show one ounce of the terror she felt.

"Yes," she agreed. "You did find me, but my point is, Harm, it was a waste of time since I'm not going back with you."

"That's where you're wrong, Tess." He slid his forefinger down the length of her cheek, pausing long enough to tuck a stray strand of hair behind her ear.

"We didn't come all this way to go home empty-handed. We've got a lot of people waiting for us back home, a lot of wedding gifts have been purchased, and I've already picked out our home."

"Again, Harm, I'm sorry you wasted your time, but as you can see," she waved her left hand in front of him, "I'm already married."

Neither Harm's nor her father's expression changed one bit, but Harm did lean closer when he spoke.

"You think we don't already know that, Tess? How stupid do you think we are?"

"You don't really want me to answer that, do you?"

Harmon's laugh was as evil as his eyes. "Haven't changed a bit, have you? You still think a woman is allowed to voice her opinion whenever she sees fit."

"Yes," she huffed. "I do. Now if you'll remove yourself from my property, I have work to do."

Harm glanced around, clearly unmoved by it all.

"It's a real shame what happened to your house. And those poor people."

Tess's heart tripped over itself. Her eyes shot up to her father, who remained in his saddle, then back to Harm. In that brief instant, the truth made itself known in her heart and in her head.

"You!" She staggered back a step, fresh fear creeping through her veins. "How could you? They never did anything to you! If it was me you wanted, why didn't you take me?"

"Well now, Tess." Harm smirked shamelessly. "We tried that, didn't we? But your husband and his brother had to play the heroes and come after you."

"What?" she cried.

"Oh, come on now, Tess, you don't honestly think Eli Gribbs is smart enough to track you down on your own, do you?"

"But how . . ."

Harm laughed bitterly. "We met up with your friend Eli on our way through Butte, didn't we, Stan?"

Tess's father nodded.

"Seems he had been arrested and was looking for some help getting out of jail."

"You helped him escape?" she gasped.

"No," Harm said, shaking his head quickly. "Not exactly. It took a little convincing, but the guard was a reasonable man and, so it seemed, in need of some quick money to pay off some loans."

"You bribed the guard?"

"Bribe is such an ugly word, Tess. I prefer to think of it as him coming over to our way of thinking is all."

"Father!" she groaned. "How could you? Have you no pride at all?"

"Pride?" roared Stan Kinley. "Most of my pride was trampled to the ground the day my youngest daughter lit out for parts unknown, leaving her father and her fiancé to explain to two hundred people why the wedding they were expecting to attend needed to be postponed."

"Canceled," she corrected.

"Postponed," Harm reiterated fiercely.

"I am married, remember? And I have no intention of leaving my husband, now or ever."

Harm shrugged. "The choice is yours this time, Tess. You can come home with us now and we'll arrange for a quiet divorce from your . . . farmer . . . or, the alternative is . . . well, let's just say either way you'll be coming back to Boston."

"What do you mean?"

"Come on, Tess," he sighed, glancing nonchalantly toward the grave site. "Do I really need to spell it out for you?"

Tess's hand clutched her chest where her breath sat frozen somewhere between her lungs and her throat.

"You wouldn't!" she cried. "You . . ."

"No," he agreed. "I wouldn't. But you'd be surprised what people around these parts will do for a few dollars."

"But why? He's done nothing! I'm the one you want, why not deal with me?"

"We are," he sighed impatiently. "This is the only way, Tess. Would you come back to Boston willingly? No, I thought not. The choice is yours then. You leave him, or he leaves you. Permanently."

"Father! How can you let him do this? I'm your own daughter, for goodness' sake!"

Stan Kinley didn't even show the courtesy of being ashamed.

"My own daughter," he retorted, "left me looking like a fool in front of all my friends and associates when she rebelled against my decision and took matters into her own hands."

"But you knew I couldn't marry Harm—look what he's done here! What do you think he'd do to me the first time I disagreed with him?"

"Put you back in your place," Stan said without flinching. "Women have a place in society, Tess, and it's behind their husbands, doing as they're told, when they're told."

"Father!" Tess clamped her mouth shut; she knew it was useless to argue further with the man.

"What's it going to be?" Harm demanded. "Are you coming peacefully, or should we call your good friend, Nate Brolin, to come and fashion another casket for that plot over yonder?"

"I can't. . . ." she faltered. Either way, she'd lose Gabriel forever, but there was simply no choice to be made. She had to leave with Harmon, despite the fact she, herself, would no doubt end up in a casket at his hands in the not too distant future. Better her death than Gabriel's, though—she'd never be able to live without him.

"You'd best decide quickly," Harm said, nodding up the road.

Tess hadn't even heard the buggy approach, and yet there it was, the old horses plodding along with their heavy load, Gabe at the reins, his handsome face looking drawn and tired.

"Do you swear to me if I go with you now, you'll leave him alone?"

"Your loyalty is very touching," Harm sneered.

"Give me your word no harm will ever come to him."

"Not unless he comes looking for it," Harm answered with a shrug.

Tess's heart raced—she'd have to put on one hell of an act to fool Gabriel, but if he ever found out the truth, he'd come after her, and Harm would not hesitate to kill him, of that Tess was certain.

"You'll have to give me some time alone with him," she said. "I'll need to explain . . ."

"Take your time." He grinned. "We leave in an hour."

Gabe stopped the horses just short of the visitors and hopped down.

"Didn't know we were expecting company." He smiled apologetically. "I'd have made a point to be here otherwise."

"They surprised me, too," Tess said, struggling to keep her voice light. "Gabriel, I'd like for you to meet my father, Stan Kinley, and th-this is Harmon Stiles."

She watched Gabe stiffen at the mention of Harm's name, but he held out his hand nonetheless and grinned broadly.

"Good to meet you both," he said. "I assume Tess has told you our good news."

Harm raised one brow and scanned the area cynically, his hands remaining at his sides.

"Good news? Doesn't seem to me you've had much of that lately."

Gabe didn't miss a beat.

"I'm not saying we haven't had our share of difficulty, Harmon, but we've had a good dose of the good, too, since she agreed to be my wife."

"Yes," Harm sneered. "We heard. How nice."

Gabe ignored the man. "So what brings you way out here?"

Harm and Stan both turned their attention to Tess whose bottom lip was being chewed raw.

"I think Tess would be better suited to answer that," Harm said. "If you don't mind, we'll just water the horses a while."

"Help yourself," Gabe said, pointing around the barn. "Water's 'round back."

Harm and Stan led their horses around to the back of the barn, leaving a curious Gabe alone with his sickened wife.

"That's Harmon Stiles?" he whispered. "Don't know what I expected him to look like, but that's not it."

"Yes, well, he's a hard man to explain really."

"So what the hell are they doing all the way out here?"

Tess swallowed, hoping it would dissolve the bile that rose in her throat. It didn't.

"Um, we need to talk."

Gabe crossed his arms over his chest. "What is it, Tess?"

"Well, Gabriel," she began, turning her back to him and slowly stepping away. "The thing is, they've come to take me home."

"You are home." She couldn't see his face but his tone told her everything she dreaded. This was *not* going to be easy.

"Home to Boston."

Gabe's hand was on her arm in a flash, whipping her around to face him.

"Stand still," he seethed. "And tell me what the hell you're talking about!"

Tess forced calm into her voice, any hint of nerves and he'd know.

"I have decided to return to Boston."

"What?" he roared.

"I can't do this anymore, Gabriel," she said, her opened hand indicating the disaster around them. "I'm sorry, I thought I was stronger, but I guess you were right all along. I don't belong here."

Gabe blinked hard—twice. He must be hearing things.

"What the hell . . . you can't leave—you're my wife and your place is here with me."

"I'm sorry," she said again. "I can't take this, it's too much."

"But you said . . ."

"I know what I said, Gabriel," she sighed, the lump rising in her throat again. "I was wrong."

"*You were wrong?*" he yelled, then took in a long breath. "Wait a minute. What did they say to you?"

"Nothing," she croaked.

"Did that son of a bitch threaten you?"

"No," she lied. She had to make him believe her—somehow, she had to convince him.

"Then what? Tess, if he said anything to you, tell me. I won't let him hurt you." He reached for her hand but she pulled back, fearing his touch would destroy her resolve. "Tess, honey, just tell me what it is."

"I'm sorry, Gabriel," she said, her voice finally cracking. "I hate to hurt you like this but it's for the best. I could never be the wife you need. Or deserve."

"Damn it, Tess, you're not making any sense!"

"I'm sorry. . . ."

"Stop saying that! They must have upset you somehow, so tell me what's happened and I'll fix it."

"You can't fix this, Gabe."

Gabe? When the hell had she started calling him Gabe? What happened to Gabriel?

"How do you know?" he asked, a note of desperation finding its way through. "I'm pretty handy at fixing most things."

His attempt to lighten the situation seared her heart even more.

"It's over," she said, shaking her lowered head. "Once we get back to Boston, my father will arrange for a quiet divorce."

"No!" Gabe's yowl could probably be heard right through the main street of town. "I will never divorce you, Tess. I don't care how good a lawyer your daddy is, it's not going to happen, do you hear me? Now stop this nonsense and talk to me."

"There's nothing else to say," Tess said, openly weeping now. "We'll be leaving in a short while."

"The hell you will!"

"I'm so sorry, Gabriel," she repeated.

"Shut up! Just shut up, okay?" He rammed his fingers through his hair and paced angrily in front of her. "What if you're carrying my child?"

A rasping sob tore through Tess. Her hands instinctively flew to her belly, protecting it from the pain she was feeling—and inflicting.

"I'm not," she lied again. "I started bleeding this morning."

Gabe eyed her suspiciously. "I don't believe you. Look at me, Tess. Look me in the eye and tell me you're not carrying."

Tess lifted her tear-streaked face to his and willed herself the strength to pull this off.

"I am telling you the truth," she said, barely above a whisper. "Please, just let me go."

"Do you love him?"

"No," she said. "I never have."

"Do you love me?"

Tess's lips trembled against the lie. She needed to lie, needed him to believe it, but the truth was stronger than she was.

"Yes," she choked. "You know I do."

"Then why are you doing this?" he cried, his own eyes glassy with unshed tears. "Did I do something? Did I *not* do something?"

"No," she sobbed. "It has nothing to do with you, you're a wonderful man. I'm just not capable of living this way anymore. It's too hard. You said it yourself, Gabe, ladies belong in cities."

Gabe's mouth opened and slammed shut. He should have known she'd throw that back in his face one day. Should have listened to his gut a long time ago, but, no, he gave in to his stupid heart and now look where it got him.

"Go," he mumbled. "Get the hell out of here."

"Gabriel, please," she sobbed, reaching for his arm.

He stormed away from her then, with long, angry strides, never once looking back.

Chapter 34

Twice Harmon Stiles threatened to shut Tess up for good if she didn't stop crying, but it was the look in his eyes the third time he turned around that did finally stifle her sobs. She knew he would kill her, maybe not today, maybe not tomorrow, but one day. Her only concern was what would happen to her unborn child. Would she live long enough to bring the child into the world, and if so, what kind of life would he have?

She covered her stomach with her hands and prayed frantically for God to save the son she was certain she carried. Once the child was born, Tess would find a way to deliver him to his father, but until then, she would have to use every little bit of knowledge she had and every ounce of courage she could muster to ensure he was born healthy. She owed Gabriel at least that much.

They rode through the day and night, stopping long enough to water the horses. When they reached Shelton, Harm purchased another horse from the livery and tied Tess to it as though she were some kind of criminal.

In the almost two days since they'd left El Cielo, Tess had not spoken once. Harm and Stan chatted away like they were taking a Sunday ride, discussing everything from local politics to the readmission of the southern states, to how—if given the opportunity—they would personally bring a halt to the whole "women suffrage" fiasco. Women needed to be kept in line by their men, and those women were obviously married to nancy-boys. What they needed was a firm hand to guide him.

More than once Tess leaned over the saddle and vomited onto the ground. Neither Harm nor her father paid her any mind at all, not even offering her a drink of water. Never had she known such despair; even when she thought Gabriel was to marry another, she had never felt this desolate. Her only reprieve was the knowledge Gabriel would not be harmed and one day, God willing, he would be united with his son.

Nothing else mattered to her anymore.

Bart had been riding fences for two days now and his poor horse was taking the brunt of his anger for it. Leave it to Joby to go and get busted up in a fight at the saloon so he couldn't ride; hell, he could hardly move for that matter. Doc Bender told Gabe it'd probably be a couple weeks before his ribs healed. Bart cussed and threw down his pouch of staples. Damn, but he hated ranching.

He hadn't seen Collette in two days, hadn't had a decent meal or a warm place to sleep, and if it weren't for the fact Gabe was his brother and he needed help, he'd be long gone.

"Bart!"

Bart spun on his heel—what the hell was Seth doin' ridin' his horse that hard? Didn't he know . . .

"Bart!" he yelled again. "You best get back to the barn—there's somethin' horrible wrong with the boss and I can't find Miss Tess anywhere!"

"Whoa down there, Seth," he hollered, taking the horse by the bit. "What're you talkin' about?"

Seth took in great gulps of air before saying anything else. Bart waited, his fury growing with each passing second.

"I done went by to see if the boss needed me for anythin' else today b'fore I left, and he was . . . he was . . ."

"He was what?" Bart bellowed.

"Can't explain it," Seth said, shaking his head. "He done tore up the barn or somethin' and there he was, sittin' right in the middle of it all, mumblin' on an' on."

"About what?" Bart was already throwing his tools back into his saddlebag.

"Don't rightly know, couldn't make out anythin' he said."

"Where's Tess?" He pulled himself into the saddle and was already turning toward home.

"Dunno. Like I said, I couldn't find 'er."

"Well, how long's he been like that?"

"Dunno that either," Seth called after him. "I ain't been near the barn since yesterday mornin' when them two fellas showed up."

Bart had no idea who he was talking about, but in the time Seth took to tell him, Bart could already be home. He spurred his horse on as fast as he could, but even at that speed it would be close to dark before he reached his brother.

The barn was a disaster. Saddles and bridles lay strewn around, pitchforks and shovels had been up-ended and hurled across the length of the room, and the ladder to the loft lay in three pieces on the floor.

Bart stared in disbelief at the mess, checking to make sure the horses hadn't been injured. He almost missed Gabe altogether until his voice crackled from behind a pile of hay.

"She left me."

Bart wandered over to the hay pile, righting pitchforks as he went.

"What're you talkin' about?"

"My wife," Gabe growled. "She left. Saddled up with her father and . . . and . . . Harmon Stiles . . . and left."

Bart's jaw just about hit the floor. "She what? When?"

"Yesterday morning." Gabe's head fell back against the wall, the heels of his hands pressed into his eyes. "Said she couldn't live like this anymore and she left."

"This is a joke, right?"

"Do I look like I'm laughing?" Gabe snapped.

"But she was so happy here with you and . . . okay, it's been a little tough lately, but you were making it work."

"I thought so."

"Ho-lee shit." He slumped down in the hay beside his brother and stared blindly at the wall. "How'd her father get here?"

Gabe shrugged. "They were here when I got back from Brolin's mill, and next thing I knew they were all three of them riding out."

"Maybe they forced her. . . ." Bart offered weakly, but Gabe shook his head.

"I asked her over and over again if they'd said or done anything to scare her, but she denied it. Kept saying how sorry she was, and how I was right, she didn't belong out west; how she was wrong about everything."

"Ho-lee shit," he whistled, knowing he was repeating himself but unable to think of anything else. "And yer sure she ain't lyin', maybe on account of bein' scared or somethin'?"

Gabe shook his head slowly. "She's the worst liar

in the world. Looked me right in the eye and told
me . . ." His voice trailed off.

"I can't believe it," Bart said. "I just can't believe it."

"Told me her father would arrange for a 'quiet'
divorce—can you believe that shit? I am not about
to divorce my wife!"

"Gabe, man, maybe you should think 'bout it. If
this is really what she wants . . ."

"What about what I want, Bart? What about that?"

"Gabe . . ."

"No!" he raged. "This is crap! We took vows, we
swore to love each other forever—not just until
someone burns down our house or kills part of our
family, and not until some fancy-pants lawyer turns
up and waves his money around. We swore to love
each other forever and I intend to hold her to that."

"But if she doesn't love you . . ."

"I don't give a shit! She's the one who came here;
she's the one who told me she was in love with me
after knowing me all of one day. She's the one who
made me love her—whether I wanted to or not—so
I'll be damned if I'm going to just let that go."

"What are you sayin'?"

"I don't know what I'm saying!" He pushed himself up and began to pace back and forth over the
same line he'd walked a million times already.
"Maybe what I'm saying is if she wants to live in the
city, then damn it, that's where we'll live."

"What?" Bart was on his feet in a heartbeat.
"You're gonna move to the city? What the hell would
you do with yourself? You hate the city."

"I don't know, I don't care. She married me and
she's damn well going to stay married to me."

He stopped pacing and stared around the barn,
not really seeing anything and yet seeing everything
for the first time.

"When will you go?" Bart asked quietly.

Gabe shrugged. "Soon. But first I need to work out what's going to happen to the ranch."

"Hell, Gabe, I'll tend the ranch. . . ."

"No, you won't." Gabe turned to face his brother. "You don't want to be a rancher, Bart, you never have. Tess told me about the sheriff's job. You should take it, it's what you want."

"But what about the ranch?"

Gabe exhaled loudly. "Well, I guess I could go talk to our new friend Wyatt. He might be interested in taking it over."

"No bloody way!" Bart erupted. "It'll end up in the hands of Stupid Frankie—or worse—and even I'm a better rancher than him."

"Is that any way to speak of a man who will be your brother-in-law one day?" Collette's soft laughter made them both jump. She stepped inside the barn, froze, and sucked in her breath. "What on earth happened here?"

"What are you doing here?" Bart asked, obviously happy she was.

"I came to see Tess," she answered slowly, still eyeing the barn. "What happened?"

Gabe looked back at Bart and shrugged. "Might as well tell her."

"Tell me what?"

Bart hurried over and took both her hands in his. "Why don't you sit down?"

"What is it, Bart?"

"Sit down," he repeated, pushing her gently toward a pile of hay.

"I will not sit down!" she snapped. "Now out with it!"

"Okay," he sighed. "But you're not going to like it."

"I gathered that already. What is it?" She glanced cautiously around the barn. "Where's Tess?"

"Tess is gone." Gabe's face was as grim as it was the

minute he saw the two strange men in his yard the day before.

"Ho-lee shit, Gabe," Bart scowled. "Couldn't you've been a little easier on 'er when you said it?"

"What? Is there an easy way to say it? I don't think so. She's gone."

Collette sank slowly into the hay beneath her. "What do you mean she's gone? Gone where?"

"I mean she's *gone* gone. Left yesterday morning."

"Yesterday?" she croaked. "She's been gone since yesterday? Why didn't anyone tell me?"

"Don't look at me," Bart said, holding up both hands. "I just got here."

"What on earth did she say?"

Gabe snorted. "She said she'd have her father arrange the divorce, that's what she said."

"No." Collette's head shook so hard Gabe was sure it would twist right off her neck. "You must have misunderstood."

Bart sat down beside her, still in shock himself.

"Nope," Gabe said. "There was no misunderstanding. She's gone."

"But how . . . where . . . I don't understand."

"That makes three of us," he said.

"Where did she go?" Collette's face was as white as the daisies she clutched in her hand.

"Boston."

"Boston?" she almost shrieked. "No, Tess would never go back there. Not as long as her father and that other horrible man are alive."

Gabe's head cocked to the side. "What other horrible man?"

"That . . . that . . . Stiles man. I think she said his name was Harmon Stiles, you know—the man her father wanted her to marry. She's scared to death of him."

"What? How do you know this, Collette?" he demanded, crouching in front of her.

"She told me. That day . . . that awful day we buried Rosa and Miguel . . . and you two rode off. I asked her about Boston and . . . she told me what an awful man he was." A sob broke from deep within her. "Oh, Gabe, she was so frightened telling me about him, there's no way she would go anywhere near him!"

"Are you absolutely sure?" he asked, peering intensely into her frightened face.

"Good Lord, yes. She told me he threatened her but she wouldn't say anything more except he was an evil, evil man. Oh, Gabe, are you certain she said Boston?"

"Yes," he groaned. "And the only reason I'm so sure is because she left here with her father *and* Stiles."

"No!" Collette cried. "You have to go after her, Gabe. There's no way she would go anywhere with that man unless . . . unless . . . go after her!"

"I asked her, Collette, over and over again if either one of them had threatened her in any way and she denied it. Said she couldn't live like this anymore."

"And you believed her?" She shot to her feet and grabbed Gabe by the arms. "Go after her!"

"She wasn't lying, Collette," he said slowly. "I made her look at me, look me right in the eye."

"Did she say she didn't love you?"

"N-no," he answered hesitantly. "She said she did love me."

Collette's face softened. "Did you ask her about the baby?"

Bart bolted upright then. "What baby?"

Gabe and Collette both ignored him.

"I asked her," Gabe said, his frown deepening. "But she told me she'd started bleeding. Do you know something I don't?"

Collette shook her head. "Nothing for sure, but haven't you noticed lately how often her hands rest on her belly?"

Gabe's heart fell right to his toes. She'd done the exact thing when he asked her about a baby.

"Oh God, no," he staggered back, falling against the wall. "She's got my baby growing inside her and . . ."

"Go, Gabe," Collette pleaded. "Go now. If that Stiles man is half the demon she thinks he is, she is in terrible danger and so is your baby!"

Gabe didn't move. He couldn't. How could he let her ride out of here with that animal? How could he not know about the baby? How could he not know she was lying? She is the worst liar in the world! Anguish gnawed a gaping hole in his stomach. Tess.

Bart leapt into action. Without even thinking about what he was doing, or who the horse was, he charged into Zeus's stall, saddled him in record time, and yanked him out of the barn.

"Gabe!" Collette's voice beckoned him from the blackness of his thoughts. "Go! Find her and bring her home."

Gabe moved as if in a dream—a horrible, terrifying dream. He couldn't remember mounting his horse or riding out, but all of a sudden his eyes refocused and the night had turned into day. Bart stood over him pouring whiskey down his throat.

"Come on, Gabe, drink it."

Gabe brushed it away with the back of his hand and stood up.

"Where are we?" he asked.

"'Bout halfway to Butte, I think."

"How long've we been riding?"

"Through the night. Wasn't sure you'd ever snap out of it."

Gabe grimaced. He'd never felt so lost before, but then he'd never had so much to lose before either.

"Any sign of them?" he asked.

"Not yet," Bart said, "but we'll find them."

"Damn right we will." Gabe nodded. "I won't lose her now."

Chapter 35

Just after midday they rode into Shelton. Bart took the left side of the street and Gabe took the right; someone must have seen them.

"Yeah." The man in the livery nodded slowly. "I think I seen 'em yesterday. Come in lookin' for a fresh horse. Two men and a scraggly lookin' woman."

Gabe's whole body tensed. If he didn't need this information so bad, he'd have cracked the guy right up his skull.

"She weren't lookin' so good. Thought maybe she was sick 'er somethin', but the one fella—the one with the cash—tol' me to mind my own business and they rode out."

Gabe thanked him shortly and hurried to hunt down Bart. He found his brother in the sheriff's office where he was relaying the events of the last several days. The sheriff, a youngish, thin man, with long legs and squinty eyes, nodded silently.

"I'll be keepin' an eye out for them," he said. "You find them, you bring them to me, you hear? I don't want any trouble with you folks now."

The brothers rode on, running their horses as long as they dared and then slowing them to a walk only long enough to cool them down. Then it was off full tilt again. Neither man spoke as they both worked and reworked plans in their heads. It would be useless to discuss their ideas because they'd just end up arguing at this point. Especially because Gabe's plan involved a lot more punching and shooting than his brother's did. When the time came, they would instinctively meld the two unspoken plans together and make it work.

Hours passed without any sign of Tess. There were tracks, of course, but they could have been made by anyone on horseback. Gabe didn't care how long it took or how far he had to ride; if he had to go clear across to Boston, he'd do that, and God help that son of a bitch Stiles if Tess had suffered so much as a broken fingernail on the trek east.

They stopped briefly to water the horses and it was then Gabe noticed Bart eyeing him.

"You okay with this?" Bart asked. "I mean, you're not gonna go squirrely on me when we catch up to them, are you?"

"I'm not making any promises," Gabe answered honestly, using his hands as a cup from which to drink.

"I'm only asking because . . ." He pulled a pistol from his saddlebag. "I brought this in case you needed one, but . . ."

"What about you?"

Bart pushed back his duster to reveal the black Colt slung low on his hip.

"Guess that was a stupid question, wasn't it?" Gabe chuckled dryly.

"I ain't gonna give you this if you're gonna go at them with it blazin'."

Gabe snatched it from his brother's hand and tucked it inside his waistband. "Thank you."

"Gabe . . ."

"Come on, Bart, we're going to lose the light in a while."

They saddled up and headed out again, ever cognizant of the fact they could trip over Tess at any minute.

Tess stared into the fire with unseeing eyes. Maybe she'd been wrong, maybe Harm had been bluffing about what he'd do to Gabriel. It wasn't a gamble Tess was willing to take. Her heart ached to see her husband one more time; her body longed to be tucked up against his, sharing their combined warmth. But the truth was, she would probably never see Gabriel again, and even if she did, it wasn't likely he would speak to her. Not after the way she'd left him.

The pain in his eyes had etched itself onto her heart. She had hurt him, and worse, she had lied to him—albeit for a good reason, but a lie was a lie nonetheless. And God help her when he discovered she was, in fact, carrying his child.

She could try to escape, go back to El Cielo and tell Gabriel everything, but then she would be risking his life and her own as well. That was the one thing she was absolutely certain of—if she did manage to escape, Harmon Stiles would track her down again, and from what he had already confessed to, she was sure he would stop at nothing to get to her.

"Go to sleep, Tess." Harm's harsh voice raked through her. "I won't have you whining and crying tomorrow because you're tired."

Tess lay down in the grass, but she did not go to sleep; she would not go to sleep. Every time she closed her eyes, Gabriel's face loomed in her subconscious, his broken and confused soul pleading with her through his storm-filled eyes. One day, perhaps, he would learn the truth and understand why she needed to do what she did, but that wasn't the least bit of comfort to her at that moment.

She rolled onto her side and studied the two men on the other side of the fire. Her own father—the man who raised her and claimed to love her—had sold her to the highest bidder, as he had done with his older daughter. How could he do that to her? She couldn't imagine doing that to her own child—couldn't imagine not protecting her child from every single thing.

But, as Harm said, you'd be surprised what people'd do for a little bit of money.

Tess's brain sparked—Harm carried a gun! She'd seen it hidden under his coat. Maybe if she waited until he was asleep—really good and asleep—she could get it away from him somehow. But then what? Shoot him? Shoot her own father?

Her mind toiled over the idea long into the night. Maybe she could tie them up with something and keep them there until somebody passed by. Surely someone would happen by and offer assistance, wouldn't they?

It was her only hope. If she stayed with Harm, she would no doubt be beaten into submission, or worse, and the life growing inside her would be in terrible jeopardy. She couldn't let that happen—this child, conceived out of a deep and mutual love, deserved the chance at a decent life.

Her soul cried out to Gabriel for strength. She had to get free of Harm, without letting him go free, so she could make her way back to her husband.

With painstaking caution, she inched her way around the fire, closer and closer to Harm. Certain the pounding of her heart would wake him, she took deep, quiet breaths, trying to calm it. One of the horses, hobbled nearby, nickered softly, but neither Harm nor her father stirred.

Another inch closer to freedom, another inch closer to death. Finally she was beside him, but her hands trembled so hard she had to sit on them for a moment to still them. Ever so slowly, with feather-light fingers, she lifted the side of his coat, revealing the smooth handle of the revolver. Tess's throat was too dry to swallow. Her tongue flicked out, trying to moisten her lips, but it, too, was dryer than the dirt.

She eased the gun from its holster with a steadiness that came from being deathly afraid. The horse nickered again, louder this time, startling Tess and making her hand jerk.

"What the . . ." Harmon's hand clamped down over hers. "What the hell do you think you're doing?"

Tess knew what was coming, tried to brace herself for it, but it wasn't enough. The force of his blow sent her reeling until she was flat on her back, blood oozing from her bottom lip. She tried to sit up but Harm was standing over her, his evil eyes flashing wickedly.

"What were you going to do, shoot me?" His lips pulled back in a threatening sneer. "You don't have what it takes to shoot a man, Tess."

She didn't answer but tried to push herself backward away from him. He grasped her by the upper arm, hauled her to her feet, and backhanded her, sending her staggering back again. Her head throbbed, the world around her spun, and the ground raced up to meet her.

"Get up!" he bellowed. "You want to fight me, Tess? Then let's fight."

He hauled her up again only to knock her back down.

Please, Tess prayed, *please don't let him hurt my baby.*

"Wh-what's going on?" Stan Kinley finally rousted himself out of sleep.

"F-father," she gasped. "Help me, please."

He rose to his feet, his eyes moving slowly over his daughter and then Harm.

"What's going on?" he repeated. "Stiles?"

Harm didn't even look at him. "She was trying to steal my gun."

"Tess?" her father said, looking back at his daughter on the ground. "Is this true?"

"Please, Father," she begged again. "Help me. . . ."

Stan shook his head slowly. "Why can't you do as you're told? Your sister was never any trouble, but you . . . you'd test the patience of the Almighty."

"Father," she pleaded. "Please . . ."

"Shut up!" Harm snapped, grasping her by the elbow. He half dragged her back to the fire and threw her down in a heap. From somewhere in his saddlebag, he produced a ball of twine and bound her, hands and feet, and left her to bleed beside the fire.

Tess's cries fell on deaf ears. Neither her father nor Harm paid her another minute's notice but returned to their bedrolls and closed their eyes. Blood trickled into her mouth, leaving a dirty metal taste. She tried to spit it out but could not, for the life of her, find the strength.

It sickened her more than anything else to realize both men were again fast asleep as if nothing had happened. The sound of their breathing reverberated inside her already pounding head. Despite her best efforts to the contrary, Tess's heavy lids eventually slid shut, partly from swelling and partly from exhaustion, and as usual, Gabriel's face loomed before her, taunting her from beyond her reach.

"Gabriel," she sobbed softly. "Oh, Gabriel."

"Shhh, it's okay."

She willed her eyes to open, but they wouldn't budge. Icy fear raced through her veins—never before had Gabriel's image spoken back to her. She must be dying and her angel had come to take her home; she was going to die right there in the dirt and so was her baby.

"No," she wailed, her raw throat barely able to whisper.

A hand clamped down over her mouth—a strong, gentle hand. She knew this hand, but still . . . she forced her mouth to open wide enough that she could sink her teeth into the fleshy part between the thumb and forefinger. This was no dream—that hand was real! But still her eyes wouldn't open.

She heard a muffled yelp and then a voice right in her ear.

"Tess, it's me," Gabriel whispered. "You need to keep still, okay?"

Gabriel! Tess's body convulsed against its binding. With the last of her willpower, she finally forced her lids open a slit and there, heaven help her, was Gabriel, his face mere inches from hers, his breath warm against her face.

"Gabr—" she started, but he clamped his hand down over her mouth.

"Shhh," he repeated. "You need to stay quiet."

Pain and exhaustion forgotten, Tess's eyes flew open wide. He really was there, really speaking to her, really touching her. Tears gushed from her eyes, rolling down her cheeks to the dust below her.

"I'm going to move my hand now," he whispered. "But don't move. Do you understand?"

Her head bobbed rapidly.

Gabe's hand slipped from her mouth, but he stayed where he was, his eyes darting across the fire.

"Stay right here," he ordered fiercely. "Right here!"

She opened her mouth to protest but slammed it shut. Gabriel was here! Relief flooded through her in one giant wave but was quickly drowned out by the fierce panic that followed. Harm was sure to kill him—she had to get him away from here.

"Gabriel!" she whispered hoarsely.

He put his finger to her lips and scowled, silencing her instantly.

He tiptoed back to Zeus, who'd been standing there the whole time, and silently removed a rope and a small silver flask. The horse tossed his head back and whinnied softly, barely audible over the gentle breeze.

In the next instant, all hell broke loose. Harm's horses caught Zeus's scent and kicked up enough ruckus to wake both Harm and Stan, who were on their feet instantly, guns drawn.

Gabe turned slowly, his hands out to his sides, and faced the two of them. Fear gripped Tess's heart and throat. Why was he acting so calm when she was scared to death.

"Harm," she cried. "Don't! Whatever you're thinking of doing, I beg you, please don't do it."

"Shut up," Harm ordered, sauntering closer. "Well, isn't this sweet? Come to rescue your little woman, have you?"

Gabe didn't answer, but his eyes never wavered.

"I thought she made it pretty clear the other day she was through with you." He took another step, then another. "Why the hell would she want a nowhere farmer when she could live the high life in the big city with money, prestige . . . power."

Again, no answer. Tess fought against the ropes, trying to get to her feet, but it was useless.

"Gabriel," she begged. "Please go. He's going to kill you if you stay here! Please!"

Still Gabe didn't move. Harm was right in front of him now, his pistol pressed against the underside of Gabe's jaw.

"Thought you'd be a hero, didn't you? Well, you heard the lady, Calloway, she asked you to leave. Now I suggest you get back on that animal you rode in on and get the hell on out of here before you make me do something you're going to regret."

"Is this where I'm supposed to start shaking?" Gabe asked, his voice steady and even.

"No," Harm sneered. "Heroes like you don't get scared, do they? Hell, you probably wouldn't care if I shot you right between the eyes, would you? No, you wouldn't, because then you'd be a martyr, too."

Gabe didn't even blink. "You're such a piece of crap, Stiles. I don't care what you do to me. . . ."

"Well, how about if I put the bullet in her instead?" He whirled the gun away from Gabe and pointed it at Tess, who trembled uncontrollably on the ground.

The next instant, the night sky exploded in gunfire and flashes of light, but Tess witnessed none of it from the safety of her cocoon. Something—no, someone—was on top of her. Gabriel's huge body sprawled over her, protecting her from flying bullets and debris. Somehow from his twisted position he managed to fire off a couple rounds himself, putting one bullet through Harm's right arm and another through Stan's left shin.

Then suddenly there was silence. Dead, eerie silence that frightened Tess more than the bullets.

Her mind clamored with fear—*why didn't Gabriel move? Why didn't he get off of her?*

Chapter 36

"Gabriel!" she cried, wriggling and squirming beneath him. Her efforts were futile, as he was far too heavy and her bindings made it impossible to move him. "Oh please, God, please . . ."

"Stay still," he rasped in her ear. "Are you hurt?"

"No," she answered in a rush of air, offering a silent prayer of thanks. "Are you?"

"I'm fine." He sat up, wrapped his arms around her, and squeezed as tight as he dared without snapping her in two. "What the hell did you think you were doing taking off with him? Why didn't you just tell me . . . ?"

"Oh, Gabriel," she sobbed, clutching his shirt in her hands. "He told me he'd kill you if I didn't go with him and after what he did to Rosa and Miguel . . ."

"He what?" Gabe roared. "You left with him, knowing full well he killed them?"

Tess nodded solemnly. "I had to. He didn't actually do it himself, but he said he paid someone to do it for him."

"Why?"

"I don't know," she answered, hanging her head. "To get to me, I guess. I'm so sorry, Gabriel. If only I'd gone away like you tried to make me do so many times, then none of this would have happened."

"Hush now," he soothed. "None of this is your fault."

"But if I'd stayed in Boston, Rosa and Miguel would still be alive and . . ."

"Stop it," he said forcefully. "Just stop it. You didn't do this, Tess, he did."

"Is he . . . ?"

"No, but he's hurt pretty bad. Just a minute," he said, tugging at the ropes. Finally freed, she flung her arms around his neck and sobbed. When her eyes opened again, the sight before her made her want to gag. Her father lay on the ground in front of her, blood pooling beneath him; his eyes rolled up in their sockets, his tight lips twitching with every breath.

"Father!" she cried. "Oh, no!"

She fell in a heap beside him, running her hands over his face and hair. Harmon Stiles lay a few feet away, swearing like a banshee. And from out of nowhere, Bart appeared, towering over Stiles.

Gabe knelt beside Tess, taking her in his arms and turning her away from her father.

"He's gone, Tess," he said softly. "I'm sorry."

"No!" she sobbed. Her tiny hands flailed against Gabe's chest, then suddenly stilled. She pushed Gabe away, rose to her feet, and flung herself at Harmon Stiles, beating him mercilessly with her balled fists.

"You did this!" she screeched. "You bastard!"

Harm cursed louder, swinging back at her with his one good arm, until Gabe lifted her in the air and pulled her out of his reach. So angry was Tess, so wild was her fury, she did the only other thing she could think of—she wound up and spat on Harmon Stiles, spat right in his face.

"I hate you," she seethed. "I hope you rot in hell!"

She lifted her head and the whole world went black around her. If Gabe hadn't been standing right behind her, she would have landed right back down in the dirt. He scooped her into his arms and stormed at Harmon.

"Gabe," Bart warned.

"So help me, Stiles," he spat through gritted teeth. "When I get through with you, you'll be wishing I killed you right here."

Stiles hurled more insults and curses at Gabe, but he had already turned and walked away, Tess's limp form pressed against him.

Without any help, Bart somehow managed to saddle the hog-tied Stiles and the lifeless Stan Kinley onto their horses before easing Tess from his brother's arm. Once Gabe was seated high on Zeus, Bart handed his wife back to him and mounted his own mare. And so began the long ride home, with a stop in Shelton to pay a visit to the sheriff and the local doctor.

The old medic pronounced Tess healthy but exhausted, and so far as he could tell, the child had not been harmed. Still, Gabe kept her right in the saddle with him, even when she weakly protested she was able to ride on her own.

Gabriel hardly spoke the rest of the ride home. His silence frightened Tess more than anything—he knew about the baby now, knew she'd lied to him. How on earth could she ever make that up to him?

"What the . . . ?" Bart's voice drifted off as he spurred his horse toward the yard.

"Holy jumpin' Jiminy," Gabe whistled. "Would you look at that?"

In the last light of day, Tess could barely make out the shape of a building—a new building—right where she'd cleared land several days before.

As they approached, Collette and Wyatt Langman stepped out of the structure, Collette rushing past to greet them.

"Welcome home, Tess," she cried, tears streaming down her face. "Are you all right?"

"Yes," she smiled wanly. "Thank you."

Gabe pushed his knee into the horse's side and urged it forward, leaving his brother and Collette to their own welcome home greeting.

"Calloway," Wyatt nodded. "Good to see you. We only got the one room together so far, but it'll give you a roof over your head for now."

Gabe was struck dumb for a moment. This was not the Wyatt Langman he'd grown up hating.

"I-I'm much obliged," he finally said, sliding down from his saddle.

"Oh, Mr. Langman," Tess choked. "I don't know what to say. You are very kind . . ."

"Bah! Weren't nothin'. Figured you'd be needin' somethin' to come home to eventually." He shrugged as if his gesture had been nothing more than offering them a cup of coffee. "We'll be back in the mornin' and we'll get to work on the rest of it."

Gabe's face tightened, his Adam's apple bobbed, but no words would form. At last he managed a short nod of thanks.

Wyatt clapped him on the shoulder as he strolled by.

"You take care of that little girl," he said, in reminiscence of Gabe and Tess's wedding day. "Or you'll have me to answer to."

Gabe finally chuckled. "Won't let her out of my sight."

"Come on, Lettie," Wyatt called, taking his horse by the reins. "Let's let these people get settled."

Collette's nervous eyes flitted from Bart to her father.

"P-Pa," she began, but he cut her off.

"I know what yer gonna say, and it ain't right."

"But Pa . . ."

"Let me finish," he growled. "It ain't right for you to be spendin' so much time with that Calloway boy unless you've set a date."

"Oh, Pa!" Collette squealed, throwing her arms around her father's neck. "Do you really mean it?"

"Now now, that's enough," he said, pulling Collette's arms away. A faint shimmer gleamed in his eyes when he turned to Bart. "Now don't you go thinkin' I'm doin' this 'cuz I like ya—'cuz I don't. Yer still a Calloway and I mean to hate the Calloway name 'til the day I die. Got that?"

Bart's face broke into that stupid Calloway grin. "Yes, sir, thank you, sir," he said. "Or can I call you Pa?"

"You cannot!" Wyatt bellowed good naturedly. "You ain't family yet, Calloway!"

Collette kissed her father on the cheek, but Wyatt wasn't finished yet—and this time his expression was sober.

"Weddin' or no weddin'," he said, pointing his crooked finger at Bart, "you git my daughter home at a respectable time, you hear?"

"Yes, sir."

Wyatt mounted up and rode off, leaving the four of them alone. Bart took Zeus by the bit and disappeared into the barn with Collette.

"Come on, Tess," Gabe murmured. "Let's go see our new house."

The small room was still bare wood, but someone—Collette, no doubt—had had the foresight to furnish it with an ample-sized mattress and fresh linens. Gabe sank down on the soft bed, falling back against the pillows with an exhausted sigh. Tess immediately crawled up beside him and snuggled up against his chest.

"Gabriel?"

"Hmmm?"

"Do you hate me?"

"What?" He laughed. "Why would you even think that?"

"I lied to you," she answered meekly. "About the baby I mean, and . . ."

"Why didn't you tell me before?" he asked softly.

"I wasn't sure myself until you asked me that day and it was as if I just knew. I'm so sorry, Gabriel. Can you ever forgive me?"

"Tess," he said, his voice like velvet. "I'm not going to lie to you, I was madder than hell when I first found out, but then I figured it out."

"Figured what out?" she asked.

"You really love me." He said it as though he had only just come to realize it. And apparently he had.

"Yes," she breathed, snuggling closer. "I really do."

"Tess?"

"Mmm?"

"Don't *ever* do that to me again." His voice was tight—almost as tight as the knot in his stomach.

Tess raised her head high enough to plant a million kisses along his jawline.

"I love you, Gabriel. I was trying to protect you," she said. "I don't know what I would do if something ever happened to you. I . . ."

"Don't ever do that to me again."

"But I was trying to keep you safe, don't you see?"

"Don't ever do that to me again."

"Gabriel . . ."

"Don't ever do that to me again."

"Okay." She laughed. "You win—even if the world is falling to pieces around us, even if you turn into a miserable old troll, even if . . ."

"Stop!" he cried, pulling her into his embrace. "Even if the world falls to pieces because I'm an old troll, I want you right beside me—not in front of me, not behind me. Beside me. You got that?"

"I got it," she said. "I got it. And I want you right

beside me—every day, every minute, every second of my life."

"Deal."

They lay in silence for a time, both marveling at their extraordinary good fortune. Tess's mind kept drifting back to their baby. A more loved child there could not possibly be, and she suddenly had the urge to start preparing for his arrival. She probably had seven months or so before he was due, but one couldn't be too organized.

She tipped her head back so she could look in her husband's handsome face.

"What do you think we should name him?" she asked.

"Who?" he said, sounding more than a little sleepy.

"Our son, Gabriel. He's going to need a name."

"Our son?" he yelped, sitting up. His huge hand rested across Tess's belly, bringing an enormous smile to his face. "This here's a daughter, Tess, you mark my words. She'll be as beautiful as her mother and as clear thinking and rational as her father."

Tess laughed for the first time in days.

"Modest, too, I bet."

"Of course."

"But I'm afraid you're wrong," she said. "It's a boy."

"Girl."

"Boy."

"Tess?"

"Yes?"

"Shut up and kiss me."

And for once in her life, Tess Kinley Calloway did as she was told without argument, without a second thought.

About the Author

Born the youngest of four girls, Laura quickly learned three important lessons: sisters are your best friends, always live in a home with more than one bathroom, and life is full of happy endings. And while Laura's own life adventures have taken her from a small logging community in Southern British Columbia to the wilds of Canada's arctic, she has always held fast to those ideas. She loves spending time with her family; made sure her home came equipped with two and a half baths; and continues to believe in, and write about, happy endings. She presently lives in the Northwest Territories with her husband and three sons.

www.lauradrewry.com